RESOUNDING PRAISE FOR
HEROES ARE MY WEAKNESS

AN NPR BOOKS GREAT READ 2014

A Best Fiction Book of 2014

A Best Romance 2014
"...heart-wrenching and uplifting..."

Kirkus Reviews (★Starred Review★)

A Best Romance 2014
"An unforgettable, deliciously spicy romance..."

Library Journal (★Starred Review★)

Top Ten Romance Fiction 2014
"...another romance to treasure
from one of the genre's superstars..."

Booklist (★Starred Review★)

A Best Contemporary Romance 2014
"...A Phillips classic ... Awesome!"

RT Reviews (★Starred Review★)

By Susan Elizabeth Phillips

HEROES ARE MY WEAKNESS

THE GREAT ESCAPE

CALL ME IRRESISTIBLE

WHAT I DID FOR LOVE

GLITTER BABY

NATURAL BORN CHARMER

MATCH ME IF YOU CAN

AIN'T SHE SWEET?

BREATHING ROOM

THIS HEART OF MINE

JUST IMAGINE

FIRST LADY

LADY BE GOOD

DREAM A LITTLE DREAM

NOBODY'S BABY BUT MINE

KISS AN ANGEL

HEAVEN, TEXAS

IT HAD TO BE YOU

SUSAN ELIZABETH PHILLIPS

Heroes Are
My
WEAKNESS

AVONBOOKS

An Imprint of HarperCollinsPublishers

AVON BOOKS
An Imprint of HarperCollins*Publishers*
195 Broadway
New York, New York 10007

Copyright © 2014 by Susan Elizabeth Phillips
ISBN 978-0-06-210609-4
www.avonromance.com

First Avon Books mass market printing: August 2015
First William Morrow mass market international printing: May 2015
First William Morrow paperback printing: May 2015
First William Morrow paperback international printing: September 2014
First William Morrow hardcover printing: September 2014

Avon Trademark Reg. U.S. Pat. Off. and in Other Countries, Marca Registrada, Hecho en U.S.A.
HarperCollins® is a registered trademark of HarperCollins Publishers.

Printed in the U.S.A.

10 9 8 7 6 5 4 3 2 1

*In memory of Mary Stewart, Anya Seton, Charlotte Brontë,
Daphne du Maurier, Victoria Holt, and Phyllis Whitney.
I owe my love of reading to your magical novels.
Without you visionary women, I would not be a writer.*

Chapter One

Annie didn't usually talk to her suitcase, but she wasn't exactly herself these days. The high beams of her headlights could barely penetrate the dark, swirling chaos of the winter blizzard, and the windshield wipers on her ancient Kia were no match for the wrath of the storm that had hit the island. "It's only a little snow," she told the oversize red suitcase wedged into the passenger seat. "Just because it feels like the end of the world doesn't mean it is."

You know I hate the cold, her suitcase replied, in the annoying whine of a child who preferred making a point by stamping her foot. *How could you bring me to this awful place?*

Because Annie had run out of options.

An icy blast rocked the car, and the branches of the old fir trees hovering over the unpaved road whipped like witches' hair. Annie decided that anybody who believed in hell as a fiery furnace had it all wrong. Hell was this bleak, hostile winter island.

You've never heard of Miami Beach? Crumpet, the spoiled princess in the suitcase retorted. *Instead you had to haul us off to a deserted island in the middle of the North Atlantic where we'll probably get eaten by* polar bears!

The gears ground as the Kia struggled up the narrow, slippery island road. Annie's head ached, her ribs hurt from coughing, and the simple act of craning her neck to peer through a clear spot on the windshield made her dizzy. She was alone in the world with only the imaginary voices of her ventriloquist dummies anchoring her to reality. As sick as she was, she didn't miss the irony.

She conjured up the more calming voice of Crumpet's counterpart, the practical Dilly, who was tucked away in the matching red suitcase in the backseat. *We're not in the middle of the Atlantic,* sensible Dilly said. *We're on an island ten miles off the New England coast, and the last I heard, Maine doesn't have polar bears. Besides, Peregrine Island isn't deserted.*

It might as well be. If Crumpet had been on Annie's arm, she would have shot her small nose up in the air. *People barely survive here in the middle of the summer let alone winter. I bet they eat their dead for food.*

The car fishtailed ever so slightly. Annie corrected the skid, gripping the wheel more tightly through her gloves. The heater barely worked, but she'd begun to perspire under her jacket.

You mustn't keep complaining, Crumpet, Dilly admonished her peevish counterpart. *Peregrine Island is a popular summer resort.*

It's not summer! Crumpet countered. *It's the first week of February, we just drove off a car ferry that made me seasick, and there can't be more than fifty people left here. Fifty stupid people!*

You know Annie had no choice but to come here, Dilly said.

Because she's a big failure, an unpleasant male voice sneered.

Leo had a bad habit of uttering Annie's deepest fears, and it was inevitable that he'd intrude into her thoughts. He was her least favorite puppet, but every story needed a villain.

Very unkind, Leo, Dilly said. *Even if it is true.*

The petulant Crumpet continued to complain. *You're the heroine, Dilly, so everything always turns out fine for you. But not for the rest of us. Not ever. We're doomed! Doomed, I say! We're forever—*

Annie's cough cut off the internal histrionics of her puppet. Sooner or later her body would heal from the lingering aftereffects of pneumonia—at least she hoped so—but what about the rest of her? She'd lost faith in herself, lost the sense that, at thirty-three, her best days still lay ahead. She was physically weak, emotionally empty, and more than a little terrified, hardly the best state for someone forced to spend the next two months on an isolated Maine island.

That's only sixty days, Dilly attempted to point out. *Besides, Annie, you don't have anywhere else to go.*

And there it was. The ugly truth. Annie had nowhere else to go. Nothing else to do but search for the legacy her mother might or might not have left her.

The Kia hit a snow-packed rut, and the seat belt seized up. The pressure on Annie's chest made her cough again. If only she could have stayed in the village for the night, but the Island Inn was closed until May. Not that she could have afforded it anyway.

The car barely crested the hill. She had years of practice transporting her puppets through every kind of weather to perform all over, but even a decent snow driver had limited control on a road like this, especially in her Kia. There was a reason the residents of Peregrine Island drove pickups.

Take it slow, another male voice advised from the suitcase in the back. *Slow and steady wins the race.* Peter, her hero puppet—her knight in shining armor—was a voice of encouragement, unlike her former actor-boyfriend-slash-lover, who'd only encouraged himself.

Annie brought the car to a full stop, then started her slow descent. Halfway down, it happened.

The apparition came from nowhere.

A man clad in black flew across the bottom of the road on a midnight horse. She'd always had a vivid imagination—witness her internal conversations with her puppets—and she thought she was imagining this. But the vision was real. Horse and rider racing through the snow, the man leaning low over the horse's streaming mane. They were demon creatures, a nightmare horse and lunatic man galloping into the storm's fury.

They disappeared as quickly as they'd appeared, but her foot automatically hit the brake, and the car began to slide. It skidded across the road and, with a sickening lurch, came to a stop in the snow-filled ditch.

You're such a loser, Leo the villain sneered.

Tears of exhaustion filled her eyes. Her hands shook. Were the man and horse indeed real or had she conjured them? She needed to focus. She put the car into reverse and attempted to rock it out, but the tires only spun deeper. Her head fell against the back of the seat. If she stayed here long enough, someone would find her. But when? Only the cottage and the main house lay at the end of this road.

She tried to think. Her single contact on the island was the man who took care of the main house and the cottage, but she'd only had an e-mail address to let him know she was arriving and ask him to turn on the cottage's utilities. Even if she had his phone number—Will Shaw—that was his name—she doubted she could get cell reception out here.

Loser. Leo never spoke in an ordinary voice. He only sneered.

Annie grabbed a tissue from a crumpled pack, but instead of thinking about her dilemma, she thought about the horse and rider. What kind of a crazy took an animal out in this weather? She squeezed her eyes shut and fought a wave of nausea. If only she could curl up and go to sleep. Would it be so terrible to admit that life had gotten the best of her?

Stop it right now, sensible Dilly said.

Annie's head pounded. She had to find Shaw and get him to pull out the car.

Never mind Shaw, Peter the hero declared. *I'll do it myself.*

But Peter—like her ex-boyfriend—was only good in a fictional crisis.

The cottage was about a mile away, an easy distance for a healthy person in decent weather. But the weather was horrible, and nothing about her was healthy.

Give up, Leo sneered. *You know you want to.*

Stop being such a douche, Leo. This voice came from Scamp, Dilly's best friend and Annie's alter ego. Even though Scamp was responsible for many of the scrapes the puppets got into—scrapes heroine Dilly and hero Peter had to sort out—Annie loved her courage and big heart.

Pull yourself together, Scamp ordered. *Get out of the car.*

Annie wanted to tell her to go to hell, but what was the point? She pushed her flyaway hair inside the collar of her quilted jacket and zipped it. Her knit gloves had a hole in the thumb, and the door handle was icy against her exposed skin. She made herself open it.

The cold slapped her in the face and stole her breath. She had to force her legs out. Her beat-up brown suede city boots sank into the snow, and her jeans were no match for the weather. Ducking her head into the wind, she made her way to the rear of the car to get her heavy coat, only to see that the trunk was wedged so tightly into the hillside that she couldn't open it. Why should she be surprised? Nothing had gone her way in so long that she'd forgotten what good fortune felt like.

She returned to the driver's side. Her puppets should be safe in the car overnight, but what if they weren't? She needed them. They were all she had left, and if she lost them, she might disappear altogether.

Pathetic, Leo sneered.

She wanted to rip him apart.

Babe . . . You need me more than I need you, he reminded her. *Without me, you don't have a show.*

She shut him out. Breathing hard, she pulled the suitcases from the car, retrieved her keys, snapped off the headlights, and closed the door.

She was immediately plunged into thick, swirling darkness. Panic clawed at her chest.

I will rescue you! Peter declared.

Annie gripped the suitcase handles tighter, trying not to let her panic paralyze her.

I can't see anything! Crumpet squealed. *I hate the dark!*

Annie had no handy flashlight app on her ancient cell phone, but she did have . . . She set a suitcase in the snow and dug in her pocket for her car keys and the small LED light attached to the ring. She hadn't tried to use the light in months, and she didn't know if it still worked. With her heart in her throat, she turned it on.

A sliver of bright blue light cut a tiny path through the snow, a path so narrow she could easily wander off the road.

Get a grip, Scamp ordered.

Give up, Leo sneered.

Annie took her first steps into the snow. The wind cut through her thin jacket and tore at her hair, whipping the curly strands onto her face. Snow slapped the back of her neck, and she started to cough. Pain compressed her ribs, and the suitcases banged against her legs. Much too soon, she had to set them down to rest her arms.

She hunched into her jacket collar, trying to protect her lungs from the icy air. Her fingers burned from the cold, and as she moved forward again, she called on her puppets' imaginary voices to keep her company.

Crumpet: *If you drop me and ruin my sparkly lavender dress, I'll sue.*

Peter: *I'm the bravest! The strongest! I'll help you.*

Leo: (sneering) *Do you know how to do anything right?*

Dilly: *Don't listen to Leo. Keep moving. We'll get there.*

And Scamp, her useless alter ego: *A woman carrying a suitcase walks into a bar . . .*

Icy tears weighed down her eyelashes, blurring what vision she had. Wind caught the suitcases, threatening to snatch them away. They were too big, too heavy. Pulling her arms from their sockets. Stupid to have brought them with her. Stupid, stupid, stupid. But she couldn't leave her puppets.

Each step felt like a mile, and she'd never been so cold. Here she'd thought her luck had begun to change, all because she'd been able to catch the car ferry over from the mainland. It only ran sporadically, unlike the converted lobster boat that provided the island with weekly service. But the farther the ferry traveled from the Maine coastline, the worse the storm had become.

She trudged on, dragging one foot after the other through

the snow, arms screaming, lungs burning as she tried not to succumb to another coughing fit. Why hadn't she put her warm down coat in the car instead of locking it in the trunk? Why hadn't she done so many things? Find a stable occupation. Be more circumspect with her money. Date decent men.

So much time had passed since she'd been on the island. The road used to stop at the turnoff that led to the cottage and to Harp House. But what if she missed it? Who knew what might have changed since then?

She stumbled and fell to her knees. The keys slipped from her hand and the light went out. She grabbed one of the suitcases for support. She was frozen. Burning up. She gasped for air and frantically felt around in the snow. If she lost her light . . .

Her fingers were so numb she nearly missed it. When she finally had the flashlight back in her grasp, she turned it on and saw the stand of trees that had always marked the road's end. She moved the beam to the right, where it fell on the big granite boulder at the turnoff. She hoisted herself back to her feet, lifted the suitcases, and stumbled through the drifts.

Her temporary relief at having found the turnoff faded. Centuries of harsh Maine weather had stripped this terrain of all but the hardiest of spruce, and without a windbreak, the blasts roaring in from the ocean caught the suitcases like spinnakers. She managed to turn her back to the wind's force without losing either one. She sank one foot and then another, struggling through the tall snowdrifts, dragging the suitcases, and fighting the urge to lie down and let the cold do what it wanted with her.

She'd bowed so far into the wind that she nearly missed it. Only as the corner of a suitcase bumped against a low snow-shrouded stone wall did she realize that she'd reached Moonraker Cottage.

The small, gray-shingled house was nothing more than an amorphous shape beneath the snow. No shoveled pathway, no welcoming lights. The last time she'd been here, the door had been painted cranberry red, but now it was a cold, periwinkle blue. An unnatural mound of snow under the front window covered a pair of old wooden lobster traps, a nod to the house's origins as a fisherman's cottage. She hauled herself through the drifts to the door and set the suitcases down. She fumbled with the key in the lock only to remember that island people seldom locked up.

The door blew open. She dragged the suitcases inside and, with the last of her strength, wrestled it shut again. The air wheezed in her lungs. She collapsed on the closest suitcase, her gasps for breath more like sobs.

Eventually she grew conscious of the musty smell of the icy room. Pressing her nose to her sleeve, she fumbled for the light switch. Nothing happened. Either the caretaker hadn't gotten her e-mail asking him to have the generator working and the small furnace fired up or he'd ignored it. Every frozen part of her throbbed. She dropped her snow-crusted gloves on the small canvas rug that lay just inside the door but didn't bother to shake the snow from the wild tangle of her hair. Her jeans were frozen to her legs, but she'd have to pull off her boots to remove them, and she was too cold to do that.

But no matter how miserable she was, she had to get her puppets out of their snow-caked suitcases. She located one of the assorted flashlights her mother always kept near the door. Before school and library budgets were slashed, her puppets had provided a steadier livelihood than her failed acting career or her part-time jobs walking dogs and serving drinks at Coffee, Coffee.

Shaking with cold, she cursed the caretaker, who apparently had no qualms about riding a horse through a storm but couldn't summon the effort to do his real job. It had to have been Shaw riding the horse. No one else lived at this end of the island during the winter. She unzipped the suitcases and pulled out the five dummies. Leaving them in their protective plastic bags, she stowed them temporarily on the sofa, then, flashlight in hand, stumbled across the frigid wood floor.

The interior of Moonraker Cottage bore no resemblance to anyone's idea of a traditional New England fishing cottage. Instead her mother's eccentric stamp was everywhere—from a creepy bowl of small animal skulls to a silver-gilded Louis XIV chest bearing the words PILE DRIVER that Mariah had spray-painted across it in black graffiti. Annie preferred a cozier space, but during Mariah's glory days, when she'd inspired fashion designers and a generation of young artists, both this cottage and her mother's Manhattan apartment had been featured in upscale decorating magazines.

Those days had ended years ago when Mariah had fallen out of favor in Manhattan's increasingly younger artistic circles. Wealthy New Yorkers had begun asking others for help compiling their private art collections, and Mariah had been forced to sell off her valuables to support her lifestyle. By the time she'd gotten sick, everything was gone. Everything except something in this cottage—something that was supposed to be Annie's mysterious "legacy."

"It's at the cottage. You'll have . . . plenty of money . . ." Mariah had said those words in the final hours before she'd died, a period in which she'd been barely lucid.

There isn't any legacy, Leo sneered. *Your mother exaggerated everything.*

Maybe if Annie had spent more time on the island she'd know whether Mariah had been telling the truth, but she'd hated it here and hadn't been back since her twenty-second birthday, eleven years ago.

She shone the flashlight around her mother's bedroom. A life-size mounted photograph of an elaborately carved Italian wooden headboard served as the actual headboard for the double bed. A pair of wall hangings made of boiled wool and what looked like remnants from a hardware store hung next to the closet door. The closet still smelled of her mother's signature fragrance, a little-known Japanese men's cologne that had cost a fortune to import. As Annie breathed in the scent, she wished she could feel the grief a daughter should experience following the loss of a parent only five weeks earlier, but she merely felt depleted.

She waited until she'd located Mariah's old scarlet woolen cloak and a pair of heavy socks before she got rid of her own clothes. After she'd piled every blanket she could find on her mother's bed, she climbed under the musty sheets, turned out the flashlight, and went to sleep.

ANNIE HADN'T THOUGHT SHE'D EVER be warm again, but she was sweating when a coughing fit awakened her sometime around two in the morning. Her ribs felt as if they'd been crushed, her head pounded, and her throat was raw. She also had to pee, another setback in a house with no water. When the coughing finally eased, she struggled out from under the blankets. Wrapped in the scarlet cloak, she turned on the flashlight and, grabbing the wall to support herself, made her way to the bathroom.

She kept the flashlight pointed down so she couldn't see her reflection in the mirror that hung over the old-fashioned sink. She knew what she'd see. A long, pale face shadowed by illness; a sharply pointed chin; big, hazel eyes; and a runaway mane of light brown hair that kinked and curled wherever it wanted. She had a face children liked, but that most men found quirky instead of seductive. Her hair and face came from her unknown father—*"A married man. He wanted nothing to do with you. Dead now, thank God."* Her shape came from Mariah: tall, thin, with knobby wrists and elbows, big feet, and long-fingered hands.

"To be a successful actress, you need to be either exceptionally beautiful or exceptionally talented," Mariah had said. *"You're pretty enough, Antoinette, and you're a talented mimic, but we have to be realistic . . ."*

Your mother wasn't exactly your cheerleader. Dilly stated the obvious.

I'll be your cheerleader, Peter proclaimed. *I'll take care of you and love you forever.*

Peter's heroic proclamations usually made Annie smile, but tonight she could think only of the emotional chasm between the men she'd chosen to give her heart to and the fictional heroes she loved. And the other chasm—the one between the life she'd imagined for herself and the one she was living.

Despite Mariah's objections, Annie had gotten her degree in theater arts and spent the next ten years plodding to auditions. She'd done showcases, community theater, and even landed a few character roles in off-off-Broadway plays. Too few. Over the past summer, she'd finally faced the truth that Mariah was right. Annie was a better ventriloquist than she'd ever be an actress. Which left her absolutely nowhere.

She found a bottle of ginseng-flavored water that had somehow escaped freezing. It hurt to swallow even a sip. Taking the water with her, she made her way back into the living room.

Mariah hadn't been to the cottage since summer, just before her cancer diagnosis, but Annie didn't see a lot of dust. The caretaker must have done at least part of his job. If only he'd done the rest.

Her dummies lay on the hot pink Victorian sofa. The puppets and her car were all she had left.

Not quite all, Dilly said.

Right. There was the staggering load of debt Annie had no way of repaying, the debt she'd picked up in the last six months of her mother's life by trying to satisfy Mariah's every need.

And finally get Mummy's approval, Leo sneered.

She began removing the puppets' protective plastic. Each figure was about two and a half feet long, with movable eyes and mouth and detachable legs. She picked up Peter and slipped her hand under his T-shirt.

"How beautiful you are, my darling Dilly," he said in his most manly voice. *"The woman of my dreams."*

"And you are the best of men." Dilly sighed. *"Brave and fearless."*

"Only in Annie's imagination," Scamp said with uncharacteristic rancor. *"Otherwise, you're as useless as her exes."*

"There are only two exes, Scamp," Dilly admonished her friend. *"And you really mustn't take out your bitterness against men on Peter. I'm sure you don't mean to, but you're starting to sound like a bully, and you know how we feel about bullies."*

Annie specialized in issue-oriented puppet shows, several of which focused on bullying. She set Peter down and moved Leo off by himself, where he whispered his sneer inside her head. *You're still afraid of me.*

Sometimes it felt as if the puppets had minds of their own.

Pulling the scarlet cloak tighter around her, she wandered to the front bay window. The storm had eased and moonlight shone through the panes. She looked out at the bleak winter landscape—the inky shadows of spruce, the desolate sheet of marsh. Then she lifted her gaze.

Harp House loomed above her in the distance, sitting at the very top of a barren cliff. The murky light of a half-moon outlined its angular roofs and dramatic turret. Except for a faint yellow light visible from high in the turret, the house was dark. The scene reminded her of the covers on the old paperback gothic novels she could still sometimes find in used-book stores. It didn't take much imagination for her to envision a barefoot heroine fleeing that ghostly house in nothing more than a filmy negligee, the menacing turret light glowing behind her. Those books were quaint compared with today's erotically charged vampires, werewolves, and shape-shifters, but she'd always loved them. They'd nourished her daydreams.

Above the jagged roofline of Harp House, storm clouds raced across the moon, their journey as wild as the flight of the horse and rider who'd charged across the road. Her skin turned to gooseflesh, not from the cold but from her own imagination. She turned away from the window and glanced over at Leo.

Heavy-lidded eyes . . . Thin-lipped sneer . . . The perfect villain. She could have avoided so much pain if she hadn't romanticized those brooding men she'd fallen in love with, imagining them as fantasy heroes instead of realizing one was a cheater and the other a narcissist. Leo, however, was a different story. She'd created him herself out of cloth and yarn. She controlled him.

That's what you think, he whispered.

She shivered and retreated to the bedroom. But even as she slipped back under the covers, she couldn't shake off the dark vision of the house on the cliff.

Last night I dreamt I went to Manderley again . . .

SHE WASN'T HUNGRY WHEN SHE awakened the next morning, but she made herself eat a handful of stale granola. The cottage was frigid, the day gloomy, and all she wanted to do was go back to bed. But she couldn't live in the cottage without heat or running water, and the more she thought about her absent caretaker, the angrier she grew. She dug out the only phone number she had, one for the island's combination town hall, post office, and library, but although her phone was charged, she couldn't get a signal. She sank down on the pink velvet couch and dropped her head in her hands. She'd have to go after Will Shaw herself, and that meant making the climb to Harp House. Back to the place she'd sworn she'd never again go near.

She pulled on as many layers of warm clothes as she could find, then wrapped herself in her mother's red cloak and knotted an ancient Hermès scarf under her chin. Summoning all her energy and willpower, she set out. The day was as gray as her future, the salt air frigid, and the distance between the cottage and the house at the top of the cliff insurmountable.

I'll carry you every step of the way, Peter announced.

Scamp blew him a raspberry.

It was low tide, but the icy rocks along the shoreline were too hazardous to walk on at this time of year, so she had to take the longer route around the saltwater marsh. But it wasn't just the distance that filled her with dread.

Dilly tried to give her courage. *It's been eighteen years since you made the climb to Harp House. The ghosts and goblins are long gone.*

Annie pressed the edge of the cloak over her nose and mouth.

Don't worry, Peter said. *I'll watch out for you.*

Peter and Dilly were doing their jobs. They were the ones responsible for untangling Scamp's scrapes and stepping in when Leo bullied. They were the ones who delivered antidrug messages, reminded kids to eat their vegetables, take care of their teeth, and not let anyone touch their private parts.

But it'll feel so good, Leo sneered, then snickered.

Sometimes she wished she'd never created him, but he was such a perfect villain. He was the bully, the drug pusher, the junk food king, and the stranger who tried to lure children away from playgrounds.

Come with me, little kiddies, and I'll give you all the candy you want.

Stop it, Annie, Dilly said. *No one in the Harp family ever comes to the island until summer. Only the caretaker lives there.*

Leo refused to leave Annie alone. *I have Skittles, M&M's, Twizzlers . . . and reminders of all your failures. How's that precious acting career working out?*

She hunched into her shoulders. She needed to start meditating or practicing yoga, doing something that would teach her to discipline her mind instead of letting it wander wherever it wanted—or didn't want—to go. So what if her acting dreams hadn't worked out the way she'd intended. Kids loved her puppet shows.

Her boots crunched in the snow. Dead cattails and hollow reeds poked their battered heads through the frozen crust of the sleeping marsh. In summer, the marsh teemed with life, but now all was bleak, gray, and as quiet as her hopes.

She stopped to rest once again as she neared the bottom of the freshly plowed gravel drive that led up the cliff to Harp House. If Shaw could plow, he could get her car out. She dragged herself on. Before the pneumonia, she could have charged uphill, but by the time she finally reached the top, her lungs were on fire and she'd started to wheeze. Far below, the cottage looked like a neglected toy left to fend for itself against the pounding sea and rugged Maine shoreline. Dragging more fire into her lungs, she made herself lift her head.

Harp House rose before her, silhouetted against the pewter sky. Rooted in granite, exposed to summer squalls and winter gales, it dared the elements to take it down. The island's other summer homes had been built on the more protected eastern side of the island, but Harp House scorned the easy way. Instead it grew from the rocky western headlands far above the sea, a shingle-sided, forbidding, brown wooden fortress with an unwelcoming turret at one end.

Everything was sharp angles: the peaked roofs, shadowed eaves, and foreboding gables. How she'd loved this Gothic gloom when she'd come to live here the summer her mother had married Elliott Harp. She'd imagined herself clad in a mousy gray dress and clutching a portmanteau—gently born, but penniless and desperate, forced to take the humble position of governess. Chin up and shoulders back, she'd confront the brutish (but exceptionally handsome) master of the house with so much courage that he would eventually fall hopelessly in love with her. They'd marry, and then she'd redecorate.

It hadn't taken long before the romantic dreams of a homely fifteen-year-old who read too much and experienced too little had met a harsher reality.

Now the swimming pool was an eerie, empty maw, and the simple sets of wooden stairs that led to the back and side entrances had been replaced with stone steps guarded by gargoyles.

She passed the stable and followed a roughly shoveled path to the back door. Shaw had better be here instead of galloping off on one of Elliott Harp's horses. She pressed the bell but couldn't hear it ring inside. The house was too big. She waited, then rang again, but no one answered. The doormat looked as though it had been recently used to stamp off snow. She rapped hard.

The door creaked open.

She was so cold that she stepped into the mudroom without hesitating. Miscellaneous pieces of outerwear, along with assorted mops and brooms, hung from a set of hooks. She rounded the corner that opened into the main kitchen and stopped.

Everything was different. The kitchen no longer held the walnut cabinets and stainless steel appliances she remembered from eighteen years ago. Instead the place looked as though it had been squeezed through a time warp back to the nineteenth century.

The wall between the kitchen and what had once been a breakfast room was gone, leaving the space twice as large as it had once been. High, horizontal windows let in light, but since the windows were now set at least six feet from the floor, only the tallest person could see through them. Rough plaster covered the top half of the walls, while the bottom was faced with four-inch-square once-white tiles, some chipped at the corners, others cracked with age. The floor was old stone, the fireplace a sooty cavern large enough to roast a wild boar . . . or a man unwise enough to have been caught poaching on his master's land.

Instead of kitchen cabinets, rough shelves held stoneware bowls and crocks. Tall, freestanding dark wood cupboards rose on each side of a dull black industrial-size AGA stove. A stone farmhouse sink held a messy stack of dirty dishes. Copper stockpots and saucepans—not shiny and polished, but dented and worn—hung above a long, scarred wooden prep table designed to chop off chicken heads, butcher mutton chops, or whip up a syllabub for his lordship's dinner.

The kitchen had to be a renovation, but what kind of renovation regressed two centuries. And why?

Run! Crumpet shrieked. *Something's very wrong here!*

Whenever Crumpet got hysterical, Annie counted on Dilly's no-nonsense manner to provide perspective, but Dilly remained silent, and not even Scamp could come up with a wisecrack.

"Mr. Shaw?" Annie's voice lacked its normal powers of projection.

When there was no reply, she moved deeper into the kitchen, leaving wet tracks on the stone floor. But no way was she taking off her boots. If she had to run, she wasn't doing it in socks. "Will?"

Not a sound.

She passed the pantry, crossed a narrow back hallway, detoured around the dining room, and stepped through the arched entry into the foyer. Only the dimmest gray light penetrated the six square panes above the front door. The heavy mahogany staircase still led to a landing with a murky stained-glass window, but the staircase carpet was now a depressing maroon instead of the multicolored floral from the past. The furniture bore a dusty film, and a cobweb hung in the corner. The walls had been paneled over in heavy, dark wood, and the seascape paintings had been replaced with gloomy oil portraits of prosperous men and women in nineteenth-century dress, none of whom could possibly have been Elliott Harp's Irish peasant ancestors. All that was missing to make the entryway even more depressing was a suit of armor and a stuffed raven.

She heard footsteps above her and moved closer to the staircase. "Mr. Shaw? It's Annie Hewitt. The door was open, so I let myself in." She looked up. "I'm going to need—" The words died on her tongue.

The master of the house stood at the top of the stairs.

Chapter Two

He descended slowly. A gothic hero come to life in a pearl gray waistcoat, snowy white cravat, and dark trousers tucked into calf-hugging black leather riding boots. Hanging languidly at his side was a steel-barreled dueling pistol.

An icy finger slithered down her spine. She briefly considered the possibility that her fever had come back—or her imagination had finally shoved her over the cliff of reality. But he wasn't a hallucination. He was all too real.

Only slowly did she tear her gaze away from the pistol, the boots, and the waistcoat to see the man himself.

In the dim gray light, his hair was raven black; his eyes a pale, imperial blue; his face chiseled and unsmiling—everything about him the embodiment of nineteenth-century haughtiness. She wanted to curtsy. To run. To tell him she didn't really need that governess job after all.

He came to the bottom of the stairs, and that was when

she saw it. The pale white scar at the corner of his eyebrow. The scar she'd given him.

Theo Harp.

Eighteen years had passed since she'd last seen him. Eighteen years of trying to bury the memories of that ugly summer.

Run! Run as fast as you can! This time it wasn't Crumpet she heard in her head but sensible, practical Dilly.

And someone else . . .

So . . . We finally meet. Leo's perpetual disdain was gone, replaced by awe.

Harp's wintry, masculine beauty was a perfect match for these Gothic surroundings. He was tall, lean, and elegantly dissolute. His white cravat emphasized the dark complexion he'd inherited from his Andalusian mother, and his teenage scrawniness was a distant memory. But his air of trust fund entitlement hadn't changed. He regarded her coldly. "What do you want?"

She'd given her name—he knew exactly who she was—but he acted as though a stranger had stepped into his house.

"I'm looking for Will Shaw," she said, hating the slight tremor in her voice.

He stepped down onto the marble floor, which was inset with black, diamond-shaped onyx. "Shaw doesn't work here any longer."

"Then who's taking care of the cottage?"

"You'd have to ask my father that."

As if Annie could simply dial up Elliott Harp, a man who spent winters in the South of France with his third wife, a woman who couldn't have been more different from Mariah. Her mother's vivid personality and eccentric, gender-bending style—pipe stem trousers, white men's shirts, beautiful scarves—had attracted half a dozen lovers as well as Elliott Harp. Marrying Mariah had been the answer to his midlife rebellion against an ultraconservative life. And Elliott had provided the sense of security Mariah had never been able to achieve for herself. They'd been doomed from the beginning.

Annie curled her toes inside her boots, ordering herself to stand her ground. "Do you know where I can find Shaw?"

His shoulder barely rose—too bored to waste energy on a real shrug. "No idea."

The ring of a very modern cell phone intruded. Unnoticed by her, he'd been cradling a sleek black smartphone in his opposite hand—the one not caressing the dueling pistol. As he glanced at the display, she realized he was the one she'd seen last night galloping across the road with no regard for the beautiful animal he'd been riding. But then, Theo Harp had a dark history when it came to the welfare of other living creatures, animal and human.

Her nausea was back. She watched a spider creep across the dirty marble floor. He silenced the call. Through the open door behind him—the one that led to the library—she glimpsed Elliott Harp's big mahogany desk. It looked unused. No coffee mugs, yellow pads, or reference books. If Theo Harp was working on his next book, he wasn't doing it there.

"I heard about your mother," he said.

Not—I was sorry to hear about your mother. But then he'd seen how Mariah had treated her daughter.

"Stand up straight, Antoinette. Look people in the eye. How do you expect anyone to respect you?"

Even worse, *"Give me that book. You're not reading any more drivel. Only the novels I give you."*

Annie had hated every one of those novels. Others might fall in love with Melville, Proust, Joyce, and Tolstoy, but Annie wanted books that depicted courageous heroines who stood their ground instead of throwing themselves under a train.

Theo Harp ran his thumb along the edge of the phone, the dueling pistol still dangling from his other hand as he studied her improvised bag-lady attire—the red cloak, the old head scarf, her worn brown suede boots. She'd fallen into a nightmare. The pistol? His bizarre outfit? Why did the house look as though it had regressed two centuries? And why had he once tried to kill her?

"He's more than a bully, Elliott," her mother had told him then husband. *"There's something seriously wrong with your son."*

Annie understood now what hadn't been clear that summer. Theo Harp was mentally ill—a psychopath. The lies, the manipulations, the cruelties . . . The incidents his father Elliott had tried to dismiss as boyish mischief hadn't been mischief at all.

Her stomach refused to settle. She hated being so frightened. He transferred the dueling pistol from his left hand to his right. "Annie, don't come up here again."

Once again, he was getting the best of her, and she hated it.

From nowhere, a ghostly moan crept into the hallway. She whipped around to find its source. "What's that?"

She looked back at him and saw he'd been taken by surprise. He quickly recovered. "It's an old house."

"That didn't sound like a house noise to me."

"It's not your concern."

He was right. Nothing about him concerned her any longer. She was more than ready to leave, but she'd barely taken half a dozen steps before the sound repeated, a softer moan this time, even eerier than the first moan and coming from a different direction. She stared back at him. His frown had deepened, his shoulders tensed.

"Crazy wife in the attic?" she managed.

"Wind," he said, daring her to refute him.

She curled her hand around the soft wool of her mother's cloak. "If I were you, I'd leave the lights on."

She kept her head up long enough to pass through the foyer into the back hallway, but when she reached the kitchen, she stopped and hugged the red cloak around her. An Eggo frozen waffle box, an empty bag of Goldfish crackers, and a ketchup bottle were visible in the overflow of the trash bin in the corner. Theo Harp was crazy. Not the funny crazy of a man who tells bad jokes, but the bad crazy of someone who keeps dead bodies stacked in the cellar. This time as she stepped out into the arctic air, it was more than the cold that made her shiver. It was despair.

She stood straighter. Theo's smartphone . . . There must be reception in the house. Was it possible to get it out here, too? She retrieved her dinosaur of a cell phone from her pocket, found a sheltered place near the deserted gazebo, and turned it on. Within seconds, she had a signal. Her hands shook as she called the number for the island's so-called town hall.

A woman who identified herself as Barbara Rose answered. "Will Shaw left the island last month with his family," she said. "A couple of days before Theo Harp got here."

Annie's heart sank.

"That's what young people do," Barbara went on. "They leave. The lobstering hasn't been good for the past few years."

At least now Annie understood why he hadn't answered her e-mail. She licked her lips. "I wonder . . . How much would someone charge to come out and help me?" She outlined the problem with her car, as well as her ignorance of how to work the small pellet furnace and generator.

"I'll send my husband out as soon as he gets back," Barbara said briskly. "That's the way we do things on the island. We help each other out. Shouldn't be more than an hour."

"Really? That'd be . . . That's really nice." Annie heard a soft whinny from inside the stable. The summer she'd lived here, the building had been painted a soft gray. Now it was a dark maroon, just like the nearby gazebo. She gazed toward the house.

"Everybody was sorry to hear about your mother," Barbara said. "We're going to miss her. She brought culture to the island, along with famous people."

"Thank you." At first Annie thought it was a trick of the light. She blinked, but there it was. A pale oval gazing down at her from an upstairs window.

"After Booker gets your car out, he'll show you how to take care of your furnace and generator." Barbara paused. "Have you seen Theo Harp yet?"

As quickly as it had appeared, the face disappeared. Annie was too far away to have made out the features, but they didn't belong to Theo. A woman? A child? The lunatic wife he'd locked away?

"Only briefly." Annie stared at the empty window. "Did Theo bring anyone with him?"

"No, he came alone. You might not've heard, but his wife died last year."

Had she? Annie drew her gaze away from the window before she let her imagination take over again. She thanked

Barbara for her help and started the return trek to Moonraker Cottage.

Despite the cold, the pain in her lungs, and the eeriness of the face she'd seen, her spirits had lifted a little. Soon she'd have her car back, along with heat and electricity. Then she could start to search in earnest for whatever Mariah had left her. The cottage was small. It shouldn't be that hard to find.

Once again, she wished she could sell the place, but everything connected with Mariah and Elliott Harp had always been complicated. She stopped to rest. Elliott's grandfather had built Harp House at the dawn of the twentieth century, and Elliott had acquired the surrounding property, including Moonraker Cottage. For some reason, Mariah had loved the cottage, and during their divorce proceedings, she'd demanded Elliott give it to her. He'd refused, but by the time the final divorce decree had been drawn up, they'd reached a compromise. The cottage was hers as long as she occupied it for sixty consecutive days each year. Otherwise, it reverted back to the Harp family. No breaks. No do-overs. If she left before the sixty days were up, she couldn't come back and start again.

Mariah was a city creature, and Elliott thought he'd gotten the best of her. If she left the island during that two-month period, even for a night, she'd lose the place forever. But to his consternation, the arrangement suited Mariah. She loved the island, if not Elliott, and since she couldn't see her friends, she invited them to stay with her. Some were well-established artists, others new talents she wanted to encourage. All of them welcomed the chance to paint, to write, to create in the cottage's studio. Mariah had nurtured the artists much better than she'd ever nurtured her own daughter.

Annie huddled into the cloak and started walking again. She'd inherited the cottage, along with the same terms her mother had agreed to. Sixty consecutive days spent here, or the cottage once again belonged to the Harp family. But unlike her mother, Annie hated the island. Right now, though, she had nowhere else to go—as long as she didn't count the moth-eaten futon in the storage room of the coffeehouse where she'd worked. Between her mother's illness and her own, she hadn't been able to keep up with her jobs, and she didn't have the strength or money to find another place to stay.

By the time she'd reached the frozen marsh, her legs were rebelling. She distracted herself by practicing variations on her eerie moans. Something almost like a laugh squeezed out of her. She might be a failure as an actress, but not as a ventriloquist.

And Theo Harp hadn't suspected a thing.

BY HER SECOND MORNING, ANNIE had water, electricity, and a house that was chilly but livable. Thanks to Barbara Rose's garrulous husband, Booker, Annie learned that the return of Theo Harp was the talk of the island. "Tragedy what happened to his wife," Booker said, after he'd taught Annie how to keep the pipes from freezing up, operate the generator, and conserve her propane. "We all feel real bad for the boy. He was an odd one, but he spent a lot of summers here. Did you read his book?"

She hated admitting she had, so she gave a noncommittal shrug.

"It gave my wife nightmares worse than Stephen King," Booker said. "Can't imagine where he got his imagination."

The Sanitarium had been an unnecessarily grisly novel about a mental hospital for the criminally insane with a room that transported its residents—especially those who got their kicks out of torture—back through time. Annie had hated it. Theo had a juicy trust fund, thanks to his grandmother, so he didn't have to write for a living, and in Annie's mind that made what he'd created more reprehensible, even if it had been a best seller. He was supposed to be working on a sequel, and this one she definitely wasn't reading.

After Booker left, Annie unpacked the groceries she'd brought from the mainland, checked all the windows, shoved a steel accent table in front of the door, and slept for twelve hours. As always, she awoke coughing and thinking about money. She was drowning in debt and sick of worrying about it. She lay under the covers, eyes on the ceiling, trying to see her way out.

After Mariah had been diagnosed, she'd needed Annie for the first time, and Annie had been there, even giving up her own jobs when it got to the point that she couldn't leave Mariah alone.

"How did I raise such a timid child?" her mother used to say. But at the end Mariah had been the fearful one, clinging to Annie and begging her not to leave.

Annie had used her small savings to pay the rent on Mariah's beloved Manhattan apartment so her mother wouldn't have to leave, then relied on credit cards for the first time in her life. She bought the herbal remedies Mariah swore made her feel better, the books that fed her mother's artistic spirit, and the special foods that kept Mariah from losing too much weight.

The weaker Mariah grew, the more appreciative she became. "I don't know what I'd do without you." The words were balm to the little girl who still lived inside Annie's adult soul yearning for her critical mother's approval.

Annie might have managed to stay afloat if she hadn't decided to fulfill her mother's dream of one last trip to London. Relying on more credit cards, she'd spent a week pushing Mariah in a wheelchair through the museums and galleries she loved the most. The moment at the Tate Modern when they'd stopped before an enormous red and gray canvas by the artist Niven Garr had made her sacrifice worthwhile. Mariah had pressed her lips to Annie's palm and uttered the words Annie had yearned to hear all her life. "I love you."

Annie dragged herself out of bed and spent the morning digging through the cottage's five rooms: a living area, kitchen, bathroom, Mariah's bedroom, and an artist's studio that had also served as a guest room. The artists who'd stayed here over the years had given Mariah paintings and small pieces of sculpture, the most valuable of which her mother had long ago sold off. But what had she saved?

Nothing and everything jumped out at her. The tufted-back hot pink Victorian sofa and futuristic taupe armchair, a stone Thai goddess, the bird skulls, a wall-size painting of an upside-down elm tree. The hodgepodge of objects and furniture styles were unified by her mother's infallible sense of color—vanilla walls and solid upholstery fabrics of periwinkle, olive, and taupe. The sofa's hit of hot pink along with an ugly iridescent painted plaster chair shaped like a mermaid provided the shock value.

As she rested over her second cup of coffee, she decided she had to be more systematic in her search. She started in the living room, listing every art object and its description in a notebook. It would be so much easier if Mariah had told her what to look for. Or if she could sell the cottage.

Crumpet pouted. *You didn't have to take your mother on that trip to London. You should have bought me a new gown instead. And a tiara.*

You did the right thing, ever-supportive Peter said. *Mariah wasn't a bad person, just a bad mother.*

Dilly spoke in her usual gentle manner, which didn't make her words sting any the less. *Did you do it for her . . . or did you do it for yourself?*

Leo simply sneered. *Anything to win Mummy's love, right, Antoinette?*

And that was the thing about her puppets . . . They spoke the truths she didn't want to confront.

She glanced out the window and saw something moving in the distance. A horse and rider, stark against a sea of gray and white, tearing across the winter landscape, as if all the demons in hell were chasing them.

AFTER ANOTHER DAY OF COUGHING spells, naps, and indulging in her hobby of sketching goofy-looking cartoon kids to cheer herself up, she could no longer ignore the problem of using her cell. More snow last night would have made the already hazardous road impassable, and that meant another trek to the top of the cliff in search of a signal. This time, however, she'd steer clear of the house.

With her puffy down-filled coat, she was better equipped for the climb than she'd been last time. Although it was still bitterly cold, the sun was temporarily out, and the fresh snow looked as though it had been dusted with glitter. But her problems were too big for her to enjoy the beauty. She needed more than a cell signal. She needed Internet access. Unless she wanted a dealer to take advantage of her, she needed to research everything she listed in her inventory notebook, and how was she going to do that? The cottage had no satellite service. The hotel and inns offered free public Internet during the summer, but they were closed now, and even if her car could handle the trips to town, she couldn't imagine randomly banging on doors, looking for someone who'd let her inside to Web surf.

Even with her coat, the red knit cap she'd pulled over her rambunctious hair, and the scarf she'd wrapped over her nose and mouth to protect her airways, she was shivering by the time she hiked to the top of the cliff. Glancing toward the house to make sure Theo wasn't in sight, she found a place behind the gazebo to make her calls—the elementary school in New Jersey that hadn't paid her for her last visit, the consignment shop where she'd left Mariah's remaining pieces of decent furniture. Her own shabby furniture hadn't been worth selling, and she'd hauled it to the curb. She was so sick of worrying about money.

I'll pay your bills, Peter declared. *I'll save you.*

A noise distracted her. She looked around and saw a child crouched under the low branches of a big red spruce. She appeared to be three or four years old, too young to be outside by herself. She wore only a puffy pink jacket and purple corduroy pants—no mittens, no boots, no hat pulled down over her stick-straight light brown hair.

Annie remembered the face in the window. This must be Theo's child.

The idea of Theo as a father horrified her. The poor little girl. She wasn't dressed warmly enough, and she didn't seem to be supervised. Considering what Annie knew of Theo's past, those might be the least of his parenting sins.

The child realized Annie had seen her and backed into the branches. Annie crouched down. "Hey there. I didn't mean to scare you. I was making some phone calls."

The child simply stared at her, but Annie had encountered more than her share of shy little ones. "I'm Annie. Antoinette, really, but no one calls me that. Who are you?"

The child didn't answer.

"Are you a snow fairy? Or maybe a snow bunny?"

Still no response.

"I'll bet you're a squirrel. But I don't see any nuts around. Maybe you're a squirrel who eats cookies?"

Usually even the shyest child responded to this kind of silliness, but the little girl didn't react. She wasn't deaf—she'd turned her head at a birdcall—but as Annie studied those big, watchful eyes, she knew something wasn't right.

"Livia . . ." It was a woman's voice, muffled, as if she didn't want anyone inside the house to hear. "Livia, where are you? Come here right now."

Annie's curiosity got the better of her, and she edged around to the front of the gazebo.

The woman was pretty, with a long swish of blond hair parted at one side and a curvy build that even jeans and a baggy sweatshirt couldn't hide. She leaned awkwardly into a pair of crutches. "Livia!"

There was something familiar about the woman. Annie stepped out of the shadows. "Jaycie?"

The woman wobbled against her crutches. "Annie?"

Jaycie Mills and her father had lived in Moonraker Cottage before Elliott had bought it. Annie hadn't seen her in years, but you didn't forget the person who'd once saved your life.

A flash of pink shot past as the little girl—Livia—ran toward the kitchen door, her snow-caked red sneakers flying. Jaycie wobbled on her crutches. "Livia, I didn't give you permission to go outside." Again, she spoke in that odd hiss-whisper. "We've talked about this before."

Livia gazed up at her but didn't say a word.

"Go take your shoes off."

Livia disappeared, and Jaycie looked at Annie. "I heard you were back on the island, but I didn't expect to see you up here."

Annie moved closer but stayed in the shadow of the trees. "I can't get cell reception at the cottage, and I needed to make some calls."

As a child, Jaycie had been as blond as Theo Harp and his twin sister were dark, and that hadn't changed. Although she was no longer the skinny rail she'd been as a young teen, her pretty features had the same softly blurred quality, as if she existed behind a breath-fogged lens. But why was she here?

Jaycie must have read her mind. "I'm the housekeeper here now."

Annie couldn't think of a more depressing job. Jaycie made an awkward gesture behind her, toward the kitchen. "Come in."

Annie couldn't go in, and she had the perfect excuse. "I've been ordered to stay away by Lord Theo." His name stuck to her lips like rancid oil.

Jaycie had always been more earnest than the rest of them, and she didn't react to Annie's jibe. Being the daughter of a drunken lobsterman had accustomed her to adult responsibilities, and even though she'd been the youngest of the four of them—a year younger than Annie and two years younger than the Harp twins—she'd seemed the most mature. "The only time Theo comes downstairs is in the middle of the night," she said. "He won't even know you're here."

Apparently Jaycie didn't realize Theo was making more than nighttime excursions downstairs. "I really can't."

"Please," she said. "It would be nice to have a grown-up to talk to for a change."

Her invitation sounded more like a plea. Annie owed her everything, and as much as she yearned to refuse, walking away would have been wrong. She pulled herself together, then moved quickly across the open expanse of the backyard in case Theo happened to be looking outside. As she mounted the gargoyle-guarded steps, she had to remind herself that his days of terrorizing her were over.

Jaycie stood just inside the open back door. She saw Annie looking at the purple hippopotamus poking incongruously from beneath one of her armpits and the pink teddy bear poking from the other. "They're my daughter's."

Livia was Jaycie's daughter, then. Not Theo's.

"The crutches hurt my armpits," Jaycie explained as she stepped back to let Annie into the mudroom. "Tying these on top for cushioning helps."

"And makes for interesting conversation."

Jaycie merely nodded, her gravity at odds with the stuffed animals.

Despite what Jaycie had done for Annie that long-ago summer, they'd never been close. During Annie's two brief visits to the island after her mother's divorce, she'd sought Jaycie out, but her rescuer's reserve had made the encounters awkward.

Annie scuffed her boots on the mat just inside the door. "How did you hurt yourself?"

"I slipped on the ice two weeks ago. Don't bother with your boots," she said as Annie bent down to pull them off. "The floor is so dirty, a little snow won't make any difference." She moved awkwardly from the mudroom into the kitchen.

Annie took her boots off anyway, only to regret it as the chill from the stone floor seeped through her socks. She coughed and blew her nose. The kitchen was even darker than she remembered, right down to the soot on the fireplace. More pots had piled up in the sink since she'd been here two days earlier, the trash was overflowing, and the floor needed sweeping. The whole place made her uneasy.

Livia had disappeared, and Jaycie collapsed into a straight-back wooden chair at the long table in the center of the kitchen. "I know everything is a mess," she said, "but since my accident, it's been hell trying to get my work done."

There was a tension about her that Annie didn't remember, not just in her chewed fingernails, but also in her quick, nervous hand movements.

"Your foot looks painful," Annie said.

"It couldn't have come at a worse time. A lot of people seem to get around on crutches just fine, but obviously I'm not one of them." She used her hands to lift her leg and prop her foot on the neighboring chair. "Theo didn't want me here anyway, and now that things are falling apart . . ." She lifted her hands, then seemed to forget where they were going and dropped them back in her lap. "Have a seat. I'd offer to make coffee, but it's too much work."

"I don't need anything." As Annie sat catty-corner to Jaycie, Livia came back into the kitchen, hugging a bedraggled pink-and-white-striped kitten. Her coat and shoes were gone, and her purple corduroy slacks were wet at the cuffs. Jaycie noticed but seemed resigned.

Annie smiled at the child. "How old are you, Livia?"

"Four." Jaycie answered for her daughter. "Livia, the floor is cold. Get your slippers."

The child disappeared again, still without saying a word.

Annie wanted to ask about Livia, but it felt like prying, so she asked about the kitchen instead. "What happened here? Everything has changed so much."

"Isn't it awful? Elliott's wife, Cynthia, is obsessed with everything British, even though she was born in North Dakota. She got it into her head to turn the place into a nineteenth-century manor house and somehow convinced Elliott to spend a fortune on the renovations, including this kitchen. All that money for something this ugly. And they weren't even here last summer."

"It does seem crazy." Annie propped her heels on the chair rung to get them off the stone floor.

"My friend Lisa— You don't know her. She was off island that summer. Lisa loves what Cynthia did, but then she doesn't have to work here." Jaycie gazed down at her bitten fingernails. "I was so excited when Lisa recommended me to Cynthia for the housekeeper's job after Will left. Work's impossible to find here in the winter." The chair creaked as she tried to find a more comfortable position. "But now that I've broken my foot, Theo's going to fire me."

Annie set her jaw. "Typical of Theo Harp to kick somebody when she's helpless."

"He seems different now. I don't know." Her wistful expression reminded Annie of something she'd nearly forgotten—the way Jaycie had watched Theo that summer, as if he were her entire world. "I guess I hoped we'd see each other more. Talk or something."

So Jaycie still had feelings for him. Annie remembered being jealous of Jaycie's soft blond prettiness, even though Theo hadn't paid much attention to her. Annie tried to be tactful. "Maybe you should consider yourself lucky. Theo isn't exactly a solid romantic prospect."

"I guess. He's gotten kind of strange. Nobody comes here, and he hardly ever goes into town. He roams around the house all night, and during the day, he's either out riding or up in the turret writing. That's where he stays, not in the main house. Maybe all writers are strange. I go for days without seeing him."

"I was here two days ago, and I ran into him right away."

"You did? That must have been when Livia and I were sick, or I would have seen you. We slept most of the day."

Annie recalled the small face in the second-floor window. Maybe Jaycie had slept, but Livia had roamed. "Theo's living in the turret where his grandmother used to stay?"

Jaycie nodded and adjusted her foot on the chair. "It has its own kitchen. Before I broke my foot, I kept it stocked. Now I can't maneuver the steps so I have to send everything up in the dumbwaiter."

Annie remembered that dumbwaiter all too well. Theo had stuffed her inside it one day and stuck her between the floors. She glanced at the round face of the old clock on the wall. How much longer before she could leave?

Jaycie pulled a cell from her pocket—another high-tech smartphone—and set it on the table. "He texts me when he needs something, but since I broke my foot, I can't do much. He didn't want me here in the first place, but Cynthia insisted. Now I've given him an excuse to get rid of me."

Annie would have liked to say something hopeful, but Jaycie had to know enough about Theo to realize he'd do exactly what he wanted.

Jaycie picked at a glittery My Little Pony sticker that had adhered to the rough-hewn servant's table. "Livia is everything to me. All I have left." She didn't say it in a self-pitying way, more as a statement of fact. "If I lose this job, there aren't any others." She rose awkwardly from the table. "Sorry to dump on you. I spend too much time with only a four-year-old to talk to."

A four-year-old who didn't seem to speak.

Jaycie hobbled toward a very large, old-fashioned icebox. "I need to get dinner started."

Annie rose. "Let me help." Despite her fatigue, it would feel good to do something for someone else.

"No, it's okay." She pulled at the latch on the icebox and opened the door, revealing the interior of a very modern refrigerator. She stared at the contents. "While I was growing up, all I wanted to do was get away. Then I married a lobsterman and got stuck here."

"Anybody I knew?"

"He was older, so probably not. Ned Grayson. The best-looking man on the island. For a while, that made me forget about how much I hated it here." She snatched a bowl covered in plastic wrap from the refrigerator. "He died last summer."

"I'm sorry."

She gave a rueful laugh. "Don't be. Turned out, he had a mean temper and big fists that he wasn't afraid of using. Mainly on me."

"Oh, Jaycie . . ." Her air of vulnerability made it doubly obscene to imagine her being abused.

Jaycie tucked the bowl under her free arm, wedging it tightly against her body. "It's ironic. I thought my broken bones were behind me when he died." She pushed the refrigerator door closed with her hip only to lose her balance at the last minute. Her crutches fell to the floor, along with the bowl. It shattered, sending glass and chili flying.

"*Shit!*" Harsh, angry tears clouded her eyes. Chili splattered the stone floor, the cupboard, her jeans and sneakers. Shards of glass were everywhere.

Annie rushed to her side. "Get cleaned up. I'll take care of this."

Jaycie sagged against the icebox and stared at the mess. "I can't depend on other people. I have to take care of myself."

"Not right now, you don't." Annie spoke as firmly as she could. "Tell me where I can find a bucket."

She stayed for the rest of the afternoon. No matter how tired she was, she wouldn't leave Jaycie like this. She cleaned up the chili mess and managed the dishes in the sink, doing her best to muffle her cough when Jaycie was nearby. All the while, she kept an eye out for Theo Harp. Knowing he was so close unnerved her, but she wouldn't let Jaycie see that. Before she left, she did something she'd never imagined. She fixed his dinner.

She gazed into the bowl of doctored tomato soup, leftover hamburger, instant white rice, and frozen corn. "I don't suppose you've seen any rat poison lying around," she said as Jaycie hobbled across the kitchen. "Never mind. This meal is already disgusting enough."

"He won't notice. He doesn't care about food."

All he cared about was hurting people.

She carried the dinner tray down the back hallway. As she placed it in the dumbwaiter, she remembered the terror of being trapped inside that tight enclosure. Everything had been pitch-black. She was squeezed into a ball, her knees squashed to her chest. Theo had been sentenced to spend two days in his room for that, and only Annie had noticed that Regan, his twin, had sneaked in to keep him company.

Regan had been as sweet and shy as Theo was mean and selfish. But unless Regan was playing her oboe or writing poetry in her purple notebook, brother and sister had been inseparable. Annie suspected she and Regan would have become real friends if Theo hadn't made sure that didn't happen.

Jaycie's eyes filled when it came time for Annie to leave. "I don't know how to thank you."

Annie hid her fatigue. "You already did. Eighteen years ago." She hesitated, knowing what she should do, not wanting to, but finally making the only choice she could live with. "I'll come back tomorrow for a little bit to help out."

Jaycie's eyes flew open. "You don't have to do that!"

"It'll be good for me," she lied. "Keep me from brooding." A new thought came to her. "Does the house have WiFi?" When Jaycie nodded, she managed a smile. "Perfect. I'll bring my laptop. You'll be helping me. There's some research I have to do."

Jaycie grabbed a tissue and pressed it to her eyes. "Thank you. It means a lot."

Jaycie disappeared to find Livia, and Annie went to get her coat. Despite her exhaustion, she was glad to have done something to help repay her old debt. She began to pull on her gloves, then hesitated. She couldn't stop thinking about that dumbwaiter.

Go on, Scamp whispered. *You know you want to.*

Don't you think that's a little immature? Dilly replied.

Definitely, Scamp said.

Annie remembered her younger self, so desperate to make Theo like her. She crept through the kitchen. Moving as quietly as she could, she stepped into the back hallway and down the narrow passage to the end. She stared at the door of the dumbwaiter. Edgar Allan Poe had a monopoly on "Nevermore," and "Rosebud" was hardly terrifying. "You will die in seven days" seemed too specific. But she'd watched a lot of television when she was sick, including *Apocalypse Now* . . .

She opened the door of the dumbwaiter, lowered her head, and uttered, in a soft, creepy moan, *"The horror . . ."* The words uncoiled like a hissing snake. *"The horrrror . . ."*

She got goose bumps.

Sick! Scamp exclaimed in delight.

Juvenile, but satisfying, Dilly said.

Annie hurried back the way she'd come and let herself out. Staying in the shadows where she couldn't be spotted from the turret, she made her way to the drive.

Harp House finally had the ghost it deserved.

Chapter Three

Annie woke up in a slightly more positive frame of mind. The idea of driving Theo Harp gradually insane was so satisfyingly twisted that she couldn't help but feel better. There was no way he could write those awful books without a powerful imagination, and what could be more well deserved than turning that imagination against him? She thought about what else she might be able to pull off and allowed herself a brief fantasy of Theo in a straitjacket, trapped behind asylum bars.

With snakes slithering across the floor! Scamp added.

You won't get him that easily, Leo sneered.

Annie hit a snag in her hair and tossed her comb aside. She pulled on jeans, a camisole, a long-sleeved gray T-shirt, and topped it all with a sweatshirt that had somehow survived her college days. As she left her bedroom for the living room, she took in what she'd done before she'd gone to bed last night. The small animal skulls Mariah had displayed in a bowl edged with barbed wire were now buried in the bottom of a trash bag. Her mother and Georgia O'Keeffe might find bones beautiful, but Annie didn't, and if she had to spend two months here, she was going to feel at least marginally at home. Unfortunately, the cottage was so compact there was nowhere to stash the iridescent plaster mermaid chair. She'd tried to sit in it and been jabbed in the back with a pair of breasts.

Two items she'd uncovered disturbed her—a copy of the *Portland Press Herald* dated exactly seven days earlier and a bag of freshly ground coffee in the kitchen. Someone had been here recently.

She drank a cup of that same coffee and made herself eat a piece of jelly toast. She dreaded the thought of going back to Harp House, but at least she'd have WiFi access. She studied the painting of the inverted tree. Maybe by the end of the day she'd know who R. Connor was and whether his or her work had any value.

She couldn't put it off any longer. She stuffed her inventory notebook, her laptop, and some other things in her backpack, wrapped herself up, and began her reluctant journey to Harp House. As she crossed the eastern edge of the marsh, she eyed the wooden footbridge. Bypassing it made the trip longer, and she needed to stop avoiding it. She would. But not today.

Annie had met Theo and Regan Harp two weeks after Mariah and Elliott had flown off to the Caribbean together and returned married. The twins were just coming up the cliff steps from the beach. Regan had appeared first, all golden tan legs and long, dark hair swinging around her pretty face. Then Annie had seen Theo. Even at sixteen, skinny, with a few breakouts on his forehead and a face not quite big enough to carry his nose, he'd been arresting, aloof, and she was instantly captivated. He, however, had regarded her with undisguised boredom.

Annie desperately wanted them to like her, but she was intimidated by their self-confidence, and that made her tongue-tied in their presence. While Regan was easy and sweet, Theo was rude and cutting. Elliott tended to indulge them both in an attempt to make up for their mother's desertion when they were five, but he insisted they include Annie in their activities. Theo begrudgingly invited her to go out with them on their sailboat. But when Annie arrived at the dock that jutted between Harp House and Moonraker Cottage, Theo, Regan, and Jaycie had already set off without her. The next day she'd shown up an hour earlier only to have them not appear at all.

One afternoon Theo told Annie she should go see an old lobster boat wreck not far down the shoreline. Annie discovered too late that the wreck had become a nesting spot for the island's gulls. They'd dive-bombed her, batting her with their wings, and one had struck her on the head in a scene straight out of Hitchcock's *The Birds*. Annie had been wary of birds ever since.

The litany of his misdeeds had been unending: dead fish in her bed, rough play in the swimming pool, abandoning her in the dark on the beach one night. Annie shook off the memories. Fortunately, she'd never be fifteen again.

She began to cough, and as she stopped to catch her breath, she realized it was her first coughing spasm of the morning. Maybe she was finally getting better. She imagined herself sitting at a warm desk in a warm office, a warm computer in front of her, as she worked away at a job that would bore her to tears but would bring a steady paycheck.

But what about us? Crumpet whined.

Annie needs a real job, sensible Dilly said. *She can't be a vent forever.*

Scamp piped up with her own words of advice. *You should have made porn puppets. You could have charged a lot more for the shows.*

The porn puppets were an idea Annie had entertained when she was running the worst of her fever.

She finally reached the top of the cliff. As she passed the stable, she heard a horse whinny. She quickly cut into the trees just in time to see Theo emerge through the stable doors. Annie was cold even in her down coat, but he wore only a charcoal sweater, jeans, and riding boots.

He stopped walking. She was behind him, but the tree cover was sparse, and she prayed he wouldn't turn around.

A gust of wind stirred up a ghostly dervish in the snow. He crossed his arms over his chest, grabbed the bottom of his sweater, and pulled it over his head. He wore nothing underneath.

She gazed at him in astonishment. He stood there barechested, the wind tearing at his thick dark hair as he defied the Maine winter. He didn't move. She might have been watching one of the old television soaps famous for using any excuse to get their heroes out of their shirts. Except it was bitterly cold, Theo Harp was no hero, and the only explanation for what he'd done was insanity.

He knotted his hands into fists at his sides, lifted his chin, and gazed at the house. How could someone so beautiful be so cruel? The hard planes of his back . . . The muscularity of his broad shoulders . . . The way he stood against the sky . . . It was all so strange. He seemed less a mortal and more a part of the landscape—a primitive creature who didn't need the simple human comforts of warmth, food . . . love.

She shivered inside her down coat and watched him disappear through the turret door, his sweater still dangling at his side.

JAYCIE WAS TOUCHINGLY GLAD TO see her. "I can't believe you came back," she said as Annie hung up her backpack and pulled off her boots.

Annie put on her happiest face. "If I stayed away, I'd miss all the fun." She glanced around the kitchen. Despite its gloom, it looked marginally better than it had yesterday, but it was still awful.

Jaycie lumbered from the stove toward the table, gnawing on her bottom lip. "Theo's going to fire me," she whispered. "I know he is. Since he stays in the turret all the time, he doesn't think anybody needs to be in the house. If it weren't for Cynthia . . ." She gripped the crutches so tightly that her knuckles turned white. "This morning he spotted Lisa McKinley here. She's been meeting the mail boat for me. I didn't think he knew about it, but I was wrong. He hates having people around."

Then how does he expect to find his next murder victim? Scamp inquired. *Unless it's Jaycie . . .*

I'll take care of her, Peter trumpeted. *That's what I do. Take care of weak women.*

Jaycie repositioned herself on her crutches, the pink hippopotamus head bobbing incongruously near her armpit, her forehead furrowing. "He . . . he sent me a text and told me he didn't want Lisa up here anymore. To have them hold the mail in town until he could get to it. But Lisa's been bringing up groceries every week, too, and what am I supposed to do about that? I can't lose this job, Annie. It's all I have."

Annie tried to be encouraging. "Your foot will be better soon, and you'll be able to drive."

"That's only part of it. He doesn't like kids here. I told him how quiet Livia is and promised he wouldn't even know she was around, but she keeps sneaking outside. I'm afraid he'll see her."

Annie shoved her feet into the sneakers she'd brought with her. "Let me get this straight. Because of Lord Theo, a four-year-old can't go outside to play? That's not right."

"I guess he can do what he wants—it's his house. Besides, as long as I'm on crutches, I can't go out with her anyway, and I don't want her out there by herself."

Annie hated the way Jaycie kept making excuses for him. She should be smart enough to see him as he really was, but after all these years, she still seemed to have a crush on him.

Kids have crushes, Dilly whispered. *Jaycie's a grown woman. Maybe it's more than a crush.*

This is not good, Scamp said. *Not good at all.*

Livia came into the kitchen. She wore her corduroy pants from yesterday and carried a clear plastic shoe box–size container of broken crayons along with a dog-eared pad of drawing paper. Annie smiled at her. "Hi, Livia."

The child ducked her head.

"She's shy," Jaycie said.

Livia brought her drawing supplies to the table, hoisted herself up onto one of the chairs, and set to work. Jaycie showed Annie where the cleaning supplies were stored, apologizing the whole time. "You don't have to do this. Really. It's my problem, not yours."

Annie cut off her apologies. "Why don't you see what you can do about his master's meals? Since you let me down with the rat poison idea, maybe you could find some deadly mushrooms?"

Jaycie smiled. "He's not that bad, Annie."

So untrue.

As Annie carried dust rags and a broom into the main hallway, she eyed the stairs uneasily. She prayed Jaycie was right and that Theo's appearance here four days ago had been an anomaly. If he found out Annie was doing Jaycie's work, he really would find another housekeeper.

Most of the downstairs rooms were closed off to conserve heat, but the foyer, Elliott's office, and the dreary sunroom all needed attending. With her limited strength, she decided to make the foyer her priority, but by the time she'd gotten rid of the cobwebs and wiped down the dusty paneled walls, she was wheezing. She returned to the kitchen and found Livia alone there, still busy at the table with her crayons.

She'd been thinking about Livia, and she went into the mudroom to find her backpack with Scamp inside. Annie made most of her puppets' outfits, including Scamp's rainbow tights, short pink skirt, and bright yellow T-shirt with its sparkly purple star. A headband with a floppy green poppy held her crazy orange yarn curls in place. Annie slipped the puppet over her hand and arm, then positioned her fingers on the levers that operated the puppet's mouth and eyes. She held Scamp behind her back and returned to the table.

As Livia peeled the paper from her red crayon, Annie took a chair catty-corner to her. Instantly, Scamp poked her head up over the side of the table and peered at Livia. "La . . . La . . . *LA!*" Scamp sang in her most attention-getting voice. "I Scamp, otherwise known as Genevieve Adelaide Josephine Brown, declare it a beee-u-tiful day!"

Livia jerked up her head and stared at the puppet. Scamp leaned forward, her wild curls tumbling around her face, and tried to peer at Livia's artwork. "I love to draw, too. Can I see your picture?"

Livia, all eyes on the puppet, covered the paper with her arm.

"I suppose some things are private," Scamp said. "But I believe in sharing my talents. Like my singing."

Livia cocked her head curiously.

"I'm a wonderful singer," Scamp chirped. "Not that I share my amazingly fabulous songs with just anybody. Like you and your drawing. You don't have to share with anyone."

Livia promptly pulled her hand away from what she'd drawn. While Scamp bent over the paper to study it, Annie had to rely on what she could see out of the corner of her eye—something approximating a human figure standing near a crudely drawn house.

"Fab-u-loso!" Scamp said. "I, too, am a great artist." Now she was the one who cocked her head. "Would you like to hear me sing?"

Livia nodded.

Scamp threw her arms wide and began to sing a comically operatic version of "The Itsy-Bitsy Spider" that always brought squeals of laughter from the kindergarten crowd.

Livia listened carefully, but she didn't crack a smile, not even when Scamp began changing the lyrics. "Out came the moon and drank up all the grasshopper juice . . . And the itsy-bitsy underpants went crazy all over again. *Olé!*"

The singing made Annie cough. She covered it up by having Scamp embark on a wild dance. At the end, Scamp threw herself down on the table. "Being fabulous is soooo exhausting."

Livia nodded solemnly.

Annie had learned it was best when dealing with children to stop when you were ahead. Scamp picked herself up and tossed her head of curls. "It's time for my nap. *Au revoir.* Until we meet again . . ." She disappeared under the table.

Livia immediately ducked her head to see where the puppet had gone, but as she leaned forward, Annie rose, tucked Scamp out of sight in front of her, and crossed the floor to return the puppet to the backpack. She didn't look at Livia, but as she left the kitchen she could feel the child watching her.

Later that day, while Theo was out riding, Annie took advantage of his absence to carry the trash that had accumulated in the house out to the metal drums that sat behind the stables. On her way back to the house, she looked toward the empty swimming pool. An unsightly collection of frozen debris had accumulated on the bottom. Even in the heart of the summer, the water around Peregrine Island was frigid, and she and Regan had done most of their swimming in the pool while Theo preferred the ocean. If the surf was up, he'd toss his board in the back of his Jeep and head toward Gull Beach. Annie had yearned to go with him but was too afraid of rejection to ask.

A black cat crept around the corner of the stable and gazed up at her through a pair of yellow eyes. Annie froze. An alarm bell rang in her head. "Get out of here!" she hissed.

The cat stared at her.

She dashed toward it, waving her arms. "Go! Go away! And don't come back. Not if you know what's good for you."

The cat scurried away.

Out of nowhere, her eyes filled with tears. She blinked them away and went back into the house.

ANNIE SLEPT ANOTHER TWELVE HOURS that night, then spent the rest of the morning working on her inventory of the cottage living room, listing the furnishings, paintings, and objects like the Thai goddess. At the house yesterday, she'd been too busy to do any research, but she'd make time today. Mariah had never depended on dealers to determine the value of what she had. She'd done her homework first, and so would Annie. In the afternoon, she tucked her laptop computer in her backpack and hiked up to Harp House. Her muscles ached from their unaccustomed exercise, but she made it to the top with only one coughing spasm.

She cleaned Elliott's office, including the ugly dark walnut gun cabinet, and washed yesterday's dishes while Jaycie worried about Theo's meals. "I'm not a very good cook," she said. "One more reason for him to fire me."

"I can't help you out there," Annie said.

Annie saw the black cat again and dashed outside without her coat to shoo it away. Later she settled at the kitchen table with her laptop, but the house's WiFi system was password protected, something she should have anticipated.

"I always use the phone Theo gave me," Jaycie said as she sat at the table, peeling some carrots. "I've never had to use a password."

Annie tried various combinations of names, birthdays, even boat names with no luck. She stretched her arms overhead to ease her shoulders, stared at the screen, then slowly typed in *Regan0630,* the summer day Regan Harp had drowned after her sailboat capsized in a squall off the island's coast. She'd been twenty-two, a new college graduate, but in Annie's mind, she'd be forever sixteen, a dark-haired angel who played the oboe and wrote poetry.

The door flew open, and Annie whipped around in her chair. Theo Harp stalked into the kitchen with Livia slung under his arm.

Chapter Four

He looked as though he'd been blown in by a fierce nor'easter. However, the most alarming part of his sudden appearance wasn't his thunderous expression but the terrified little girl tucked under his arm, her small mouth open in a chilling silent scream.

"Livia!" Jaycie lurched toward her daughter, lost her balance, and fell awkwardly to the stone floor, taking her crutches with her.

Annie jumped up from the table and sprang toward him, moving automatically, too horrified by what was unfolding to wait for Jaycie to recover. "What do you think you're doing?"

His dark brows knit in outrage. "What am *I* doing? She was in the stable!"

"Give her to me!" Annie pulled Livia away from him, but the child was just as frightened of her. Jaycie had managed to push herself into a sitting position. Annie deposited Livia in

Jaycie's lap, then instinctively positioned herself between them and Theo. "Stay where you are," she warned him.

Hey! I'm the hero, Peter protested. *Protecting people is my job.*

"She was *in my stable*!" Theo exclaimed.

His presence filled the cavernous kitchen, taking up all the air. Gulping for a thread of oxygen, Annie planted her feet. "Could you please use your inside voice?"

Jaycie gasped. Theo's volume didn't change. "She wasn't just standing in the doorway. She was in the stall with Dancer. In the *stall*. That horse is skittish. Do you have any idea what could have happened to her in there? And I told you to stay away. Why are you here?"

She ordered herself not to let him browbeat her—not this time around—but she couldn't match him in ferocity. "How did she get in the stall?"

His eyes flashed accusation. "How do I know? Maybe it wasn't latched."

"In other words, you forgot to latch it." Her legs had begun to shake. "Maybe you were thinking too hard about taking your horse out in another blizzard?"

She'd managed to deflect his attention from Jaycie and Livia. Unfortunately, all his focus was now on her. He flexed his hands, as if he were getting ready to swing a punch. "What the hell are you doing here?"

The puppets saved her. "Language," she said, using Dilly's disapproving voice but, fortunately, remembering to move her lips as she said it.

"Why are you in my house?" He enunciated each syllable in the same unpleasant manner as Leo.

She couldn't let him know she'd been helping Jaycie. "There's no WiFi at the cottage, and I need it."

"Find it somewhere else."

If you don't stand up to him, Scamp said, *he'll win all over again.*

Annie lifted her chin. "I'd appreciate it if you'd give me the password."

He stared at her as if she'd crawled out of a sewer. "I told you to stay away."

"Did you? I don't remember." She had to cover up for Jaycie. "Jaycie told me I couldn't be here," she lied, "but I ignored her." She needed to make sure he understood. "I'm not as nice as I used to be."

Jaycie made a small noise instead of keeping quiet as she should have, which sent Theo's attention back to her. "You know what our deal is, Jaycie."

Jaycie curled Livia against her breasts. "I tried to keep Livia out of your way, but . . ."

"This isn't going to work," he said flatly. "We'll have to come up with another arrangement." And with that lofty proclamation, he turned to leave, as if there was no more to say.

Let him go! Crumpet urged.

But Annie couldn't, and she dashed in front of him. "What bad movie did you step out of? Look at her!" She pointed her finger toward Jaycie, hoping he wouldn't notice that it wasn't altogether steady. "You're really thinking about throwing a penniless widow and her child out into the snow? Has your heart completely turned to stone? Never mind. Rhetorical question."

He regarded her with the annoyed expression of someone being buzzed by a pesky mosquito. "What part of this is your business?"

She hated confrontation, but Scamp didn't, so she channeled her alter ego. "The part of me that's a compassionate human being. Stop me if 'compassionate' is a word you don't understand." His imperial blue eyes darkened. "Livia won't be going into the stable again because you're going to remember to lock the door. And your housekeeper has been doing a great job, despite her broken foot. You've been getting your meals, haven't you? Look at this kitchen. It's spotless." An exaggeration, so she zeroed in on what she suspected was his weak spot. "If you fire Jaycie, Cynthia will hire someone else. Just think. Another stranger invading your privacy. Poking around Harp House. Watching you. Disturbing your work. Even trying to have a *conversation* with you. Is that what you want?"

Even as she drew a wheezy breath, she read her victory in the slight tightening of his eyelids, the vague downward tilt at the corners of his too-beautiful mouth.

He glanced toward Jaycie, who was still sitting on the floor with Livia cradled in her arms. "I'm going out for a couple of hours," he said brusquely. "Clean up the turret while I'm gone. Leave the third floor alone."

He stormed out the door with nearly as much force as when he'd come in.

Livia had her thumb in her mouth. Jaycie kissed both of her cheeks before setting her aside and pulling herself up with her crutches. "I can't believe you talked to him like that."

Annie couldn't believe it either.

The turret had two entrances: one from the outside and another from the second floor of the house. Jaycie's difficulty managing steps meant Annie was the one who had to do the job.

The turret was built on a higher foundation than the rest of Harp House, so its first floor was on the same level as Harp House's second floor, and the door at the end of the house's upstairs hallway opened directly into the turret's main living area. Nothing seemed to have changed since the days when the twins' grandmother had stayed here. The angular, beige walls served as a backdrop for overstuffed furnishings from the 1980s, pieces that were worn in places and sun-faded from the row of windows facing the ocean.

A worn Persian rug covered most of the wooden parquet floor, and a beige couch with big rolled arms and fringed pillows sat beneath a pair of amateur landscape oil paintings. A set of big wooden floor candlesticks holding tall, chunky white candles with unlit wicks and dusty tops stood beneath a pendulum clock whose hands had stopped at eleven and four. This was the only part of Harp House that didn't seem to have regressed two hundred years, but it was just as gloomy.

She made her way into the small galley kitchen where the dumbwaiter occupied the end wall. Instead of a pile of dirty dishes, the crockery that had been sent up from the main kitchen with Theo's meals was clean and sitting in a blue plastic dish drainer. She pulled a bottle of spray cleaner from under the sink, but she didn't immediately use it. Jaycie only cooked dinner for him. What did the Lord of the Underworld eat the rest of the time? She set down the bottle and opened the closest cupboards.

No eye of newt or toe of frog. No sautéed eyeballs or French-fried fingernails. Instead she found boxes of shredded wheat, Cheerios, and Wheaties. Nothing overly sweet. Nothing fun. But then again, no preserved human body parts.

This might be her only chance to explore, so she continued her snooping. Some uninteresting canned goods. A six-pack of high-end carbonated mineral water, a large bag of premium coffee beans, and a bottle of good Scotch. A few pieces of fruit sat out on the counter, and as she gazed at them, her Wicked Queen voice cackled in her head. *Have an apple, my pretty . . .*

She turned away and went to the refrigerator, where she found bloodred tomato juice, a block of hard cheese, oily black olives, and unopened containers of some disgusting pâté. She shuddered. Not surprising that he liked organ meats.

The freezer was virtually empty, and the hydrator drawer held only carrots and radishes. She gazed around the kitchen. Where was the junk food? The bags of tortilla chips and tubs of Ben & Jerry's? Where was the stockpile of potato chips, the stash of peanut butter cups? No salty, crunchy things. No sweet indulgences. In its own way, this kitchen was as creepy as the other one.

She picked up the spray cleaner, then hesitated. Hadn't she read somewhere that you were supposed to clean from the top down?

Nobody likes a snoop, Crumpet said in her superior voice.

Like you don't have any faults, Annie retorted.

Vanity isn't a fault, Crumpet retorted. *It's a calling.*

Yes, Annie wanted to snoop, and she was going to do it now. While Theo was safely out of the house, she could see exactly what he kept in his lair.

Her sore calf muscles protested as she climbed the steps to the second floor. If she craned her neck, she could see the closed door that led to the third-floor attic, where he was supposed to be writing his next, sadistic novel. Or maybe chopping up dead bodies.

The bedroom door was open. She peered inside. With the

exception of jeans and a sweatshirt tossed across the bottom of the badly made bed, it looked as though an old lady still lived here. Off-white walls, drapes printed with cabbage roses, a raspberry slipper chair with a tufted round ottoman, and a double bed covered in a beige spread. He certainly hadn't done anything to make himself feel at home.

She went back out into the tiny hallway and hesitated for only a moment before making her way up the remaining six steps to the forbidden third floor. She pushed open the door.

The pentagonal room had an exposed wooden ceiling and five bare, narrow windows with pointed arches. The human touches that were missing everywhere else were visible here. An L-shaped desk jutted out from one wall, its top cluttered with papers, empty CD cases, a couple of notebooks, a desktop computer, and headphones. Across the room, black metal industrial shelving held various electronics including a sound system and a small flat-screen television. Stacks of books sat on the floor beneath some of the windows, and a laptop computer lay next to a slouchy easy chair.

The door squeaked open.

She gave a hiss of alarm and spun around.

Theo came inside, a black knit scarf in his hands.

He tried to kill you once, Leo sneered. *He can do it again.*

She swallowed. Pulled her eyes away from the small white scar at the corner of his eyebrow, the scar she'd given him.

He came toward her, no longer simply holding the black scarf, but passing it through his hands like a garrote . . . or a gag . . . or maybe a chloroform-soaked rag. How long would he have to hold it over her face before she was unconscious?

"This floor is off-limits," he said. "But then you know that. Yet here you are."

He looped the scarf around his neck, holding the ends in his fists. Her tongue was frozen. Once again, she had to call on Scamp for courage. "You're the one who's not supposed to be here." She hoped he didn't hear the squeak in her normally reliable voice. "How am I supposed to snoop if you don't leave when you say you're going to?"

"You're kidding, right?" He pulled on the ends of the scarf.

"It's— It's really your fault." She needed to come up with something quickly. "I wouldn't have come in here if you'd given me your password when I asked."

"Fortunately, I'm not following you."

"A lot of people tape it to their computers." She gripped her hands behind her back.

"I don't."

Hold your ground, Scamp ordered. *Make him understand he's dealing with a woman now, not a grossly insecure fifteen-year-old.*

She'd aced her improv classes, and she gave it her best. "Don't you think that's a little moronic?"

"Moronic?"

"Bad word choice," she said hastily. "But . . . Say you forget the password. Do you really want to have to call your satellite company?" She coughed and sucked in some air. "You know what that experience is like. You'll be on the phone for hours listening to a recording telling you how important your call is. Or that their menu has changed, and you're supposed to listen carefully. I mean, isn't changing the menu their problem, not yours? After a few minutes of that, I usually feel like killing myself. Do you really want to go through that kind of hell when a simple Post-it note solves the whole problem?"

"Or a simple e-mail," he said with the sarcasm her ramble deserved. "Dirigo."

"What?"

Dropping his hands from the scarf, he wandered to the nearest window, where a telescope was pointed toward the ocean. "You convinced me. The password is *Dirigo.*"

"What kind of password is that?"

"The state motto of Maine. It means 'I direct.' It also means you've lost your excuse to snoop."

Nothing much she could say to that. She edged backward toward the door.

He lifted the telescope from its tripod and carried it to another window. "Do you really think I don't know you're doing Jaycie's work for her?"

She should have realized he'd figure that out. "What do you care, as long as the work gets done?"

"Because I don't want you around."

"Got it. You'd rather fire Jaycie."

"I don't need anybody here."

"Sure you do. Who's going to answer the door while you're asleep in your casket?"

He ignored her, peering through the eyepiece of the telescope instead and adjusting it. She felt a prickling at the back of her neck. The window he'd moved to was the one that looked down on the cottage.

That's what you get for challenging a scoundrel, Leo sneered.

"I have a new telescope," he said. "When the light's just right, it's amazing how much I can see." He shifted the telescope ever so slightly. "I hope that furniture you moved wasn't too heavy for you."

The chill traveled all the way to her toes.

"Don't forget to change the sheets in my bedroom," he said without turning. "There's nothing better than the feel of clean sheets against bare skin."

She wouldn't let him see how much he still frightened her. She made herself turn away slowly and head for the stairs. She had every reason to tell Jaycie she couldn't do this anymore. Every reason except an absolute certainty that she couldn't live with herself if she let her fear of Theo Harp force her into abandoning the girl who'd once saved her life.

She worked as quickly as she could. She dusted the living room furniture, vacuumed the rug, scoured the kitchen, and then, her stomach pitching with foreboding, she moved to his bedroom. She found clean linens, but stripping the old sheets from his bed was too personal, too intimate. She set her jaw and did it anyway.

As she reached for a dust rag, she heard the attic door close above her followed by the click of a lock and the sound of footsteps coming down the stairs. She told herself not to turn around, but she did anyway.

He stood in the doorway, one shoulder propped against the doorjamb. His gaze moved from her untidy hair to her breasts—barely visible beneath her heavy sweater—then glided over her hips, lingered, moved on. There was something calculating about his inspection. Something invasive and disturbing. Finally, he turned away.

And that's when it happened.

An unearthly sound—half moan, half growl, and totally chilling—seeped into the room.

He stopped in his tracks. She twisted her head to look up toward the attic. "What's *that*?"

His brow knit. He opened his mouth, as if he wanted to offer an explanation, but no words came out. Moments later he was gone.

The door slammed below. She set her jaw.

Bastard. Serves you right.

THEO'S BREATH FOGGED THE AIR as he unlatched the door to the stable, the place where he'd always go when he needed to think. He'd thought he'd anticipated everything, but he hadn't anticipated that she'd be back, and he wouldn't tolerate it.

The interior smelled of hay, manure, dust, and cold. In past years his father had kept as many as four horses here, animals boarded at the island stable when the family wasn't on Peregrine. Now Theo's black gelding was the only horse.

Dancer gave a soft whinny and poked his head over the stall. Theo had never imagined he'd have to see her again, yet here she was. In his house. In his life. Bringing the past with her. He rubbed Dancer's muzzle. "It's just you and me, boy," he said. "You and me . . . and whatever new devils have shown up to haunt us."

The horse tossed its head. Theo opened the stall door. He couldn't let this go on. He had to get rid of her.

Chapter Five

Being alone in the cottage at night had spooked Annie from the beginning, but that night was the worst yet. The windows had no curtains, and Theo could be watching her at any time through his telescope. She left the lights off, stumbled around in the dark, and pulled the covers over her head when she went to bed. But the dark only stirred her memories of the way everything had changed.

It had happened not long after the dumbwaiter incident. Regan was either at a riding lesson or locked in her room writing poetry. Annie had been perched on the rocks at the beach, daydreaming about being a beautiful, talented actress starring in a major motion picture when Theo had come along. He'd settled next to her, his long legs emerging from a pair of khaki shorts a little too big for him. A hermit crab had scampered through a tidal pool at their feet. He'd gazed out toward the break where the waves began to curl. "I'm sorry about some of the stuff that's happened, Annie. Things have been weird."

Sap that she was, she'd instantly forgiven him.

From then on, whenever Regan was occupied, Theo and Annie had hung out. He showed her some of his favorite spots on the island. He began confiding in her, at first hesitantly but gradually being more forthcoming. He told her how much he hated his boarding school and how he was writing short stories that he wouldn't show anyone. They talked about their favorite books. She convinced herself she was the only girl he'd ever confided in. She showed him some of the drawings she now did in secret so Mariah couldn't critique them. Finally, he'd kissed her. *Her.* Annie Hewitt, a gangly scarecrow of a fifteen-year-old with a too long face, too big eyes, and too curly hair.

After that, every moment that Regan was away found them together, usually inside the cave at low tide making out in the wet sand. He touched her breast through her swimsuit, and she thought she'd die of happiness. When he'd pushed the top down, she'd been embarrassed because her breasts weren't bigger, and she'd tried to cover them with her hands. He moved her hands away and stroked each nipple with his fingers.

She was in ecstasy.

Soon they were touching each other everywhere. He unzipped her shorts and pushed his hand in her underpants. No boy had ever touched her there. His finger went inside her. She was bursting with hormones. Instantly orgasmic.

She touched him, too, and the first time she felt the wetness on her hand, she thought she'd hurt him. She was in love.

But then things changed. For no reason, he began to avoid her. He started putting her down in front of his sister and Jaycie. "Annie, don't be such a dork. You act like a kid."

Annie tried to talk to him alone, find out why he was being like this, but he avoided her. She found half a dozen of her precious paperback gothic novels on the bottom of the swimming pool.

One sunny July afternoon, they'd been crossing the marsh footbridge, with Annie slightly ahead of the twins and Jaycie trailing. Annie had been trying to impress Theo with how sophisticated she was by talking about her life in Manhattan. "I've been using the subway since I was ten, and——"

"Stop bragging," Theo had said. And then his hand had slammed into her back.

She'd flown off the footbridge and hit the murky water facedown, her hands and forearms sinking into the muck, ooze sucking at her legs. As she tried to pull herself out, rotting strands of eel-like cordgrass and clots of blue-green algae clung to her hair, her clothes. She spat out the mud, tried to rub her eyes but couldn't, and started to cry.

Regan and Jaycie were as horrified as Annie, and in the end, it had taken both of them to pull her from the marsh. Annie had badly skinned one knee and lost the leather sandals she'd bought with her own money. Tears slid through the muck on her cheeks as she stood on the bridge like a creature from a horror movie. "Why did you do that?"

Theo had regarded her stonily. "I don't like braggers."

Regan's eyes had filled with tears. "Don't tell, Annie! Please don't tell. Theo will get in so much trouble. He won't ever do anything like that again. Promise her, Theo."

Theo had stalked away, not promising anything.

Annie hadn't told. Not then. Not until much later.

THE NEXT MORNING, SHE WANDERED through the cottage trying to wake herself up after a fitful night's sleep before she made the dreaded trek to Harp House. She ended up in the studio, safely out of range of Theo's telescope. Mariah had expanded the back of the cottage to make this a spacious, well-lit workspace. The paint spatters on the bare wooden floor testified to the parade of artists who'd worked here over the years. A bright red bedspread peeked out from beneath half a dozen cardboard boxes stacked on the bed shoved into the corner. Next to the bed was a pair of cane-seated wooden chairs painted yellow.

The room's light blue walls, red bedspread, and yellow chairs were supposed to evoke van Gogh's painting *Bedroom in Arles,* while the life-size trompe l'oeil mural on the longest wall depicted the front end of a taxi crashing through a storefront window. She hoped to God that mural wasn't the legacy because she couldn't imagine how she'd get away with selling an entire wall.

She imagined her mother in this room, feeding the artists' egos in ways she never did her own daughter's. Mariah believed artists needed nurturing, but she'd refused to encourage her daughter to draw or act, even though Annie had loved doing both.

"The art world is a vipers' pit. Even if you're enormously talented—which you aren't—it eats people alive. I don't want that for you."

Mariah would have done so much better with one of those naturally feisty little girls who didn't care about others' opinions. Instead she'd given birth to a shy child who lived on daydreams. Yet, in the end, Annie had been the strong one, supporting a mother who could no longer care for herself.

She set her coffee mug aside as she heard the unfamiliar sound of a vehicle approaching. She went to the living room and gazed out the window in time to see a battered white pickup stop at the end of the walk. The door opened and a woman who looked to be in her early sixties climbed down. Her bulky figure was wrapped in a gray down coat, and a serviceable pair of black boots sank into the snow. She wore no hat over her big blond bouffant but had looped a diamond-patterned black and green knit scarf around her neck. She leaned into the truck and withdrew a pink gift bag with raspberry tissue paper frothing from the top.

Annie was so happy to see a face not connected with Harp House that she nearly tripped over the painted canvas rug in her hurry to get to the door. As she opened it, a dusting of snow blew off the roof.

"I'm Barbara Rose," the woman said with a friendly wave. "You've been here nearly a week. I thought it was time somebody checked in to see how you're doing." Her bright red lipstick stood out against her winter-pale complexion, and as she came up the steps, Annie saw a few flecks of mascara lodging in the faint puffiness under her eyes.

Annie welcomed her inside and took her coat. "Thanks for sending your husband out to help me that first day. Would you like some coffee?"

"Love it." Beneath the coat, stretchy black pants and a royal blue sweater clung to her ample body. She took off her boots, then followed Annie into the kitchen, bringing along the gift bag and the strong floral scent of her perfume. "It's lonely for any woman by herself on this island, but out here in the middle of nowhere . . ." The quick hunch of her shoulders turned into a shudder. "Too many things can go wrong when you're alone."

Not exactly the words Annie wanted to hear from a seasoned islander.

As Annie made a fresh pot of coffee, Barbara gazed around the kitchen, taking in the collection of kitschy salt and pepper shakers on the windowsill, the series of black-and-white lithographs on the wall. She seemed almost wistful. "All kinds of famous people used to come here during the summer, but I don't remember seeing much of you."

Annie switched on the coffeemaker. "I'm more a city person."

"Peregrine sure isn't a good place for a city person in the dead of winter." Barbara liked to talk, and as the coffeemaker began to gurgle, she spoke of the exceptionally cold weather and how hard it was for the island women during the winter when their men were out in rough seas. Annie had forgotten about the complicated laws regarding when and where commercial lobstermen could set their traps, and Barbara was more than happy to fill her in.

"We only fish here from early October to the first of June. Then we concentrate on the tourists. Most of the other islands fish from May to December."

"Wouldn't it be easier when the weather's warmer?"

"That's for sure. Although, when it comes to pulling up traps, a lot of things can go wrong, even when the weather's good. But lobster fetches a higher price during the winter, so there are advantages to fishing now."

Annie finished making the coffee. They carried the mugs out to the table that sat in the front bay. Barbara handed Annie the pink gift bag, then took the chair across from her. It held a black-and-white scarf knitted in the same diamond-pattern as Barbara's.

Barbara used her hand to sweep the leftover toast crumbs

from Annie's breakfast into her palm. "Knitting keeps a lot of us busy during the winter. Otherwise I start fretting. My son's living in Bangor now. I used to see my grandson every day, but now I'm lucky if I see him every couple of months." Her eyes clouded, as if she wanted to cry. She stood abruptly and carried the crumbs she'd collected into the kitchen. When she returned, she hadn't quite regained her composure. "My daughter Lisa's talking about leaving. If that happens, I'll lose my two granddaughters."

"Jaycie's friend?"

Barbara nodded. "It seems like the fire at the school might be the last straw for her."

Annie dimly recalled the small frame building that had served as the island schoolhouse. It perched just up the hill from the wharf. "I didn't know there'd been a fire."

"It happened in early December, right after Theo Harp arrived. An electrical fire. Burned the place to the ground." She tapped the table with the tips of lacquer-red fingernails. "That school educated island kids for fifty years, right up to the time they left for high school on the mainland. Now we're using an old double-wide—all the town can afford—and Lisa says she's not goin' to let her girls keep going to school in a trailer."

Annie didn't blame the women who wanted to leave. Life on a small island was more romantic in concept than in real life.

Barbara toyed with her wedding ring, a thin gold band with a very small diamond. "I'm not the only one. Judy Kester's son's getting lots of pressure from his wife to move in with her parents someplace in Vermont, and Tildy—" She waved her hand as if she didn't want to keep thinking about it. "How long are you staying?"

"Till the end of March?"

"In winter, that's a long time."

Annie shrugged. The terms of her ownership of the cottage didn't seem to be common knowledge, and she intended to keep it that way. Otherwise, she'd look as if she were being controlled by someone else, just like one of her puppets.

"My husband's always telling me to butt out of other people's business," Barbara said, "but I couldn't live with myself if I didn't warn you that staying out here by yourself is going to be hard."

"I'll be fine." Annie said it as if she believed it.

Barbara's worried expression wasn't encouraging. "You're far from town. And I saw that car of yours . . . With no paved roads, it won't be any use this winter."

Something Annie had already figured out.

Before she left, Barbara invited Annie to the island Bunco game. "It's mainly us grandmas, but I'll make Lisa play. She's closer to your age."

Annie quickly accepted. She had no desire to play Bunco, but she needed to talk to someone other than her puppets and Jaycie who, for all her sweetness, wasn't exactly a stimulating conversationalist.

A NOISE AWAKENED THEO. NOT another nightmare this time, but a sound that didn't belong. He opened his eyes and listened.

Even through the fog of leftover sleep, it didn't take long to figure out what he was hearing. The sound of the downstairs clock chiming.

Three . . . Four . . . Five . . .

He sat up in bed. That clock hadn't worked since his grandmother Hildy had died a good six years ago.

He pushed back the covers and listened. The melodic chimes were muted, but still clearly audible. He counted. *Seven . . . Eight . . .* It went on. *Nine . . . Ten . . .* Finally, at twelve, the chimes stopped.

He looked at his bedside clock. It was three in the morning. *What the hell?*

He got out of bed and made his way downstairs. He was naked, but the cold air didn't bother him. He liked discomfort. It made him feel alive.

The light from a quarter moon seeped through the windows and painted jail bars across the carpet. The living room smelled dusty, unused, but the pendulum of Hildy's wall clock swung in a rhythmic *ticktock,* its hands pointing to midnight. The clock that had been silent for years.

He might spend his working life with time-traveling villains, but he didn't believe in the supernatural. Yet he'd walked through this room before he'd gone to bed, and if the clock had been ticking, he'd have noticed it. Then there were the unexplained noises.

There had to be an explanation for all of it, but he had no clue what it was. He'd have plenty of time to think about it, though, because he'd never get back to sleep tonight. Just as well. Sleep had become his enemy, a sinister place inhabited by the ghosts of his past, ghosts that had grown all the more menacing ever since Annie had shown up.

THE ROAD WASN'T AS ICY as it had been eight nights ago when Annie had arrived, but the potholes were more pronounced, and it took her forty minutes to make the fifteen-minute trip to the village for the women's Bunco game. She tried not to think about Theo Harp as she drove, but he was never far from her thoughts. It had been three days since their confrontation in the turret, and she'd only seen him from a distance. She wanted to keep it that way, but something told her it wouldn't be that easy.

She was grateful for the chance to get away from the cottage. Despite her hikes up to Harp House, she'd begun to feel better physically, if not emotionally. She'd put on her best pair of jeans and one of her mother's white menswear shirts. Pulling her renegade hair up in a messy, curly twist; slicking on some toffee-colored lipstick; and swiping her lashes with mascara was the best she could do with what she had. Sometimes she thought she should give up mascara to make her eyes less prominent, but her friends said she was too critical and that her hazel eyes were her best feature.

On the right side of the road, the big stone wharf jutted into the harbor where the lobster boats were moored. Enclosed boathouses had replaced the open sheds she remembered. If things were as they used to be, summer visitors still stored their pleasure craft inside, right along with the lobstermen's traps and buoys awaiting fresh paint jobs.

Across the road from the wharf, a few small eateries were shuttered for the winter, along with a gift shop and a couple of art galleries. The island town hall, a small, multipurpose, gray-shingled building that also served as post office and library, was open year-round. On the hill rising behind the town, she could just make out the snow-topped headstones of the cemetery. Higher up the slope and looking out over the harbor, the gray-shingled Peregrine Island Inn sat dark and empty, waiting for May to bring it to life again.

The village's houses had been built close to the road. Their side yards held stacks of wire lobster traps, reels of cable, and junk cars that hadn't yet found their way to an off-island dump. The Rose home looked much like the others: square, shingled, and functional. Barbara let her in and took her coat, then led her to the kitchen through a serviceable living room that smelled of woodsmoke and the hostess's floral perfume.

Mint green tieback curtains framed the window over the sink, and a souvenir plate collection hung above the dark wood cabinets. Barbara's pride in her grandchildren was evident in the numerous photos displayed on the refrigerator.

A still-handsome octogenarian whose high cheekbones and broad nose suggested she might be some combination of African and Native American sat at the kitchen table with the only young woman other than Annie, a petite brunette with a snub nose, black-framed, rectangular glasses, and a medium-length bob. Barbara introduced her as her daughter, Lisa McKinley. This was Jaycie's friend, and the one who'd recommended Jaycie to Cynthia Harp for the housekeeping job.

Annie soon learned that Lisa was both Peregrine's volunteer librarian and the owner of the island's only coffeehouse and bakery. "Bakery's closed until May first," Lisa told Annie. "And I hate Bunco, but I wanted to meet you."

Barbara gestured toward her refrigerator photo gallery. "Lisa has two beautiful girls. My granddaughters. They were born here."

"My punishment for marrying a lobsterman instead of taking off with Jimmy Timkins when I had the chance," Lisa said.

"Don't mind her. She loves her husband," Barbara said, before she introduced Annie to the other women.

"Doesn't it bother you, being out in that cottage all alone?"

The question came from Marie, a woman whose deeply etched lines descended downward from the corners of her mouth, giving her a sour expression. "Especially with Theo Harp as your only neighbor."

"I'm pretty fearless," Annie replied.

The puppets in her head fell all over themselves laughing.

"Get your drinks, everybody," Barbara ordered.

"You couldn't pay me to stay there," Marie said. "Not while Theo's at Harp House. Regan Harp was the sweetest girl."

Barbara jiggled the dispenser on the wine box. "Marie has a suspicious nature. Don't pay attention."

Marie wasn't deterred. "All I'm saying is that Regan Harp was as good a sailor as her brother. And I'm not the only one who thinks it's strange that she took that boat out with a squall blowing in."

As Annie tried to take this in, Barbara directed her toward a seat at one of the two tables. "Don't worry if you've never played. There's not a steep learning curve."

"Bunco is mainly an excuse for us to drink wine and get away from the men." Judy Kester's comment didn't merit her big laugh, but Judy seemed to laugh at almost everything. Between her good humor and the dyed, bright red hair that projected from her head like a clown's yarn wig, it was hard not to like her.

"Real intellectual stimulation isn't allowed on Peregrine," Lisa said tartly. "At least not during the winter."

"You're still mad because Mrs. Harp didn't come back last summer." Barbara rolled the dice.

"Cynthia's my friend," Lisa said. "I don't want to hear anything bad about her."

"Like the fact that she's a snob?" Barbara rolled again.

"She's not," Lisa countered. "Just because she's cultured doesn't mean she's a snob."

"Mariah Hewitt was a lot more cultured than Cynthia Harp," Marie said sourly, "but she didn't go around looking down her nose at everybody."

Despite Annie's own issues with her mother, it was nice to hear her spoken of fondly.

As Lisa took her turn, she explained to Annie, "Cynthia and I became friends because we like so many of the same things."

Annie wondered if that included their decorating tastes.

"Mini-Bunco," someone said at the next table.

The game was as easy to learn as Barbara had said, and Annie gradually sorted out the names and personalities of the women seated at both tables. Lisa fancied herself an intellectual; Louise, the octogenarian, had come to the island as a bride. Marie's personality was as sour as her face, while Judy Kester was naturally funny and cheerful.

As the island's volunteer librarian, Lisa soon turned the conversation to Theo Harp. "He's a gifted writer. He shouldn't be wasting his time writing trash like *The Sanitarium*."

"Oh, I loved that book," Judy said, her boundless good humor as bright as the purple sweatshirt that proclaimed her WORLD'S BEST GRANDMA. "Scared me so bad I slept with the light on for a week."

"What kind of man writes about all that torture?" Marie said, pursing her lips. "I've never read anything so grisly in my life."

"It was the sex that made the book sell so good." This observation came from a ruddy-faced woman named Naomi. Her towering height, harshly dyed black bowl cut, and big voice made her an imposing figure, and Annie wasn't surprised to learn she captained her own lobster boat.

The most stylish member of the group—and the owner of the local gift shop—was Naomi's Bunco partner Tildy, a sixty-year-old with a thinning blond crop, cherry red V-neck sweater, and layered silver necklaces. "The sex was the best part," she said. "That man has some imagination."

Although Lisa was about Annie's age, she was nearly as puritanical as Marie. "It embarrassed his family. I don't object to well-written sex scenes, but—"

"But"—Tildy cut in—"you don't like sex scenes that actually turn people on."

Lisa had the grace to laugh.

Barbara rolled the dice. "The only reason you didn't like it was because Cindy didn't approve."

"Cynthia," Lisa corrected her. "Nobody calls her Cindy."

"Bunco!" Silver crosses bobbed at Judy's earlobes as she slapped her hand down on the bell at her table. The others groaned.

They switched partners. The conversation drifted to the price of propane and the frequency of power failures, then to lobstering. In addition to learning that Naomi had her own boat, Annie discovered that most of the women, at one time or another, had served as sternmen on their husband's boats, a hazardous job that entailed emptying heavy traps, sorting the contents for keepers, and rebaiting the traps with grotesquely smelly bait. If Annie hadn't already dismissed any fantasies about island life, their conversations would have brought her back to hard reality.

But the primary topic was the marine forecast and how it affected the transport of supplies. The big ferry that had brought Annie to the island ran only once every six weeks during the winter, but a smaller boat was supposed to come over weekly with groceries, mail, and supplies. Unfortunately twelve-foot swells had kept the boat on the mainland last week, so the islanders had to wait another week for the next scheduled run. "If anybody has extra butter, I'll buy it off you," Tildy said, tugging on her silver necklaces.

"I have butter, but I need eggs."

"No eggs. But I have some extra zucchini bread in the freezer."

Tildy rolled her eyes. "We all have zucchini bread."

They laughed.

Annie thought about how little food she had left and how much more organized she needed to be when it came to ordering groceries. Unless she wanted to end up eating from cans all winter, she'd better call in her order first thing tomorrow. And pay for it with more credit card debt . . .

Judy rolled the dice. "If the ferry doesn't make it next week, I swear I'm going to roast my grandkids' guinea pigs."

"You're lucky to still have all your grandkids here," Marie said.

Judy's cheery expression faded. "I can't imagine what I'll do if they leave."

Louise, the octogenarian, hadn't commented, but Tildy reached over and patted her frail arm. "Johnny won't leave. You'll see. He'd divorce Galeann before he'd let her talk him into going."

"I hope you're right," the old lady said. "Lord knows, I hope you're right."

As the evening came to an end and the women gathered their coats, Barbara gestured Annie away from the door. "I've been thinking about you ever since our visit, and I wouldn't feel right if I didn't warn you . . . A lot of people believe we're all one big family out here, but the island has its dark side."

Tell me about it, Annie thought.

"I'm not talking about Marie and her obsession with Regan Harp's death. Nobody believes Theo was responsible. But Peregrine's a place for people who want to slip off the radar. The captains hire sternmen from the mainland without asking too many questions. Your mother had vandals break in a couple of times out there. I've seen fights, knifings. Tires get slashed. And not all our full-timers are stand-up citizens. If you drop your traps in somebody else's fishing area once too often, you might find your lines cut and all your equipment on the ocean floor."

Annie started to point out that she had no intention of dropping lobster traps anywhere, but Barbara wasn't done. "That kind of trouble spills over onto the land. I love most everybody here, but we do have our share of drunks and un-desirables. Like Jaycie's husband. Because Ned Grayson was good-looking and his family went back three generations, he decided he could do whatever he wanted."

Just like Theo, Annie thought.

Barbara patted her arm. "All I'm saying is, you're cut off out there. You've got no phone, and you're too far away from town to get help fast. Keep your guard up, and don't let yourself get complacent."

No worries about that.

ANNIE LEFT THE HOUSE WITH a serious case of the scaredy-cats. She checked the backseat of her car twice before she got behind the wheel and kept one eye on the rearview mirror as she drove home. Other than a few minor skids and nearly losing her front end in a pothole, she made it back without incident. That gave her the confidence to make a return trip to town three days later to borrow some books.

When Annie entered the tiny library, Lisa McKinley was manning the desk while one of her red-haired daughters raced around the room. Lisa greeted Annie, then gestured toward a list mounted in a Plexiglas frame propped on the corner of the desk. "These are my recommendations for February."

Annie scanned the titles. They reminded her of the heavy, depressing books Mariah had forced her to read. "I like books that are a little more entertaining," she said.

Lisa's shoulders sagged with disappointment. "Jaycie's the same way. When Cynthia was here, we organized book recommendations for every month of the year, but hardly anybody pays attention."

"I guess people have different tastes."

Just then Lisa's daughter knocked over a stack of children's books and Lisa hurried off to clean up the mess.

Annie left town with a stack of paperbacks and Lisa's disapproval. She was halfway to the cottage when a crater of a pothole loomed in front of her. "Shit." She barely tapped the brakes, but the Kia began to slide, and she was off the road again.

She tried to rock her way free and was no more successful this time than she'd been the last time. She got out to look. She wasn't dug in as deeply as before, but she was deep enough that she needed help. And did she have a way of getting help? Did she have an emergency kit packed away or a couple of bags of sand stashed in the trunk like any sensible islander? Not her. She was completely ill-equipped to live in a place that depended on self-sufficiency.

Loser, Leo whispered.

Peter, her hero, stayed silent.

She gazed down the road. The wind that never seemed to stop blowing lashed her. "I hate this place!" she yelled, which only made her cough.

She started to walk. The day was overcast as usual. Did the sun ever shine on this godforsaken island? She shoved her gloved hands in her pockets and hunched her shoulders, trying not to think about her warm, red knit cap lying on her bed at the cottage. Theo was probably staring at it right now through his telescope.

Her head shot up as she heard branches snap followed by the pounding that could only come from the hooves of a very large animal. It was a sound that didn't belong on an island with nothing larger than a cat or dog. And a midnight-black horse.

Chapter Six

Horse and rider emerged from a patch of old-growth spruce. Theo reined in as he saw her. She tasted cold metal in the back of her throat. She was alone on a lawless island at the end of a deserted road with a man who had once tried to kill her.

And just might have it on his mind again.

Eeek! Eeek! Crumpet's silent shrieks matched the rhythm of Annie's heartbeat.

Don't you dare wimp out, Scamp ordered as Theo came toward her.

Annie wasn't generally afraid of horses, but this one was huge, and she thought she detected a crazy look in his eyes. She felt as if she were revisiting an old nightmare, and despite Scamp's orders, she took a few steps back.

Wimp, Scamp taunted.

"Going someplace special?" He wasn't dressed as he should be for such cold weather. Only a black suede jacket and gloves. No hat. No warm muffler wrapped around his neck. But at least everything was comfortably twenty-first century. She still didn't understand what she'd seen that first night.

Marie's words at the Bunco game came back. *"All I'm saying is that Regan Harp was as good a sailor as her brother. And I'm not the only one who thinks it's strange that she took that boat out with a squall blowing in."*

She beat back her trepidation by channeling her favorite puppet. "I'm heading for a soiree with my many island friends. And if I don't show up, they'll come looking for me."

He cocked his head.

She hurried on. "Unfortunately, my car's in a ditch, and I could use some help getting it out." Being forced to ask him for help was worse than her worst coughing fit, and she couldn't leave it like that. "Or maybe I need to find someone with a little more muscle?"

He had more than enough muscle, and it was foolish of her to goad him.

He gazed along the road toward her car, then peered down at her. "I don't think I like your attitude."

"You're not the first."

His eyelids flickered in one of those facial tics she imagined psychopaths developed over time. "You have a strange way of asking for help."

"We all have our quirks. How about a push?" Turning her back on him gave her the willies, but she did it anyway.

Dancer's hooves struck the gravel as Theo trotted alongside her toward the car. She wondered if he'd started to believe Harp House was haunted. She hoped so. *Ticktock goes the clock.*

"Let's put it this way," he said. "I'll help you if you help me."

"I'd be glad to, except I have trouble cutting up dead bodies. All that bone." *Damn it!* This was what happened when she spent too much time alone with her puppets. Their personalities took over.

Our personalities come from you, Dilly pointed out.

Theo pretended to look mystified. "What are you talking about?"

She backtracked. "What kind of help do you need?" *Other than psychiatric?*

"I want to rent the cottage from you."

She came to a dead stop. She didn't know what she'd expected, but it wasn't this. "And where am I supposed to stay?"

"Go back to New York. You don't belong here. I'll make it worth your while."

Did he really think she was that stupid? She shoved her hands in her jacket pockets. "Do you really think I'm that stupid?"

"I've never thought you were stupid."

She picked up her steps, but kept her distance. "Why would I leave before my sixty days are over?"

He looked down at her, at first pretending to be puzzled and then acting upset, as though he'd finally remembered. "I forgot about that."

"Sure you did." She stopped walking. "Why do you want to rent the cottage? You already have more rooms than you know what to do with."

He sneered just like Leo. "To get away from it all."

I'd punch him for you, Peter said uneasily. *But he's awfully big.*

He studied her Kia, then dismounted and tied Dancer to a branch on the other side of the road. "A car like this is useless around here. You should know that."

"I'll buy another one right away."

He gave her a long look, then opened the car door and slid in. "Give it a push."

"Me?"

"It's your car."

Jerkoff. She wasn't strong enough to do the job, as he very well knew, but he kept her shoving away at the rear end as he called out orders. Only when she began to cough did he relinquish his spot behind the wheel and push her car out on his first try.

Her clothes were a mess, her face smudged, but he'd barely gotten his hands dirty. On the bright side, he hadn't dragged her into the trees and slit her throat, so she had no reason to complain.

SHE WAS STILL THINKING ABOUT her encounter with Theo the next day as she hung her coat and backpack on the hooks by the back door of Harp House and exchanged her boots for sneakers. Just because he hadn't tried to harm her physically didn't mean he wouldn't do it. For all she knew, he'd left her unharmed only because he didn't want the inconvenience of a potential police visit caused by a dead female body washing up on the beach.

Just like Regan . . . She shoved the thought aside. Regan was the only person Theo had ever cared about.

She rounded the corner into the kitchen and saw Jaycie sitting motionless at the table. She wore her customary jeans and sweatshirt—all Annie had seen her in—but those casual clothes never looked quite right on her. Jaycie should be wearing flirty summer dresses and big sunglasses as she drove a red convertible down an Alabama road.

Annie set her laptop on the kitchen table. Jaycie didn't look at her but said wearily, "It's over." She rested her elbows on the table and rubbed her temples. "He sent me a text this morning after he got back from his ride. He said he had to drive into town, and when he got back, we needed to talk about making another arrangement."

Annie suppressed the urge to launch into a diatribe. "That doesn't necessarily mean he's going to fire you." That was exactly what it meant.

Jaycie finally looked at her, a long piece of blond hair falling over her pale cheek. "We both know he's going to. I can stay with Lisa for a couple of days, but what do I do after that? My baby . . ." Her face crumpled. "Livia's already been through so much."

"I'll talk to him." It was the last thing Annie wanted to do, but she couldn't think of any other way to offer Jaycie comfort. "He's . . . still in town?"

Jaycie nodded. "He took the recycling in because I couldn't do it. I can't blame him for wanting to get rid of me. It's impossible for me to do what I was hired to do."

Annie could blame him, and she didn't like the wistful softening in Jaycie's eyes. Was being attracted to cruel men her pattern?

Jaycie pushed herself up from the table and reached for her crutches. "I need to check on Livia."

Annie wanted to hurt him. Now, while he was away

from the house. Send him back to the mainland. She grabbed a bottle from the refrigerator and went upstairs, entering the turret through the door at the end of the hallway. She made her way to the turret's only bathroom, where a damp towel hung next to the shower stall.

The sink looked as though it had been wiped clean since his morning shave. She turned the ketchup bottle she'd brought with her upside down and squirted a few drips in her hand. Not a lot. Only a trace. Spreading her fingers, she ran them down the bottom left corner of the mirror leaving the faintest red smudge behind. Nothing too obvious. Something that might or might not look like a bloody handprint. Something so faint he'd have to wonder if he'd overlooked it that morning or, if he hadn't, what had happened since then to put it there.

It would be so much more satisfying to leave a knife plunged into his bed pillow, but if she went too far, he'd stop suspecting ghosts and start suspecting her. She wanted to make him question his sanity, not look for a perpetrator, exactly what she hoped she'd accomplished when she'd sabotaged his grandmother's clock last week.

She'd made the trek back to Harp House in the dead of night, a treacherous trip she'd had to talk herself into. But her trepidation had been more than worth it. Earlier that day she'd checked the hinges on the turret's outside door to make sure they wouldn't squeak. They hadn't, and nothing had given her away when she'd let herself in shortly before two in the morning. It had been a simple task to creep into the living room while Theo slept upstairs. She'd pulled the clock just far enough away from the wall to slip in the fresh battery she'd brought to replace the dead one she'd removed earlier. Once that was done, she reset the time so the clock would chime midnight, but only after she was safely back at the cottage. Pure genius.

But the memory didn't cheer her. After everything he'd done, these pranks felt more juvenile than menacing. She needed to up her game, but she couldn't figure out how to do that without getting caught.

She heard a noise from behind. Sucking in her breath, she spun around.

It was the black cat.

"Oh, my god . . ." She fell to her knees. The cat stared at her out of golden eyes. "How did you get in here? Did he lure you in? You have to stay away from him. You can't come in here."

The cat turned its head and flounced off into Theo's bedroom. She went after him, but he'd gone under the bed. She got down on her stomach and tried to convince him to come out. "Come here, kitty. Here, kitty."

The cat wouldn't budge.

"He's feeding you, isn't he?" she said. "Don't let him feed you. You have no idea what he's putting in your Fancy Feast."

As the cat continued to elude her efforts, she grew increasingly frustrated. "You stupid cat! I'm trying to help you."

The cat dug its claws into the rug, stretched, and yawned in her face.

She reached under the bed, extending her arm. The cat lifted his head, and then, miraculously, started to crawl toward her. She held her breath. The cat approached her hand, sniffed, and began licking her fingers.

A ketchup-loving cat.

As long as she kept a little ketchup on her fingers, the cat was content to let her pick him up, carry him back into the main house and down to the kitchen. Jaycie was still with Livia, so there were no witnesses to Annie's struggle getting an extremely pissed-off animal into the lidded picnic basket she found in the pantry. The cat howled like a car siren all the way down to the cottage.

By the time she got him inside, her nerves were scraped as raw as the scratches on her arms. "Believe me, I don't like this any better than you do." She flipped open the lid. The cat jumped out, arched his back, and hissed at her.

She filled a bowl with water. A pile of newspapers on the floor was the best she could do for a litter box. This evening, she'd feed him her last can of tuna, the one she'd intended for her own dinner.

She wanted to go to bed, but she'd stupidly promised Jaycie she'd talk to Theo. As she trudged back up to the top of the cliff, a scarf wrapped over her nose and mouth, she wondered how much longer she'd have to keep doing this before she paid off her debt to Jaycie.

Who was she kidding? She'd barely started.

She smelled the fire even before she saw the smoke rising from the trash drums behind the garage. Jaycie couldn't have managed that icy path, so Theo was back from town and satisfying his unhealthy fascination with fire.

When they were kids, he'd kept a supply of driftwood above the tide line so they could build beach fires whenever they wanted. "If you look into the flames," he'd say, "you can see the future." But one day Annie had spied him alone on the beach tossing what she thought was a piece of driftwood on the fire he'd built until she'd caught a flash of purple and realized he'd thrown Regan's precious purple poetry notebook into the flames.

That night she'd heard them fighting in Theo's room. "You did it!" Regan had cried. "I know you did it. Why are you so mean?"

Whatever response Theo had made was lost in the sound of the argument Elliott and Mariah were having at the bottom of the stairs.

A few weeks later, Regan's beloved oboe went missing. Eventually a visiting houseguest spotted the charred remains in one of the trash drums. Was it so impossible to believe that he'd played a part in Regan's death?

Annie wanted to snatch back the promise she'd made to Jaycie that she'd talk to him. Instead she steeled herself and rounded the garage. His jacket lay across a tree stump, and he wore only jeans and a long-sleeved gray T-shirt. As she moved closer, she realized that confronting him right now, when she'd just come up from the cottage, worked to her favor. He didn't know this was her second trip, so he'd have no reason to connect her with the handprint on his mirror. Jaycie couldn't maneuver the steps, and Livia was too small to have reached the mirror. That left only a not-so-friendly creature from the other world.

A shower of sparks erupted from the drum. Seeing him through those glowing red embers—that dramatic dark hair, those feral blue eyes and saber-sharp features—was like catching a glimpse of the devil's lieutenant out for a winter romp.

She curled her hands in her coat pockets and stepped inside the burning circle. "Jaycie says you're going to fire her."

"Does she?" He picked up a chicken carcass that had fallen on the ground.

"I told you last week that I'd help her, and I have. The house is decent, and you're getting your meals."

"If you can call what the two of you send up 'meals.'" He tossed the carcass into the fire. "The world's a tough place for a bleeding heart like you."

"Better a bleeding heart than no heart at all. Even if you gave her a big severance check, how long would it last? It's not like there are other jobs waiting for her. And she's one of your oldest friends."

"This morning, I was the one who had to drive the recycling into town." He gathered up a handful of withered orange peels.

"I would have taken it in."

"Right." He threw in the orange peels. "We saw how well yesterday's trip worked out for you."

"An aberration." She said the words with a straight face and some serious attitude.

He gazed at her, taking in her undoubtedly flushed cheeks and the tangled mayhem poking out from beneath her red knit hat. She didn't like the way he was looking at her. Not threatening, but more as if he were really seeing her. All of her. Bumps and bruises. Scars. Even— She tried to shake off the impression. Even . . . a few holy spots.

Instead of the fear and disgust his scrutiny should have elicited, she had a disturbing desire to sit down on one of the tree stumps and tell him her troubles, as if she were fifteen all over again. Exactly how he'd roped her in the first time. Her hatred spewed over. "Why did you burn Regan's poetry notebook?"

The fire flared. "I don't remember."

"She was always trying to protect you. No matter what horrible thing you did, she'd defend you."

"Twins are weird." He almost sneered, reminding her so much of Leo that she shivered. "Tell you what," he said. "Maybe we can work something out."

The calculation in his eyes made her suspect he'd set another one of his traps. "No way."

He shrugged. "All right." He pitched a full trash bag into the fire. "I'll go talk to Jaycie."

The trap snapped shut. "You haven't changed a bit! What do you want?"

He turned his devil's eyes on her. "I want to use the cottage."

"I'm not leaving the island," she said as the acrid smell of burning plastic filled the clearing.

"Not a problem. I only need it during the day." The waves of heat rising from the fire between them distorted his features. "You stay at Harp House in the daytime. Use the WiFi. Do whatever you want. When evening comes, we trade places."

He'd set a trap, and the jaws had snapped. Had he ever said that he was going to fire Jaycie, or had she and Jaycie merely assumed that was the case? As she considered the likelihood that this was a ploy designed to manipulate her into doing his bidding, she was struck by something else. "*You're* the one who was using the cottage before I got here. That coffee I found belonged to you. And the newspaper."

He threw the last of the trash into the fiery drum. "So what? Your mother never minded lending out the cottage."

"My mother's gone," Annie countered. She remembered the newspaper she'd found that had been dated a few days before her arrival. "You must have known when I was arriving—everybody on this island seemed to know. But when I got here, there was no water, no heat. That was deliberate."

"I didn't want you to stay."

He exhibited not even a trace of shame, but under the circumstances, she wasn't handing him a gold star for honesty. "What's so special about the cottage?"

He grabbed his jacket from the stump. "It's not Harp House."

"But if you hate the place so much, why are you here?"

"I could ask you the same."

"I didn't have a choice." She jerked her hat over her ears. "That's not the way it is with you."

"Isn't it?" He hooked his jacket over his shoulder and headed toward the house.

"I'll only agree on one condition," she called after him, knowing as she did that she was in no position to make conditions. "I can use your Range Rover whenever I want."

He kept going. "The key's on a hook next to the back door."

She remembered the underwear she'd left scattered around the bedroom and the book of pornographic art photos lying open on the couch. Then there was the black cat. "Fine. But our deal doesn't start until tomorrow. I'll bring you a key to the cottage in the morning."

"No need. I already have one." In two long strides he'd rounded the stables and was out of sight.

ANNIE HAD BEEN BLACKMAILED, BUT she'd also gotten something out of it. Not only did she now have reliable transportation, but she also wouldn't have to worry about bumping into Theo during the day. She wondered if he'd discovered the handprint she'd left on the bathroom mirror. If only she could hear him scream.

Maybe tonight she'd scratch claw marks into the turret door. Let him figure that one out.

When Annie got inside, Jaycie was sitting at the table, sorting a pile of clean laundry. Livia looked up from a big jigsaw puzzle on the floor, her attention on Annie for the first time. Annie smiled and vowed to bring Scamp out again before the day was over.

She made her way to the table to help with the laundry. "I talked to Theo. You don't have to worry."

Jaycie's debutante eyes brightened. "Really? Are you sure?"

"I'm sure." Annie picked up a bath towel and began to fold it. "I'll run the errands into town from now on, so let me know what I need to do."

"I should have had more faith in him." She sounded almost breathless. "He's been so nice to me."

Annie bit her tongue. Hard.

They worked in silence for a while. Annie dealt with the sheets and towels so she wouldn't have to handle his personal items. Jaycie took her time folding a pile of silky boxer briefs, fingering the material. "I'll bet these cost a lot."

"Amazing that such delicate fabric can hold up against all those clawing female hands." *Not to mention a large body part . . .*

Jaycie took Annie's comment seriously. "I don't think so. His wife died just a year ago, and the only females around here are you, me, and Livia."

Annie gazed toward the four-year-old. Livia's forehead was knit in concentration as she pressed the giant jigsaw pieces into their proper places. There was nothing wrong with her intelligence, and Annie had heard her humming softly to herself, so her vocal cords were working. Why wouldn't she talk? Was it shyness or something more complicated? Whatever the cause, her muteness made her more vulnerable than the average four-year-old.

Livia finished her puzzle and left the kitchen. Annie was here too much to be kept in the dark about the little girl. "I saw Livia writing her numbers. She's really smart."

"She gets some of them backward," Jaycie said, but she was clearly proud.

Annie couldn't think of any way to handle this other than to be direct. "I haven't heard her talk. Maybe she talks to you when I'm not around?"

Jaycie lips tightened. "I was a late talker."

She spoke with a finality that didn't encourage more questions, but Annie wasn't ready to give up. "I don't mean to be intrusive, but I feel like I need to know more."

"She'll be fine." Jaycie hauled herself up on her crutches. "Do you think I should make sloppy joes for Theo's dinner?"

Annie didn't want to imagine what Theo would think of Jaycie's sloppy joes. "Sure." She steadied herself to broach a more difficult topic. "Jaycie, I think you need to make sure Theo doesn't get too near Livia again."

"I know. He was really mad about the stable."

"Not just the stable. He's . . . unpredictable."

"What do you mean?"

She couldn't outright accuse him of intending to harm Livia when she didn't know if that was true, but she also couldn't ignore the possibility. "He's . . . not good with kids. And Harp House isn't the safest place for a child."

"You're not an islander, Annie, so you don't know how it is here." Jaycie sounded almost condescending. "Island kids aren't pampered. I was hauling traps when I was eight, and I don't think there's a kid here who can't drive a car by their tenth birthday. It's not like on the mainland. Peregrine kids learn to be independent. That's why keeping her inside is so awful."

Annie doubted whether any of those independent island kids were mute. Still, for all she knew Livia talked to Jaycie when Annie wasn't around. And maybe Annie's concern was for nothing. Theo had seemed genuinely upset about the possibility of Livia getting hurt in the stable.

She separated out the dish towels. "Theo wants to use the cottage during the day."

"He worked there a lot until you came back."

"Why didn't you tell me?"

"I thought you knew."

She started to say that Theo had a fully equipped office in the turret, then remembered Jaycie didn't know Annie had been up there. The only way she could stomach the idea of working for him was by reminding herself she wasn't working for him. She was paying off her debt to Jaycie.

When she was done stacking the folded laundry in the basket ready to be put away the next time Theo left the house, she carried her laptop into what had once been a pleasant sunroom but now, with its dark-paneled walls and thick wine carpet, looked more like a man cave for Dracula. At least it had a view of the ocean, unlike Elliott's office. She chose a deep leather armchair that looked out across the big front porch to the water, which was slate gray today with angry whitecaps.

She opened the inventory file she'd created and set to work, hoping this time not to hit so many dead ends. She'd been able to track down most of the artists whose work hung on the cottage walls. The artist who'd painted the studio mural was a part-time college professor whose work had never caught on, so she wouldn't have to deal with trying to sell off a wall. The black-and-white lithographs in the kitchen should bring her a few hundred dollars. R. Connor, the painter of the upside-down tree, sold his paintings at summer art fairs for modest prices, and considering the commission she'd have to pay a dealer, she would barely put a dent in her bills.

She let herself Google Theo's name. It wasn't as though she'd never Googled him, but now she added another word to her search. *Wife.*

She found only one clear photo. It had been taken a year and a half ago at a black-tie benefit for the Philadelphia Orchestra. Theo looked as though he'd been born to wear a tuxedo, and his wife—the photo identified her as Kenley Adler Harp—was his perfect match—a patrician beauty with finely carved features and long dark hair. There was something familiar about her, but Annie couldn't put her finger on what.

A little more digging pulled up her obituary. She'd died last February, just as Jaycie had said. She'd been three years older than Theo. She had an undergraduate degree from Bryn Mawr and an MBA from Dartmouth, so she was both beautiful and smart. She'd worked in finance and was survived by her husband, her mother, and a couple of aunts. Not exactly a fertile family. The cause of death wasn't listed.

Why did she look so familiar? The dark hair, perfectly symmetrical features . . . It finally hit her. Regan Harp might have looked like this if she'd lived to her thirties.

The uneven tap of crutches interrupted that creepy thought. Jaycie appeared in the door of the sunroom. "Livia's gone. She's gotten out again."

Annie set her laptop aside. "I'll get her."

Jaycie braced herself against the doorframe. "She wouldn't do this if I could take her out myself once in a while. I know it's wrong to keep her cooped up like this. God, I'm a terrible mother."

"You're a great mother, and I need some fresh air anyway."

Fresh air was the last thing Annie needed. She was sick of fresh air. Sick of the wind cutting her face and of her muscles aching from crawling after cats and climbing up the cliff drive to Harp House twice in one day. But at least her strength was beginning to return.

She gave Jaycie a reassuring smile and went to the kitchen to bundle up. She gazed at her backpack for a few moments, then decided it was finally time to pull out Scamp.

Livia was crouched under the branches of her favorite tree. The snow had melted away from the trunk, and she sat cross-legged on the bare ground dancing a pair of pinecones around as if they were play figures.

Annie slipped Scamp over her hand and arranged the puppet's pink skirt to fall down over her own forearm. Livia pretended not to see her approach. Sitting on an old ledge stone close to the tree, Annie propped her elbow on one leg and let Scamp loose. "Pssttt . . . Pssttt . . ."

The *p* sound was one that amateur ventriloquists tended to avoid, along with letters such as *m, b, f, q, v,* and *w*—all of which required lip movement. But Annie had years of practice with sound substitutions, and even adults weren't aware that she used a softened version of the *t* sound for *p*.

Livia looked up, her eyes fixed on the puppet.

"How do you like my outfit?" Scamp bobbed about, showing off her multicolored tights and star-decked T-shirt. Movement was another distraction that kept audiences from noticing sound substitutions. For example, pronouncing "*my*" as "*ny*."

Scamp tossed her chaotic yarn hair. "I should have worn my leopard jeans. Skirts get in my way when I want to turn a somersault or hop on one leg. Not that you'd know. You're too little to hop on one leg."

Livia shook her head ferociously.

"You're not?"

More head shaking. Livia scrambled out from under the branches, tucked up one leg, and hopped awkwardly on the other.

"*Magnifico!*" Scamp clapped her small cloth hands. "Can you touch your toes?"

Livia bent her knees and touched her toes, the tips of her straight brown hair brushing the ground.

They continued this way for a while, Scamp putting Livia through her paces. Finally, after Livia had completed a series of laps around the spruce tree, with Scamp urging her to go faster, the puppet said, "You're amazingly athletic for someone who's only three."

That stopped Livia in her tracks. She scowled at Scamp and, with a frown, held up four fingers.

"My mistake," Scamp said. "I guess I thought you were younger because you can't talk."

Annie was relieved to see that Livia seemed more insulted than ashamed. Scamp tilted her head so a chunk of curly orange yarn fell over one eye. "It must be hard not talking. I talk all the time. Talk, talk, talk. I find myself quite fascinating. Do you?"

Livia nodded solemnly.

Scamp gazed up toward the sky, as if she were thinking something over. "Did you ever hear of . . . free secret?"

Livia shook her head, keeping her focus on Scamp, as if Annie didn't exist.

"I love free secret," the puppet said. "If I say 'free secret,' I can tell you anything, and you're not allowed to get mad. Annie and I play it, and, boy, has she ever told me some bad secrets, like the time she broke my favorite purple crayon." Scamp threw her head back, opened her mouth wide, and yelled, *"Free secret!"*

Livia's eyes grew huge, expectant.

"My turn first!" Scamp said. "And remember . . . You're not allowed to get mad when I tell you. Just like I won't get mad if you tell me something." Scamp hung her head and spoke in a soft, confessional term. "My free secret is . . . At first I didn't like you because your hair is pretty and brown and mine is orange. It made me jealous." She looked up. "Are you mad?"

Livia shook her head.

"That's good." It was time to see if Livia would accept the connection between vent and puppet. She pretended to whisper something in the puppet's ear.

Scamp turned to her. "Do we have to, Annie?"

Annie spoke for the first time. "Yes, we really do."

Scamp sighed and returned her attention to Livia. "Annie says we have to go inside."

Livia picked up her pinecones and rose.

Annie hesitated, then made Scamp lean toward the child and speak in a loud whisper. "Annie also said that if you're by yourself and you see Theo, you should run to your mom because he doesn't understand little kids."

Livia scurried toward the house, giving Annie no clue how she felt about that.

IT HAD JUST GOTTEN DARK when Annie left Harp House, but this time she wasn't walking back to the cottage with only a flashlight as a weapon against her vivid imagination. Instead she'd grabbed the key to Theo's Range Rover from the hook in the kitchen and driven herself home.

The cottage had no garage, only a graveled spot off to the side. She parked there, let herself in through the side door, and flicked on the light.

The kitchen had been trashed.

Chapter Seven

ANNIE TOOK IN THE DESTRUCTION. The cupboards and drawers hung open, with silverware, dish towels, boxes, and cans littering the floor. She dropped her backpack. The messy contents of her overturned trash was spread everywhere, along with paper napkins, plastic wrap, and a bag of noodles. Mariah's kitschy salt and pepper shakers were still lined up on the windowsill, but colanders, measuring cups, and cookbooks lay on a bed of spilled rice.

She looked toward the dark living room, and the back of her neck prickled. What if someone were still in the house? She backed out the door she'd just entered, rushed to the car, and locked herself in.

The sound of her ragged breathing filled the interior. There was no 911 to call. No friendly neighbor she could run to. What was she supposed to do? Drive into town for help? And exactly who was going to help her on a lawless island with no police force? If any serious crime occurred, police came over from the mainland.

No police. No neighborhood watch. Regardless of what the maps said, she'd left the state of Maine for the State of Anarchy.

Her other option was to drive back to Harp House, but that was the last place she could turn for help. She'd thought she was being so subtle with her scary noises and ghostly pranks. Obviously not. This was Theo's doing. His retaliation.

She wanted a gun just like the other islanders. Even if she ended up shooting herself, a gun would make her feel less vulnerable.

She investigated the interior of Theo's car. A high-end sound system, GPS, a phone charger, and a glove box with registration papers and a car manual. A windshield scraper lay on the floor in front of the passenger seat, a travel umbrella in the back. All of it useless.

She couldn't sit here forever.

I would, Crumpet said. *I'd sit here until somebody came to rescue me.*

Which wasn't going to happen. Annie flipped the trunk switch and inched out of the car. Looking around to make sure no one was sneaking up on her, she crept to the trunk. There she found a small shovel with a short handle. Exactly the sort of thing a smart islander carried around to dig out his car if he got stuck.

Or if he needed to bury a dead body, whispered Crumpet.

What about the cat? Was it still inside, or had Annie rescued it from imagined danger only to drag it to its actual death?

She grabbed the shovel, pulled out the flashlight she kept in her coat pocket, and crept toward the house.

It's awfully dark out here, Peter said. *I think I'll go back to the car.*

The snow had gone through a thaw and freeze yesterday, and the icy surface wasn't likely to reveal much in the way of footprints, even if she had enough light to see them. She made her way to the front of the house. Surely Theo wouldn't have hung around after he'd done this, but how could she be certain? She maneuvered past the old-fashioned wooden lobster traps near the front door and crouched beneath the living room window. Slowly she raised her head and peered inside.

It was dark, but she could see just enough to realize this room hadn't been spared. The taupe armchair that looked like an airline seat had been turned on its side, the couch was askew, its pillows scattered, and the tree painting hung crookedly against the wall.

Her breath frosted the glass. Carefully she raised the flashlight higher and directed it toward the back of the room. Books had been thrown off the shelves, and two drawers of the Louis XIV graffiti chest gaped open. The cat was nowhere to be seen, dead or alive.

She ducked and felt her way around to the rear of the cottage. It was even darker here, more isolated. Lifting her head inch by inch, she finally had a clear view into her bedroom, but it was too dark to see anything. For all she knew, Theo could be lurking under the window on the other side.

She braced herself, drew up the flashlight, and shone it into the room. It was exactly as she'd left it—no mess other than the one she'd made herself this morning.

"What in the *hell* are you doing?"

She screamed, dropped the shovel, and whirled around.

Theo stood in the dark not twenty feet away.

She started to run. Back the way she'd come. Racing around the side of the house, trying to get to the car. Feet churning, brain screaming. She slipped and lost the flashlight as she fell. She clambered back up and kept running.

Get inside. Hit the locks. Get away before he catches you. She'd run over his feet if she had to. Run over *him*.

Heart hammering, she rounded the front of the cottage. Changed direction. Looked up . . .

He was leaning against the passenger door of the Range Rover, arms crossed over his chest, looking as relaxed as could be.

She jerked to a stop. He wore his heavy black suede jacket and jeans. No hat or gloves. "It's strange," he said calmly, the light from the kitchen window cutting across his face. "I don't remember you being this crazy when you were a kid."

"*Me? You're* the psychopath!" She hadn't meant to scream

it—hadn't meant to say it at all. The word hung in the air between them.

But he didn't come after her. Instead, he said calmly, "This has to stop. You realize that, don't you?"

The surest way for him to make everything stop was to kill her. Her chest heaved. "You're right. Whatever you say." She began to back up, moving slowly, carefully.

"I get it." He uncrossed his arms. "I was a monster when I was sixteen. Don't think I've forgotten. But a few years with a shrink straightened me out."

Shrinks couldn't straighten out his kind of pathology. She gave a shaky nod. "Good. Great. I'm glad for you." She inched backward another step.

"It happened years ago. You're making yourself look ridiculous."

That sent an angry rush through her. "Go away! You've done enough."

He pushed himself away from the car. "I haven't done a damn thing. And you're the one who needs to go away!"

"I've been inside the cottage. I got your message." She lowered her voice, struggling to sound calm. "Just tell me . . ." She spoke even more softly, her voice barely trembling. "Did you— Did you hurt the cat?"

He cocked his head. "Mariah's death must have been hard on you. Maybe you should talk to somebody."

Did he really believe she was the one with mental problems? She needed to placate him. "I will. I'll talk to somebody. So you can go on home now. Take the car."

"You mean *my* car? The car you drove off in without asking permission?"

He'd told her she could take the car when she needed it, but she wasn't going to argue with him about it. "I won't do it again. Now it's late, and I'm sure you have work to do. I'll see you in the morning." Not after this. She'd have to find another way to repay Jaycie because she absolutely couldn't go up there again.

"I'll leave as soon as you tell me why you were skulking around the cottage?"

"I wasn't skulking. Just . . . getting a little exercise."

"Bull." He strode toward the cottage's side door, pulled it open, and disappeared inside.

She made a dash for the car, but she wasn't quick enough. He shot back out of the house. "What the hell happened in there?"

His outrage was so convincing that she would have believed him if she hadn't known better. "It's okay," she said quietly. "I won't tell anyone."

He jabbed his finger toward the cottage. "You think I did that?"

"No, no. Of course, I don't."

"You *do* think I did it." His frown turned to a glower. "You can't imagine how much I want to walk away right now and let you deal with this yourself."

"F-follow your instincts."

"Don't tempt me." In two long strides he was beside her. She jumped as his fingers clamped around her wrist. As she struggled, he pulled her toward the door. "Will you shut up?" he said. "You're hurting my ears. Not to mention terrifying the entire seagull population."

The fact that he sounded exasperated instead of ominous had an odd effect on her. She began to feel stupid instead of threatened. Like one of those dimwitted heroines in old black-and-white movies who were always being dragged around by John Wayne or Gary Cooper. She didn't like the feeling, and when they were inside, she stopped struggling.

He let her go, but his eyes were on her, and they were deadly serious. "Who did this?"

She told herself he was conning her, but she didn't feel conned, and she couldn't think of anything to say but the truth. "I thought you did."

"Me?" He seemed genuinely confused. "You're a pain in the ass, and I wish like hell you hadn't shown up here, but why would I trash the place where I like to work?"

She heard a mew. The cat crept into the kitchen.

One mystery solved.

Seconds ticked by as he stared at the animal. Then at

her. Finally he spoke, using the overly patient manner people employ when they're dealing with a child or the mentally impaired. "What are you doing with my cat?"

The traitorous animal rubbed against his ankles.

"It . . . followed me home."

"Like hell." He picked up the cat and scratched it behind the ears. "What did this crazy lady do to you, Hannibal?"

Hannibal?

The cat tucked his head against Theo's jacket and closed his eyes. Theo carried it with him into the living room. Feeling more and more confused, she followed him. He switched on the lights. "Does anything seem to be missing?"

"I— I don't know. I had my cell and my laptop with me, but . . ." *Her puppets!* Scamp was still in her backpack, but what about the rest?

She rushed past him to the studio. A low shelf for storing art supplies ran beneath the windows. She'd cleaned it up last week and set them there. They looked exactly as they had when she'd left that morning. Dilly and Leo separated by Crumpet and Peter.

He poked his head inside. "Nice friends."

She wanted to pick them up, talk to them, but not with him watching. He moved toward her bedroom. She went after him.

A messy stack of clothes waited for her to finish clearing out the rest of Mariah's things to make more room for her own. A bra hung over the chair between the windows along with last night's pajamas. She usually made her bed, but this morning she'd neglected to do it and had even left a bath towel on the edge of the mattress. Worst of all, yesterday's bright orange underpants lay in the middle of the floor.

He took it all in. "They did a real job in here."

Was he actually cracking a joke?

The cat had fallen asleep in his arms, but Theo continued to stroke its back, his long fingers sinking into the black fur. He wandered back into the living room and then the kitchen. She kicked the book of pornographic art under the sofa and followed him.

"Do you notice anything strange?" he asked.

"Yes! My house has been trashed."

"That's not what I mean. Look around. Do you see anything odd?"

"My life flashing before my eyes?"

"Stop screwing around."

"I can't help it. I tend to joke when I'm terrified." She tried to see whatever it was he wanted her to see, but she was too confused. Was Theo genuinely innocent or simply a good actor? She couldn't think of anyone else who would have done this. Barbara had warned her about strangers on the island, but wouldn't a stranger have stolen something? Not that there was much to steal.

Except Mariah's legacy.

The idea that someone else might know about the legacy stopped her in her tracks. She gazed at the kitchen. The biggest mess came from the overturned trash can and spilled bags of rice and noodles. Nothing seemed to be broken. "I guess it could have been worse," she said.

"Exactly. There's no broken glass. As far as you can tell, nothing is missing. This seems calculated. Does someone on the island have a grudge against you?"

She stared at him. Seconds ticked by before he got it.

"Don't look at me," he said. "You're the one holding the grudge."

"For good reason!"

"I'm not saying I blame you for it. I was a rotten kid. All I'm saying is that I don't have a motive."

"Sure you do. More than one. You want the cottage. I bring back bad memories. You're—" She stopped herself just before she spilled out what she was thinking.

He read her mind. "I'm not a psychopath."

"I didn't say you were." But, oh, was she thinking it.

"Annie, I was a kid, and I had big problems that summer."

"You think?" She wanted to say so much more, but this wasn't the time.

"Let's temporarily eliminate me from your list of suspects." He held up his hand, disturbing the cat. "Just as an exercise. You can put my name right back at the top as soon as we're done."

He was making fun of her. That should have made her furious, but it was oddly comforting. "There are no other suspects," she said. Except whoever knew that something valuable was supposed to be here. Had they found it? She'd been through everything in the bookcase, but she hadn't done a systematic inventory of the contents of the boxes in the studio or of everything in the closets. How would she even know?

"Have you had a run-in with anyone since you arrived?" Again that hand went up. "Other than me."

She shook her head. "But I've been warned about drifters."

He set the cat down. "I don't like what's happened. You need to report it to the mainland police."

"From what I remember, nothing short of murder brings them out here."

"You're right about that." He unzipped his jacket. "Let's get this mess cleaned up."

"I'll handle it," she said quickly. "You go on."

He gave her a faintly pitying look. "If I intended to kill you or rape you or whatever you think I might do, it would have happened by now."

"So glad it hasn't."

He muttered something under his breath and stalked off into the living room.

As she removed her coat, she thought about the self-help gurus and the way they told people to follow their instincts. But instincts could be wrong. Right now, for example. Because she felt almost safe.

BY THE TIME ANNIE CURLED into bed that night, she'd begun coughing again, which made it even harder to fall asleep, but how could she relax with Theo Harp sprawled on the pink couch? He'd refused to go home, even after she'd ordered him out. And the awful thing was, some part of her had wanted him to stay. This was exactly how it had been when she was fifteen. He'd acted like a friend, gained her confidence, and then turned into a monster.

The day had been exhausting, and when she finally drifted off, she slept deeply. As the faint gray morning light seeped through her eyelids, she experienced one of those blissful, sleep-fogged moments when it was too early to get up and she could stay where she was. Warm and cozy, she pulled up her knees. And brushed against something.

Her eyes flew open.

Theo lay in bed next to her. Right there. On his back. Only inches away.

The air stuck in her throat, then came out in a wheeze.

His eyes stayed shut, but his lips moved. "Warn me if you're going to scream," he muttered. "So I can kill myself first."

"What are you *doing* here?" she screeched. Not screamed.

"The couch was killing my back. Too damned short."

"I told you to use the bed in the studio!"

"Boxes on it. No blankets. Too much trouble."

He lay on top of the covers, still wearing his jeans and sweater, with the quilt she'd given him last night pulled to his chest. Unlike the rat's snarl that awaited her in the morning, his hair was perfectly rumpled, his jaw attractively stubbled, the bronze complexion he'd inherited from his mother showcased by the snowy white pillowcase. He probably didn't even have bad breath. And he showed no inclination to move.

Any urge she'd felt to fall back asleep had vanished. She thought of all kinds of things she wanted to say. *Damn you! How dare you!* But both sounded like bad dialogue from one of her old gothic novels. She gritted her teeth. "Please get out of my bed."

"You got anything on under the covers?" he asked, eyes still shut.

"Yes, I have something on!" She hit the perfect note of righteous outrage.

"Great. Then we don't have a problem."

"We wouldn't have a problem even if I *didn't* have anything on."

"Are you sure about that?"

Was he coming on to her? If she hadn't already been wide awake, that would have done the trick. She thrust herself out of bed, immediately conscious of her yellow flannel Santa pajamas, a joke present from a girlfriend. She grabbed Mariah's robe, snatched up yesterday's socks, and left him alone.

ANNIE'S FOOTSTEPS FADED. THEO SMILED. He'd had his first good night's sleep in longer than he could remember. He felt almost rested. Just lying here irritating Annie had been . . .

He searched for the word, finally found it. But it felt so unfamiliar, he had to examine it for a moment to make sure it fit.

Irritating Annie had been . . . fun.

She was scared to death of him—no mystery why—but she hadn't backed down. Even as an awkward, insecure teen, she'd had more courage than she gave herself credit for—more than she should have had, considering the way her mother had undermined her. She'd also possessed a strong sense of right and wrong. No messy gray areas for Antoinette Hewitt. Maybe that's what had drawn him to her when they were kids.

He couldn't abide having her here, but it was becoming increasingly apparent she wasn't going anywhere for a while. That damned divorce agreement. He wanted to be able to use the cottage whenever he liked, and she'd screwed that up. But it was more than the cottage. It was Annie herself, with her ridiculous naïveté and her link to a past he wanted to forget. Annie, who knew too much.

He'd been pissed when he'd discovered her stuck on the road. That's why he'd baited her into trying to push the car out herself, even though he knew she couldn't. As he'd sat behind the wheel badgering her to push harder, he'd experienced the oddest sensation. He'd almost felt as if he were slipping into another man's skin. A regular Joe who liked to have a little fun with people.

An illusion. Nothing about him was normal. But this morning he almost felt that way.

HE FOUND HER STANDING AT the kitchen sink. Last night, they'd cleaned up the worst of the mess, and now she was washing the silverware that had been strewn across the floor. She had her back to him, her run-amok honey brown curls in their customary free-for-all. He'd always been drawn to classically beautiful women, and Annie wasn't that. His arousal bothered him. But he'd been living without sex for longer than he cared to remember, and it was automatic.

He remembered her at fifteen—awkward, funny, and so smitten with him that he'd felt no pressure to try to impress her. His sexual fumblings were comic now, normal for a horny teenage boy. Maybe the only thing that had been normal about him.

Her plain navy robe came to midcalf with yellow flannel pajamas sticking out beneath. They showed Santa trying to squeeze into a chimney. "Nice jammies."

"You can go home now," she retorted.

"Do you have any with the Easter Bunny?"

She turned, one hand on her hip. "I like sexy nightwear. Sue me."

He laughed. Not much of one—rusty at its core—but still a laugh. There was no darkness about Annie Hewitt. With her big eyes, freckled nose, and scallywag's hair, she reminded him of a fairy. Not one of those fragile fairies who flitted gracefully from flower to flower, but a preoccupied fairy. The kind of fairy more likely to tumble over a dozing cricket than sprinkle any magic glitter. He felt himself uncoil, just a bit.

She swept her eyes from head to toe. He was used to women staring at him, but they weren't generally scowling at the time. True, he'd slept in his clothes and needed a shave, but how bad could he look? She frowned. "Do you even have bad breath?"

He had no idea what she was talking about. "I just used your toothpaste, so I don't think so. Any reason you want to know?"

"I'm keeping a list of disgusting things about you."

"Since 'psychopath' is already at the top of your list, it doesn't seem like you need to add much more." He said it lightly, as if it were a joke, even though they both knew it wasn't.

She grabbed the broom and began sweeping up some rice they'd missed. "Interesting the way you showed up at just the right time last night."

"I came down to get my car. You remember my car. The one you *stole*." He'd told her she could borrow it, but so what?

She was smart enough to pick her battles, and she ignored the accusation. "You made it here awfully fast."

"I took the beach path."

She jabbed the broom into the corner. "Too bad you weren't using your little spy telescope last night. Maybe you'd know who did this."

"I'll be more conscientious in the future."

She went after a noodle wedged under the stove. "Why were you dressed like Beau Brummell that first day?"

It took him a moment to remember what she meant. "Research. Getting a sense of what it feels like to move around in those clothes." And then, because he could be a real prick . . . "I like to slip inside my characters as much as possible. Especially the more twisted ones."

She looked so horrified he almost apologized. But why? He gazed toward the cupboards. "I'm hungry. Where's the cereal?"

She shoved the broom in the cupboard. "I'm out."

"How about some eggs?"

"Out."

"Bread?"

"Gone."

"Leftovers?"

"I wish."

"Tell me my coffee's still here."

"Only a little, and I'm not sharing."

He began opening cupboards, looking for it. "You obviously haven't gotten used to island grocery shopping."

"Stay out of my stuff."

He found what was left of his bag of ground coffee on top of the refrigerator. She made a lunge for it, but he held it over her head. "Be nice."

Nice. A rubbish word. One he hardly ever used. The word had no moral weight. A person didn't need courage for "nice." "Nice" called for no sacrifice, no strength of character. If only all he'd ever had to do was be nice . . .

He dropped his arm, and with his free hand tugged at the sash on her robe. As the sides separated, he pressed his palm to the skin exposed by the open V at the neck of her flannel pajama top. Her eyes grew wide and startled. "Forget the coffee," he said. "Take this off so I can see if what's underneath has gotten any bigger."

Not nice. Not nice at all.

But instead of slapping him as he deserved, she regarded him with an unsettling disgust. "You're demented." With a scowl, she stomped away.

You got that right, he thought. *And don't forget it.*

Chapter Eight

Annie stood off to the side of the kitchen window, watching as the cat jumped willingly into Theo's car and the two of them drove off together. *Don't turn your back, Hannibal,* she thought.

There was nothing sexy about Theo pulling her robe open. A bastard's nature was to act like a bastard, and he'd done what came naturally. But as she turned away from the window, she thought about the calculation she'd seen in his eyes when he'd done it. He'd deliberately tried to unhinge her, but it hadn't worked. He was a devious jerk, but was he a dangerous one? Her instincts said no, but her reliable brain was flashing enough warning signals to stop a freight train.

She headed for her bedroom. His so-called rental of her cottage was supposed to start today, and she needed to get out of here before he came back. She pulled on what had become her standard island uniform—jeans and wool socks with a long-sleeved top and heavy sweater. She missed the floaty fabrics and colorful prints of her summer boho dresses. She missed her vintage 1950s frocks with their fitted bodices and full skirts. One of her favorites was printed with ripe summer cherries. Another had a border of dancing martini glasses. Unlike Mariah, Annie loved colorful clothes with whimsical trims and decorative buttons. None of which enlivened the jeans and ratty sweaters she'd brought with her.

She returned to the living room and glanced out the window but saw no sign of Theo's car. She dressed quickly, grabbed her inventory notebook, and began going through the cottage room by room to see if anything was missing. She'd wanted to do this last night, but she wasn't letting Theo know anything about the legacy or her suspicion that the break-in was tied to it.

Everything on her list was still in place, but for all she knew, what she was looking for could be tucked in the back of a drawer or in one of the closets she hadn't yet thoroughly investigated. Had her housebreaker found what Annie couldn't locate?

Theo worried her. As she zipped up her coat, she made herself reexamine the possibility that the break-in had nothing to do with Mariah's legacy and everything to do with Theo trying to pay her back for spooking him. She'd thought she'd gotten away with the clock incident, but what if she hadn't? What if he'd seen through her and this was his payback? Should she follow her head or her instincts?

Definitely her head. Trusting Theo Harp was like trusting a poisonous snake not to bite.

She circled the cottage. Theo had done the same before he'd left, ostensibly to look for tracks . . . or maybe to wipe out any evidence he might have left himself. He'd told her the lack of fresh snow and the confusion from her footprints made it impossible to see anything unusual. She didn't quite believe him, but as she searched the same area, she couldn't find anything suspicious either. She turned toward the ocean. The morning tide was going out. If Theo had made it along the beach path last night, she should be able to make it in daylight.

Wet, jagged rocks guarded the shoreline near the cottage, and the icy ocean wind carried the smell of salt and seaweed. In warmer weather, she could have walked right along the water's edge, but now she stayed farther back, carefully picking her way along a narrow path that was sandy during the summer but was now icy with hard-packed snow.

The path wasn't as well defined as it had once been, and she had to climb over a few of the boulders that used to serve as her reading perches. She'd spent hours here daydreaming about the characters in whichever novel she was reading. The heroines were fueled only by strength of character as they faced down these forbidding men with their noble lineages, savage moods, and aquiline noses. Not unlike a certain Theo Harp. Although Theo's nose wasn't aquiline. She remembered how disappointed she'd been when she'd looked up that romantic-sounding word and seen what it really meant.

A pair of seagulls battled the cut of the wind. She stopped for a moment to take in the fierce beauty of the ocean as it pounded toward the shoreline, the foamy gray crests plunging into roiling dark valleys. She'd lived in the city so long that she'd forgotten this sense of being absolutely alone in the universe. It was a pleasant, dreamy sensation in the summer, but unsettling in the winter.

She moved on. The icy crust cracked beneath her feet as she reached the Harp House beach. She hadn't been here since the day she'd almost died.

The memory she'd tried so hard to suppress came flooding back.

She and Regan had found the litter of pups a few weeks before the end of the summer. Annie was still miserable from Theo's hostile withdrawal, and she'd been staying away from him as much as she could. On that particular morning while he was out surfing, she, Regan, and Jaycie were in the stable with the new pups. The pregnant mongrel who hung around the yard had delivered them during the night.

The pups, cuddled against their mother, were only a few hours old, six squirmy masses of black and white fur with their eyes still closed and their soft pink tummies rising and falling with each new breath. Their mother, a short-haired mix of so many breeds it was impossible to guess her pedigree, had shown up at the beginning of the summer. Theo had initially claimed her as his own, then lost interest after the dog had hurt its foot.

The three girls had sat cross-legged in the straw, their soft chatter drifting back and forth as they examined each tiny pup. "That one is the cutest," Jaycie declared.

"I wish we could take them with us when we leave."

"I want to name them."

Eventually, Regan had fallen silent. When Annie asked if something was wrong, Regan twisted a strand of her shiny dark hair around her finger and poked at the floor with a piece of straw. "Let's not tell Theo about them."

Annie didn't intend to tell Theo anything, but she still wanted to know what Regan meant. "Why not?"

Regan pulled the lock across her cheek. "Sometimes he——"

Jaycie jumped in. "He's a boy. Boys are rougher than girls."

Annie thought of Regan's oboe and the purple notebook full of her poetry. She thought of herself—locked in the dumbwaiter, attacked by the gulls, pushed into the marsh. Regan jumped to her feet as if she wanted to change the subject. "Come on. Let's go."

The three of them had left the stable, but later that afternoon, when she and Regan had returned to check on the pups, Theo was already there.

Annie hung back while Regan went to his side. He was crouched in the straw stroking one of the small, wriggling bodies. Regan settled next to him. "They're cute, aren't they?" She framed it as a question, as if she needed him to validate her opinions.

"They're mutts," he said. "Nothing special. I don't like dogs." He rose from the straw and stalked out of the stable, not even glancing at Annie.

The next day Annie found him in the stable again. It was raining outside, the smell of fall already in the air. Regan was off packing the last of her things for the next day's trip home, and Theo had one of the pups in his hands. Regan's words came rushing back, and Annie leaped forward. "Put it down!" she'd exclaimed.

He didn't argue with her, just set the pup back with the rest. As he looked at her, his normal sulky expression disappeared, and in her imaginative eyes, he seemed more tragic than sullen. The romantic bookworm inside her forgot about his cruelty and thought only of her beloved misunderstood heroes with their dark secrets, hidden nobility, and prodigious passions. "What's wrong?"

He shrugged. "The summer's over. Sucks that it's raining on our last day."

Annie liked the rain. It gave her a good excuse to curl up and read. And she was glad to leave. The past few months had been too hard.

All three of them would be going back to their old schools. Theo and Regan to fancy boarding schools in Connecticut, and Annie to her junior year at LaGuardia High, the *Fame* school.

He dug his fists into the pockets of his shorts. "Things aren't going too great with your mom and my dad."

She'd heard the quarrels, too. The quirkiness Elliott had originally found so charming in Mariah had gotten under his skin, and she'd overheard her mother accuse Elliott of being stuffy, which he was, but his stability was what Mariah had wanted, even more than his money. Now Mariah was saying she and Annie were going back to their old apartment when they returned to the city. Just to pack things up, she'd said, but Annie didn't believe her.

Rain clicked against the dusty stable windows. Theo nudged the toe of his sneaker into the straw. "I'm . . . sorry things got weird with us this summer."

Things hadn't gotten weird. *He'd* gotten weird. But she wasn't big on confrontation, and she'd merely muttered, "It's okay."

"I—I liked talking to you."

She'd liked talking to him, too, and she'd liked their make-out sessions even more. "Me, too."

She didn't know exactly how it happened, but they ended up sitting on one of the wood benches, their backs against the stable wall, talking about school, about their parents, about the books they had to read next year. It was exactly as it used to be, and she could have talked to him for hours, but Jaycie and Regan appeared. Theo jumped up from the bench, spat in the straw, and jerked his head toward the door. "Let's go into town," he told them. "I want some fried clams."

He didn't invite Annie to come along.

She felt ugly and stupid for talking to him again. But that night, right after she'd finished packing the last of her things, she found a note from him slipped under her bedroom door.

Tide's out. Meet me in the cave. Please.
                                         T.

She'd pulled a fresh top and a clean pair of shorts from her suitcase, fluffed her hair, dabbed on some lip gloss, and slipped out of the house.

He wasn't on the beach, but she hadn't really expected to see him there. They always met by a small, sandy area toward the back where there was a tidal pool to poke around in.

He was wrong about the tide. It was coming in strong. But they'd been in the cave before when the tide shifted, and there was no danger of being trapped. Even though the water was deeper at the back of the cave, they had no trouble swimming out.

Cold seawater soaked her sneakers and splashed her bare legs as she scrambled over the rocks to the entrance. When she got there, she turned on the small pink flashlight she'd brought down with her. "Theo?" Her voice echoed around the rocky chamber.

He didn't answer.

A wave splashed her knees. Disappointed, she was about to turn back when she heard it. Not his response, but the frantic yips of the pups.

Her first thought was that Theo had brought them down so they could play with them. "Theo?" she called for him again, and when he didn't answer, she moved deeper into the cave, searching it with the flashlight she'd brought with her.

The sandy crescent in the back near where she and Theo used to make out was underwater. The waves lapped at the ledge just above. On that ledge sat a cardboard box, and from inside the box came the sounds she was hearing.

"Theo!" She got a sick feeling in her stomach, a feeling that grew worse when he didn't respond. She began wading toward the back of the cave until the rising water was at her waist.

The ledge was cut into the rock wall a few inches over her head. The old cardboard box was already getting soaked from the spray. If she tried to pull it off the ledge, the bottom would drop out and the pups would fall in the water. But she couldn't leave them here. In no time at all, the waves would sweep the box away.

Theo, what have you done?

She couldn't think about that, not with the pups' yips growing more frantic. She felt along the cave wall with the toe of her sneaker until she found a niche to use as a step. She pulled herself up and shone the flashlight into the box. All six of the pups were there, yipping, terrified, scampering frenetically on a scrap of brown towel already soggy with seawater. She set the flashlight on the ledge, grabbed two of them, and tried to secure them against her chest so she could step down. Their sharp claws scratched her through her T-shirt, and she lost her grip. With terrified yelps, both pups tumbled back into the box.

She'd have to take them out one at a time. She snatched up the biggest and stepped off the ledge, wincing as his claws dug into her arm. So easy to swim out of the cave. So hard to wade through the swirling water with a struggling puppy in her arms.

She dragged herself toward the fading light at the cave opening. The water sucked at her legs. The pup was frantic, and its claws hurt. "Please be still. Please, please . . ."

By the time she reached the mouth of the cave, the scratches on her arm had begun to bleed, and five more pups were still inside. But before she could go back for any of them, she had to find someplace safe to put this one. She stumbled across the rocks toward their fire circle.

The pit held the ashes of last week's fire, but the inside was dry, and the stones around the perimeter were high enough to keep the pup from getting out. She set it down, raced to the cave, and rushed back inside. She'd never stayed in there long enough to see how high the tide reached, but the water was still rising. As the cave floor sloped down, she began to swim. Even though it was summer, the water was icy. Her hands touched the wall, and she found her foothold under the ledge. Shivering, she reached into the box for the second pup and winced when a new set of claws scored her skin.

She managed to get this pup safely to the fire pit, but the water was growing deeper, and she had to struggle to reach the back of the cave for the third one. The flashlight she'd left on the ledge had grown dimmer, but she could see enough to tell that the cardboard box was close to collapsing. She'd never get them all out in time. But she had to.

She lifted the third pup and stepped off the ledge. A wave caught her, the dog struggled, and she lost her grip. It slipped into the water.

With a sob, she plunged her arms into the churning salt water and reached frantically around for the small body. She felt something and snatched the pup up.

The undertow dragged at her as she tried to wade toward the fading light at the mouth of the cave. She was having trouble breathing. The pup had stopped struggling, and she didn't know if it was dead or alive until she placed it in the fire pit and saw it move.

Three more. She couldn't go back in yet. She had to rest. But if she did, the animals would drown.

The undertow was growing stronger instead of weaker, and the water was rising higher. She lost a sneaker somewhere and kicked off the other. Every breath was a struggle, and by the time she reached the water-sodden box, she'd gone under twice. The second time, she swallowed so much salt water, she was still choking when she climbed up.

Before she could grab hold of the fourth pup, a wave knocked her back. She found her footing and climbed again, gasping for breath. She made a wild grab and pulled out another pup. The pain from the scratches on her arms and chest, the fire in her lungs, were excruciating. Her legs were giving out, and her muscles screamed for her to stop. A wave pulled her feet out from under her, and she and the pup were swamped, but somehow she managed to hold on. She tried to cough out the water she'd swallowed. The muscles in her arms and legs burned. Somehow she reached the fire pit.

Two more . . .

If she'd been thinking clearly, she would have stopped, but she was acting on instinct. Her entire life had led to this moment when her only purpose was to save the pups. She fell on the rocks as she scrambled back to the cave, and a long gash opened on her calf. She staggered inside. An icy wave pushed her down. She struggled to swim.

Only the faintest glow came from the flashlight on the ledge. The wet cardboard box sagged precariously. Her knee scraped the rock as she pulled herself up.

Two pups. She couldn't do this twice. She had to get them both out. She tried to pick them up together but couldn't make her hands work. Her foot slipped again, and again she fell back in the water. Gasping, she fought her way to the surface, but she was choking and disoriented. She barely managed to hoist herself up to the ledge again. She reached inside.

Only one. She could only save one.

Her fingers closed around wet fur. With a wrenching sob, she took the pup and started to swim only to discover that her legs wouldn't move. She tried to get them under her so she could stand, but the undertow was too strong. And then, in the dim light coming from outside, she saw the monster wave barreling toward the cave. Rising higher and higher still. Scudding inside, engulfing her, and throwing her against the rocky cave wall. She twisted and tumbled, her arms flailing, knowing she was drowning.

A hand pulled at her. She fought, struggled. The arms were strong. Insistent. They dragged at her until she felt clean air on her face.

Theo.

It wasn't Theo. It was Jaycie. "Stop fighting!" the girl cried.

"The dogs . . ." Annie gasped. "There's another——" She ran out of oxygen.

Another wave crashed over them. Jaycie's grip stayed firm.

She dragged Annie and the pup against the current and out of the cave.

When they reached the rocks, Annie collapsed, but Jaycie didn't. As Annie struggled to sit up, her rescuer rushed back to the cave. It didn't take her long to return carrying a wet, wriggling puppy.

Annie was dimly aware of the blood streaming from the gash in her calf, of her scratched arms, and the stains blooming like crimson roses through her T-shirt. She heard the dogs' yips coming from the fire pit, but the sound brought her no pleasure.

Jaycie hovered over the pit, the pup she'd rescued still in her arms. Annie slowly absorbed the fact that Jaycie had saved her life, and through her chattering teeth she mustered a ragged "Thank you."

Jaycie shrugged. "I guess you should thank my old man for getting drunk. I had to get out."

"Annie! Annie, are you down there?"

It was too dark to see, but Annie had no trouble recognizing Regan's voice. "She's here," Jaycie called up when Annie couldn't answer.

Regan scampered down the shallow stone steps and rushed to Annie. "Are you all right? Please don't tell my dad. Please!"

Anger coursed through Annie. She came to her feet as Regan hurried to the puppies. She lifted one to her cheek and started to cry. "You can't tell, Annie."

All the emotions Annie had suppressed exploded inside her. She left the pups, left Regan and Jaycie, and climbed awkwardly over the rocks to the cliff stairs. Her legs were still weak, she was shivering, and she had to grip the rope handrail to pull herself up.

The lights were still on around the deserted swimming pool. Annie's pain and fury gave her legs fresh strength. She rushed across the lawn and into the house. She flew up the stairs, her feet pounding on the treads.

Theo's room was toward the back, next to his sister's. She flung open the door. He lay on his bed, reading. The sight of her, with her matted hair, bloody scratches, and gashed calf brought him to his feet.

There were always bits of riding gear lying around his bedroom. She didn't consciously snatch up the riding crop, but a force she couldn't control had taken over. The crop was in her hand, and she was rushing toward him. He stood there, not moving, almost as if he knew what was coming. She brought up her arm and swung the crop at him as hard as she could. It caught the side of his face and split the thin skin over his brow bone.

"Annie!" Her mother, drawn by the noise, raced into the room with Elliott right behind. Elliott wore his customary starched long-sleeved blue dress shirt while her mother wore a narrow black caftan and long silver earrings. Mariah gasped as she saw the blood streaming down Theo's face and then Annie's condition. "My God . . ."

"He's a monster!" Annie cried.

"Annie, you're hysterical," Elliott proclaimed, hurrying to his son.

"The dogs nearly died because of you!" she screamed. "Are you sorry they didn't? Are you sorry they're still alive?" Tears streaming down her face, she lunged at him again, but Elliott twisted the riding crop from her grasp. "Stop it!"

"Annie, what happened?" Her mother was staring at her as if she no longer recognized her.

Annie poured out the story. As Theo stood there, his eyes on the floor, blood running from the cut, she told them everything—about the note he'd written, the pups. She told them how he'd locked her in the dumbwaiter and set the birds on her at the boat wreck. How he'd pushed her into the marsh. The words rushed out of her in a torrent.

"Annie, you should have told me all this earlier." Mariah pulled her daughter from the room, leaving Elliott to stanch the flow of blood from his son's wound.

Both the gash in Annie's calf and the cut in Theo's forehead needed stitches, but there was no doctor on the island and simple bandages had to do. This left each of them with a permanent scar—Theo's small, almost rakish, Annie's longer but eventually fading more than the memory ever could.

Later that night, after the puppies were resettled in the

stable with their mother and everyone had gone to bed, Annie was still awake, listening to the faintest sound of voices coming from the adults' bedroom. They were speaking too softly for her to hear, so she crept out into the hallway to eavesdrop.

"Face facts, Elliott," she heard her mother say. "There's something seriously wrong with your son. A normal kid doesn't do things like this."

"He needs discipline, that's all," Elliott had retorted. "I'm finding a military school for him. No more coddling."

Her mother didn't relent. "He doesn't need a military school. He needs a psychiatrist!"

"Stop exaggerating. You always exaggerate, and I hate it."

The argument gathered steam, and Annie cried herself to sleep.

THEO GAZED DOWN FROM THE turret. Annie stood on the beach, the ends of her hair whipping from beneath her red knit cap as she stared toward the cave. A rockslide a few years ago had blocked the entrance, but she still knew exactly where it was. He rubbed the thin white scar on his eyebrow.

He'd sworn to his father that he hadn't meant to hurt anyone—that he'd only taken the pups to the beach that afternoon so he and Annie could play with them, but that he'd started watching TV and forgotten about them.

The military school he was then sent to was committed to reforming troubled boys, and his classmates survived the austerity by tormenting one another. His solitary nature, preoccupation with books, and status as a newcomer made him a target. He was forced into fights. Most of them he won, but not all. He didn't much care either way. Regan, however, did, and she staged a hunger strike.

Her boarding school was the sister institution of his former school, and she wanted Theo back. At first Elliott had ignored her hunger strike, but when the school threatened to send her home for anorexia, he'd relented. Theo had gone back to his old school.

He turned away from the turret window and packed up his laptop along with a couple of yellow legal pads he was taking to the cottage. He'd never liked to write in an office. In Manhattan, he'd traded his home office for a library cubicle or a table at one of his favorite coffee shops. If Kenley was at work, he'd move to the kitchen or an easy chair in the living room. Kenley had never been able to understand it.

You'd be a lot more productive, Theo, if you'd stay in one spot.

Ironic words from a woman whose emotions could race from manic highs to paralyzing lows in the span of a day.

He wasn't going to let Kenley haunt him today. Not after having his first restful sleep since he'd come to Peregrine Island. He had a career to rescue, and today he was going to write.

The Sanitarium had been an unexpected blockbuster, a circumstance that hadn't impressed his father. "It's a bit difficult to explain to our friends why my son has such a grisly imagination. If it weren't for your grandmother's foolishness, you'd be working at the company, where you belong."

His grandmother's foolishness, as Elliott called it, was her decision to leave her estate to Theo, and, in his father's estimation, take away Theo's need to have a real occupation. In other words, go to work for Harp Industries.

The company had its roots in Elliott's grandfather's button manufacturing business but now made the titanium pins and bolts built of super alloys that helped hold together Black Hawk helicopters and stealth bombers. But Theo didn't want to make pins and bolts. He wanted to write books where the boundaries between good and evil were blazingly clear. Where there was at least a chance that order would win out over chaos and madness. That's what he'd done in *The Sanitarium,* his horror novel about a sinister mental hospital for the criminally insane with a room that transported its residents, including Dr. Quentin Pierce, a particularly sadistic serial killer, back through time.

Now he was working on the sequel to *The Sanitarium.* With the background already established from the first book and his intention to send Pierce back to nineteenth-century London, his task should have been easier. But he was having trouble, and he wasn't sure why. He did know he'd have a better chance of breaking through his block at the cottage, and he was glad he'd been able to bully Annie into letting him work there.

Something rubbed against his ankles. He looked down to see that Hannibal had brought him a gift. A limp gray mouse carcass. He grimaced. "I know you're doing it out of love, pal, but would you mind knocking it off?"

Hannibal purred and scratched his chin against Theo's leg.

"Another day, another corpse," Theo muttered. It was time to get to work.

Chapter Nine

Theo had left his Range Rover for her at Harp House. Driving it over the treacherous road into town to meet the weekly supply boat should have been a lot more relaxing than driving her Kia, but she was too wound up from waking that morning and finding Theo sleeping next to her. She parked the car at the wharf and cheered herself up thinking about the real salad she'd fix herself for dinner.

Several dozen people waited at the wharf, most of them women. The disproportionate number of older residents testified to what Barbara had said about younger families leaving. Peregrine Island was beautiful during the summer, but who'd want to stay here year-round? Although today's clear, sunny sky and bright light reflecting off the water had a particular kind of beauty.

She spotted Barbara and waved. Lisa, bundled up in an oversize coat that probably belonged to her husband, was talking with Judy Kester, whose bright red-orange hair was as loud and cheery as her laugh. Seeing the Bunco women together made Annie desperately miss her own friends.

Marie Cameron hurried over, looking as though she'd been sucking on lemons. "How are you doing out there by yourself?" she asked as dolefully as if Annie were in the final stages of a terminal illness.

"Fine. No problems." Annie wasn't mentioning last night's break-in to anyone.

Marie leaned closer. She smelled of clove and mothballs. "You watch out for Theo. I know what I know, and anybody with eyes could see a squall was coming in. Regan wouldn't have taken her boat out in that weather, not voluntarily."

Fortunately, the converted lobster boat that served as the weekly supply ferry was pulling up to the wharf, and Annie didn't have to respond. The boat held plastic crates filled with grocery bags, as well as a spool of electrical cable, roofing shingles, and a shiny white toilet. The islanders automatically formed a bucket brigade to unload the boat, then reloaded it in the same fashion with the mail, packages, and empty plastic crates from the previous shipment of groceries.

When that was done, everyone headed to the parking lot. Each plastic grocery crate had a white index card attached with the recipient's name printed in black marker. Annie had no trouble locating the three crates marked HARP HOUSE. They were packed so full she had to struggle to get them to the car.

"It's always a good day when the ferry makes it," Barbara called out from the tailgate of her pickup.

"The first thing I'm going to do is eat an apple," Annie replied as she settled the last crate into the Range Rover.

She went back to get her own meager order from the dozen or so crates waiting to be claimed. She inspected the names on each one but couldn't find hers. She checked again. NORTON . . . CARMINE . . . GIBSON . . . ALVAREZ . . . No HEWITT. No MOONRAKER COTTAGE.

As she searched for the third time, she caught the scent of Barbara's floral cologne behind her. "Something wrong?"

"My groceries aren't here," Annie said. "Only the ones for Harp House. Somebody must have taken mine by mistake."

"More likely the new girl at the grocery messed up again," Barbara said. "Last month she forgot half of my order."

Annie's good mood vanished. First the break-in at the cottage and now this. She'd been here two weeks. She had no bread, no milk, nothing but a few canned goods left and some rice. How was she going to wait another week for the next ferry, providing the boat could even make the crossing?

"It's cold enough for your things to hold in the car for half an hour," Barbara said. "Come to the house with me, and I'll give you a cup of coffee. You can call the store from there."

"Could you give me one of your apples, too?" Annie asked glumly.

The older woman smiled. "Sure."

The kitchen smelled of bacon and Barbara's perfume. She handed Annie an apple and began putting away her own groceries. Annie called the clerk on the mainland who was in charge of the islanders' orders and explained what had happened, but the clerk sounded more annoyed than apologetic. "I got a message saying you'd canceled your order."

"But I didn't."

"Then I guess somebody doesn't like you."

Barbara put a pair of floral coffee mugs on the table as Annie hung up. "Somebody canceled my order."

"Are you sure? That girl screws up all the time." Barbara retrieved a cookie tin from the cupboard. "Still . . . Things like that do happen around here. If somebody has a grudge, they make a phone call." She opened the lid revealing a waxed paper nest filled with frosted sugar cookies.

Annie sat down, but she'd lost her appetite, even for the apple. Barbara took a cookie for herself. She'd penciled in one eyebrow a little crookedly, which made her look slightly barmy, but there wasn't anything crazy about her straightforward gaze. "I'd like to say that things will get better for you, but who knows?"

Not what Annie wanted to hear. "There's no reason for anyone to hold a grudge against me." *Except maybe Theo.*

"And no reason why feuds spring up. I love Peregrine, but it isn't for everyone." She held the cookie tin out to Annie, shaking it to encourage her, but Annie shook her head. Barbara snapped the lid back on. "I'm probably nosing in where I don't belong, but you're about the same age as Lisa, and it's obvious you're not happy here. I'd hate to see you leave, but you don't have family on the island, and you shouldn't be miserable, either."

Barbara's concern meant everything to her, and Annie fought the urge to confide about the forty-six days she still had to spend here and the debts she couldn't pay off, about her distrust of Theo and her fears for her future, but she wouldn't do any of that.

"Thanks, Barbara. I'll be fine."

As she drove back to Harp House, she thought about how much smarter age and debt were making her. No more trying to patch a living together with puppets and odd jobs. No more worries about a nine-to-five job conflicting with auditions. She'd find something with a regular paycheck and a nice, cushy 401(k).

You'll hate it, Scamp said.

"Not as much as I hate being poor," Annie retorted.

Even Scamp couldn't argue with that.

ANNIE SPENT THE REST OF the day at Harp House. On a trip to dump the trash, she spotted something odd in front of the tree stump near Livia's hideout. Two rows of short sticks had been stuck in the ground in front of the gnarled hollow at the base of the stump. Half a dozen strips of bark lay across the top like a roof. She hadn't seen this yesterday, so Livia must have sneaked out today. Annie wished Jaycie would talk about her daughter's muteness. The child was such a mystery.

The Range Rover disappeared later that afternoon, so Annie left in plenty of time to get back to the cottage on foot before dark. But since she'd filled both a plastic bag and her backpack with groceries from Harp House, she had to keep stopping to rest. Even from a distance, she could see the Range Rover parked in front of the cottage. That wasn't fair. He was supposed to be gone by the time she returned home. The last thing she wanted was a battle with Theo, but if she didn't stand up to him now, he'd plow her down.

She entered the cottage through the front door and found Theo with his legs propped up on the arm of her pink couch and Leo slipped over his arm. Theo dropped his feet to the floor. "I like this guy."

"Of course you do," Annie said. *Two of a kind.*

Theo addressed the puppet. "What's your name, big guy?"

"His name is Bob," she said. "And now that the second shift's arrived—that would be me—it's past time for you to go home."

He pointed Leo toward the grocery sack. "Anything good in there?"

"Yes." She got rid of her coat and went to the kitchen. Fully conscious that she'd walked off with his food, she set her backpack on the floor and put the plastic bag on the counter. He followed her, Leo still on his arm, something she found profoundly disturbing. "Put Bob down. And from now on, leave my puppets alone. They're valuable, and nobody touches them but me. You're supposed to be working today, not nosing around in my stuff."

"I worked." He peered into the plastic grocery bag. "I killed off a runaway teenage girl and a homeless man. They were torn apart by a wolf pack. And since the scene's set in civilized Hyde Park, I have to say, I'm feeling pretty good about myself."

"Give me that!" She grabbed Leo from him. The last thing she needed was Theo putting images of wolf pack attacks in her head.

First, I ripped out her throat . . .

She deposited Leo in the living room, then returned to the kitchen. The sight of Leo and Theo together called for retaliation. "A strange thing happened at the house today when I was upstairs. I heard . . . I shouldn't say anything. I don't want to upset you."

"Since when?"

"Well . . . I was at the end of the hall, right by the turret door, and I felt this chill coming from the other side." She'd always been a truthful person, and she couldn't imagine how she'd gotten so comfortable with lying. "It was as though somebody had left a window open, except ten times colder." She had no trouble manufacturing a slight shiver. "I don't know how you can stand living in that place."

He took out a carton with half a dozen eggs. "I guess some people are more comfortable with ghosts than others."

She looked at him sharply, but he seemed more interested in inspecting the contents of the grocery bag than in being spooked. "Interesting that we like so many of the same brands," he said.

He'd find out as soon as he talked to Jaycie, so she might as well tell him herself. "Somebody canceled my grocery order. I'll replace everything when the ferry arrives next week."

"This is *my* food?"

"Only a few things. A loan." She began pulling out the groceries she'd stuffed in her backpack.

He grabbed the package closest to him. "You took my *bacon*?"

"You had two of them. You won't miss one."

"I can't believe you took my bacon."

"I'd liked to have taken your doughnuts or your frozen pizza, but I couldn't. And do you know why? Because you didn't order either one. What kind of man are you?"

"A man who likes real food." He pushed her out of the way so he could see what her backpack held and picked up a small chunk of Parmesan—a piece she'd cut from the wedge he'd ordered. "Excellent." He tossed it from one hand to the other, then set it on the counter and began opening her cupboards.

"Hey! What are you doing?"

He pulled out a saucepan. "I'm making my dinner. With *my* groceries. If you don't piss me off, I might share with you. Or not."

"No! Go home. The cottage is mine now, remember?"

"You're right." He began tossing the packages back in the plastic bag. "I'll take these with me."

Damn it. Along with coughing less, her appetite had begun to return, and she'd barely eaten all day. "Fine," she said begrudgingly. "You cook. I'll eat. Then you're out of here."

He was already rummaging through the bottom cupboard for another pot.

She put Leo away in the studio, then went to her bedroom. Theo didn't like her—definitely didn't want her around—so why was he doing this? She traded her boots for sock monkey slippers and straightened up the clothes she'd left lying on the bed. She didn't want to be around a man she was more than a little afraid of. Even worse, a man some part of her still wanted to trust, despite all the evidence stacked against him. It was too much like being fifteen all over again.

The smell of sizzling bacon began to fill the air, along with the faintest scent of garlic. Her stomach growled. "Screw it." She went back into the kitchen.

The delicious odors were coming from the iron skillet. Spaghetti boiled in the saucepan, and he was beating some of her precious eggs in a big yellow mixing bowl. Two wineglasses sat on the counter, along with a dusty bottle from the cupboard over the sink. "Where's the corkscrew?" he said.

She drank good wine so seldom that she hadn't thought about opening any of the bottles Mariah had stored. Now the lure was irresistible. She rummaged through the junk drawer and handed over the corkscrew. "What are you making?"

"One of my specialties."

"Human liver with fava beans and a nice Chianti?"

He cocked an eyebrow at her. "You're adorable."

She wouldn't let him dismiss her so easily. "You do remember I have a lot of reasons to expect the worst from you."

He pulled out the wine cork with one efficient twist. "It was a long time ago, Annie. I told you. I was a screwed-up kid."

"Take this in the spirit with which it's intended . . . . You're still screwed up."

"You don't know anything about who I am now." He filled her glass with bloodred wine.

"You live in a haunted house. You terrify small children. You take your horse out in the middle of a blizzard. You—"

He set down the bottle a little too hard. "I lost my wife a year ago this month. What the hell do you expect? Party hats and noisemakers?"

She felt a stab of remorse. "I'm sorry about that."

He shrugged off her sympathy. "And I'm not abusing Dancer. The wilder the weather is, the more he loves it."

She thought of Theo standing bare-chested in the snow. "Just like you?"

"Yeah," he said flatly. "Just like me." He grabbed a cheese grater he'd found somewhere and the wedge of Parmesan, shutting her out.

She sipped her wine. It was a delicious cabernet, fruity and full-bodied. He clearly didn't want to talk, which made her determined to force the issue. "Tell me about your new book."

Seconds ticked by. "I don't like to talk about a book while I'm writing it. It takes away the energy that belongs on the page."

A challenge similar to the one that actors faced performing the same role night after night. She watched him grate the cheese into an oblong glass bowl. "A lot of people hated *The Sanitarium*." Her comment was so rude she was almost ashamed.

He grabbed the boiling pot of spaghetti from the stove and dumped the contents into a colander in the sink. "Did you read it?"

"Didn't get around to it." It went against her nature to be so blunt, but she wanted him to know she wasn't the same timid mouse she'd been at fifteen. "How did your wife die?"

He transferred the hot pasta to the mixing bowl and beaten eggs without losing a beat. "Despair. She killed herself."

His words made her queasy. There was so much more she wanted to know. *How did she do it? Did you see it coming? Were you the reason?* That last question most of all. But she didn't have the stomach to ask any of it.

He added the bacon and garlic to the pasta and tossed the mixture with a pair of forks. She grabbed some silverware and napkins and carried them to the table set in the living room bay window. After she'd fetched the wineglasses, she took her place. He emerged from the kitchen with their loaded plates and frowned at the garishly painted plaster mermaid chair. "Hard to believe your mother was an art expert."

"It's not any worse than a dozen other things in the cottage." She inhaled the scents of garlic, bacon, and the roughly grated Parmesan on top. "This smells delicious."

He put down her plate and sat across from her. "Spaghetti carbonara."

Hunger must have fried her brain because she did the stupidest thing. She automatically lifted her glass. "To the chef."

He locked eyes with her but didn't lift his own glass. She quickly set hers down, but his gaze held, and she felt an odd prickling, as if something more than the draft coming through the bay window had stirred the air between them. It took her only a moment to figure out exactly what was happening.

Certain women were drawn to volatile men, sometimes out of neuroses, sometimes—if the woman was a romantic—out of the naive fantasy that her particular brand of femininity was powerful enough to tame one of these rogue males. In novels, the fantasy was irresistible. In real life, it was total bull. Of course she felt a sexual pull from all that dangerous masculinity. Her body had been through a lot lately, and this reawakening meant she was healing. On the flip side, her reaction was also a reminder that he still held a destructive fascination for her.

She concentrated on the food, twirling her fork in the pasta and pushing a messy bite into her mouth. It was the best thing she'd ever tasted. Rich and gooey, savory with garlic and smoky with bacon. Completely satisfying. "When did you learn to cook?"

"When I started writing. I discovered that cooking was a great way for me to untangle plot problems in my head."

"Nothing quite as inspiring as a butcher knife, right?"

He raised his unscarred eyebrow at her.

She was starting to feel a little too snarky, so she relented. "This might be the best meal I've ever eaten."

"Only compared with what you and Jaycie have been fixing."

"There's nothing wrong with our food." She couldn't muster up much conviction.

"Nothing much right with it, either. The best you can say is that it's serviceable."

"I'll take serviceable. Serviceable's good." She chased a bacon morsel with her fork. "Why don't you cook for yourself."

"Too much trouble."

Not an entirely satisfying answer, since he seemed to enjoy cooking, but she wasn't going to show enough interest to inquire further.

He leaned back in his chair. Unlike her, he wasn't wolfing down his meal but savoring it. "Why didn't you order groceries for yourself?"

"I ordered," she said around another mouthful. "Apparently someone left a message canceling it."

He cradled his wineglass. "Here's what I don't get. You haven't even been here a full two weeks. How have you managed to piss off somebody that fast?"

She'd give anything to know whether or not he was aware that she might have something valuable hidden here. "I have no idea," she said, twisting a strand of pasta around her fork.

"There's something you're not telling me."

She dabbed at her mouth. "There are a lot of things I'm not telling you."

"You have a theory about this, don't you?"

"Yes, but unfortunately, I can't prove you're the one behind the trouble."

"Cut the bullshit," he said harshly. "You know I didn't trash this place. But I'm starting to believe you might have some idea who did."

"None. Swear." That part was true, at least.

"Then why did it happen? Despite the company you keep, you're no dummy. I think you have your suspicions."

"I might. And no, I'm not sharing."

He regarded her with a shuttered expression that was impossible to read. "You really don't trust me, do you?"

It was such a ludicrous question that she didn't bother answering, although she couldn't resist rolling her eyes. Which he didn't find amusing.

"I can't help if you won't level with me," he said in the voice of someone used to instant obedience.

No chance he'd get that from her. It would take more than fabulous food and great wine to wipe out her memory bank.

"Tell me what's happening," he went on. "Why is someone after you? What do they want?"

She placed her palm on her chest and drawled, "The key to my heart."

A muscle ticked in his jaw. "Keep your secrets then. I don't care."

"No reason you should."

They finished eating in silence. She carried her plate and wineglass into the kitchen. The cupboard door above the sink was still ajar displaying the bottles stacked inside. Her mother had always kept good wine around, thanks to the gifts people brought her. Rare vintages. Highly sought after collectibles. Who knew what she had stored in there? Maybe—

The wine! Annie gripped the edge of the sink. What if these bottles of wine were her legacy? She'd been so focused on the art in the cottage that she hadn't thought beyond. Rare bottles of wine fetched exorbitant sums at auction. She'd heard of a single bottle going for twenty or thirty thousand dollars. What if she and Theo had just polished off part of her legacy?

The wine started to come back up in her throat. She heard him walking into the kitchen behind her. "You have to go now," she said unsteadily. "I appreciate the food, but I'm serious. You have to get out of here."

"Fine by me." He set his plate on the counter, showing no more emotion about being kicked out than he did about anything else.

As soon as he was gone, she grabbed her notebook, wrote down the information from the label of each wine bottle, then carefully boxed them all up. She found a marker and wrote CLOTHES TO DONATE on the flap, then tucked the box away in the back of her closet. If there was another break-in, she wouldn't make it easy on whoever was out to get her.

"I KEEP THINKING IF THIS room looked better," Jaycie said, leaning precariously on her crutches, "Theo might want to relax here."

Which meant Jaycie would have a better chance of spending time with him the way she wanted to. Annie flipped the sunroom couch cushions. Jaycie wasn't a smitten teenager any longer. Hadn't she learned anything about making better choices in men?

"Theo didn't come back to the house for dinner last night?"

Annie heard the question in Jaycie's voice but decided it was best to keep last night's meal to herself. "He stayed around for a while to give me a hard time. I finally kicked him out."

Jaycie moved her dust rag across the bookshelves. "Oh. That was probably good."

THE WINE WAS ONE MORE disappointment. Annie tracked each bottle online. The most expensive was a hundred dollars, definitely pricey, but all of them together weren't enough to qualify as a legacy. As she closed the lid to her laptop, she heard Jaycie at the kitchen door. "Livia! You're not supposed to be outside. Come here right now!"

Annie sighed. "I'll get her."

Jaycie hobbled out into the hallway. "I'm going to have to start punishing her."

Jaycie was too softhearted. Besides, they both recognized that it wasn't right to keep an active child inside all day. As Annie put on her coat and gathered up Scamp, she decided that being a decent person was a pain in the ass.

She found Livia crouched on her heels by the tree stump. The little girl had added something new to the double row of sticks stuck in the ground in front of the hollow stump. A small pavement of stones now formed a pathway under the stick canopy to the tree hollow entrance.

Annie finally realized what she was looking at. Livia had built a fairy house. They were common in Maine, handmade dwellings for any fanciful creatures who might dwell in the woodlands. Made of sticks, moss, pebbles, pinecones—whatever was available in nature.

Annie sat cross-legged on the cold ledge stone and propped Scamp on her knee. "It's me," Scamp said, "Genevieve Adelaide Josephine Brown, otherwise known as Scamp. Whatcha doing?"

Livia touched her new stone pavement, almost as if she wanted to say something. When she didn't, Scamp said, "It looks like you built a fairy house. I like to build things. I made alphabet letters out of Popsicle sticks once, and I made tissue paper flowers, and I made a Thanksgiving turkey from a cutout of my hand. I'm quite artistic. But I never built a fairy house."

Livia kept her attention firmly fixed on Scamp, as if Annie didn't exist.

"Have the fairies visited?" Scamp asked.

Livia's lips began to part, as if she wanted to say something. Annie held her breath. The child's brow furrowed. Her mouth closed, opened again, and then everything about her seemed to wilt. Her shoulders sagged, her head dropped. She looked so miserable that Annie regretted trying to push her.

"Free secret!" Scamp shouted.

Livia looked up, her gray eyes coming alive again.

Scamp pressed one of her small cloth hands to her mouth. "This is a bad one. Remember you're not allowed to get mad."

Livia nodded solemnly.

"My free secret is . . ." Scamp lowered her voice to a near whisper. "One time I was supposed to pick up my toys, but I didn't want to, so I decided to go exploring instead, even though Annie told me not to go outside. But I did anyway, and she didn't know where I was, and it made her really scared." Scamp paused for breath. "I told you it was bad. Do you still like me?"

Livia's head bobbed in an emphatic nod.

Scamp leaned back against Annie's chest. "It's not fair. I told two free secrets, but you haven't told me even one."

Annie could feel Livia's longing to communicate—the tension gathering in her small body, the misery etched into her delicate features.

"Never mind!" Scamp exclaimed. "I have a new song. Did I mention that I'm an amazing singer? I will now perform for you. Do not sing along—I'm a solo artist—but feel free to dance."

Scamp launched into an enthusiastic version of "Girls Just Want to Have Fun." During the first chorus, Annie came to her feet and danced along, Scamp bobbing above her crossed arm.

Livia soon joined in. By the time Scamp delivered the final chorus, Livia and Annie were dancing together, and Annie hadn't coughed once.

ANNIE DIDN'T SEE THEO THAT day, but the next afternoon, as she and Jaycie continued attacking the sunroom, he made his presence known. "It's a text from Theo." Jaycie looked down at her phone. "He wants all the fireplaces cleaned. He's forgotten I can't do this."

"He hasn't forgotten anything," Annie retorted. Trust Theo to find a new way to torture her.

Jaycie gazed at Annie over the purple hippopotamus tied to the top of her crutch. "It's my job. You shouldn't have to do this kind of thing."

"If I don't, I'll deprive Theo of his entertainment."

Jaycie collapsed against the bookcases, sending a leather-bound volume tumbling to its side. "I don't understand why the two of you don't get along. I mean . . . I remember what happened, but that was a long time ago. He was just a kid. And I never heard about him getting into trouble again."

Because Elliott would have hushed it up, Annie thought. "Time doesn't change a person's basic character."

Jaycie regarded her earnestly, the most naive woman on earth. "There's nothing wrong with his character. If there was, he'd have fired me."

Annie bit back a pointed retort. She wouldn't inflict her own cynicism on the only real friend she had here. And maybe she was the one with the character flaw. After everything Jaycie had been through in her marriage, it was admirable that she could still maintain her optimism about men.

WHEN ANNIE ENTERED THE COTTAGE that night covered with soot, she was greeted with the sight of Leo straddling the back of her couch like a cowboy riding a horse. Dilly sat in a chair, the empty wine bottle from two nights ago in her lap. Crumpet was sprawled on the floor in front of an open copy of the pornographic art photo book, while Peter had crept up behind her to look under her skirt.

Theo came out of the kitchen, a dish towel in his hands. She looked from the puppets to him. He shrugged. "They were bored."

"*You* were bored. You didn't want to write, and this was your way of procrastinating. Didn't I tell you to leave my puppets alone?"

"Did you? I don't remember."

"I could argue with you about that, but I have to take a bath. For some reason, I seem to be covered in fireplace ash."

He smiled. An honest-to-God smile that didn't quite fit on his brooding face. She stalked toward the bedroom. "You'd better be gone when I come out."

"Are you sure you want me to leave?" she heard him say. "I picked up a couple of lobsters in town today."

Damn it! She was ravenous, but that didn't mean she was going to sell herself out for food. Not for ordinary food, anyway. But lobster . . . ? She slammed her bedroom door, which made her feel like a twit.

I don't see why you'd feel that way, Crumpet said petulantly. *I slam doors all the time.*

Annie stripped off her dirty jeans. *Exactly my point.*

She took a bath, washed the soot out of her hair, and dressed in a clean pair of jeans and one of Mariah's black turtleneck sweaters. She tried to tame her wet hair by putting it up in a ponytail, knowing as she did that her curls would soon pop out like demented mattress springs. She eyed her meager supply of makeup but refused to apply even lip gloss.

The kitchen smelled like a four-star restaurant, and Theo was peering into the cabinet over the sink. "What happened to the wine that was here?"

She pushed up the sleeves of her sweater. "It's boxed up and waiting for my next trip to the post office." The value of the whole batch was around four hundred dollars, not a legacy, but still welcome. "I'm selling it. Turns out, I'm too poor to drink hundreds of dollars' worth of wine myself. Or offer it to an unwanted houseguest."

"I'll buy a bottle from you. Better yet, I'll trade it for the food you stole from me."

"I didn't steal anything. I told you. I'll replace it all when the supply boat comes in next week." She made a hasty amendment. "Except for what you ate."

"I don't want it replaced. I want your wine."

Scamp butted in. *Give him your body instead.*

Damn it, Scamp. Shut up. Annie gazed toward the pots on the stove. "Even the least expensive bottle is worth more than the food I borrowed."

"You're forgetting tonight's lobster."

"On Peregrine, hamburger is more expensive than lobster. But nice try."

"Fine. I'll buy a bottle from you."

"Great. Let me get my price list."

He muttered something under his breath as she made her way to the bedroom.

"How much do you want to pay?" she called out.

"Surprise me," he said from the kitchen. "And you can't have any. I'm drinking the whole thing myself."

She pulled the box from the rear of the closet. "Then I'll have to add a corking fee. It'll be cheaper to share."

She heard something that was either a cough or a rough laugh.

Theo had made mashed potatoes to go with the lobster—creamy, garlicky mashed potatoes—indisputable evidence that his offer to fix dinner was premeditated, since there hadn't been any potatoes in the cottage that morning. What was his motivation for hanging around here? It definitely wasn't altruistic.

She set the table, grabbed a sweatshirt against the draft coming in through the bay window, and helped carry the dishes in from the kitchen. "Did you really sweep out all those fireplaces?" he asked as they started to eat.

"I did."

Something happened at the corner of his mouth as he filled her wineglass and lifted his own in a toast. "To good women everywhere."

She wasn't getting into an argument with him—not while she had a rosy red lobster and ramekin of warm butter in front of her, so she pretended she was alone.

They ate in silence. Only after she'd finished her last bite—a particularly sweet morsel from the tail—and dabbed at the smear of butter on her chin did she break it. "You made a deal with the devil, didn't you? You traded your soul for the ability to cook."

He dropped an empty claw into the shell bowl. "Plus being able to see through women's clothes."

Those imperial blue eyes had been designed for cynicism, and the sparks in the irises took her aback. She wadded up her napkin. "Too bad about that. There isn't much around here that's worth seeing."

He ran his thumb across the edge of his wineglass, his eyes on her. "I wouldn't say that."

A jolt of sexual electricity zipped through her body. Her skin burned, and for a moment, it was as if she was fifteen all over again. It was the wine. She pushed her plate back from the edge of the table. "That's right. The prettiest woman on the island is right under your roof. I forgot about Jaycie."

He looked momentarily confused—a monumental fake-out on his part. She tightened her ponytail. "Don't practice your sexual mojo on her, Theo. She's lost her husband, she has a mute child, and—thanks to you—she has no job security."

"I was never going to fire her. You knew that."

She hadn't known it at all, and she didn't trust him. But then something occurred to her. "You won't fire her as long as you can make me jump through hoops. Is that it?"

"I can't believe you really swept out those fireplaces." The slight lift of one indolent eyebrow said she'd been played for a sucker. "If she stayed in town instead of living at the house, she could come out a couple of times a week," he said. "I can still do that, you know."

"Where in town? A room in somebody's house? That's worse than what she has now."

"It shouldn't be a problem as long as I can work here." He drained his wineglass. "And Jaycie's kid will talk when she's ready."

"The great child psychologist has spoken."

"Who better to recognize a troubled kid than me?"

She played at wide-eyed innocence. "But Livia isn't a psychopath."

You think just because I'm a bad guy, I don't have feelings?

She'd definitely had too much wine because the voice belonged to Leo.

"I had some problems that summer. I acted out."

His lack of emotion infuriated her, and she jumped up from the table. "You tried to *kill* me. If Jaycie hadn't been walking on the beach that night, I would have drowned."

"Do you think I don't know that?" he said with an unsettling intensity.

She hated her own uncertainty about him. She should feel more threatened when they were together, but the only threat she felt came from confusion. Still, was that so different from being fifteen? She hadn't wanted to believe she was in danger then, either. Not until she'd almost drowned.

"Tell me about Regan," she said.

He balled his napkin and stood. "There's no point."

If he had been anybody else, compassion would have made her stop. But she needed to understand. "Regan was a good sailor," she said. "Why would she take the boat out when she knew it was getting ready to storm? Why would she do that?"

He strode across the room and grabbed his jacket. "I don't talk about Regan. *Ever.*"

Seconds later, he was out the door.

SHE FINISHED OFF THE LAST of the wine before she went to bed and awoke with a giant thirst and an even bigger headache. She didn't want to go to Harp House today. Hadn't Theo said he wouldn't fire Jaycie? But she didn't trust him. And even if he had meant it, Jaycie still needed help. Annie couldn't abandon her.

As she left the cottage, she vowed not to let Theo make her jump through hoops with any more jobs like cleaning fireplaces. There was only room for one puppet master on Peregrine Island, and that was herself.

Something whizzed by her head. With a gasp, she fell to the ground.

She lay there breathing hard, the dirt cold and rough beneath her cheek, the world spinning around her. She squeezed her eyes shut. Felt her heart pounding.

Someone had just tried to shoot her. Someone who might, even now, be coming after her with a gun.

Chapter Ten

Annie tested her arms and legs, only moving them enough to make sure she hadn't been hit. She listened hard but heard nothing except the ragged sound of her breath and the pound of surf. A seabird called out. Slowly, carefully, she lifted her head.

The bullet had come from the west. She saw nothing unusual in the thicket of red spruce and stunted hardwoods that lay between where she was lying and the road. She pushed herself higher, the weight of her backpack shifting, and gazed back toward the cottage, then the ocean, then up at Harp House looming at the top of the cliff. Everything looked as cold and isolated as always.

She came to her knees slowly. With only a backpack for protection, she was too exposed. She had no experience with firearms. How did she know that had really been a bullet?

Because she knew.

Was it a hunter's errant shot? Peregrine Island had no game animals, but every home had guns. According to Barbara, more than a few islanders had shot either themselves or each other. Generally, they'd been accidents, she'd said, but not always.

Annie heard something behind her—a noise that didn't belong—the sound of a horse's hooves. A fresh rush of adrenaline sent her to the ground again.

Theo was coming after her to finish the job.

As soon as the thought took shape, she struggled to her feet. She'd be damned if she'd let him shoot her while she was cowering in the dirt. If he was going to kill her, he'd have to look her in the eye when he pulled the trigger. As she spun around and saw the powerful animal galloping toward her from the beach, a terrible sense of betrayal ripped through her, along with a desperate need to believe this wasn't happening.

Theo pulled up and threw himself off Dancer. There was no gun in his hand. No weapon of any kind. Maybe he'd dropped it. Or . . .

His cheeks were ruddy from the cold, but his jacket was unzipped, and it opened as he dashed toward her. "What happened? I saw you fall. Are you all right?"

Her teeth were chattering, and she was shaking all over. "Did you just try to *shoot me*?"

"*No!* What the hell? Are you saying somebody tried to shoot you?"

"Yes, somebody tried to shoot me!" she cried.

"Are you sure?"

She gritted her teeth. "I've never been shot at, but yes, I'm sure. How could you not have heard?"

"I was too close to the water to hear anything. Tell me exactly what happened."

The heels of her hands stung through her gloves. She clenched her fingers. "I was on my way to the house, and a bullet flew past my head."

"Where did it come from?"

She tried to remember. "I think it was over there." She pointed a shaking hand toward the road, the opposite direction from the way he had just come.

He studied her, as if he was trying to see how badly she'd been hurt, then took a quick survey of the landscape. "Stay where I can see you. We'll go up to the house together." Moments later, he was riding toward the trees.

She felt too vulnerable to stay where she was, but she'd be even more exposed if she walked back across the open expanse of the marsh to the cottage. She waited for her legs to steady, then ran toward the trees at the base of the drive leading to Harp House.

It didn't take Theo long to pull up next to her. She expected him to chew her out for not staying put, but he didn't. Instead he dismounted and, taking Dancer by the lead, walked with her.

"Did you see anything?" she asked.

"Nothing. Whoever did this was long gone by the time I got there."

When they got to the top of the drive he told her he had to cool Dancer down. "I'll meet you in the house," he said. "And then we're going to have a conversation."

She wasn't ready to go inside, where she'd have to talk to Jaycie. Instead she slipped into the stable while Theo walked Dancer around the yard. The stable still smelled of animals and dust, although with only one horse housed here now, the smells were fainter than they'd once been. Spidery light seeped through the window above the rickety wooden bench where she and Theo had talked that afternoon, not long before she'd gone down to the cave to meet him.

She slipped off her backpack and called the mainland police number she'd stored in her phone after the break-in. The officer she reached dutifully listened to the information she gave him, but didn't seem interested. "It was kids. It's the Wild West out there on Peregrine, but I guess you already know that."

"The kids are in school," she replied, trying not to sound as impatient as she felt.

"Not today. The teachers from all the islands are on Monhegan for their winter conference. The kids have the day off."

It was mildly comforting to think the shot might have come from a kid messing around with guns instead of an adult with a more sinister purpose. The officer promised he'd make inquiries the next time he came to the island. "If anything else happens," he said, "you be sure to notify us."

"Like if a bullet actually hits me?"

He chuckled. "I don't think you need to worry about that, ma'am. The islanders are a rough bunch, but they don't generally kill each other."

"Dumbass," she murmured, disconnecting as Theo led Dancer into the stable.

"What did I do this time?" Theo said.

"Not you. I called the mainland police."

"I can imagine how well that conversation went." He took Dancer into the only stall with bedding. Even though the stables weren't heated, he tossed his jacket on a hook and began to unsaddle his horse. "You're positive someone tried to shoot you?"

She rose from the bench. "You don't believe me?"

"Why wouldn't I?"

Because I never believe what you tell me. She moved closer to Dancer's stall. "I don't suppose you found footprints? Or a bullet casing?"

He removed the saddle blanket. "Oh, yeah. With all the muck lying on the ground, that was the first thing I saw. A bullet casing."

"You don't have to be so sarcastic." Since she was almost always sarcastic with him, she expected him to turn on her, but he only growled that she watched too many cop shows.

As he finished taking off Dancer's tack, she gazed into the next stall, the one where she and Regan had found the pups. Now it held only a push broom, a stack of buckets, and bad memories. She looked away.

Eventually she stopped fidgeting and simply watched Theo work—those long even brushstrokes, the gentle touch of his fingers as he made sure he didn't miss any burrs or mud clots, the way he'd stop what he was doing to scratch Dancer behind his ears and talk softly to him. His obvious care made her say something she instantly regretted. "I didn't really think it was you."

"Yeah, you probably did." He set aside the brush and knelt down to check Dancer's hooves. After he was assured that the horse hadn't picked up any stones, he came out of the stall and turned those laser-focused eyes on her. "No more bullshit," he said. "You need to tell me right now what's going on."

She pulled off her cap and ran it through her hands. "How am I supposed to know?"

"You know more than you're letting on. You don't trust me? Fine. But you're going to have to get over that because right now I'm the only person you *can* trust."

"That doesn't exactly make sense."

"Deal with it."

It was time for a quick reminder. "When I came back to the island . . . The first time I saw you, you were carrying a gun."

"An antique dueling pistol."

"From your father's gun collection."

"That's right. There's a whole cabinet full of guns in the house. Shotguns, rifles, handguns." He paused, his eyes narrowing. "And I know how to fire every one of them."

She shoved her hat in her pocket. "That makes me feel ever so much better."

But, ironically, it did. If he truly wanted to kill her for some twisted reason only he knew, he would have done it by now. As for her legacy . . . He was a Harp, and she hadn't seen any signs that he needed money.

Then why is he living on the island? Dilly asked. *Unless he has no place else to go.*

Just like you, Crumpet pointed out.

Annie suppressed the puppets' voices. She might not like it—she didn't like it—but right now Theo was the only one she could talk to.

Just the way it was when you were fifteen, Dilly said.

He curled his fingers over the stall door. "This has gotten out of hand. Tell me whatever it is you're hiding."

"It could have been a kid. The island teacher is at a conference, so there was no school today."

"A kid? You think a kid tossed the cottage, too?"

"Maybe." No, she didn't think that at all.

"If a kid had done it, there would have been a lot more destruction."

"We don't know that." She slipped past him. "I've got to go. Jaycie was expecting me an hour ago."

She'd barely managed a step before he'd planted himself in front of her, his body an immovable wall of hard tendon and solid muscle. "You have two options," he said. "You either need to get off the island . . ."

Leaving him the cottage? No way was she doing that.

". . . or," he said, "you can level with me and let me try to help."

The offer seemed so genuine, so seductive. But instead of burying her face in his sweater as she wanted to, she channeled Crumpet at her most peevish. "What do you care? You don't even like me."

"I like you very much."

He said it with a straight face, but she wasn't buying. "Bull."

One of those dark arched eyebrows inched upward. "You don't believe me?"

"I do not."

"Okay, then." He stuffed his hands into the pockets of his jeans. "You're kind of a mess. But . . ." His voice turned soft and husky. "You're a woman, and that's what I need. It's been a long time."

He was playing games. She could see it in his eyes, but that didn't prevent the hot kick of her senses. The sensation was unwelcome and unsettling, but understandable. He was a dark-haired, blue-eyed sexual fantasy come to life right from her books, and she was a tall, thin, thirty-three-year-old woman with a peculiar face, berserker hair, and a fatal attraction to men who weren't as noble as they seemed. She fought his black magic with a crucifix of sarcasm. "Why didn't you say so earlier? I'll take my clothes off right now."

He was all inky silk and plush black velvet. "Too cold out here. We need a warm bed."

"Not really." *Shut up! Just shut the hell up!* "I'm plenty hot enough. At least that's what I've been told." She tossed her hair, grabbed her backpack, and swept past him.

This time he let her go.

WITH SOMETHING HALFWAY BETWEEN A grin and a grimace, Theo watched the stable door slam shut. He shouldn't have baited her, even if she was in on the game. But those big eyes kept sucking him in, making him want to play games. Have a little dirty fun. There was also something about the way she smelled, not of the ruthlessly expensive perfumes he'd grown so used to, but basic bar soap and fruity drugstore shampoo.

Dancer nudged him in the shoulder. "I know, fella. She got me good. And it's my own fault." His horse poked him in the jaw in agreement.

Theo put away the tack and filled Dancer's bucket with fresh water. Last night, when he'd tried to get into the laptop Annie had left at the house, he couldn't break her password. For now, her secrets were her own, but he couldn't let that go on much longer.

He needed to stop messing with her. Besides, baiting her the way he'd just done seemed to throw him off balance more than it bothered her. The last thing he wanted on his mind right now was a naked woman, let alone a naked Annie Hewitt.

Having her on Peregrine again was like being shoved back into a nightmare, so why did he look forward to being with her? Maybe because he found a certain bizarre safety in her company. She didn't possess any of the polished beauty he was always drawn to. Unlike Kenley, Annie had a quirky amusement park of a face. Annie was also smart as a whip, and although she wasn't needy, she didn't present herself as being indomitable, either.

Those were her good points. As for the bad . . .

Annie regarded life as a puppet show. She had no experience with soul-crushing nights or despair so thick it clung to everything you touched. Annie might deny it, but she still believed in happy endings. That was the illusion trapping him into wanting to be with her.

He grabbed his jacket. He needed to start thinking about

the next scene he couldn't seem to write instead of the naked
body lurking underneath Annie's heavy sweaters and bulky
coat. She wore too damned many clothes. If it were summer,
he'd see her in a bathing suit, and his writer's imagination
would be satisfied enough so that he could move on to more
productive thoughts. Instead he kept conjuring up images of
the skinny teenage body he barely remembered and curiosity
about what it looked like now.

Horny bastard.

He gave Dancer one last pat. "You're luckier than you
know, pal. Living without a set of balls makes life a lot less
complicated."

ANNIE SPENT A FEW HOURS researching the oldest of the art
books she'd found in the bookcase, but none of them turned out
to be rare, not the David Hockney volume, or the Niven Garr
collection, or Julian Schnabel's book. When she'd had enough
frustration, she helped Jaycie clean.

Jaycie had been quieter than usual all day. She looked tired,
and as they moved into Elliott's office, Annie ordered her to sit
down. Jaycie propped her crutches against the arm of the leather
couch and sagged into the sofa. "Theo sent a text telling me to
make sure you take the Range Rover back to the cottage tonight."

Annie hadn't told Jaycie about getting shot at, and she
didn't intend to. Her purpose was to make Jaycie's life easier,
not add to her worries.

Jaycie tucked a lock of blond hair behind her ear. "He also
told me not to send up dinner tonight. That's the third time
this week."

Annie moved the vacuum to the front windows and said
carefully, "I haven't invited him, Jaycie. But Theo does what he
wants."

"He likes you. I don't understand it. You say terrible things
about him."

Annie tried to explain. "He doesn't like me. What he likes
is giving me a hard time. There's a big difference."

"I don't think so." Jaycie pulled herself back up and fumbled with her crutches. "I'd better go see what Livia is up to."

Annie gazed after her in dismay. She was hurting the last person in the world she wanted to upset. Life on an almost deserted island was getting more complicated by the day.

That evening, just before she went to get her coat, Annie saw Livia pull a footstool across the kitchen floor, climb up on it, and push a rolled tube of drawing paper into Annie's backpack. She intended to investigate as soon as she got to the cottage, but the first thing she saw when she opened the door was Leo sprawled on the couch with a drinking straw tied around his arm like a drug user's tourniquet. Dilly lounged at the other end, a tiny paper cylinder rolled like a cigarette dangling from her hand, her legs crossed like a man's, ankle over knee.

Annie yanked off her hat. "Will you leave my puppets *alone*?!"

Theo wandered out from the kitchen, a lavender dish towel tucked in the waistband of his jeans. "Until now, I didn't know I had such bad impulse control."

Annie hated the thrum of pleasure she felt at the sight of him. Still, what woman with a heartbeat wouldn't enjoy feasting her eyes on a man like him, lavender tea towel and all? She punished him for his ridiculous good looks by getting snooty. "Dilly would never smoke. She specializes in preventing substance abuse."

"Admirable."

"And you're supposed to be out of here by the time I get home."

"Am I?" He looked vague, a matinee idol prone to memory lapses. Hannibal wandered out from the kitchen and draped himself over Theo's shoe.

She gazed at the cat. "What's your familiar doing here?"

"I need him while I work."

"To help cast spells?"

"Writers have this thing for cats. You couldn't possibly understand." He stared down his perfectly sculpted nose at her, his expression so deliberately condescending that she knew he was trying to rile her. Instead she rescued her puppets from their newfound vices and took them back to the studio.

The boxes were no longer on the bed but set along the wall underneath the taxi mural, which her research had proven to be worthless, like so much else. She'd begun going through the boxes' contents, inventorying everything inside, but the only interesting items she'd found so far were the cottage guest book and her Dreambook, the name she'd given the scrapbook she'd kept when she was a young teen. She'd filled its pages with her drawings, *Playbill*s from shows she'd seen, photos of her favorite actresses, and reviews she'd written herself of her own imaginary Broadway triumphs. It was depressing to see how far short her adult life had fallen from the fantasies of that young girl, and she put it away.

The smell of something delicious wafted in from the kitchen. After dragging a comb through her hair and dabbing on a little lip gloss because she was pathetic, she returned to the living room, where she found Theo lounging on the couch in the same place he'd positioned Leo earlier. Even from across the room, she could see he was holding one of her drawings. "I'd forgotten you were such a good artist," he said.

Seeing him examining something she'd done to entertain herself made her uncomfortable. "I'm not any good. I do it for fun."

"You're selling yourself way short." He looked at the drawing again. "I like this kid. He's got character."

It was a sketch she'd done of a studious young boy with straight, dark hair and a cowlick sprouting like a fountain from the crown of his head. Bony ankles showed beneath the cuffs of his jeans, as if he might be going through one of those preteen growth spurts. Square-rimmed glasses sat on a lightly freckled nose. His shirt was buttoned wrong, and he wore an adult watch that was too big for his wrist. Definitely not great art, but he had potential as a future puppet.

Theo tilted the paper, looking at it from another angle. "How old do you think he is?"

"No idea."

"Twelve, maybe. Struggling with puberty."

"If you say so."

As he set the drawing down, she realized he'd poured himself a glass of wine. She began to protest, but he gestured toward the open bottle on the Louis XIV chest. "I brought it down from the house. And you can't have any until you answer a few questions."

Something she really didn't want to do. "What are we having for dinner?"

"*I'm* having meat loaf. And not just any meat loaf. One with a little pancetta tucked inside, two special cheeses, and a glaze with a mystery ingredient that might be Guinness. Interested?"

Even thinking about it made her mouth water. "I might be."

"Good. But you're going to have to talk first. That means time's run out, and you're up against the wall. Decide right now whether or not you're going to trust me."

How was she supposed to do that? He couldn't have shot at her, not from where he'd been. But that didn't mean he was trustworthy, not with his history. She took her time settling in the airplane seat armchair and tucked her legs under her. "Too bad the critics hated your book. I can only imagine what those brutal reviews did to your self-confidence."

He took a sip of wine, as indolent as a playboy relaxing on the Costa del Sol. "Shattered it. Are you sure you didn't read the book?"

Time to pay him back for his earlier condescension. "I prefer loftier literature."

"Yes, I saw some of that loftier literature in your bedroom. Definitely intimidating to a hack like me."

She frowned. "What were you doing in my bedroom?"

"Searching it. More successfully than when I tried to get into your computer. One of these days you're going to have to give me your password. It's only fair."

"Not going to happen."

"Then I'll have to keep prying until you level with me." He pointed toward her with his wine goblet. "By the way, you need some new panties."

Considering the snooping she'd done in the turret, she had a hard time summoning up as much righteous indignation as she should. "There is nothing wrong with my underpants."

"Said by a woman who hasn't gotten laid in a very long time."

"I have so!"

"I don't believe you."

She experienced a contradictory desire to play games and be honest. "For your information, I've gotten down and dirty with a long line of loser boyfriends." Not that long a line, but since he'd burst out laughing, she wasn't going to clarify.

When he finally sobered, he gave his head a rueful shake. "I see you're still selling yourself short. Why is that, by the way, and when are you going to grow out of it?"

The idea that he thought more of her than she sometimes thought of herself took her aback.

Trust him, Scamp urged.

Don't be a fool, Dilly said.

Forget about him! Peter exclaimed. *I shall save you!*

Dude, Leo sneered. *Stop being such a tool. She can save herself.*

The reminder of the men who hadn't stood by her might have been what tipped the scale in Theo's direction. Even as she told herself that psychopaths had a special talent for earning the trust of their victims, she untucked her legs and told him the truth. "Right before Mariah died, she said she'd left something valuable for me at the cottage. A legacy. And once I found it, I'd have money."

She had his full attention. He dropped his legs to the floor and sat up straight. "What kind of legacy?"

"I don't know. She could barely breathe. She slipped into a coma right after and died before morning."

"And you haven't found what it is?"

"I've researched all the major art pieces, but she'd been selling off her collection for years, and nothing that's left seems to be worth much. For a few glorious hours, I thought it might be the wine."

"Writers stayed here. Musicians."

Annie nodded. "If only she'd been more specific."

"Mariah had a habit of making things hard for you. I never understood it."

"Her way of expressing love," she said without any bitterness. "I was too ordinary for her, too quiet."

"The good old days," he said drily.

"I think she was afraid for me because I was so different from her. Beige to her crimson." Hannibal jumped into her lap, and she rubbed his head. "Mariah was worried I wouldn't be able to cope with life. She thought criticism was the best way to toughen me up."

"Twisted," he said, "but it seems to have worked."

Before she could ask him what he meant by that, he went on. "Did you look in the attic?"

"What attic?"

"That space above the ceiling?"

"That's not an attic. It's a——" But of course it was an attic. "There's no way to get to it."

"Sure there is. There's an access trap in the studio closet."

She'd seen that trap dozens of times. She'd just never thought about what it led to. She sprang out of the chair, displacing Hannibal. "I'm going to look right now."

"Hold up. One wrong step, and you'll fall through the ceiling. I'll check it tomorrow."

Not before she looked herself. She dropped back into the chair. "Can I have my wine now? And my meat loaf."

He made his way toward the wine bottle. "Who else knows about this?"

"I haven't told anyone. Until now. And I hope I don't regret it."

He ignored that. "Somebody broke into the cottage, and you've been shot at. Let's assume the person who's done these things is after whatever Mariah left here."

"Nobody puts anything over on you."

"Are you going to keep taking potshots or do you want to figure this out?"

She thought about it. "Take potshots."

He stood there. Waiting patiently. She threw up her hands. "All right! I'm listening."

"That's a first." He brought the wine to her and handed it over. "Assuming you haven't told anyone else about this . . ."

"I haven't."

"Not Jaycie? Or one of your girlfriends?"

"Or a loser boyfriend? No one." She sipped her wine. "Mariah must have told someone. Or . . . And I like this idea best . . . A random derelict broke into the cottage because he was looking for money, and, in a totally unrelated event, a kid messing with a gun accidentally shot at me."

"Still looking for the happy ending."

"Better than going around looking like the Lord of Gloom all the time."

"You mean being a realist?"

"A realist or a cynic?" She frowned. "Here's what I don't like about cynics . . ."

Obviously he didn't care about what she didn't like because he was on his way to the kitchen. But cynicism was one of her hot buttons, and she followed him. "Cynics are cop-outs," she said, thinking of her most recent ex, who'd hidden his actor's insecurity behind condescension. "Being a cynic gives a person an excuse to stay above the fray. You don't have to get your hands dirty working to solve a problem because, what's the point? Instead, you can stay in bed all day and put down all the naive fools who are trying to make a difference. It's so manipulative. Cynics are the laziest people I know."

"Hey, don't look at me. I'm the guy who made you a great meat loaf." The sight of him leaning over to open the oven door derailed her tirade. He was lean, but not skinny. Muscular, but not pumped up. Suddenly the cottage seemed too small, too secluded.

She grabbed the silverware and carried it out to the table. All the while, sensible Dilly cried out in her head, *Danger! Danger!*

Chapter Eleven

THE MEAT LOAF WAS EVEN better than advertised, the accompanying roasted potatoes perfectly seasoned. By her third glass of wine, the cottage had become a place out of time where proper codes of behavior were suspended and secrets could stay secret. A place where a woman could let go of doubts and indulge every sensual whim with no one being the wiser. She tried to shake herself out of her reverie, but the wine made it too much trouble.

Theo twisted the stem of his glass between his thumb and index finger. His voice was low, as quiet as the night. "Do you remember what we used to do in the cave?"

She made a play of cutting a piece of potato in half. "Hardly anything. It was so long ago."

"I remember."

She cut the potato wedge smaller. "I can't imagine why."

He gazed at her, long and steadily, as if he knew she'd been thinking about erotic hideaways. "Everybody remembers their first time."

"There wasn't any first time," she said. "We didn't make it that far."

"Near enough. And I thought you didn't remember."

"I remember that much."

He kicked back in his chair. "We used to make out for hours. Do you remember that?"

How could she forget? Their kisses had gone on and on—cheeks, neck, mouth, and tongue. Seconds . . . minutes . . . hours. Then they'd start all over again. Adults were too fixed on the final goal to take that kind of time. Only teenagers afraid of the next step exchanged kisses that lasted forever.

She wasn't drunk, but she was buzzed, and she didn't want to linger in that bewildering cave of memory. "Kissing has turned into a lost art."

"Do you think?"

"Um." She took another sip of the rich, heady wine.

"You're probably right," he said. "I know I'm lousy at it."

She barely suppressed the urge to correct him. "Most men wouldn't admit it."

"I'm too anxious to get to the next step."

"You and every other guy."

A black tail poked up over the edge of the table. Hannibal had jumped in his lap. He stroked the cat, then set him back down.

She pushed a piece of meat loaf around on her plate, no longer hungry, no longer wary. "I don't understand. You love animals."

He didn't ask what she meant. He knew they were still back in the cave, but now the tide had turned and the weather had grown treacherous. He rose from the table and wandered toward the bookshelves. "How do you explain something you don't understand yourself?"

She rested her elbow on the table. "Was it the pups? Was it me? Who were you trying to hurt?"

He took his time answering. "Ultimately, I guess it was myself."

Which revealed nothing at all.

He said, "You should have let me know about Mariah's legacy the night of the break-in."

She rose and picked up her wineglass. "Like you tell me everything. Or anything, for that matter."

"Nobody's going around firing a gun at me."

"I don't— I didn't trust you."

He turned toward her, his gaze seductive without being lecherous. "If you knew what I was thinking right now, you'd have good reason not to trust me, because some of my happiest memories happened in that cave. I know you don't feel that way."

If it hadn't been for what had happened that last night, she might almost have agreed. The wine hummed through her veins. "It's hard to feel nostalgic about the place where you almost died."

"Understandable."

She was tired of being on edge, and she loved the way the wine had made her relax. She wanted to seal away the past, undo it so it never happened. Pretend they'd just met. She wanted to be like the women she knew who could see an attractive guy in a bar, tumble into bed with him, and walk out a few hours later with no regrets and no self-flagellation. *"I'm basically a guy,"* her friend Rachel had once said. *"I don't need emotional attachment. I just want to get off."*

Annie wanted to be a guy, too.

"I've got an idea." Theo leaned against the bookcase, and the corner of his mouth kicked up. "Let's make out. For old times' sake."

Because she'd had three glasses of wine, she didn't answer him with nearly enough conviction. "I don't think so."

"Are you sure?" He moved away from the bookcase. "We won't be breaking any new ground, the two of us. And since you can't completely shake the feeling that I'm out to kill you, you won't need to pretend you have any deep fondness for me. And frankly . . . I could use the practice."

The wine in her bloodstream couldn't resist the mischief beneath all that smoky velvet seductiveness. But even though she was drunk enough to do this, she wasn't so drunk that she didn't have a few conditions. "No hands."

He came toward her slowly. "I don't know about that."

"No hands," she said more firmly.

"All right. No hands. Below the waist."

She cocked her head. "No hands below the neck."

"I'm fairly sure that's not realistic." He stopped in front of her and removed the wineglass from her hand as intimately as unfastening a bra clasp.

She liked almost-drunk Annie. "Take it or leave it."

"You're making me a little nervous," he said. "I told you I'm not confident about my kissing. Other things, yes. But just kissing? No confidence at all."

His eyes were laughing at her. Brooding, wicked Theo Harp was snaring her in a net of erotic whimsy. Her hand moved to her hair. She pulled off her ponytail holder. "Call on your inner sixteen-year-old for help. He was very good at kissing."

He gazed at her hair, drained the last drops from her glass, and closed the final few inches between them. "I'll try."

Theo had never been a jerk about it, but when he'd wanted a woman, he'd always been able to get her. That kind of sexual arrogance, however, was dangerous with someone like Annie. Why hadn't she called him on his game? She knew better.

He didn't remember the last time he and Kenley had kissed, but he did remember the last time they'd fucked. A middle-of-the-night fuck—she hating him and making sure he knew it. He hating her and trying not to show it.

He gazed down at Annie's closed eyelids. They reminded him of pale seashells washed up on the beach. She'd grown some sharp edges over the years, but she still wouldn't know how to be a ballbuster, not even if she read the manual. She clung to her puppets and her fairyland of good intentions and happy endings. Now here she was, ripe for kissing. And here he was. About to take advantage when he should walk away.

He ran his thumbs across her cheekbones. Her lips parted ever so slightly. Annie didn't expect good behavior from him.

She'd seen his worst, and she didn't expect him to save her, to shield her, to do the right thing. Most important, she wasn't expecting him to love her. That was what he liked most. That and her total lack of faith in his decency. It had been so long since he'd had the freedom to let down his guard and be who he wanted to be.

A man with no decency at all.

He lowered his mouth over hers. Lips barely touching. Wine-scented breath mingling. She arched her neck, looking for firmer contact. He forced himself to draw back, a bare millimeter. Their lips brushed, but that was all.

She saw his game and pulled back ever so slightly, creating a space he quickly filled, but only with the lightest touch. She had every reason to fear him, and letting him get so close was ludicrous, but she moved her head so her lips skimmed his like floating feathers. Only seconds had passed, but he was already hard. He sealed his mouth against hers, parted his lips, tongue thrusting, going in for the kill.

The heels of her hands slammed into his chest. A pair of outraged hazel eyes seared him. "You're so right. You're a terrible kisser."

Him? A terrible kisser? No way was he letting that pass. He brushed the inside of his arm against her hair as he braced one hand on the wall behind her head. "Sorry. I got a cramp in my leg and lost my balance."

"You lost your chance, that's what."

Big talk from somebody who hadn't moved a step away from him. He'd never admit defeat this early in the game. Not with Annie. Feisty, softhearted Annie Hewitt, who'd never think of demanding a man's last drop of blood. "Deepest apologies." He tilted his head and blew gently on the tender skin behind her ear.

Her hair ruffled. "That's better."

He moved closer, exploring the soft place with his lips. The closeness was agonizing, but he wasn't going to let a hard-on get the best of him.

Her hands slipped around his waist and slid under his sweater, violating her own rule, something he had no intention of pointing out. She turned her head, bringing her mouth closer to his, but he'd always been a competitor, and the game was on, so he moved his kisses to the line of her jaw.

She arched her neck. He accepted the invitation and kissed her there. Her palms slid higher beneath his sweater. The touch of a decent woman felt so good. So unfamiliar. He fought against raising the stakes. Eventually she was the one who pressed her body hard against him, met his mouth with open lips.

He wasn't sure how they ended up on the floor. Had he pulled her there? Had she pulled him? He only knew that she was on her back, and he was on top of her. Just as it had been during those sweet, hot cave days.

He wanted her naked, legs splayed, wet and open. The quickness of her breathing, the way her hands gripped his bare back, told him she wanted it, too. Holding on to the last measure of his self-control, he returned to their kisses. Temples, cheeks, mouth. Deep, soulful penetrations. On and on.

She was moaning now, sounds of entreaty as she wrapped one of her legs around his. His hands tangled in the silky hullabaloo of her hair. He settled deeper into the narrow saddle of her hips. Their jeans abraded, and her moans moved deeper in her throat. He was losing control. He couldn't hold back a moment longer.

He jerked at her zipper, at his. She arched her back. He shoved at her jeans awkwardly, pushing them off one ankle. Her fist clutched a handful of his sweater. He settled between her thighs, freed himself, drove into her.

She cried out and collapsed, her low, guttural moan fierce and defenseless. He went deeper. Pulled back. Deep again. And that was all.

The universe cracked open around him.

The next thing he knew, she was cursing like crazy.

"You bastard! Son of a bitch!" She shoved him off her, yanking up her jeans and coming to her feet at the same time. "Oh, God, I hate myself. I hate you!" She was doing some kind of weird demon dance as she jerked on her zipper. Flapping her elbows. Stomping the floor. He got up, zipped his own jeans as her tirade continued. "I'm an idiot! Somebody should put me down. I swear to God! Just like a dumb, sick animal. The stupidest, dumbest . . ."

He ordered himself not to say a word.

She turned on him—red-faced and furious. "I'm not this easy! I'm not!"

"Kind of easy," he said before he could stop himself.

She grabbed a pillow from the couch and swung it at him. He was used to a woman's rages, and this was so small-time, he didn't bother to duck.

She stomped the floor again. Beyond pissed, her arms waving, curls hopping. "I know exactly what's going to happen next! The second I turn my back, I'll be facedown in the marsh. Or locked inside the dumbwaiter. Or drowning in that cave!" She gasped for air. "I don't trust you! I don't like you. And now you— You—"

"Had the best time I've had in longer than I can remember?" He'd never been a wiseass, but there was something about Annie that drew out his worst. Or maybe it was his best.

She glared at him. "You came inside me!"

His amusement vanished. He'd never been careless, and now he was the one who felt stupid. It put him on the defensive. "I wasn't exactly planning on this happening."

"You should have! Even now, one of your little swimmers could be doing a backstroke right to my—egg!"

The way she said it was funnier than hell, but he had no desire to laugh. He rubbed the back of his fist over his jaw. "You're . . . on the pill, right?"

"It's a little late to ask!" She turned and stomped away. "And, no, I'm not!"

An icy vise clamped around his rib cage. He could barely move. He heard her in the bedroom, and then in the bathroom. He needed to clean up himself, but all he could think about was what he'd done and the terrible price he might pay for what he could only think of as the most unsatisfying sexual encounter of his life.

When she finally emerged, she was wearing her navy robe,

Santa pajamas, and a pair of sweat socks. Her face was scrubbed clean, her hair pulled up with a tie that left damp tendrils corkscrewing here and there. Mercifully, she seemed calmer. "I had pneumonia," she said. "My pill schedule got screwed up."

A cold trickle slid down his spine. "When did you have your last period?"

She sneered at him. "What are you? My gynecologist? Go to hell."

"Annie . . ."

She spun on him. "Look. I know this is as much my fault as yours, but right now I'm too furious to take my share of the responsibility."

"Damn right, it's your fault, too! You and your kissing game."

"Which you *flunked*."

"Of course I flunked it. Do you think I'm made of ice?"

"You! What about me? And since when do you think it's all right to have sex without a condom?"

"I don't, damn it. But I'm not used to carrying them around in my pocket."

"You should! Look at you. You shouldn't go anywhere without a dozen of them!" She shook her head, closed her eyes, and when she opened them again, she was mercifully calmer. "Just go," she said. "I can't stand looking at you a moment longer."

His wife had delivered nearly those exact words a dozen times, but while Kenley had looked feral, Annie merely looked tired.

"I can't go, Annie," he said carefully. "I thought you'd have figured that out by now."

"Of course you can. And that's what you're going to do. Now."

"Do you really think I'll leave you here alone at night after somebody tried to shoot you?"

She stared at him. He waited for her to start the foot stomping again or throw another pillow, but she didn't. "I don't want you here."

"I know."

She crossed her arms and curled her hands around her elbows. "Do what you like. I'm too upset to argue. And sleep in the studio because I'm not sharing. Understand?" A moment later she was gone, her bedroom door shut firmly behind her.

He used the bathroom, and when he came out, faced the dinner mess. Since he'd done the cooking, he shouldn't have to clean up, but he didn't mind. Unlike real life, cleaning a kitchen was a task with a clear beginning, middle, and end. Just like a book.

ANNIE BARELY AVOIDED TRIPPING OVER Hannibal as she got out of bed in the morning. In addition to everything else, it seemed she'd acquired a part-time cat. She'd fallen asleep last night counting and recounting the days since her last period. She should be safe, but "should" was far from a guarantee. For all she knew, she could right now be incubating the devil's spawn. And if that happened . . . She couldn't bear thinking about it.

She'd thought she'd freed herself from the power these handsome, brooding fake heroes had over her. But no. All Theo had to do was show a little interest, and there she was, eyes closed, legs spread, like the dumbest heroine ever written. It was so stupid. However hopeless the quest might be, she wanted a forever love. She wanted children and the conventional family life she'd never known, but she'd never find that with these damaged, aloof men. Yet here she was, slipping right back into her old pattern, except so much worse. She'd been caught in Theo Harp's web—not because he'd diabolically cast it around her, but because she'd run into it with her arms outstretched.

She had to get to the attic before he did, and as soon as she heard him in the bathroom, she pulled the stepladder from the storage closet and carried it into the studio. He'd already made the bed, and her puppets were still arranged on the shelf under the window. Once she had the ladder into position in the closet, she climbed up and pushed open the trap. She gingerly poked her head into the cold attic space, then shone around the flashlight she'd brought with her, but she could see only construction beams and insulation.

One more dead end.

She heard the water stop in the bathroom and headed for the kitchen to make a quick bowl of cereal, then carried it back to her bedroom to eat. She didn't like hiding out in her own home, but she couldn't bear the idea of seeing him right now.

Only after he left the cottage did she remember the paper Livia had put in her backpack. She removed the roll and carried it over to the table, where she smoothed it out. Livia had used her black marker to draw a trio of stick figures, two large and one very small. The smallest figure, drawn off to the side of the page, had ruler-straight hair. Beneath it, Livia had printed her own name in crooked capital letters. The other two figures weren't labeled. One lay prone with a red flower shirt decoration, the other stood with arms outstretched. At the bottom of the paper, Livia had laboriously printed out crooked letters:

FRESEK

Annie studied the drawing more closely. The small figure, she noticed, had no mouth.

FRESEK

Annie finally understood. She didn't know exactly what she was seeing, but she knew why Livia had given this to her. This drawing was Livia's free secret.

Chapter Twelve

ANNIE PARKED THE RANGE ROVER in the garage at Harp House. Thinking about Livia's drawing would have been a welcome distraction from worrying about being pregnant if there weren't something so unsettling about what the little girl had depicted. She wanted to show the drawing to Jaycie to see if she could decipher it, but Annie had made a pact, and even though she'd done it with a four-year-old, she wouldn't break it.

She closed the garage door and wandered toward the edge of the drive. She'd made it to Harp House before Theo, and as she looked down, she saw him on the beach path, a solitary figure silhouetted against the vastness of the sea. His head was bare as usual, with nothing more than his black suede jacket as protection against the wind. He crouched down to examine a tidal pool. Eventually he leaned back on his heels and gazed out at the water. What was he thinking about? Some gruesome plot line? His dead wife? Or maybe he was considering how to get rid of an inconvenient woman he might have accidentally gotten pregnant?

Theo was not going to kill her. She was certain of that. But he could hurt her in a lot of other ways. She understood her tendency to romanticize men like Theo, and she had to be on her guard. She'd had sex with a fantasy last night. A romantic bookworm's fantasy.

ANNIE WASHED JAYCIE'S AND LIVIA'S breakfast dishes and straightened the kitchen. By the time she was done, she still hadn't seen Jaycie, and she went to look for her.

They lived in the old housekeeper's apartment on the opposite side of the house from the turret. Annie wound through the back hallway until she reached the door at the end. It was closed, and she knocked. "Jaycie?"

There was no answer, and she knocked again. Just as she was about to turn the knob, Livia opened the door. She looked adorable with a homemade paper crown pushed so far down on her head that her ears stuck out. "Hey, Liv. I like your crown."

Livia was only interested in seeing if Annie had brought Scamp along, and she was clearly disappointed not to see the puppet on Annie's arm. "Scamp's taking a nap," Annie said. "But I'm sure she'll want to visit you later. Is Mommy here?"

Livia opened the door all the way to let Annie inside.

The housekeeper's apartment had been designed in an L shape to provide both a sitting room and sleeping area. Prior to breaking her foot, Jaycie had converted the sitting room into Livia's bedroom. Her own room was austere—a bed, chair, dresser, and lamp, all castoffs from the house. Livia's space was more cheerful, with a bright pink bookcase, child's table and chairs, a pink and green rug, and a bed with a Strawberry Shortcake comforter.

Jaycie stood at the window, staring outside. The hippopotamus she'd tied to the top of her crutch had twisted so it was facedown. Jaycie turned slowly from the window, her jeans and cherry red sweater clinging to her curves. "I was—straightening up in here."

Since Livia's toys were strewn about, and half a dozen

stuffed animals poked out from the rumple of blankets on the unmade bed, Annie didn't believe her. "I was afraid you were sick," Annie said.

"No. I'm not sick."

Annie realized she didn't know Jaycie any better now than when she'd first come here not quite three weeks ago. Instead she felt as if she were looking at a photo that was slightly out of focus. Jaycie leaned on her good foot. "Theo didn't come home last night."

The skin on Annie's neck grew hot with guilt. That explained why Jaycie was hiding out. Even though Annie didn't believe Theo had any personal interest in Jaycie, she felt as if she'd broken the girlfriend code. She had to tell Jaycie at least part of the truth, but not with Livia taking in everything they were saying. "Scamp really likes your drawings, Liv. Maybe you could make one for us to hang in the kitchen while Mommy and I go talk."

Livia didn't protest. She went to her table and opened her crayon box. Annie stepped out into the hallway, and Jaycie followed. Annie wasn't going to lie to her, but it would be cruel to tell her too much. "Some odd things have been happening," she said, guilt clinging to her like sticky syrup. "I didn't want to bother you, but I guess you need to know. When I got back to the cottage on Saturday night, it had been trashed."

"What do you mean?"

Annie told her what she'd found. And then she told her the rest. "Yesterday morning on my way over here, someone shot at me."

"Shot at you?"

"The bullet barely missed. Theo found me right after. That's why he didn't come home last night. He didn't want to leave me alone, even though I told him he didn't need to stay."

Jaycie leaned against the wall behind her. "It was an accident, I'm sure. Some fool shooting at birds."

"I was in the open. It was pretty clear I wasn't a bird."

But Jaycie wasn't listening. "I'll bet it was Danny Keen. He's always doing things like this. He probably broke into the cottage with a couple of his friends. I'll call his mother."

Annie didn't believe the explanation was that simple, but Jaycie had already taken off down the hall, moving more easily on the crutches than she had when Annie had arrived. Annie reminded herself that Jaycie never had to know what had happened at the cottage. No one ever had to know. Not unless she really was pregnant . . .

Stop! demanded Dilly. *You are not going to think that way.*

I'll marry you, Peter said. *Heroes always do the right thing.*

Peter was starting to get on her nerves.

LIVIA CAME INTO THE LIBRARY wearing her pink coat, crooked paper crown still on her head, and dragging Annie's backpack. It didn't take detective skills to figure out what she wanted. Annie closed down her laptop and went to fetch her own coat.

The temperature had risen into the high thirties, and as they stepped outside, the gutters were dripping and the snow was beginning to disappear from all but the shadiest spots. As they neared the fairy house, she saw that an egg-size rock topped with a tiny carpet of green winter moss had appeared, a cushy perch for a tiny woodland creature. She wondered if Jaycie knew Livia had slipped out earlier. "Looks like the fairies have a new place to sit."

Livia leaned back on her heels to examine the rock.

Annie started to reprimand her for coming out alone, then thought better of it. Livia didn't seem to stray any farther than the tree. As long as Theo kept the stable locked, she shouldn't come to any harm.

Annie sat on the ledge stone and pulled out Scamp. "*Buon giorno,* Livia. It is I, *Scamperino.* I'm practicing my *Italiano.* That means 'Italian.' Do you speak any foreign languages?"

Livia shook her head.

"A pity," Scamp said. "Italian is the language of pizza, which I simply adore. And gelato. That's like ice cream. And badly built towers. Alas . . ." She dropped her head. "Neither pizza nor gelato is available on Peregrine Island."

Livia looked sorry about that.

"I have a brilliant idea!" Scamp exclaimed. "Maybe you and Annie could make fake pizzas this afternoon with English muffins."

Annie expected Livia to object, but instead, she nodded. Scamp shook her head to fluff her orange curls. "The drawing you left for me last night was *eccellente*. That's Italian for 'excellent.'"

Livia dipped her head and gazed at her feet, but Scamp wasn't deterred. "I am exceptionally clever, and I have deduced—that means I've figured out—I have deduced . . ." She dropped her voice to a whisper. ". . . that the drawing is your free secret."

Livia's small face tightened with apprehension.

Scamp cocked her head and said softly, "Don't worry. I'm not mad at you."

Livia finally looked at her.

"That's you in the picture, isn't it? But I'm not sure who the others are . . ." She hesitated. "Maybe your mother?"

Livia gave a tiny, almost indecipherable nod.

Annie felt as though she were wandering through a dark room with her arms outstretched trying not to bump into anything. "It looks like she's wearing something pretty. Is it a flower or maybe a valentine? Did you give it to her?"

Livia shook her head violently. Tears sprang to her eyes, as if the puppet had betrayed her. With a hiccuping sob, she ran toward the house.

Annie winced as the kitchen door banged shut. A couple of college psychology classes hadn't equipped her to meddle in something like this. She wasn't a child psychologist. She wasn't a mother . . .

But she might be.

Her chest started to hurt. She put Scamp away and went back into the kitchen, but she couldn't face another hour inside Harp House.

The bright winter sunlight mocked the darkness of her mood as she left again. Shoulders hunched, she walked around to the front of the house and stood at the top of the cliff. The front porch stretched behind her. Below, the granite steps carved into the rock face led to the beach. She began her descent.

The steps were slippery and shallow, and she held on to the rope rail. How had her life gotten to be such a mess? For now, the cottage was the only home she had, but once she got back on her feet . . . *If she got back on her feet . . .* Once she found a steady job, she wouldn't be able to leave for two months to come here. Sooner or later, the cottage would fall back into Harp hands.

But not yet, Dilly said. *Right now, you're here, and you have a job to do. No more whining. Nose to the grindstone. Stay positive.*

Shut up, Dilly, Leo sneered. *For all your supposed sensibility, you don't have a clue how messy life can be.*

Annie blinked. Had that really been Leo? The voices were getting mixed up in her head. Peter was her support. Leo only attacked.

She shoved her hands into her pockets. The wind plastered her coat against her and whipped the ends of her hair from beneath her knit hat. She faced the water, imagining herself in command of the waves, the currents, the rise and fall of the tides. Imagining power when she'd never felt more powerless.

Finally, she made herself turn around.

A rockslide had covered the mouth, but Annie knew exactly where it was. In her mind the cave would always be a secret hideaway issuing its siren's call to everyone who passed. *Come inside. Bring your picnics and your playthings, your daydreams and your fantasies. Reflect . . . Explore . . . Make love . . . Die.*

A gust of wind tugged at her hat. She grabbed it before it could sail into the sea and shoved it in her pocket. She wasn't going back up to the house today, not with this emotional tornado spinning inside her. She scrambled over the rocks and made her way to the cottage.

Neither the Range Rover nor Theo was there. She made a cup of tea to warm up and sat at the table in the window, petting Hannibal and thinking about the possibility of being pregnant. If she were in the city, she could run to the closest drugstore and pick up an EPT. Now she'd have to order one and wait for the ferry to arrive.

Except as she remembered the crates of open grocery bags being passed from one islander to the next, she knew she couldn't do that. She'd spotted Tampax, liquor, adult incontinence diapers. Did she really want everyone on the island to know she'd ordered an EPT? She yearned for the anonymity of the big city.

After she finished her tea, she gathered up her inventory notebook and headed to the studio. She'd needed to go through the boxes more methodically. She turned the corner and froze just inside the studio door.

Crumpet hung by a noose from the ceiling.

Crumpet. Her silly, vain, spoiled little puppet princess . . . Her head hung at a macabre angle, yellow yarn sausage curls flopping to the side. Her small cloth legs dangled helplessly, and one of her tiny, raspberry-pink patent leather shoes lay on the floor.

With a sob, Annie rushed across the room and grabbed a chair to get her down from the rope that had been nailed to the ceiling.

"Annie!" The front door banged open.

She spun around and charged out of the studio. "You *creep*! You ugly, insensitive *jerk*!"

He stormed into the living room like a lion after a wildebeest. "Have you lost your mind?"

Unwanted tears sprang to her eyes. "Did you think that was funny? You haven't changed at all."

"Why didn't you wait? Do you want to get shot at again?"

She bared her teeth. "Is that a threat?"

"Threat? Are you so naive that you think it can't happen again?"

"If it happens again, I swear to God I will kill you!"

That stopped them both. She'd never imagined herself capable of such ferocity, but she'd been attacked at the most elemental level. However self-centered Crumpet might be, she was part of Annie, and Annie was her guardian.

"If what happens again?" he asked in a quieter voice.

"At first, all those positions you put my puppets in were funny." She thrust her hand in the direction of the studio. "But this is cruel."

"Cruel?" He strode past her. She turned to see him peer into her bedroom and then advance toward the studio. "Son of a bitch," he muttered.

She went after him, then stopped in the studio doorway to watch as he reached up and pulled the piece of rope down.

He slipped the noose off Crumpet's head, carried her to Annie, and handed the puppet over. "I'm getting a locksmith out here as soon as I can," he said grimly.

Her gaze followed him as he moved to the corner of the room. She clutched Crumpet tighter as she saw what she'd missed. Instead of being on the shelf under the windows, her other puppets were stuffed inside the wastebasket, heads and limbs dangling over the sides.

"Don't." She rushed to them. Sinking down on her heels with Crumpet on her lap, she took them out one by one. She straightened their clothes and their hair. When she was done, she looked up at Theo, searching his face, his eyes, seeing nothing she hadn't seen before.

His mouth tightened. "You should have waited at the house for the car. I wasn't gone long. Don't walk down here by yourself again." He stalked from the studio.

This was what he'd been so angry about when he'd charged in.

She arranged Dilly, Leo, and Peter on the shelf.

Thank you, Peter whispered. *I'm not as brave as I thought.*

She wasn't quite ready to abandon Crumpet, and she carried her into the living room where Theo was taking off his coat. "I don't have money for a locksmith," she said quietly.

"I do," he retorted, "and I'm having a new lock installed. Nobody is going to poke around in my stuff when I'm not here."

Was he really that self-absorbed, or was this his way of letting her save face?

She slipped Crumpet on her arm. The familiar feeling of the puppet's frilly dress calmed her. She raised her arm, not thinking anything through. "Thank you for saving me," Crumpet said in her breathy, coquette's voice.

Theo cocked his head, but Annie addressed the puppet instead of him. "Is that all you have to say, Crumpet?"

Crumpet took Theo in from head to toe. "You are smokin'."

"Crumpet!" Annie scolded. "Where are your manners?"

Crumpet blinked her long lashes at Theo and cooed, "You are smokin' . . . sir."

"That's enough, Crumpet!" Annie exclaimed.

The puppet tossed her curls, clearly in a huff. "What do you want me to say?"

Annie spoke patiently. "I want you to say you're sorry."

Crumpet grew petulant. "What do I have to be sorry for?"

"You know very well."

Crumpet leaned toward Annie's ear, speaking in a faux whisper. "I'd rather ask him who does his hair. You know what a disaster my last visit was."

"Only because you insulted the shampoo girl," Annie reminded her.

Crumpet's nose went up in the air. "She thought she was prettier than I."

"Prettier than 'me.'"

"She *was* prettier than you," Crumpet said triumphantly.

Annie sighed. "Stop stalling and say what you need to."

"Oh, all right." Crumpet gave a begrudging *humph*. And then, even more begrudgingly, "I'm sorry I thought you were the one who hung me from the ceiling."

"Me?" Theo was actually addressing the puppet.

"In my defense . . ." Crumpet sniffed. "You do have a history. I still haven't recovered from the way you made Peter look up my skirt."

"You loved that, and you know it," Annie told her.

Theo shook his head, as if he were clearing out cobwebs. "How do you know I'm not the one who hung you up?"

Annie finally spoke directly to him. "Did you?"

This time he remembered to look at Annie. "It's like your friend here said . . . I have a history."

"And I wouldn't have been surprised if I'd come home and found Crumpet and Dilly going at it in my bed." She pulled the puppet from her hand. "But not this."

"You still have too much faith in people." His mouth twisted unpleasantly. "It hasn't even been a month, and you've already forgotten who the villain is in your fairy tale."

"Maybe. Maybe not," she said.

He stared at her, then moved past her to the studio. "I have work to do."

He disappeared without defending himself, without denying anything.

THERE WAS NO COZY DINNER for two that night, so Annie made herself a sandwich, then moved some of the boxes from the studio into the living room. Settling cross-legged on the floor, she opened the flaps of the first box. It was full of magazines ranging from upscale glossies to long-defunct photocopied zines. Some of them contained feature stories Mariah had written or stories about her. Annie listed the name of each magazine in her notebook, along with its publication date. It seemed unlikely that any of these were collectibles, but she wouldn't know until she checked.

The second box contained books. She surveyed them for autographs and to make sure nothing important was pressed between the pages, then added the individual titles to her notebook. It would take forever to check all of this, and she still had two more boxes to sort through.

Although she felt better physically than when she'd come to the island, she still needed more sleep than normal. She changed into a pair of Mariah's menswear pajamas and pulled her sock monkey slippers out from under the bed. But as she stuck her foot into the first slipper, she felt something—

She yelped and jerked her foot out.

The studio door banged open. A shudder wracked her body. Theo barged in. "What's wrong?"

"Everything!" She reached down and gingerly plucked up the slipper between her thumb and forefinger. "Look at this!" She tilted the slipper, and a dead mouse tumbled to the floor. "What kind of depraved mind does something like this!" She threw the slipper down. "I hate this place! I hate this island! I hate this cottage!" She rounded on him. "And don't think I'm afraid of a little mouse. I've lived in too many rat-hole apartments for that. But I didn't expect some sicko to leave one in my shoe!"

Theo slipped a hand into the pocket of his jeans. "It . . . might not have been a sicko."

"You think doing something like this is normal?" She was screeching again, and she didn't care.

"Maybe." He rubbed his jaw. "If . . . you're a cat."

"Are you telling me—" She glared at Hannibal.

"Think of it as a love letter," Theo said. "He only gives these special gifts to the people he cares about."

Annie turned on the cat. "Don't you ever do anything like that again, do you hear me? It's revolting!"

Hannibal lifted his rear quarters in a long stretch, then came across the room and nudged her bare foot with his nose.

She moaned. "Is this day ever going to end?"

Theo smiled and picked up his cat. He put it out of the room into the hall and closed the door, leaving himself inside with her.

She'd grabbed her robe from a hook on the closet door. As she wrapped it around herself, she remembered an incident she'd tried to forget. "You left a dead fish in my bed."

"Yes, I did." He walked over to inspect the life-size mounted photograph of the carved wooden headboard that served as the real headboard of her bed.

"Why?" she asked, as Hannibal yowled outside the door.

"Because I thought it was funny." He ran his thumb over the top edge of the photograph, giving it more attention than it deserved.

She stepped past the mouse carcass. "Who else did you torture besides me?"

"Don't you think one victim was enough?"

She upended a wastebasket over the mouse, then went to the door and let Hannibal back in so he'd stop yowling. She didn't need a cozy chat with Theo tonight, especially not in her bedroom, but she had so many questions. "I'm starting to believe you hate Harp House nearly as much as I do, so why did you come to the island?"

He walked to the window and looked out onto the bleak winter meadow. "I have a book to finish, and I needed a place to write where nobody would bother me."

She didn't miss the irony. "How's that working out so far?"

His breath fogged the glass. "Not my best plan."

"There's plenty of winter left," she pointed out. "You could still rent a beach house in the Caribbean."

"I'm fine where I am."

But he wasn't. She was sick of the mysteries surrounding him, sick of how powerless not knowing more about him made her feel. "Why did you come to Peregrine? The real story. I want to understand."

He turned toward her, his expression as cold as the frost on the window. "I can't imagine why."

His haughty lord-of-the-manor act didn't intimidate her, and she managed something she hoped resembled a sneer. "Chalk it up to my never-ending curiosity about the inner workings of a pathological mind."

He lifted an eyebrow at her, but didn't seem overly offended. "There's nothing more unpleasant than listening to someone with a big trust fund and a book deal whine about how tough they've got it."

"True," she said. "But the fact is, you lost your wife."

He shrugged. "I'm not the only man that's happened to."

Either he was covering up, or he was as emotionally detached as she'd always believed. "You also lost your twin. And your mother."

"She took off when I was five. I barely remember her."

"Tell me about your wife? I saw a photo of her online. She was beautiful."

"Beautiful and independent. Those are the women I'm attracted to."

Qualities Annie knew little about.

"Kenley was also brilliant," he said. "Off-the-chart smart. And ambitious. But what attracted me the most was that fierce independence."

In the game of life, the score was clear. Kenley Harp, 4. Annie Hewitt, 0. Not that she was jealous of a dead woman, but she yearned to be fiercely independent, too. And possessing extreme beauty along with a megabrain wouldn't hurt either.

If it had been anyone other than Theo, Annie would have

changed the subject, but their relationship existed so far outside the borders of normalcy that she could say what she wanted. "If your wife had all those qualities, why did she kill herself?"

He took his time answering—nudging Hannibal away from the overturned wastebasket, checking the latch on the window. Finally, he said, "Because she wanted to punish me for making her miserable."

His indifference fit perfectly with everything she'd once believed about him, but no longer quite rang true. She spoke lightly, "You make me miserable, too, but I'm not going to kill myself."

"Reassuring. But unlike Kenley, your independence isn't a false facade."

She was trying to absorb that when he staged his own attack.

"Enough of this bullshit. Take off your clothes."

Chapter Thirteen

"TAKE OFF MY CLOTHES? YOU'RE DELUSIONAL."

Theo stepped around the cat. "Am I? After last night, we don't seem to have anything to lose. And you'll be happy to know that your cottage is now fully stocked with condoms. Every room."

He really was the devil. She looked around her bedroom. "You put condoms in here?"

He inclined his head. "The top drawer of your bedside table. Right next to your teddy bear."

"That," she said, "is a Beanie Baby collectible."

"Apologies." He was cool, easy, a man with nothing more complicated on his mind than seduction. "I also put them in the studio, the kitchen, the bathroom, and my pockets." He let his eyes skim over her. "Although . . . Not everything I'm thinking about doing to you requires a condom."

Her nerve endings sparked, and her imagination took off

on a pornographic expedition just as he'd intended. She pulled herself back to reality. "You're assuming an awful lot."

"Like you said. There's plenty of winter left."

This was a bogus seduction, his pathetic attempt to put a stop to her questioning. Or maybe it wasn't. She tightened the sash on her robe. "The thing about me is . . . Without some kind of emotional intimacy, I'm not interested."

"Remind me of what kind of emotional intimacy we had last night . . . because you seemed very interested."

"That whole episode was an alcohol-induced aberration." Not completely true, and he didn't look as though he was buying it, but it was true enough. Hannibal pawed at the trash basket again, threatening to turn it over, and she picked him up. "Knock it off and tell me why you came to Peregrine instead of going someplace more pleasant."

His silky seductiveness vanished. "Stop prying. It has nothing to do with you."

"If you want me to take off my clothes, it does." She actually managed something close to a purr. Was she really trying to use sex as currency? She should be ashamed of herself, but since he wasn't falling over laughing, she didn't even flush. "Sex for honesty. That's my offer."

"You're not serious."

Not one bit. She stroked the cat between his ears. "I don't like secrecy. If you want to see me naked, you'll have to give me something in exchange."

He glowered at her. "I don't want to see you naked that badly."

"Your loss." Where had she gotten this confidence? This feistiness? Here she stood in all her messy glory, wearing too-big men's pajamas, a ratty old bathrobe, and—not to forget—possibly pregnant. Yet she was acting as if she'd just sashayed down a Victoria's Secret runway. "Hold your cat while I take care of our dearly departed friend," she said.

"I'll handle it."

"Suit yourself." She lifted the cat until they were nose to nose. "Come on, Hannibal. Your daddy has another corpse to get rid of."

She swept from the room, cat in her arms, satisfaction warming her heart. She hadn't learned much, but she'd somehow managed to even the playing field. As she set the cat down, she mulled over what he'd said about her independence not being a false facade. What if he were right? What if she weren't as much of a wreck as she believed herself to be?

It was a new idea, but she'd been so beaten down lately that she automatically rejected it. Except . . . If it really was true, she'd have to readjust her whole view of herself.

"Backbone, Antoinette. That's what you're lacking. A sturdy backbone."

No, Mother, she thought. *Just because I'm not you doesn't mean I don't have plenty of backbone. I had enough to give you everything you needed before you died, didn't I?*

And now she was paying the price.

The kitchen door opened and closed. A moment later he came into the living room. He spoke so softly she almost missed what he said. "I couldn't write. I had to get away from everyone."

She turned. Alert.

He stood by the bookcase, his hair a little tousled from his trip outside to dispose of the mouse. "I couldn't stand all the pity coming from my friends and all the hatred coming from hers." He gave a brutal laugh. "Her father told me I might as well have pushed those pills down her throat. And maybe he was right. Have you heard enough?"

As he turned away and headed for the studio, she went after him. "The thing is, if you wanted to get away, why didn't you go someplace you didn't hate? The French Riviera. The Virgin Islands. God knows, you can afford it. Instead you came here."

"I love Peregrine. I just don't love Harp House. Which made it the perfect place to start writing again. No distractions. At least not until you showed up." He disappeared inside the studio.

That made sense, but something was missing. She followed him through the door. "A couple of weeks ago, I saw you coming out of the stable. It was bitter that day, but you took your sweater off. Why did you do that?"

He studied a scratch on the floor. She didn't think he was going to answer. But then he did. "Because I wanted to *feel* something."

One of the classic signs of a psychopath was an inability to experience normal emotions, but the pain etched into the lines of his face testified that he felt everything. An uneasiness came over her. She didn't want to hear more, so she turned away. "I'll leave you alone."

"We were happy at first," he said. "At least I thought so."

She looked back at him.

He gazed toward the wall mural, but she had the sense he wasn't seeing the painted taxi crashing through the storefront window. "After a while, she started calling me more frequently from work. I didn't think anything of it, but before long, I was getting dozens of messages every day—every hour. Texts, phone calls, e-mails. She wanted to know where I was, what I was doing. If I didn't reply right away, she'd fly into a rage and accuse me of being with other women. I was never unfaithful to her. Never."

He finally looked at Annie. "She quit her job. Or maybe she was forced out. I've never been sure. Her behavior became more bizarre. She told her family and some of her friends that I was screwing around on her, that I'd threatened her. I finally got her to a shrink. He put her on medication, and things were better for a while until she stopped taking her pills because she said I was trying to poison her. I tried to get her family to help, but she was never at her worst with them, and they refused to believe anything was really wrong. She started attacking me physically—punching and scratching. I was afraid I was going to hurt her, and I moved out." His hands fisted at his sides. "She killed herself a week later. How's that for a real-life fairy tale?"

Annie was appalled, yet everything about him rejected pity, so she kept her cool. "Leave it to you to marry a psycho."

He looked startled. Then his shoulders relaxed. "Yeah, well, takes one to know one, right?"

"So they say." She glanced over at her puppets resting on the shelf, then back at him. "Remind me what part of this is your fault. Other than marrying her in the first place."

His tension came back, along with his anger. "Come on, Annie. Don't be naive. I knew exactly how sick she was. I should never have left her. If I'd stood up to her family and gotten her into a hospital where she belonged, she might still be alive."

"It's a little hard to get anyone committed these days who doesn't want to be."

"I could have found a way."

"Maybe. Maybe not." Hannibal brushed against her. "I had no idea you were such a sexist."

His head jerked up. "What are you talking about?"

"Any rational woman married to a man who was abusing her the way your wife was abusing you would have gotten out, gone to a shelter, whatever it took to get away. But because you're male, you were supposed to stick around? Is that how it is?"

He seemed momentarily confused. "You don't understand."

"Don't I? If you're determined to go on a guilt trip, do it for a real sin—like not making me dinner tonight."

The faintest shadow of a smile softened his features. "What is it about you?"

"My taste in pajamas? I have no idea."

"How about your decency?" Then, more severely, "And stupidity. Promise me you won't make any more treks on foot. And when you're driving, keep your eyes open."

"Wide open." She finally knew the truth about his marriage only to wish she didn't. In the process of satisfying her curiosity, she'd allowed one more crack to form in the wall between them, one more brick to fall. "Good night," she said. "I'll see you in the morning."

"Hey, we had a deal. Aren't you supposed to take off your clothes now?"

"It would only be pity sex," she said, in a mock confessional. "I won't insult you like that."

"Go ahead. Insult me."

"You're much too evolved. You'll thank me later."

"I seriously doubt that," he muttered as she left him alone.

SATURDAY NIGHT WAS THE VILLAGE'S monthly Lobster Boil, and Jaycie had asked Annie to take her. "It's not so much for me," she'd said. "But Livia hardly ever gets to be with other kids. And I'll be able to introduce you to everyone you haven't met."

This was Jaycie's first night off since she'd broken her foot. Her ready smiles as she baked the chocolate pecan sheet cake for the event indicated how much she was looking forward to it for her own sake, not just for Livia's.

Jaycie's run-down Chevy Suburban was parked in the garage. As with so many of the island's road-weary vehicles, rust patches were eating through the body, hubcaps were missing, and there was no license plate, but it did have a properly attached car seat for Livia, so they were taking it.

Annie buckled Livia in, put the cake on the floor behind the passenger seat, then helped Jaycie get settled. The night was windy, but with no fresh snow and the worst of the icy patches gone, the road wasn't as treacherous as it had been. Still, Annie was glad to be driving the Suburban instead of her own car.

She'd dressed up in the only skirt she'd brought with her, a slim-fitting dark green pencil skirt with a soft, three-inch wool flounce that brushed her knees. She'd paired the skirt with one of Mariah's white, long-sleeved ballet tops, her own cranberry tights, and designer boots that laced to just above her ankles. She'd spotted them in the window of a resale shop last winter and bought them for next to nothing. With a good cleaning and fresh laces, they looked almost new.

As they turned out onto the road, Annie addressed Livia over her shoulder. "Scamp is sorry she couldn't come with you tonight. She has a sore throat."

Livia glowered and kicked the heels of her sneakers hard against her seat, making the brown velvet cat ears on her headband wobble. She didn't need words to communicate how she felt about the puppet's absence. "Maybe I can meet Scamp someday," Jaycie said. She toyed with her coat zipper. "How's Theo?"

Even in the dim light, her too-bright smile was painful. Annie hated seeing her like this. As pretty as she was, Jaycie didn't have a chance with Theo. He was attracted to beautiful, brilliant, and crazy, three qualities neither Jaycie nor Annie possessed. For Annie, that was a bonus, but Jaycie wouldn't see it the same way.

Annie skirted the truth. "He was in the studio working when I went to bed last night, and I barely saw him this morning."

But she'd seen enough. The sight of him coming out of her bathroom with a towel wrapped around his waist, beads of water still glistening on his shoulders, had stopped her in her tracks. Exactly the kind of reaction to him that might have gotten her pregnant.

She swallowed her trepidation. "Someone broke into the cottage again yesterday when no one was there." Conscious of Livia in the backseat, she didn't say any more. "I'll tell you later."

Jaycie twisted her hands on her lap. "I haven't been able to get hold of Laura Keen to talk to her about Danny. Maybe she'll be here tonight."

They pulled up at the brightly lit town hall. The flag on the flagpole was blowing straight up, and people were streaming inside holding plastic cupcake carriers, six-packs of beer, and liter bottles of soda. Jaycie seemed nervous, and Annie rescued the crutch she dropped as she climbed out of the car.

They battled the wind to get to the door. Livia clutched her pink stuffed kitten, and her thumb crept to her mouth. Maybe it was Annie's imagination, but a momentary lull seemed to fall over the crowd as the three of them entered. Seconds passed, and then several of the older women came toward them—Barbara Rose, Judy Kester, and boat captain Naomi.

Barbara gave Jaycie a gentle hug, enveloping her in a cloud of floral perfume. "We were afraid you wouldn't make it tonight."

"You've been out of touch too long," Naomi said.

Judy squatted down in front of Livia. "Look what a big girl you are," she squealed, her red hair brighter than ever. "Can I have a hug?"

Definitely not. Livia ducked behind Annie for protection. Annie reached back and rubbed her shoulder. She loved that Livia viewed her as a safe haven.

Judy backed off with a laugh, took Jaycie's cake, and carried it to the dessert table while they got rid of their coats. Jaycie's black slacks and royal blue sweater were well worn but still flattering. Her long blond hair swung from a side part, and her carefully applied makeup included mascara, eye shadow, and cherry lipstick.

The meeting room at the town hall was barely as big as the living room at Harp House and crowded with long tables covered in white paper. The scuffed gray walls displayed the community bulletin board, yellowed historical photographs, an amateurish oil painting of the harbor, first-aid posters, and a fire extinguisher. One doorway led to the closet-size library, the other to the combined clerk's office, post office, and—judging from the savory smells—kitchen.

Lobster Boil, Jaycie explained, was a misnomer for the monthly event, since no lobster was involved. "We eat so much of it that about twenty years ago people decided to change the menu to a traditional New England boiled dinner. Beef brisket or ham during the winter, clams and corn on the cob in the summer. I don't know why we still call it a Lobster Boil."

"Let no one ever accuse the islanders of not hanging on to their traditions," Annie said.

Jaycie tugged at her bottom lip with her teeth. "Sometimes I think I'm going to suffocate if I have to stay here another day."

Lisa McKinley came through the doorway from the kitchen area. She wore jeans and a V-neck blouse that showcased a Victorian-style necklace, a present—she was quick to announce—from Cynthia Harp. Annie drifted off so she and Jaycie could catch up. As she moved among the tables, bits of conversation swirled around her.

". . . five hundred pounds behind where my catch was this time last year."

". . . forgot to order Bisquick, so I have to make them from scratch."

"That's more than the price of a new helm pump."

Annie studied a black-and-white print hanging crookedly on the wall. It showed figures in seventeenth-century garb standing by the sea. Naomi came up behind her and nodded toward the print. "Lobsters washed right up on the beach during colonial times. They had so many they fed them to their pigs and the prisoners in jail."

"They're still a treat for me," Annie said.

"They are for most people, and that's good news for us. But we have to keep the crop sustainable or we're out of business."

"How do you do that?"

"With a lot of regulation about when and where people can fish. And breeders are off-limits. If we catch a breeding female, we cut a V in its tail fin to identify it and throw it back in. Eighty percent of the lobsters we catch have to be thrown back either because they're undersize, oversize, V-notched, or they're carrying eggs."

"Hard life."

"You have to love it, that's for sure." She tugged on one of the silver studs in her earlobes. "If you're interested, you can come out on my boat. The weather looks like it'll be fairly decent at the beginning of the week, and not many city people can say they've worked as a sternman on a Maine lobster boat."

The invitation took Annie aback. "I'd love that."

Naomi seemed genuinely pleased. "You'll have to get up early. And don't wear your good clothes."

They'd just made arrangements for Annie to meet Naomi at the boathouse dock on Monday morning when the outside door swung open bringing a fresh blast of cold air. Theo walked in.

The noise level in the room dropped as people grew aware of his presence. Theo nodded, and the chatter picked up again, but most of the crowd continued to watch him surreptitiously. Jaycie paused in her conversation with Lisa to gaze at him. A group of men with weather-beaten faces gestured him over to join them.

Annie felt something tug on her skirt and looked down to see Livia trying to get her attention. The child had grown bored with the company of adults, and her attention was fixed on a group of children in the corner, three boys and two girls, the youngest of whom Annie recognized from her library visit as Lisa's daughter. Annie had no trouble interpreting the entreaty in Livia's expression. She wanted to play with the children but was too shy to approach them by herself.

Annie took her hand, and they approached the group together. The girls were putting stickers in a book while the boys argued over a handheld video game. She smiled at the girls, their round cheeks and red hair clearly identifying them as sisters. "I'm Annie. And you know Livia."

The older one looked up. "We didn't see you for a long time. I'm Kaitlin and this is my sister, Alyssa."

Alyssa gazed at Livia. "How old are you now?"

Livia held up four fingers.

"I'm five. What's your middle name? Mine is Rosalind."

Livia dipped her head.

When it became obvious Livia wasn't going to respond, Alyssa looked at Annie. "What's wrong with her? Why won't she talk?"

"Shut up, Alyssa," her sister admonished. "You know you're not supposed to ask about that."

Annie had grown used to thinking of Jaycie and Livia as being somehow separate from the community, but they weren't. They were as deeply entrenched as anyone here.

The video game tussle between the three boys was getting out of hand. "It's my turn!" one of them shouted.

"Is not! It's my game." The largest boy landed a hard punch on the one who'd complained, and then all three of them were on their feet ready to swing at one another.

"*Avast,* ye ragged curs!"

The boys froze, then gazed around, trying to find the source of the Captain Jack Sparrow voice. Livia was way ahead of the game, and she smiled.

"Stop yer caterwaulin' or I'll throw ye all in the bilge."

The boys slowly turned their attention to Annie, who'd formed a puppet from her right hand. She eased down and settled her weight back on her calves, moving her thumb to make the puppet talk. "A good thing I left me cutlass on the poop deck, ye sorry excuses for sea dogs."

Boys were the same everywhere. One mention of "poop," and she had them in the palm of her hand.

She directed her makeshift puppet toward the smallest boy, a cherubic little towhead with a black eye. "What about it, bucko? Ye look strong enough ta sail on the *Jolly Roger*. Searchin' fer the treasure of the Lost City of Atlantis, I am. And 'oo wants to go wi' me?"

Livia was the first to raise her hand, and Annie nearly abandoned Cap'n Jack to give her a hug. "Are ye sure, me beauty? There be fierce sea serpents. It'll take a brave lass. Are ye a brave lass?"

Livia gleefully nodded her head.

"Me, too!" said Kaitlin. "I'm a brave lass."

"You're not as brave as me, stupid!" Cherub face said.

Cap'n Jack growled. "Keep a civil tongue in yer head, lad, or I be keelhaulin' you." And then, out of habit, "There be no bullyin' on the *Jolly Roger*. When yer fightin' sea dragons, it's all fer one and one fer all. Anybody on my ship who's actin' like a bully gets tossed overboard ta feed the sharks."

They looked suitably impressed.

She had nothing but an unadorned hand for a puppet—not even a set of eyes drawn in with a marker—but the kids were enthralled. The largest boy, however, was no fool. "You don't look like a pirate. You look like a hand."

"Aye. And ye're a smart one to notice. Me enemies cast a spell o'er me, and the only way I can unlock it is ter find the lost treasure. What say ye, mateys? Are ye brave enough?"

"I'll sail with you, Captain."

Not a child's voice. But one that was exceedingly familiar.

She turned. A group of adults had gathered behind her to watch the show. Theo stood with them, his arms crossed over his chest, amusement dancing in his eyes.

Cap'n Jack gave him the once-over. "I'm only takin' on strappin' lads. Yer a bit too long in the tooth."

"Pity," Theo said, looking every bit the Regency buck. "And I was so looking forward to those sea serpents."

The dinner bell rang, and a voice called out, "Food's ready. Line up!"

"Avast, me hearties. Time fer ye ta eat yer hardtack and fer me to get back to me ship." She splayed her fingers dramatically, giving Cap'n Jack a royal send-off.

Applause rang out from both the kids and the adults. Livia snuggled up at her side. The older kids began pestering her with questions and comments.

"How d'you talk without moving your lips?"

"Can you do it again?"

"I go out on my dad's lobster boat."

"I want to talk like that."

"I was a pirate for Halloween."

The adults began claiming their offspring and steering them into the food line that had formed to the serving counter in the next room.

Theo came up to her. "So much is now clear to me that was heretofore murky."

"Heretofore?"

"It slipped out. But there's one thing I still don't understand. How did you manage the clock?"

"I have no idea what you're talking about."

He gave her a look announcing that her denial was demeaning and that, if she had any character at all, she'd come clean.

The jig was clearly up. She smiled, sidled closer to him, then emitted one of her best moans, so quietly eerie only he could hear.

"Cute," he said.

"Call it 'Revenge of the Dumbwaiter.'"

She expected him to ignore her. Instead, he looked genuinely remorseful. "I really am sorry about that."

It occurred to her that neither one of her two long-term boyfriends had ever said "I'm sorry" about anything.

Livia ran off to join her mother. Jaycie was still with Lisa, but her attention was on Theo. As Annie went over to join them, she overheard Lisa. "You need to take her back to the doctor. She should be talking by now."

Annie couldn't hear Jaycie's response.

They all lined up to fill their plates. Marie and Tildy from the Bunco group pulled Theo in with them and began peppering him with questions about his writing, but after he'd filled his plate, he left them to join Annie at the table where she was sitting with Jaycie and Livia. He took the chair next to Annie and across from Lisa and her husband, Darren, who was both a lobsterman and the island's electrician. Livia eyed Theo warily, and Jaycie lost track of the conversation she was having with Lisa.

Theo and Darren knew each other from past summers and began talking about fishing. Annie noticed how easily Theo conversed with everyone, which she found interesting, considering how fiercely he guarded his privacy.

She was sick of thinking about Theo's contradictions, and she turned her attention to her meal. In addition to a well-seasoned beef brisket, the boiled dinner included potatoes, cabbage wedges, onions, and a variety of root vegetables. With the exception of the rutabagas, which both she and Livia avoided like the plague, the rest was delicious.

For all Jaycie's infatuation with Theo, she did nothing to catch his attention beyond bestowing occasional longing gazes. Eventually Theo turned to Annie. "You slipped in the turret while I was asleep and changed the clock battery. I should have figured that out a long time ago."

"It's not your fault that you're slow. I'm sure it's hard to recover from being hit on the head with a silver spoon."

He raised an eyebrow.

Livia poked Annie, lifted her arm, and made a miniature hand puppet, awkwardly moving her small fingers to indicate she wanted another puppet show. "Later, sweetheart," Annie said, depositing a kiss on her head just behind the cat ears.

"You seem to have a friend there," Theo said.

"It's more Scamp. She and Liv are best friends. Isn't that right, bucko?"

Livia nodded and took a delicate sip of milk.

The islanders had begun lining up at the dessert table, and Jaycie rose. "I'll get you some of my chocolate pecan cake, Theo."

Theo was undoubtedly looking for an escape from Jaycie's cooking, but he nodded.

"I'm surprised to see you here," Annie said. "You're not exactly Mr. Social."

"Somebody has to keep an eye on you."

"I was with Jaycie in the car, and I'm in the middle of a crowd here."

"Still . . ."

A piercing whistle cut through the room, bringing the crowd to silence. A barrel-chested man in a parka stood by the front door, lowering his fingers from his mouth. "Listen up, everybody. The Coast Guard got a distress call about twenty minutes ago from a trawler a couple miles off Jackspar Point. They're heading out, but we can get there faster."

He nodded toward a burly, flannel-shirted lobsterman at the next table and to Lisa's husband, Darren. Both men rose. To Annie's surprise, Theo got up, too. He clasped the back of her chair and leaned down. "Don't go back to the cottage tonight," he said. "Spend the night at Harp House with Jaycie. Promise me."

He didn't wait for her answer but joined the three men at the door. He said something to them. One gave him a quick slap on the back, and all four headed outside.

Annie was startled. Jaycie looked like she wanted to cry. "I don't understand. Why is Theo going with them?"

Annie didn't understand either. Theo was a recreational sailor. Why would he be going out on a rescue mission?

Lisa bit her bottom lip. "I hate this," she said. "It has to be gusting forty knots out there."

Naomi overheard and sat next to her. "Darren's going to be fine, Lisa. Ed's one of the best seamen on the island, and his boat's as sound as they come."

"But what about Theo?" Jaycie said. "He's not used to these conditions."

"I'll find out." Naomi got back up.

Barbara came over to comfort her daughter. Lisa grabbed her hand. "Darren's just getting over the stomach flu. It's bad out there tonight. If the *Val Jane* ices up . . ."

"It's a solid boat," Barbara said, although she looked as worried as her daughter.

Naomi came back and addressed Jaycie. "Theo's an EMT. That's why he's going with them."

An EMT? Annie couldn't believe it. Theo's work involved the decapitation of bodies, not patching them together. "Did you know about this?" she asked Jaycie, who shook her head.

"We haven't had anybody on the island trained in medical care for almost two years," Naomi said. "Not since Jenny Schaeffer left with her kids. This is the best news we've had here all winter."

Jaycie grew more agitated. "Theo doesn't have any experience going out in this kind of weather. He should have stayed here."

Annie couldn't have agreed more.

The islanders' concern for their first responders and the missing boat took the pleasure out of the gathering, and everyone began packing up. Annie helped the women collect trash while Jaycie sat with Livia and Lisa's girls. Annie was just about to enter the kitchen with a load of dirty plates when she overheard a fragment of conversation that stopped her in her tracks.

". . . shouldn't be surprised that Livia still isn't talking," one of the women inside said. "Not after what she saw."

"She might never talk," another commented. "And it'll break Jaycie's heart."

The first woman spoke up again. "Jaycie has to be prepared for that. It isn't every day a little girl sees her mother murder her father."

Water splashed in the kitchen sink, and Annie could hear no more.

Chapter Fourteen

T HEO STEADIED HIMSELF AS A monster wave crashed over the bow of the *Val Jane*. He'd grown up on sailboats and been out on more than a few lobster boats. He'd experienced summer squalls, but never anything like this. The big fiberglass hull pitched into another trough, and an exhilarating rush of adrenaline surged through him. For the first time in what seemed like forever, he felt totally alive.

The lobster boat reared up on the swell, hung there for a moment, then plunged again. Even in the boat's heavy orange Grundens foul weather gear, he was bone-deep cold. Salt water trickled down his neck, and every exposed patch of his skin was wet and numb, but the shelter of the pilothouse didn't tempt him. He wanted to live this. Gulp it in. Sop it up. He needed this pump of his pulses, this rip of his senses.

Another mass of water towered before them. The Coast Guard had radioed that the missing fishing trawler, the *Sham-*

rock, had lost power after its engine flooded, and that there were two men aboard. Neither would last long if they were in the water, not with these frigid ocean temperatures. Even survival suits wouldn't protect them. Theo mentally reviewed everything he knew about treating hypothermia.

He'd backed into EMT training while he was researching *The Sanitarium.* The idea of being able to work in crisis situations stimulated his writer's imagination and eased his growing sense of suffocation. He'd begun his training over Kenley's objections.

"You need to spend your time with me!"

After he was certified, he'd volunteered to work in Philly's Center City, where he'd dealt with everything from tourists' broken bones and joggers' heart attacks to inline skating injuries and dog bites. He'd driven to New York during the hurricane that had hit the city so hard to help evacuate Manhattan's VA hospital and a Queens nursing home. One thing he'd never done, though, was treat men who'd been fished out of the North Atlantic in the dead of winter. He hoped that it wasn't already too late.

The *Val Jane* came upon the *Shamrock* suddenly. The trawler was barely afloat, listing heavily toward starboard and pitching on the ocean like an empty plastic water bottle. One man clung to the gunwale. Theo couldn't see the other.

He heard the grind of the diesel engine as Ed worked the *Val Jane* closer, even as the powerful waves tried to drive the boats apart. Darren and Jim Garcia, the other crew member Ed had chosen for tonight's mission, struggled on the icy deck in their efforts to secure the sinking fishing trawler to the *Val Jane.* Like Theo, they both wore life jackets over their foul weather gear.

Theo caught sight of the panicked face of the man barely holding on to the gunwale, then glimpsed a second crew member, who was motionless and tangled in the lines. Darren was beginning to tie a safety line around his own waist so he could board the sinking boat. Theo scrambled toward him and pulled the line away.

"What are you doing?" Darren shouted above the noise of the engine.

"I need the exercise!" Theo yelled back, and he began wrapping the rope around his own waist.

"Are you out of your—"

But Theo was already tying the knot, and instead of wasting time arguing, Darren lashed the free end around a deck cleat. Reluctantly, he handed over his knife to Theo. "Don't make us rescue you, too," he growled.

"Not a chance," Theo said, cocky as hell, an emotion he was far from feeling. The truth was, who'd be hurt if he didn't make it out of this? His old man. A few friends. They'd all get over it. And Annie?

Annie would celebrate with a bottle of champagne.

Except she wouldn't. That was the problem with her. She wasn't smart about people. He hoped like hell she'd gone to Harp House like he'd told her to. If she was carrying his baby—

He couldn't afford this kind of distraction. The *Shamrock* was sinking. Any minute now, they'd have to cast off or they'd endanger the *Val Jane*. As he gazed across the gap between the two boats, he hoped like hell he was back on board before that happened.

He studied the waves, waited for his opportunity, and took a leap of faith. Somehow he managed to bridge the roiling gap between the two vessels and scramble onto the *Shamrock*'s slick, half-submerged hull. The fisherman clinging to the gunwale had just enough strength to reach out one arm. "My son . . ." he gasped.

Theo gazed down into the cockpit. The kid trapped there was maybe sixteen and unconscious. Theo focused on the older man first. Signaling to Darren, he helped lift the man high enough so Darren and Jim could grab him and pull him aboard the *Val Jane*. The fisherman's lips were blue, and he needed tending right away, but Theo had to free the kid first.

He eased into the cockpit, his rubber boots sloshing in seawater. The boy's eyes were closed, and he wasn't moving. With the boat sinking, Theo didn't waste time trying to find a pulse. There was one basic rule in dealing with extreme hypothermia. *Nobody is dead until they're warm and dead.*

Bracing himself, he cut through the tangled lines binding

the kid's legs while he gripped the boy's survival jacket. He'd be damned if he freed him only to have his body wash overboard.

Jim and Darren wrestled with the boat hooks, doing their best to keep the two vessels close. Theo hoisted the boy's dead-weight up onto the hull. A wave crashed over his head, blinding him. He held on to the boy with all his strength and blinked his vision clear only to be hit again. Finally, Darren and Jim could reach out far enough to pull the boy aboard the *Val Jane*.

Moments later, Theo collapsed on the *Val Jane*'s deck himself, but every tick of the clock brought these men closer to death, and he immediately struggled back to his feet. While Jim and Ed dealt with the sinking trawler, Darren helped him get the men into the cabin.

Unlike the kid, who was barely old enough to shave, the older man had a full beard and the weathered skin of someone who had spent much of his life outdoors. He'd begun to shiver, a good sign. "My son . . ."

"I'll take care of him," Theo said, hoping like hell the Coast Guard got to them soon. He kept an EMT first responder kit in his car, but it didn't have the revival equipment these men needed.

In other circumstances, he'd have performed CPR on the kid, but that could be disastrous for someone with extreme hypothermia. Without stopping to get out of his own gear, he cut the men from their survival suits and wrapped them in dry blankets. He put together some makeshift heat packs and pressed them into the kid's armpits. Finally, he caught a faint pulse.

By the time the Coast Guard cutter arrived, Theo had both men covered and warming with more heat packs. To his relief, the boy had begun to stir, while his father was managing short sentences.

Theo filled in the Coast Guard paramedic as she began starting IVs and giving the men warm, humidified oxygen. The boy's eyes were open, and the father was trying to sit up. "You saved . . . his life. You saved my boy's life."

"Steady there," Theo said, gently pushing the man back down. "Glad we could help."

IT WAS NEARLY TWO IN the morning by the time he reached Harp House. Even with the Range Rover's heater running at full blast, his teeth were chattering. Only a few weeks ago, he'd craved this kind of discomfort, but something had happened to him tonight, and now he yearned to be dry and warm. Still, he made himself stop at Moonraker Cottage. To his relief, the place was empty. Hard to believe she'd done as he asked.

Harder to believe where he found her.

Instead of being curled up in one of Harp House's bedrooms, she was asleep on the couch in the turret, the lights on, a copy of *History of Peregrine Island* lying open on the floor at her side. She must have stopped at the cottage first, though, because she'd changed into her customary jeans and sweater. As tired as he was, the sight of those rambunctious curls looping across the old damask couch cushion made him begin to unwind.

She rolled to her side and blinked. He couldn't help himself. "Honey, I'm home."

She'd used his gray parka to cover herself, and it slipped to the carpet as she sat up. She pushed the hair out of her face. "Did you find the boat? What happened?"

He peeled off his jacket. "We got the men. The boat sank."

She came to her feet, taking in his disheveled hair, the wet, dark V at the neck of his sweater, his soggy jeans. "You're soaked."

"I was a lot wetter a few hours ago."

"And you're shivering."

"Hypothermia. Stage One. Best treatment is bare skin to bare skin."

She ignored his lame attempt at humor, seeing his fatigue instead, and regarding him with real concern. "How about a nice warm shower? Get upstairs."

He didn't have the energy to argue.

She went ahead of him, and by the time he reached the top of the steps, she had his robe. She pushed him into the bathroom and turned on the shower, as if he were incapable of doing it himself. He wanted to tell her to leave him alone, that he didn't need a mother. She shouldn't be here. Waiting up for him. Trusting him. Her gullibility drove him crazy. At the same time, he wanted to thank her. The last person he could remember trying to take care of him was Regan.

"I'll make you something hot to drink," she said as she turned to leave.

"Whiskey." Exactly the wrong thing to drink when you were as cold as he was, but maybe she didn't know that.

She did. As he came out of the bathroom freshly showered and wrapped in his robe, she was waiting at the door with a mug of hot chocolate. He gazed into it with disgust. "This had better be spiked."

"Not even a marshmallow. Why didn't you tell me you're an EMT?"

"I was afraid you'd ask for a free pelvic exam. Happens all the time."

"You're depraved."

"Thank you." He wandered to his bedroom, taking a sip of the hot chocolate on the way. It tasted great.

He stopped in the doorway. She'd turned down the freaking covers and even fluffed his damn pillows. He took another swig of chocolate and gazed back at her as she stood in the hallway. Her green sweater was wrinkled, and the cuff of one jean leg had caught on top of a sweat sock. She was rumpled and flushed, and she'd never looked sexier. "I'm still cold," he said, even as he told himself to back off. "Really cold."

She cocked her head. "Good try. I'm not getting into bed with you."

"But you want to. Admit it."

"Oh, sure. Why not jump right back into the lion's den?" Her irises shot gold-specked fireworks at him. "Look where it's gotten me so far. Probably pregnant. How's that for a bucket of ice water over those steaming private parts, Mr. Horn Dog?"

It wasn't funny. It was horrifying. Except the way she said it, with all that bristly outrage . . . He wanted to kiss the hell out of her. Instead, he said, a lot more assuredly than he felt, "You're not pregnant." And then, because she'd refused to tell him the first time he'd asked, "When are you getting your period?"

"That's my business."

She was all badass. Her way of distracting them from what they both wanted to do. Or maybe he was the only one?

She looped a coil of hair behind her ear. "Did you know Jaycie killed her husband?"

The abrupt change of subject momentarily took him aback. He picked up the mug. He still couldn't believe she'd made him hot chocolate. "Sure. The guy was a real bastard. Which was why I would *never* have fired her."

"Stop looking so righteous," she retorted. "We both know you set me up." She rubbed her arm through her sweater. "Why didn't Jaycie tell me?"

"I doubt she's eager to talk about it."

"Still, we've been working together for weeks now. Don't you think she might have said something?"

"Apparently not." He set the chocolate back down. "Grayson was a few years older than me. A surly kid. Wasn't too popular even then, and it doesn't seem as though anybody misses him much."

"She should have told me."

He didn't like seeing her upset, this curly-haired woman who played with puppets and trusted unreliable people. He wanted to pull her into bed. He'd even promise not to touch her if that would wipe away those frown lines. But he didn't get a chance. She flicked off the light switch and headed down the steps. He should have thanked her for taking care of him, but she wasn't the only badass around.

ANNIE COULDN'T GET BACK TO sleep, so she grabbed her coat and the keys to the Range Rover and went outside. On their way back from the Lobster Boil, she hadn't talked to Jaycie about what she'd learned. And Jaycie didn't know Annie had gone to the turret to wait for Theo.

The night sky had cleared, and the starry blanket of the Milky Way stretched above her. She didn't want to talk to either Jaycie or Theo in the morning, but instead of getting in the car, she walked to the edge of the drive and gazed down. It was too dark to see the cottage, but if someone had been there making trouble, they would have left by now. Weeks ago, she would have been afraid to go to the cottage in the middle of the night, but the island had toughened her. Now she almost hoped someone would be there. At least she'd know who her tormenter was.

The interior of the Range Rover smelled like Theo: leather and winter's cold. Her defenses were coming down so fast she could hardly keep the barriers in place. And then there was Jaycie. She and Annie had been together for nearly a month, yet Jaycie hadn't once mentioned the small fact that she'd killed her husband. Granted, it wasn't the kind of detail easily worked into a conversation, but she should have found a way. Annie was used to exchanging confidences with her friends, yet her conversations with Jaycie never went below the surface. It was as if Jaycie had a NO ADMITTANCE sign hanging around her neck.

Annie pulled up to the dark cottage and got out of the car. The locksmith she couldn't afford wasn't due until next week. She could find anything inside. She eased the door open, stepped into the kitchen, and flicked on the light. Everything was exactly as she'd left it. She made her way through the cottage, turning on lights, peeking in the storage closet.

Scaredy-cat, Peter scoffed.

"Shut up, butthead," she retorted. "I'm here, aren't I?" Leo hadn't tormented her lately, while Peter, her hero, was growing increasingly belligerent. One more thing out of balance in her life.

THE NEXT MORNING, HER HEAD ached and she needed coffee. She stepped out of the shower, wrapped a towel around herself, and padded across the cold floor toward the kitchen. Iced lemon sunlight spilled in through the front windows making the iridescent scales of the mermaid chair sparkle. How had Mariah ended up with that ugly thing? The mermaid reminded Annie of one of Jeff Koons's kitschy, and incredibly expensive, sculptures. His statues of the Pink Panther, Michael Jackson, the stainless steel animals that looked as though they'd been blown from colorful Mylar balloons . . . They'd made him famous. The mermaid could have come right out of Koons's imagination if—

She gasped and raced across the living room toward the boxes she'd left there. What if the mermaid were one of Koons's pieces? Going down on her knees, she dropped her towel as she fumbled through the cartons, looking for the cottage's guest book. Mariah could never have afforded one of Koons's statues, so it would have to have been a gift. She located the guest book and frantically thumbed through the pages, looking for Koons's name. When she couldn't find it, she started all over again.

It wasn't there. But just because he hadn't visited the cottage didn't mean the chair couldn't be one of his creations. She'd researched the paintings, the small sculptural pieces, and most of the books, and she hadn't found anything. Maybe—

"I like it here so much better than Harp House," a silky voice said behind her.

She whirled toward the kitchen doorway. Theo stood there, fingertips in his front pockets, wearing the dark gray parka she'd napped under last night, while the towel she'd been wrapped in lay on the floor.

Despite their crazy sex in this very room, he hadn't seen her naked, but she fought her natural urge to snatch up the towel and clutch it in front of her like a Victorian virgin. Instead she reached for it slowly, as if it were no big deal.

"You are one gorgeous creature," he said. "Did any of those loser boyfriends ever tell you that?"

Not in so many words. Not in any words, really. And it was nice to hear, even if it came from Theo. She tucked in the towel, but—being herself—instead of rising gracefully to her feet, she lost her balance and sprawled back on her heels.

"Fortunately," he said, "I'm practically a doctor, so none of what I'm seeing is unfamiliar."

She maintained a firm grip on both the towel and herself. "You're not practically a doctor, and I hope you enjoyed what you saw because you're not seeing any more."

"Highly doubtful."

"Really? You're really going to go there?"

"It's hard to believe you've forgotten what I did last night."
She cocked her head.

He shook his head sadly. "The heroic way I faced those menacing sharks and hundred-foot waves . . . The icebergs. And did I mention the pirates? But then, I suppose heroism should be its own reward. One shouldn't expect more."

"Nice try. Go make me coffee."

He came toward her lazily, hand outstretched. "Let me help you to your feet first."

"Back off." She got up without another pratfall. "Why are you down here so early?"

"It's not that early, and you shouldn't have come here by yourself."

"Sorry," she said, with all kinds of sincerity.

He gazed from her bare legs to the mess she'd strewn on the floor. "Another break-in?"

She started to tell him about the mermaid chair, but his eyes were back on her legs again, and being the only person wearing a towel put her at a disadvantage. "I'll have poached quail eggs and fresh mango juice. If it's not too much trouble."

"Drop that towel, and I'll throw in champagne."

"Tempting." She made her way toward her bedroom. "But since I might be *pregnant,* I shouldn't drink."

He gave a long sigh. "And with those chilling words, the raging fire in his loins vanished."

WHILE THEO WROTE IN THE studio, Annie photographed the mermaid chair from every angle. As soon as she got to Harp House, she'd e-mail the photos to Koons's Manhattan dealer. If this really was a Koons, selling it would cover her debts and then some.

She zipped her backpack, her thoughts drifting toward the man closed up in the studio.

"You are one gorgeous creature."

Even though it wasn't true, it was nice to hear.

SHE'D GOTTEN IN THE HABIT of checking the fairy house every day, and now a seagull feather swung from a pair of sticks to make a delicate hammock. As Annie took in the new addition, she thought about Livia's "free secret" drawing. The crude blob at the end of the outstretched arm of the standing adult figure hadn't been a mistake at all. It was a gun. And the body on the ground? The red smear on the chest wasn't a flower or a heart. It was blood. Livia had drawn her father's killing.

The back door opened and Lisa stepped out. She spotted Annie and waved, then headed for the muddy SUV parked in front of the garage. Annie braced herself as she went inside.

The kitchen smelled of toast, and Jaycie wore her all-too-frequent anxious expression. "Please don't tell Theo that Lisa came up here. You know how he is."

"Theo's not going to fire you, Jaycie. I guarantee it."

Jaycie turned toward the sink, speaking softly. "I saw him leave for the cottage this morning."

Annie wasn't going to talk about Theo. What could she say? That she might be pregnant with his child? A onetime occurrence.

Do you really believe that? Dilly said, with a *tsk-tsk.*

Our Annie's becoming a bit of a slut. Peter, her former hero, had turned on her.

Now who's the bully? Leo said. *Watch the name-calling, pal.* He spoke with his habitual sneer, but still . . .

She didn't know what was happening in her head. And with Jaycie standing in front of her, now wasn't the time to sort it out. "I heard how your husband died," she said.

Jaycie hobbled over to the table and sank into a chair, not looking at her. "And now you think I'm a horrible person."

"I don't know what to think. I wish you'd told me."

"I don't like to talk about it."

"I get that. But we're friends. If I'd known, I'd have understood from the beginning why Livia is mute."

Jaycie flinched. "I don't know for sure that's why."

"Stop it, Jaycie. I've done some research on mutism."

Jaycie pressed her face into her hands. "You can't imagine what it's like knowing how badly you've hurt the child you love so much."

Annie couldn't endure her unhappiness, and she backed off. "You weren't under any obligation to tell me."

Jaycie gazed up at her. "I'm . . . not good at friendships. There weren't a lot of girls my age when I was growing up. And I didn't want anybody to know how bad things were with my dad, so I shut out everybody who tried to get too close. Even Lisa . . . She's my oldest friend, but we don't talk much about anything personal. Sometimes I think the only reason she comes up here is to check things out for Cynthia."

The idea of Lisa as Cynthia's mole was something Annie hadn't considered.

Jaycie rubbed her leg. "I liked being with Regan because she never asked questions. But she was so much smarter than me, and she lived in a different world."

Annie recalled Jaycie as a background figure that summer, someone she might not have remembered if it hadn't been for what happened in the cave.

"I could have ended up in prison," Jaycie said. "Every night I thank God that Booker Rose heard me screaming and ran to the house in time to see everything through the window." She closed her eyes, then opened them again. "Ned was drunk. He came toward me waving his gun, threatening me. Livia was playing on the floor. She started to cry, but Ned didn't care. He put the gun right to my head. I don't think he would have shot me. He just wanted me to understand who was boss. But I couldn't stand hearing Livia cry, and I grabbed his arm, and . . . It was terrible. He looked so shocked when the gun went off, like he couldn't believe he wasn't in charge anymore."

"Oh, Jaycie . . ."

"I've never known how to talk to Livia about it. Whenever I tried, she struggled to get away, so I stopped trying, hoping she'd forget."

"She needs to talk to a therapist," Annie said gently.

"How am I supposed to manage that? It's not like we have one here on the island, and even if I could get her to the mainland for appointments, I can't afford it." She looked defeated, older than her years. "The only person she's really connected with since it happened is you."

Not me, Annie thought. Livia's attachment was to Scamp.

Jaycie's eyes filled with tears. "I can't believe I've hurt you, too. After everything you've done for me."

Livia raced into the room, her presence putting an end to their conversation.

AFTER ANNIE HAD LEFT FOR Harp House, Theo moved into the living room to write, but the change of scenery hadn't helped. The damned kid wouldn't die.

The boy stared back at him from Annie's drawing. Theo loved the oversize adult watch on the kid's wrist, the cowlick the boy couldn't control, those faint worry lines on his forehead. Annie had dismissed her talent as an artist, and while she might not be a master, she was one hell of an illustrator.

The kid had sucked him in right away, becoming as vivid in his mind as any of the characters he'd created. Without planning it, he'd ended up sticking him in his manuscript as a minor character, a twelve-year-old kid named Diggity Swift who'd been transported from modern-day New York City to the streets of nineteenth-century London. Diggity was supposed to be Dr. Quentin Pierce's next victim, but so far the kid had managed to do what the adults couldn't, elude Quentin's pursuit. Now Quentin was in a psychopathic rage bent on destroying the little urchin in the most painful way.

Theo had decided not to show the boy's death, something he might well have done in *The Sanitarium,* but this time around, he didn't have the stomach for it. A fleeting reference to the smell coming from the baker's oven would be more than enough.

But the kid was cunning. Even though he'd been transported into an environment that couldn't be more foreign—an environment that transcended both time and space—he'd managed to stay alive. And he was doing it without the help of social workers, child endangerment laws, or a single supportive adult, not to mention a cell phone or computer.

At first, Theo couldn't figure out how the kid was pulling

off his miraculous escapes, but then it had come to him. Video games. Playing hours of video games while his wealthy, worka-holic parents were conquering Wall Street had given Diggity quick reflexes, keen deductive skills, and a certain comfort level with the bizarre. Diggity was terrified, but he wasn't giving up.

Theo had never written a kid into a book, and he was damned if he'd ever do it again. He hit the delete key, wiping out two hours of work. This wasn't the kid's story, and Theo had to get back in control before the little prick took over.

He stretched his legs and rubbed his hand over his jaw. Annie had repacked the boxes on the floor, but she hadn't yet put them away. She lived on rainbows. He didn't believe Mariah had left her anything.

But she didn't live on rainbows where he was concerned. He wished she'd either stop taunting him with the possibility she was pregnant or give him some idea of when she'd know for sure. Kenley had never wanted kids, which had turned out to be one of the few things they'd had in common. Just the idea of ever again being responsible for another human being made him break out in a cold sweat. He'd as soon put a gun to his head.

He'd barely thought about Kenley since the night he'd told Annie about her, and he didn't like that. Annie wanted to give him a free pass for Kenley's death, but that only said something about Annie and nothing about him. He needed his guilt. It was the only way he could live with himself.

Chapter Fifteen

On Monday morning, Annie stumbled out of bed while it was still dark so she could get ready to go out on Naomi's boat, but she hadn't taken three steps across the room before she jolted wide-awake. *Go out on Naomi's boat?* She groaned and buried her face in her hands. What had she been thinking? She hadn't been thinking! That was the problem. She couldn't go out on the water with Naomi. What part of her brain had failed to register that? Once the *Ladyslipper* left the harbor, Annie would be officially off the island. But because the boat was anchored at Peregrine, departing and returning every day—because Naomi was part of the island—because Annie had been distracted—she'd somehow failed to make the connection. She must be pregnant. How else to account for such a monumental lapse?

If you didn't spend so much time mooning over Theo Harp, Crumpet said, *you'd have your brain back.*

Even Crumpet wasn't this dim-witted. Annie was supposed to meet Naomi at the dock, and she couldn't not show up without an explanation. She threw on some clothes and drove into town in the Suburban, which Jaycie had let her borrow.

The road was pitted with frozen February mud after Saturday night's storm, and she drove carefully, still shaken by how scatterbrained she'd been. For twenty-two days, she'd been trapped on an island that existed because of the sea, but she couldn't venture out into that sea. She could never make such a basic mistake again.

The sky had just begun to lighten when she found Naomi at the boathouse dock throwing some gear into the skiff that would take her to the *Ladyslipper,* which was anchored in the harbor. "There you are!" Naomi called out with a cheerful wave. "I was afraid you'd changed your mind."

Before Annie could explain, Naomi launched into the day's weather forecast. Finally, Annie had to interrupt. "Naomi, I can't go with you."

Just then a speeding car skidded into a parking space next to the boathouse, sending gravel flying. The door flew open and Theo jumped out. "Annie! Stay where you are!"

Both of them turned to watch as he charged toward them along the dock. His rumpled hair stood up in the back, and he had a pillow crease across his cheek. "Sorry, Naomi," he said as he came to a stop next to the boat captain. "Annie can't leave the island."

Another mistake. Annie had forgotten to tear up the quick note she'd left for Theo last night, and now here he was.

Naomi splayed a hand on her ample hip, showing the steel that had made her a successful lobsterman. "Why the hell not?"

As Annie began to plead an upset stomach, she struggled to come up with an explanation, Theo's hand clamped her shoulder. "Annie's under house arrest."

Naomi's other hand found her opposite hip. "What are you talking about?"

"She got into some trouble before she came here," he said. "Nothing big. Doing puppet shows without a license. New York has strict laws about that kind of thing. Unfortunately for her, it was a repeat offense."

Annie glared at him, but he was on a roll. "Instead of going to jail, the judge gave her the option of leaving the city for a couple of months. He agreed to her coming here, but only under the condition that she not leave the island. Sort of like a house arrest. Something she obviously forgot."

His explanation both fascinated and appalled her. She drew away from his hand on her shoulder. "What's it to you?"

The hand returned. "Now, Annie. You know the court made me your guardian. I'm going to overlook this little breach, but only if you swear it won't happen again."

"You city people are crazy," Naomi grumbled.

"Especially New Yorkers," Theo agreed solemnly. "Come on, Annie. Let's get you away from temptation."

Naomi wasn't having it. "Ease up, Theo. It's just a day on my boat. Nobody will be any the wiser."

"Sorry, Naomi, but I take my duty to the court seriously."

Annie fought between the desire to laugh and the urge to shove him in the harbor.

"That kind of stuff doesn't count for shit here," Naomi argued.

She was genuinely angry, but Theo didn't budge. "Right is right." He implanted his fingers in Annie's shoulder. "I'm going to overlook this little incident, but don't let it happen again." He led her off the dock.

The moment they were out of earshot, Annie looked up at him. "Doing puppet shows without a license?"

"Do you really want everybody to know your business?"

"No. Just like I don't want them to think I'm a convicted felon."

"Don't exaggerate. The puppet show thing is only a misdemeanor."

She threw up her hands. "You couldn't have come up with something better? Like an urgent phone call from my agent?"

"Do you have an agent?"

"Not any longer. But Naomi doesn't know that."

"Apologies," he said with a nineteenth-century drawl. "I just woke up, and I was under pressure." And then he went on the attack. "You were really going to climb blissfully into that boat and sail away? Honest to God, Annie, you need a keeper."

"I wasn't going on the boat. I was telling her I couldn't go when the cavalry rode up."

"Then why did you accept in the first place?"

"I've got a lot on my mind, okay?"

"Tell me about it." He steered her across the parking lot toward the town hall. "I need coffee."

A few local fishermen were still lingering around the community pot inside the door. Theo nodded at them while he filled two Styrofoam cups with something that looked like engine sludge and snapped on the lids.

Once they were outside again, they headed toward their cars. His was crookedly parked a couple of yards from hers. As he took a sip of his coffee, the curl of steam pulled her attention to the sharply defined borders of his lips. Between those perfect lips, his rumpled hair, beard stubble, and slightly red nose from the cold, he looked like a scruffy Ralph Lauren ad. "Are you in a hurry to get back?" he asked.

"Not particularly." Not until she understood why he hadn't shoved her on that boat and happily waved good-bye.

"Then get in. I have something to show you."

"Does it involve a torture chamber or an unmarked grave?"

He shot her a disgusted look.

She gave him her newly patented smirk-smile.

He rolled his eyes and opened the passenger door.

Instead of driving back toward the house, he drove in the opposite direction. The dilapidated yellow schoolhouse trailer clung to the hill next to the ruins of the old building. They passed a closed art gallery and a pair of shuttered eateries advertising lobster rolls and steamed clams. The fish house sat next to Christmas Beach, where the fishermen hauled out their boats for maintenance.

The bumpy road made drinking a hot beverage, even with a lid, difficult, and Annie sipped carefully at the bitter coffee. "What Peregrine needs is a good Starbucks."

"And a deli." He slipped on a pair of aviators. "I'd sell my soul for a decent bagel."

"You mean you still have one?"

"Are you done yet?"

"Sorry. My tongue keeps getting away from me." She squinted against the bright winter sun. "One question, Theo . . ."

"Later." He turned onto a badly rutted lane that quickly grew impassable. He parked in a grove of spruces. "We have to walk from here."

Only a few weeks ago, even a short walk had been daunting, but she couldn't remember her last coughing fit. The island had given her back her health. At least until the next time somebody shot at her.

Theo shortened his long-legged gait and held her elbow as they walked across the frozen ground. She didn't need the support, but she liked the simple courtesy of his Old World manners. Twin ruts marked what was left of a lane that cut through a pine thicket. From there the lane sloped slightly downward past a felled tree, curved around a slight bend, and then opened into what, in summer, would be a glorious meadow. At the center sat an abandoned stone farmhouse with a slate roof and a pair of chimneys. A patch of what might be blueberries grew against an old stone icehouse. The ocean lay in the distance—close enough for a breathtaking view, but too far to inflict the worst of its fury. Even on a cold winter day, the secluded, sheltered meadow felt enchanted.

She released a long, slow breath. "This is a fantasy of what a Maine island should be."

"A lot cozier than Harp House."

"A crypt is cozier than Harp House."

"I'm not arguing with you about that. This is the island's oldest working farm. Or at least it was. They kept sheep here, grew some grain and vegetables. It's been abandoned since the early 1980s."

She observed the solid roof and unbroken windows. "Somebody's still taking care of it."

He took a slow sip of coffee, saying nothing.

She tilted her head toward him, but his eyes were hidden behind the lenses of his sunglasses. "You," she said. "You're the one who's been taking care of it."

He shrugged, as if it were no big deal. "I bought the place. Got it for a song."

She wasn't fooled by his dismissive tone. He might hate Harp House, but he loved this place.

He continued to gaze across the meadow and out at the ocean. "There's no heat, no electricity. A well, but no functioning plumbing. It's not worth much."

But it was to him. The meadow's shady spots held a few still-pristine patches of snow. She gazed past them toward the water, where the morning sun decked the waves' crests with silver tinsel. "Why didn't you want me to get on Naomi's boat? Once I cleared the harbor, the cottage would have been yours."

"The cottage would have been my father's."

"So?"

"Can you imagine what Cynthia would do with it? Turn it into a peasant's hovel or tear it down to build an English village. Who the hell knows what she'd come up with?"

Another piece of what she'd thought she knew about him broke away. He wanted her to keep the cottage. She had to shake the cobwebs from her brain. "You know it's only a matter of time before I lose the cottage. Once I find a steady job, I won't be able to come here for two months every year."

"We'll cross that bridge when we get to it."

We. Not just her.

"Come on," he said. "I'll show you the place."

She followed him toward the farmhouse. She'd grown so used to the sound of the surf that the meadow's birdcalls and deeper silences seemed enchanted. As they approached the front door, she knelt to examine a cluster of snowdrops. Their tiny, bell-shaped petals dipped in apology for showing off their beauty when so much winter remained. She touched one of the snowy blooms. "There's still hope in the world."

"Is there?"

"There has to be. Otherwise, what's the point?"

His harsh bark of laughter held no merriment. "You remind me of this kid I know. He can't win, but he keeps fighting."

She tilted her head quizzically. "Are you talking about yourself?"

He seemed startled. "Me? No. The kid is— Forget it. Writers tend to blur the line between reality and fiction."

Ventriloquists, too, she thought.

I have no idea what you're talking about, Scamp sniffed.

Theo located the key he wanted and slipped it into the lock, which turned easily.

"I thought nobody on the island locked their doors," she said.

"You can take the boy out of the city . . ."

She followed him into an empty room with worn, wide-plank wooden floors and a big stone fireplace. A chorus of dust motes, disturbed by the air currents, danced in front of a sunny window. The room smelled of woodsmoke and age, but not neglect. There were no piles of trash, no holes in the walls, which were papered in a faded, old-fashioned floral design that curled at the seams.

She unzipped her coat. He stood in the center of the room, his hands in the pockets of his gray parka, almost as if he were embarrassed for her to see this. She moved past him into the kitchen. The appliances were gone, with only a stone sink left and some dented hanging metal cupboards. An old fireplace occupied the end wall. It had been swept, and fresh wood lay in the grate. *I love this place,* she thought. The house was of the island but set apart from its conflicts.

She pulled off her hat and stuffed it in her pocket. A window above the sink looked out across a clearing that must have once held a garden. She imagined it in bloom—hollyhocks and gladiolas coexisting with snap peas, cabbage, and beets, all of it flourishing.

THEO CAME INTO THE KITCHEN behind Annie and watched her gazing through the window, her open coat falling slightly off one shoulder. She hadn't bothered with makeup, and standing in this kitchen from the past, she could have been a farm woman from the 1930s. Her bold eyes and abundance of unruly hair didn't conform to contemporary standards of manufactured beauty. She was a creature unto herself.

He could imagine the makeover Kenley and her fashion-forward friends would have ordered up if they'd had the chance. Chemically straightening Annie's hair, fillers to plump her lips to porn star proportions, breast implants, and a little liposuction, although he couldn't imagine where. But the only thing wrong with the way Annie looked was . . .

Absolutely nothing.

"You belong here." As soon as the words were out, he wanted to snatch them back. He manufactured something approaching a drawl. "All ready to plow the fields, slop the hogs, and paint the outhouse."

"Gee, thanks." She should have been insulted. Instead she gazed at her surroundings and smiled. "I like your house."

"It's okay, I guess."

"More than okay. You know exactly how special it is. Why do you always have to act like such a tough-ass?"

"No acting necessary."

She thought it over. "I guess you are. But in all the wrong ways."

"In your opinion." He didn't like her insights into his weak spots, her bleeding heart opinion about his relationship with Kenley, her willingness to set aside everything that had happened during that summer all those years ago. It made him afraid for her.

A beam of sunlight skipped across the tips of her eyelashes, and he felt a primitive urge to dominate her. Prove to himself that he was still in control. He wandered toward her, taking his time, gazing into her eyes.

"Stop it," she said.

He lifted a curl that lay by her ear and ran it through his fingers. "Stop what?"

She shoved his hand away. "Stop going all bloody Heathcliff on me."

"If I had any idea what you were talking about . . ."

"The saunter. The hooded eyes, the whole broody-arrogant thing."

"I've never sauntered in my life." Despite her protests, she hadn't moved an inch. He brushed her cheek with his thumb . . .

HE WAS CASTING HIS DEVIL'S spell over her. Or maybe it was the farmhouse. Whatever the cause, she couldn't seem to move away from him, even though there was something disquieting in his gaze. Something she didn't entirely like.

All she had to do was turn her back. She didn't. Nor did she stop him as he pushed her coat from her shoulders, then shrugged off his own. They landed in the puddle of winter sunshine spilling through the window.

As they stood there, arms at their sides, gazes locked, she grew aware of every inch of her skin. Her sensitivity was so sharp that she could feel the hum of her veins and arteries. Of his. She wasn't made for mindless sex. She wasn't designed to take what a man had to offer and forget about him afterward. In these womanpower times, that lack of detachment was a weakness. A defect. One more giant thing wrong with her.

He touched her cheek.

Don't touch me like that. Don't touch me anywhere. Touch me everywhere.

He did. With a kiss that seemed almost angry. Because she wasn't someone as beautiful as he? As privileged? As successful?

His tongue invaded, and she gripped his arms. Parted her lips. Gave herself up to the seductive power of the kiss. He pressed against her. He was taller, and they shouldn't have fit together so well, but their bodies meshed perfectly.

His hands slipped under her sweater, splayed over her back. His thumbs marked a path along her spine. He'd taken charge, and she needed to stop it. To step up and assert herself the way today's woman should. Use him, instead of the other way around. But it felt so good to be desired.

"I want to see you," he murmured against her lips. "Your body. Golden in the sunlight."

His writer's words poured over her like poetry, and she couldn't find a single wisecrack to put up between them. She even lifted her arms as he tugged her sweater over her head. He unhooked her bra. It fell to the floor. He pulled off his own sweater, never taking his eyes from her breasts. The sunlight bathed her body, and although the farmhouse was cold, she was warm. Hot.

She wanted more of his poetry. More of him. She bent

down and took off her shoes. As she slipped off her socks, his fingertips glided over the bumps of her curved spine. "Like a strand of pearls," he whispered.

Her skin pebbled. Men didn't talk like this during sex. They barely talked at all. When they did, it tended to be coarse, unimaginative, and libido-dulling.

She kept her eyes locked with his as she slid down the zipper of her jeans. With the shadow of a smile, he went to his knees. Kissed the skin of her belly just above the waistband of her underpants. She slipped her hands into his hair. Felt his scalp under the pads of her fingers. Gripped the strands. Not pulling it but experiencing its texture, its feel.

He took his time, finding her hip bones and her navel, the stubble on his jaw lightly abrading her skin. Through the thin nylon fabric, his fingers traced the crack between her buttocks. She braced her hands on his shoulders as he grew impatient, tugging on her underpants, her jeans, shoving both to her ankles, then inhaling and nuzzling all that was exposed.

He wanted more, and he tried to push her knees apart. They yearned to open, but her jeans still manacled her ankles, something he quickly took care of.

She gripped his shoulders tighter as he clasped the backs of her thighs, opened them as he wished, and delved deeper.

She arched her neck. Tried to find the oxygen she needed. Her knees threatened to give out. And did.

She fell back onto their coats, her legs awkwardly splayed. He stepped between them and gazed down at all she'd revealed. "A ruffled rose garden. Full bloom."

He was killing her with his dirty poetry. She wanted to kill him back. Conquer. But it felt so good to receive.

He loomed over her; pulling off the rest of his clothes; standing between her knees; large, naked. Daring her?

Oh, yes . . .

He went to his knees. Braced her ankles on his shoulders. Parted her with his thumbs. Found her with his mouth.

Her eyes drifted closed. Neck arched.

Oh, he was thorough. So thorough. Stopping. Beginning again. Touching with fingers. Touching with lips. Tongue.

Breath cooling, then heating. She traveled the rise. Journeyed higher. Higher still. Reaching . . . Suspending . . . Seize up . . .

And the long, blissful burn.

He didn't let her close her legs. "You're not done. Quiet. Shhh . . . Don't fight me."

He owned her body.

How many times? The rise, the throb, the burn . . . He was seeing her at her most vulnerable, her most defenseless. And she was allowing it.

Only when she could handle no more did she struggle. He gave her room, then began to lower his own body over hers, all his focus on claiming what was so clearly his. On top. Still dominant. In control of his own satisfaction.

They weren't real lovers, and she couldn't permit it. She twisted from beneath him before he could pin her to the floor. Now he was the one on top of the pile of coats. He rolled to his side and reached out to gather her beneath him once again. But in the release he'd given her, she possessed an energy he didn't have. She splayed her hands on his chest and pushed him hard, sending him to his back where she could practice her own magic.

She studied the musculature of his chest, the hard plane of his abdomen. And below. She bent over him. Her hair brushed his skin. He lifted his hands and crumpled the curly strands in his fists, not pulling it. Almost . . . savoring it.

She did to him as he'd done to her. Playing. Stopping. Playing again, her skin pale against his darker complexion. Sunlight and dust, the smell of sex, of her and him. He pressed the back of her head, but she resisted, refusing to let him fly. She was the most practiced courtesan on earth. Able to give satisfaction. Or to withhold it.

He'd long ago closed his eyes. He arched his back. His features contorted. At her mercy.

Finally, she gave him the release he sought.

THAT WASN'T THE END OF IT. A coat zipper soon dug into her back, and she was on the bottom. Then on top. Then on the bottom again. At some point he abandoned her long enough to light the fire. He hadn't been kidding about the condoms. He had them with him, and he seemed to want to use them all.

As the old farmhouse creaked around them, they explored each other more slowly. He seemed to love her idiotic hair, and she rubbed his body with it. She adored his lips. He called her a "beautiful creature" again, and she wanted to cry.

The sun was high in the sky before they were sated. "Consider this makeup sex," he murmured in her ear.

It broke the spell that had captured her. She lifted her head from his shoulder. "Making up for what? We haven't been fighting. For a change."

He rolled to his side and slipped his finger in a curl by her cheek. "I'm making up for all that clumsy fumbling around I did when I was sixteen. It's a miracle you weren't turned off sex forever."

"Obviously not." A blade of light cut across his face, highlighting the scar at the corner of his eyebrow. She touched it and said, more harshly than she'd intended, "I'm not sorry about this."

"No reason you should be." He dropped her curl and rose from the floor. "You didn't do it."

She propped herself up. A red mark from the coats—or her fingernails—crossed his back. "I did," she said. "I hit you across the face with your riding crop."

He pulled on his jeans. "You didn't give me that scar. It was a surfing accident. Stupid on my part."

Now she was on her feet. "That's not true. I gave it to you."

He tugged on his zipper. "It's my face. Don't you think I should know?"

He was lying. She'd grabbed the riding crop and swung it at him in a blistering rage, punishing him for the pups, for what he'd done to her, for the cave and the note he'd written and her broken heart.

"Why are you saying this?" She snatched up her coat and pulled it on over her nakedness. "I know what happened."

"You hit me. I remember that. But you got me somewhere around here." He pointed toward a tiny white dash below the larger scar.

Why was he lying? Being in this enchanted cottage had made her drop her guard. A mistake and a sharp reminder that sex wasn't the same as either trust or intimacy. She reached for her clothes. "Let's get out of here."

IT WAS A SILENT TRIP back to town. Theo pulled into the harbor parking lot so Annie could get the Suburban, and as he stopped, a middle-aged woman with a baseball cap pulled over her fried blond hair ran up to the driver's door. She started to talk even before Theo had rolled his window down all the way.

"I just came from my father's place. Les Childers. You remember him? He owns the *Lucky Charm*. He's got a bad cut on his hand. It's been bleeding like crazy, and it's deep. It's going to need stitches."

Theo rested his elbow on the window frame. "I'll look at it, Jessie, but EMTs aren't licensed for that. Until I finish my paramedic's training, all I can do is bandage him up. He'll have to go to the mainland."

Theo was training as a paramedic? One more thing he hadn't mentioned.

Jessie leaned back on her heels, ready to do battle. "This is Peregrine, Theo. You think anybody here gives a rat's ass about what kind of license you have? You know how it works."

So did Annie. Islanders took care of their own, and in their eyes, Theo's medical training was something they expected him to use.

Jessie wasn't done. "I'd also appreciate your stopping in to see my sister. She has to give her dog injections for diabetes, but she's afraid to use the needle, and she needs help getting started. I wish we'd known you had medical training last month when Jack Brownie had his heart attack."

Whether he wanted to or not, Theo had been sucked into island life. "I'll look in on both of them," he said reluctantly.

"Follow my truck." Jessie gave Annie a brusque nod and headed toward the rusty skeleton of a once-red pickup.

Annie opened the Range Rover's door. "Congratulations, Theo. It looks like you're the new island doctor. And the vet."

He pulled off his sunglasses with one hand and rubbed the bridge of his nose with the other. "I'm in way over my head."

"Looks like it," she said. "You might want to brush up on deworming dogs. And birthing cows."

"There aren't any cows on Peregrine."

"Not now there aren't." She stepped out of the car. "But wait till everybody hears there's a new vet."

Chapter Sixteen

SOMETHING WAS VERY WRONG. THE cottage's front door hung open, and Hannibal crouched on the stoop not far from the old wooden lobster traps left partially exposed by the melting snow. Annie shot out of the Suburban and stomped across the yard to the open door. She was too angry to be cautious. She wanted someone to be inside so she could tear them apart.

Paintings hung crookedly on the walls and books were strewn on the floor. Most chilling, the intruder had scrawled a message across the wall in bright red paint.

I'm coming for u

"Like hell you are!" Annie stormed through the cottage. The kitchen and studio looked the same as when she'd last been here. Her puppets were unharmed, Theo's things untouched, but the drawers had been pulled out of her bedroom dresser, their contents flung on the floor.

The violation of her privacy infuriated her, the outrage of knowing someone felt free to break in whenever they wanted, to go through her things, to paint a cheesy message on her wall. It was too much. Either someone in the Harp family wanted to scare her away, or one of the islanders knew about Mariah's legacy and wanted Annie out of here so they could tear the place apart until they found what they wanted.

Although Elliott had bad taste in wives, she'd never regarded him as unethical. But Cynthia Harp was more problematic. She had money, motive, and local connections. Just because she was living in the South of France didn't mean she couldn't be orchestrating all this. But would she really go to so much trouble for a tiny cottage when she already had Harp House at her disposal? As for Mariah's legacy . . . With Annie out of the cottage, the intruder could spend as much time as he or she wanted searching for it with no worries of Annie walking in on them.

But Annie had had all the time in the world, and she still hadn't found what she was looking for. Still, she hadn't pried up floorboards or poked holes in walls, and maybe that was what the intruder wanted time to do. Whoever was behind this couldn't have found out about the legacy until after Annie had arrived, or they'd have already searched for it. As Hannibal hid under her bed, she skirted the sheets that had been torn from her mattress and marched back into the living room.

I'm coming for u

The red paint was still tacky. Someone wanted to frighten her, and if she wasn't so furious, it might have worked.

There was another possibility, one she was reluctant to consider but could no longer avoid, not as long as she kept hearing the sound of that bullet whizzing past her head. What if this wasn't about the legacy at all? What if someone simply hated her?

SHE FOUND A CAN OF leftover paint in the storage closet and painted over the hateful message, then headed for Harp House in the Suburban. She almost missed walking. Three weeks ago, the climb to the house had been like ascending Mount Everest, but her coughing had finally disappeared, and the exertion had started to feel good.

As Annie got out, Livia dashed outside in her socks and ran toward her, a big smile on her face. "Livia! You don't have your shoes on!" Jaycie called after her. "Come back here, you dickens."

Annie brushed Livia's cheek with her fingertips and followed her inside. Jaycie moved awkwardly toward the sink. "Lisa called. She saw you and Theo driving through town this morning."

Annie dodged Jaycie's implied question. "A woman stopped him and asked him to check on her father. Jessie somebody. Apparently the news has spread that Theo's an EMT."

Jaycie turned on the water in the sink and gave Livia a drink. "Jessie Childers. We haven't had medical help on the island since Jenny Schaeffer moved."

"That's what I heard."

Annie went off to Elliott's office to check her e-mail. She received an invitation to an old roommate's baby shower, a message from another friend, and a one-line response from Jeff Koons's dealer.

This is not his piece.

She wanted to cry. She'd told herself not to get her hopes up, but she had been certain the mermaid chair was a Koons. Instead, she'd hit another dead end.

A thud came from the kitchen, and she made herself get up to investigate. She found Jaycie trying to right one of the straight-backed chairs. "No more running, Livie. You're going to break something."

Livia kicked the corner of the chair with her sneaker. Jaycie leaned against the table with a defeated sigh. "It's not her fault. She has no place to work off her energy."

"I'll take her out," Annie said. "How 'bout it, Liv? Want to go for a walk?"

Livia nodded so vigorously that her lavender plastic headband slipped over her eyes.

Annie decided to take her down to the beach. The sun had emerged and the tide was out. Livia was an island kid. She needed to be near the water.

Annie held tightly to her hand as they descended the stone steps. Livia tried to pull away, anxious to get to the bottom, but Annie held on to her. As they cleared the last step, however, Livia stalled, taking it all in, almost as if she couldn't believe she had so much space to run free.

Annie pointed down the beach. "See if you can catch those gulls."

Livia didn't need encouragement. She started to run, her short legs churning, hair flying from beneath her pink pompom hat. She darted through the rocks toward the sand, but stayed away from the breaking waves.

Annie found a flat-top boulder far from the old cave entrance. Dropping her backpack, she watched Livia climb rocks, chase the shorebirds, and dig in the sand. When the four-year-old finally got tired, she came to sit next to Annie and her backpack. Annie smiled, removed Scamp, and slipped the puppet onto her arm.

Scamp wasted no time. "Free secret?"

Livia nodded.

"I'm scared." And then, more dramatically, "Terrified."

Livia's forehead knit.

"The ocean is so big," Scamp whispered, "and I can't swim. That's scary."

Livia shook her head.

"You don't think the water is scary?" Scamp said.

Livia didn't.

"I s'pose different things are scary to different people." Scamp tapped her cheek. "Like some things are good to be scared of—going in the ocean if there aren't any grown-ups around. And some things aren't good to be scared of because they're not real, like monsters."

Livia seemed to agree.

As Annie had watched Livia play, she'd thought over what she now knew about Livia's trauma. She wasn't sure whether this was a good idea or not, but she was going to try. "Like watching your dad try to hurt your mom," Scamp said. "That was really, really scary."

Livia poked her finger into a tiny hole in her jeans.

Annie wasn't a child psychologist, and the only thing she knew about treating childhood trauma was what she'd picked up on the Internet. This situation was too complicated, and she needed to stop right here. But . . .

Jaycie couldn't talk to Livia about what had happened. Maybe Scamp could make the topic less forbidden. "A lot scarier than the ocean," Scamp said. "If I saw my mommy have to shoot my dad with a gun, I would be so scared I might not want to talk either."

Eyes wide, Livia abandoned the hole in her jeans and turned all her attention to the puppet.

Annie backed off and let Scamp speak in her most cheerful voice. "But then, after a while, I'd get bored not talking. Especially if I had something important to say. Or if I wanted to sing. Did I ever tell you that I'm a magnificent singer?"

Livia nodded vigorously.

A wild idea occurred to Annie. An idea she had no business pursuing. But, what if . . .

Scamp began to sing, bobbing her curly yarn hair to the rhythm of the makeshift tune Annie improvised on the spot.

"A scary, scary thing happened to me.
A thing I want to forget.
Times are good and times are bad,
And that was the baddest yet!
Oh . . . That was the baddest yet!"

Livia remained attentive, not seeming upset, so Annie plunged on with her ridiculous, improvised lyrics.

"Some daddies are good and some are bad
You're stuck with what you get.
Liv's dad was bad, the very, very worst
But . . . she didn't want to see him die, oh!
She didn't want to see him die."

Ohmygod! The reality of what she'd just done sent her stomach plummeting. It was like a bad *Saturday Night Live* skit! The happy little tune, the gruesome lyrics . . . She'd just treated Livia's trauma as if it were a stand-up comedy routine.

Livia seemed to be waiting to hear more, but Annie was appalled, and she lost her courage. However good her intentions might be, she could be doing serious psychological damage to this precious little girl. Scamp hung her head. "I guess I shouldn't sing a song about something so terrible."

Livia studied her, then climbed down off the rock and scurried away to chase a seagull.

Theo found her at the cottage just as she finished giving Hannibal his evening meal. "You're not supposed to be here by yourself." He sounded crankier than usual. "Why do I smell wet paint?"

"A little touch-up." She spoke coolly, determined to re-establish the distance between them. "How did the wound repair go?"

"Not well. Stitching someone up without numbing them first isn't my idea of a good time."

"Don't tell your readers. They'll be disappointed in you."

He scowled. "If I'm not here, you need to stay at Harp House."

Good advice, except that she was experiencing an increasingly powerful urge to be here the next time her perpetrator showed up. This cat-and-mouse game had gone on long enough. She wanted a showdown.

"I refuse to raise a timid child, Antoinette."

How many of Mariah's judgments had Annie believed about herself?

"You're naturally shy . . ." "You're naturally clumsy . . ." "You need to stop being such a daydreamer . . ."

And then, "Of course I love you, Antoinette. I wouldn't be concerned about you if I didn't."

Living on this bleak winter island so far removed from her city life was making Annie think about herself in new ways. In ways—

"What the *hell*?"

She turned to see Theo examining the wall she'd painted earlier. She grimaced. "I need to put on a second coat."

He jabbed his finger at the faint red letters bleeding through the white paint. "Are you trying to be funny? This is not funny!"

"Make up your mind. I can either be funny or scream. Take your pick." She didn't feel like screaming. She'd rather punch someone.

He uttered a blistering obscenity, then asked her exactly what she'd found. When she finished, he made his proclamation. "That's it. You're moving up to Harp House. And I'm going over to the mainland to talk to the police."

"A waste of time. Even when somebody shot at me, they weren't interested. They'll be even less interested in this."

He pulled out his phone only to remember he couldn't get a signal. "Pack up. You're getting out of here."

"As much as I appreciate your concern, I'm staying right here. And I want a gun."

"A gun?"

"Only as a loan."

"You want me to lend you a gun?"

"And show me how to use it."

"That is not a good idea."

"You'd rather I face whoever is doing this unarmed?"

"I'd rather you didn't face *whoever* at all."

"I'm not running."

"Damn it, Annie. You're as reckless now as you were at fifteen."

She stared at him. She'd never thought of herself as reckless, and she liked the image. She considered it in light of her habit of falling in love with the wrong men, her belief that she could be a great actress, her determination to take Mariah to London for one last trip. And—not to forget—letting Theo Harp possibly get her pregnant.

Mariah, you didn't know me at all.

He looked frazzled, and the novelty of it made her dig in. "I want a gun, Theo. And I want to learn how to shoot it."

"It's too dangerous. You'll be safe at the house."

"I don't want to stay at Hell House. I want to stay here."

He gazed at her long and hard, then thrust his finger in her face. "All right. Target practice tomorrow afternoon. But you'd better pay attention to every word I say." He stalked away to the studio.

Annie made herself a sandwich for dinner and went back to sorting through the boxes, but it had been a long day, and she was tired. As she brushed her teeth, she gazed at the closed studio door. Despite everything she'd been telling herself about keeping her distance, she wanted him lying next to her. She wanted him so much that she grabbed a pad of Post-it notes from the kitchen, scrawled on the top one, and stuck it to her bedroom door. Then she closed herself in and went to sleep.

DIGGITY SWIFT WAS DEAD. THEO had done it. The kid had finally slipped up, Dr. Quentin Pierce had caught him, and Theo hadn't written a word since.

He closed his laptop and rubbed his eyes. His brain was fried, that was all. Tomorrow he'd be able to start with a clear head. By then, the tightness in his chest would have disappeared, and he'd be able to make headway. The middle of any book was the hardest to write, but with Diggity gone, he'd be able to see his way clear of the muddle he'd created and find a pathway to the next chapters. As long as he didn't start thinking about Annie and what had happened at his farmhouse today . . .

He wouldn't wake her tonight when he got in bed next to her. He wasn't some kind of animal with no self-control, even though that was how he felt. The novelty of making love with a woman he hadn't grown to detest fascinated him. A woman who didn't fall into a crying jag afterward. Or attack him for some imaginary offense.

Because Annie was so different from the women in his past, he wondered whether he would have noticed her if he'd passed her on the street? Damn right, he would have. The uniqueness of that quirky face would have caught his attention, the way she walked, as if she intended to conquer the ground under her. He liked her height, the funny way she had of looking at people as if she really saw them. He liked her legs——he definitely liked her legs. Annie was an original. And he needed to do a better job of protecting her.

He'd talked to Jessie and her father today, trying to get a feel for how people regarded Annie, but he hadn't learned anything that raised his suspicions. They were curious about why she'd come to the island, but they were more interested in sharing their stories about Mariah. After the boats got in tomorrow, he intended to hang out at the fish house. He'd take the men some beer, see what he could pick up. He'd also make sure they knew Annie would be armed, a disturbing prospect, but necessary.

He'd come to the island because he couldn't tolerate being around people, yet here he was, involved with everything. It had been over an hour since he'd heard her go to her room. She'd be wearing those awful pajamas. Or maybe not.

His good intentions vanished. He set aside his laptop and left the studio. But as he saw the Post-it note on her door, he stopped cold. It had one word.

No.

THEO DIDN'T MENTION THE NOTE to her the next morning. He didn't say much of anything except that he needed his car that day. Only later did she discover he'd driven to the dock to pick up the locksmith. Knowing she didn't have the money to pay the bill made her feel ashamed.

He was in the studio when she returned to the cottage. She took the box of wine from her closet and carried it out to his car.

He opened the kitchen door for her as she came back in. "What did you put in my car?"

"Some excellent wine. You're welcome. And thanks for taking care of the locks."

He saw right through her. "I had the locks changed for myself. I can't chance having my laptop stolen while I'm out."

He was trying to let her save face, which only made her more indebted. "Uh-huh."

"Annie, I don't want your wine. This isn't a big deal to me."

"It's a big deal to me."

"All right. How's this? No more Post-it notes on your door, and we'll call it even."

"Enjoy your wine." She couldn't think straight with him standing in front of her, oozing all those male pheromones, not after what had happened at the farmhouse. "Did you bring a gun?"

He didn't press. "I've got it. Grab your coat."

They went out on the marsh. After he'd gone through the basic rules of gun safety, he showed her how to load and fire the automatic pistol he'd chosen for her. The gun should have repelled Annie, but she liked shooting it. What she didn't like was the unexpected eroticism of having Theo so close. They were barely inside the cottage before they were tearing off each other's clothes.

"I don't want to talk about it," she snarled at him later that night as they lay in her bed.

He yawned. "Fine by me. More than fine."

"You can't sleep here. You have to sleep in your own bed."

He tried to settle her against his naked body. "I don't want to sleep in my own bed."

She didn't want him to, either, but however murky some things might be, this was clear. "I want sex, not intimacy."

He curled his hand around her rear. "Sex it is."

She wiggled away. "You have two options. You can either sleep by yourself, or you can lie here for the next three hours and listen to the details of every crappy relationship I've ever had, why they were crappy, and why men suck. Warning. I cry ugly."

He threw back the cover. "I'll see you in the morning."

"I thought so."

ANNIE HAD GOTTEN WHAT SHE wanted from Theo—the best sex of her life—but she'd also set boundaries.

Very sensible, Dilly said. *You've finally learned your lesson.*

The next afternoon, Annie took Livia outside again. It was too windy for the beach, so they hung out on the front porch steps. Annie needed to know if she'd done any damage yesterday, and she propped Scamp on her knee. The puppet got straight to the point. "Are you mad at me for talking your daddy when we went down to the beach?"

Livia pursed her lips, thinking it over, then slowly shook her head.

"Good," Scamp said, "because I was worried you'd be mad."

Livia shook her head again, then climbed up on the stone balustrade that had replaced the wooden spindles. She straddled the balustrade, her back to Annie.

Should she drop the subject or keep it on the table? She needed to do more research on mutism and childhood trauma. In the meantime, she would trust her instincts.

"I would hate it if I had a daddy that did bad things to my mommy," Scamp said. "Especially if I couldn't talk about it."

Livia began riding the balustrade horse.

"Or sing about it. I believe I've mentioned that I'm an accomplished vocalist." Scamp began singing a series of scales. It had taken Annie endless years of practice to sing well in the vocal registers of all her puppets, something that set her apart from most vents. Scamp finally stopped. "If you ever want me to sing another song about what happened, let me know."

Livia quit riding her horse and turned around. She stared at Annie, then at Scamp.

"Yes or no?" Scamp chirped. "I shall abide by your wise decision."

Livia dropped her head and picked at some residual pink nail polish on her thumbnail. A definite no. What had Annie expected? Did she really think her clumsy interference could unlock such a deep trauma?

Livia shifted her position on the balustrade so she was facing Annie. She slowly moved her head. A hesitant nod.

Annie felt as if her heart skipped a beat. "Very well," Scamp said. "I shall call my song 'The Ballad of Livia's Terrible Experience.'" Annie stalled for time with some dramatic throat clearing. The best she could hope to do was drag the topic out of the darkness into the light. Maybe that would make it less taboo. She also needed to tell Jaycie about this. She began to sing softly.

> *"Little girls shouldn't see bad things*
> *But sometimes they do . . ."*

She continued her song, making it up as she'd done yesterday, but this time keeping the tune more serious and avoiding any *Olés*. Livia listened to every word, then nodded at the end and went back to riding her balustrade horse.

Annie heard a noise behind her and turned.

Theo leaned against the corner of the house at the far end of the porch. Even from where she was, she could see the frown etched between his eyebrows. He'd overheard, and he was judging her for it.

Livia saw him, too, and stopped riding the balustrade. He came forward, the collar of his parka turned up, his footsteps silent on the stone porch floor.

Screw his judgment, Annie thought. At least she was trying to help Livia. What had he done, other than scare her?

Scamp was still on her arm, and she thrust the puppet forward. "*Halt!* Identify yourself!"

He halted. "Theo Harp. I live here."

"So you say. Prove it."

"Well . . . My initials are carved in the floor of the gazebo."

His initials as well as his twin's.

Scamp thrust her chin forward. "Are you good or bad, Mr. Theo Harp?"

One dark eyebrow shot toward his hairline, but he kept his focus on the puppet. "I try to be good, but it's not always easy."

"Do you eat your vegetables?"

"Everything except rutabaga."

Scamp turned toward Livia and said in a stage whisper, "He doesn't like rutabaga either." Then back to Theo. "Do you take a bath without making a big fuss about it?"

"I take showers. I like 'em."

"Do you run outside in your socks?"

"No." ˙

"Do you sneak candy when nobody's looking?"

"Only peanut butter cups."

"Your horse is scary."

He glanced over at Livia. "That's why kids need to stay out of the stable if I'm not there."

"Do you ever yell?"

He returned his attention to Scamp. "I try not to. Unless the Sixers are losing."

"Do you know how to comb your hair by yourself?"

"I do."

"Do you bite your fingernails?"

"Absolutely not."

Scamp took a deep breath, dropped her head, and lowered her voice. "Do you ever hit mommies?"

Theo didn't blink. "Never. Absolutely never. Nobody should ever hit mommies."

Scamp turned to Livia and cocked her head. "What do you think? Can he stay?"

Livia nodded agreeably—no hesitation, firm nod—and slipped down off the balustrade.

"Could I speak with Annie now?" Theo asked Scamp.

"I guess," Scamp replied. "I'll go make up songs in my head."

"You do that."

Annie returned Scamp to her backpack. She expected Livia to go inside, now that the puppet wasn't part of the conversation, but instead she wandered along the porch and down the three front steps. Annie started to tell her to come back, but Livia didn't stray. Instead she poked around in the frozen dirt next to the house.

Theo tilted his head toward the end of the porch, clearly indicating they needed a private conversation. Annie went over to him, still keeping her eye on Livia. He spoke quietly, so the child couldn't hear. "How long has this been going on?"

"She and Scamp have been friends for a while, but I only started talking about her father a couple of days ago. And, no, I don't know what I'm doing. And, yes, I realize I'm meddling with a problem that's too complicated for someone who's not a professional. Do you think I'm crazy?"

He considered. "She's definitely not as skittish as she was. And she seems to like being around you."

"She likes being around Scamp."

"Scamp is the one who started talking to her about what she saw, right? It was Scamp, not you?"

Annie nodded.

"And she wants to be with Scamp?" he said.

"She seems to."

He frowned. "How do you do it? I'm a grown man. I know damn well you're the one who's making that puppet talk, but I still look at the puppet."

"I'm good at what I do." She'd intended to be sarcastic, but it didn't come out that way.

"Damn right you are." He tilted his head toward the little girl. "I say keep going. If she's had enough, she'll let you know."

His confidence made her feel better.

He turned to leave only to have Livia come scampering up the stairs after him. She'd brought something with her. Looking up at him, she opened her hands, showing him a couple of small rocks and some clamshells. He gazed down at her. She gazed back, her lips setting in their familiar mulish line. She extended her hands. He smiled and took what she'd given him, then rubbed the top of her head. "See you later, kiddo." He disappeared down the cliff steps to the beach.

How odd. Livia was afraid of Theo, so why had she given him what she'd collected?

Rocks, clamshells . . .

Annie understood. Livia had given him her offerings because he was the one building her fairy house.

ANNIE WAS FINDING IT INCREASINGLY difficult to connect the Theo she remembered from the past with the man she now knew. She understood that people changed as they grew older, but his disturbing teenage behavior had seemed too deep rooted in psychosis to be easily fixed. He'd told her he'd had therapy. Apparently, it had worked, although he refused to talk about Regan and continued to shut down when the conversation got personal. She couldn't lose sight of the fact that he was still deeply troubled.

Later, as she was taking out the trash, she glanced down at the cottage and saw something that made her stop in her tracks. A car moved slowly, almost stealthily, toward the cottage.

Theo wrote in the studio. Sometimes he blasted music while he worked. He wouldn't even know he had a visitor.

She raced inside the house, grabbed the car keys, and sped down the cliff.

Chapter Seventeen

YOU WERE PREPARED TO DEFEND me with an ice scraper?"
Theo tossed his parka over the back of the pink velvet couch.
Two hours had passed since the unfortunate incident, and he
was just returning from his second trip to town.

"It was all I could find in your car," Annie said. "We
Ninjas have to use whatever's on hand."

"You practically gave Wade Carter a heart attack."

"He was skulking around behind the cottage," she retorted. "What was I supposed to do?"

"Don't you think jumping him was a bit extreme?"

"Not if he was getting ready to break in, and seriously,
Theo, how well do you know him?"

"Well enough to know that his wife didn't fracture her
arm just so he'd have an excuse to break into the cottage." He
dropped his car keys on the table and headed for the kitchen.
"He's lucky you didn't give him a concussion."

Annie was more than a little proud of herself. Yes, she was glad she hadn't actually hurt the man, but after feeling beat down for so long, she liked knowing she wasn't afraid to act. "Next time he'll knock on the door," she said, following him.

He opened the flaps on the box of wine bottles he'd brought back inside. "We have new locks. And he did knock, remember?"

But Theo hadn't answered, so Carter had circled the cottage, trying to figure out if anyone was inside. Annie hadn't known that. "From now on, no more loud music when you work," she said. "Anybody could sneak up on you, and you wouldn't know until it was too late."

"Why should I worry, with Wonder Woman on the job?"

She grinned. "I was pretty awesome."

His laugh was still tarnished at the edges. "At least the word's out that you're not an easy mark."

She considered asking him about the fairy house, but talking about it would destroy the magic. Besides, that was between him and Livia. "How did the bone setting go?"

"I stabilized her arm. Wade promised he'd take her over to the mainland tomorrow." He examined the label on the wine bottle. "Then Lisa McKinley saw my car and asked me to look at her youngest daughter."

"Alyssa."

"Yes, well, *Alyssa* shoved something up her nose and it won't come out. Ask me what I know about extracting a jelly bean from a kid's nose." He located the corkscrew. "I tell them all the same thing. I'm an EMT, not a doctor, but they act as if I have a medical degree from Harvard."

"Did you get it out?"

"No, and Lisa's really pissed at me." Unlike the jelly bean, the wine cork came out with a soft pop. "I don't carry around a nasal speculum, and I could do serious damage if I started poking at it. She's going to the mainland with the Carters." He pulled down two wine goblets.

"No wine for me," she said quickly. "I'm having tea. Chamomile."

The familiar hard grooves had reappeared at the corners of his unsmiling mouth. "You haven't gotten your period."

"No, I haven't." Her rejection of the wine wasn't only about a possible pregnancy, but also about his decision to bring the wine back into the cottage. If she shared, it would no longer be a gift.

He set both glasses hard on the counter. "Stop screwing with me and tell me when you're supposed to get your period?"

She couldn't play games any longer. "Next week, but I feel fine. I'm sure I'm not . . . You know."

"You're not sure of anything." He turned away to fill his own glass, not looking at her. "If you are pregnant, I'll see a lawyer, set up a trust. I'll make sure you have whatever you . . . you and the kid need."

No mention of getting rid of "the kid." "I'm not talking about this," she said.

He turned back to her, cupping the bowl of the wineglass. "It's not my favorite topic, either, but you need to know—"

"Stop talking about it!" She gestured toward the stove. "I made dinner. It won't be as good as yours, but it's food."

"Target practice first."

This time he was all-business.

THEIR GLOOMY MOODS DIDN'T LIFT until dinner. The weekly supply boat had brought groceries for Moonraker Cottage, most of which Theo had ordered, and she'd stuck with what she did well—meatballs and homemade spaghetti sauce. It wasn't haute cuisine, but his enjoyment was obvious. "Why didn't you make this for me when you were helping Jaycie with dinner?"

"I wanted you to suffer," she said.

"Mission accomplished."

He put down his fork. "So how do you want this to play out? More Post-it notes on the bedroom door, or are we going to act like adults and do what we both want?"

Leave it to Theo to get to the point. "I told you. I'm not good at emotionally detaching from sex," she said. "I know that makes me old-fashioned, but that's who I am."

"I have news for you, Annie. You're not good at emotionally detaching from anything."

"Yes, well, there's that."

He lifted his glass to her. "Have I remembered to say thank you?"

"For me being a sex goddess?"

"That, too. But . . ." He set the glass down and abruptly pushed back from the table. "Hell, I don't know. My writing's gone to hell, I have no idea how to protect you from whatever crap is happening here, and pretty soon somebody's going to ask me to do a fucking heart transplant. But . . . The thing is, I'm not exactly unhappy."

"Gee. With that kind of progress, you'll have your own special on Comedy Central in no time."

"Sensitively put." He almost smiled. "Now how about it? Are you done with Post-it notes or not?"

Was she? She carried her dirty plate into the kitchen and thought about what was right for her. Not him. Only her. She moved to the kitchen doorway. "Okay, this is what I want. Sex and lots of it."

"My world just got so much brighter."

"But impersonal. No cuddling afterward. And absolutely no sleeping in the same bed." She came back toward the table. "As soon as you've satisfied me, we're done. No cozy little chats. Sleep in your own bed."

He tilted his chair back. "Harsh, but I can live with that."

"Totally impersonal," she insisted. "Like you're a male prostitute."

He lifted one of those imperious eyebrows. "Don't you think that's a little . . . degrading?"

"Not my problem." The fantasy was delicious . . . and perfect for the message she wanted to deliver. "You're a male prostitute working in a brothel designed for an exclusive female clientele." She wandered toward the bookcases, letting the fantasy unfold, not caring how he felt about it or whether he was judging her. "The place is sparse, but luxurious. All white walls and black leather chairs. Not the overstuffed ones," she added. "Those sleek ones with chrome frames."

"Something tells me you've thought about this before," he said drily.

"All you men are sitting around in various stages of dishabille. And no one is saying a word."

"Dishabille?"

"Look it up."

"I know what it means. I'm just—"

"Each man is more beautiful than the last," she said. "I walk around the room." She walked around the room. "Everything is absolutely silent. I'm taking my time." She stopped. "There's a round platform in the exact center of the room. The platform is set six inches off the floor . . ."

Again his eyebrow went up. "You really have thought this through."

She ignored him. "That's where the men go. To be inspected."

All four legs of his chair hit the ground. "Okay, I'm getting seriously turned on."

"I choose the three I'm most aroused by. One by one, I gesture them to the platform."

"That would be the round platform set exactly six inches from the floor?"

"I carefully inspect them. I run my hands over their bodies, check them for flaws—"

"Look at their teeth?"

"—assess them for strength and, most important, endurance."

"Ah."

"But I already know who I want. And I bring him up last."

"I've never been so turned on and so horrified at the same time."

"This man is magnificent. Exactly what I need. Thick, dark hair; a chiseled profile; hard muscles. Best of all, I can see by the intelligence in his eyes that he's more than a stud. I select him."

He rose from his chair and gave her a mocking nod. "Thank you."

"No, not you." She dismissed him with a wave of her hand. "Unfortunately, the man I've chosen is already booked for the night. *Then* I take you." She gave him a triumphant smile. "You're not as expensive, and who can resist a bargain?"

"Apparently, not you." The slight hoarseness in his voice ruined his attempt at humor.

She felt like Scheherazade. She lowered her pitch, taking it to the border of sultry but not quite crossing over. "I'm wearing a filmy piece of black lace. And all I have on underneath is a tiny pair of scarlet panties."

"Bedroom!" he ordered. "Right now." It was a command, but she pretended to think it over—for about three seconds until he grabbed her by the arm and hauled her there.

After he'd pulled her through the door, she planted her feet, not yet ready to give up her control. "The room has a large bed with fur-lined shackles dangling from the head and foot boards."

"Just when you think you know someone . . ."

"And a wall of glass-fronted cabinets displaying every sex toy imaginable."

"I am way out of my league here." But the smoke mingling with the amusement in his eyes said that wasn't quite true.

"Except for those creepy gag-things," she said quickly. "You know the ones."

"I'm afraid I don't."

"Well, they're disgusting."

"I'll take your word for it."

She gestured toward the imaginary display cabinets. "Everything is tastefully arranged."

"And why not? It's a first-rate establishment."

She took a few steps away from him. "We open the glass doors and examine each item together."

"Taking our time . . ."

"You pull several out," she said.

"Which ones?"

"The ones you've noticed I've looked at the longest."

"Which would be . . ."

She narrowed her eyes at him. "I gesture toward the display of whips."

"I am not whipping you!"

She ignored his outrage, which might or might not be phony. "You get the whip I've selected and bring it to me." She pulled at her bottom lip with her teeth. "I take it from you."

"Like hell you do!" The devil inside him took over. "Unknown to you," he said, closing the distance between them, "I am not just any highly paid male prostitute. I am the *king* of male prostitutes. And now I'm taking over."

She wasn't certain how she felt about that.

He twisted a long strand of her hair around his fingers. "I yank one strip of leather free from the whip."

She stopped breathing.

"I use it to tie up your hair . . ."

Goose bumps skittered down her spine. "I'm not sure I like where this is going." She loved where this was going.

He brushed the nape of her neck with his lips, then lightly nipped the flesh. "Oh, you like it. You like it a lot." He released her hair. "Especially when I use the butt of the whip to open your legs."

Her clothes were burning her up. She had to get them off. Right now.

"I run it up your calf . . ." He moved his fingers along the inseam of her jeans. "Then up the inside of your thigh . . ."

"Take off your clothes!" She yanked her sweater over her head.

He crossed his arms over his chest and she did the same, then locked his eyes with hers. "I make you take off your clothes."

"You cad."

She was undressed first, which gave her time to drink in the sight of his body. The muscle and tendon, ridges and hollows. He was perfect, and if she wasn't, she didn't care. Apparently, neither did he.

"What happened to that whip?" she inquired. Just in case he'd forgotten . . .

"I'm glad you asked." He tilted his head. "You. On the bed."

It was only a game, but she'd never felt more desirable. She sauntered over, Sex Queen of the World, and knelt on the mattress to watch him approach.

In all his magnificent glory . . .

She sat back on her heels. The gleam in his eyes told her he was enjoying this as much as she. But was he enjoying it too much? This was, after all, a man who'd built a career on sadism.

He pushed her to her back. As he explored her body, he whispered all the perverted, crude . . . and absolutely thrilling things he intended to do to her.

She struggled to find enough air to whisper back, "And I say nothing. I let you do whatever you want, touch whatever you want. I'm completely submissive." She dug her fingernails hard into his buttocks. "Until I'm not."

And the Sex Queen of the World took over.

It was glorious.

Their role-playing liberated them. Stripped away their seriousness. Let them snarl and play and threaten and tussle. They had no scruples and every scruple. The blankets tangled around them as their threats grew more dire, their caresses more thrilling.

Outside the window of their erotic cave, fresh snow began to fall. Inside, they were lost in the wildness they'd unleashed.

THEO HAD NEVER BEEN so foolish with a woman. As he lay back in the pillows, he tried on the unfamiliar notion that sex could be fun. A sharp elbow jabbed him in the ribs. "I'm done with you," she said. "Out."

Kenley could never get enough of him. She'd wanted him with her every second. And all he'd wanted was to get away. "I'm too tired to move," he murmured.

"Fine." She flipped out of bed and flounced from the room. She'd meant what she said about not sleeping together. He should have been a gentleman and done what she'd asked, but he was feeling ill used, and he stayed where he was.

Much later, when he still hadn't fallen back asleep, he found her curled in his bed in the studio. He resisted the urge to crawl in with her and got his laptop instead. He carried it out into the living room and settled down to write. But he kept thinking about Diggity Swift. He'd killed off the kid on the page, but not in his head, and he didn't like that. Disgusted with himself, he set the laptop aside, stared out the window, and watched the snow fall.

AFTER ANNIE HAD SHOWERED AND dressed for the day in jeans and her green sweater, she found Theo in the kitchen.

"Would you like another cup of coffee?" he asked.

"No, thank you. But thank you for offering."

"My pleasure."

He'd showered before her, and he, too, was fully dressed. They had their best manners on display, making up for last night's debauchery with Old World courtesy, as if they needed to reclaim their dignity and prove they were, indeed, civilized.

As he retired to the table with his coffee, she found an old sheet, located a can of black paint in the storage closet, and carried it all into the studio where there were enough splatters on the floor not to make a difference. Half an hour later, Theo stood in the fresh snow and gazed at the banner she'd hung on the front of the cottage.

**TRESPASSERS WILL BE SHOT ON SIGHT.
NO QUESTIONS ASKED.**

She climbed down from the ladder and scowled at him, daring him to make fun of her, but he merely shrugged. "Works for me."

OVER THE COURSE OF THE next few days, Annie came to a decision. Not about Theo. Her relationship with him was as clear-cut as she could wish. She loved being Sex Queen of the World, and insisting on separate beds kept her from becoming a chump. Instead, her decision involved the legacy. She'd found nothing, and it was time to face reality. Mariah had been on so many painkillers that she hadn't known what she was saying. There was no legacy, and Annie could either fall apart because her money problems weren't going to magically disappear, or she could keep moving forward, one step at a time.

The interisland ferry was due to arrive on the first of March, only a few days away, and she began packing up everything in the cottage that had value to ship to the mainland. She arranged for a van to meet the ferry and take it all to Manhattan. Her mother's name was still worth something, and her things were going to the best resale shop in the city.

Annie had sent photos of everything to the owner, including the paintings, lithographs, art books, the Louis XIV "Pile Driver" chest, and barbed-wire bowl. He'd agreed to advance the money for transportation against future sales.

The centerpiece of the collection and the item the dealer was certain would fetch the most money was one she'd nearly overlooked. The cottage guest book. Some of the autographs were of well-known artists, and a few signatures had small doodles next to the names. The dealer hoped to get as much as two thousand dollars for it, but he took a 40 percent commission. Even if everything sold, Annie wouldn't be able to settle her debts, but she'd put a dent in them. She was also healthy again. When her sixty days were up, she'd try to get her old jobs back and start all over again. A depressing thought.

Then something happened on the last day of February that cheered her up.

Theo had been out riding longer than usual, and she kept dashing to the windows at Harp House looking for him. It was nearly dusk when she spotted him riding up the drive. She hurried out the side door, grabbing her coat on the way but not bothering with her hat and gloves.

He reined up as he saw her running toward him. "What's wrong?"

"Not a thing. Put your happy face on. I got my period!"

He nodded. "That's a relief."

No big smile. No high fives or "Thank Gods." She regarded him curiously. "Somehow I expected a little more enthusiasm."

"Trust me. I couldn't be more enthusiastic."

"You don't look it."

"Unlike you, I'm not in the habit of jumping up and down like a twelve-year-old." He rode off toward the stable.

"You should try it sometime," she called after him.

As he disappeared she shook her head in disgust. One more reminder that the only connection between them was physical. Did he let anybody see what was going on inside his head?

Of course he was relieved. Annie had a lot of gall suggesting he wasn't. A pregnant Annie would have screwed up his life in more ways than he could begin to fathom. He was irritable because of his work. He always got testy when his writing wasn't going well, and it definitely wasn't going well now. He'd killed off Diggity Swift a week ago and been blocked ever since.

He didn't understand it. He'd never had a problem killing off a character, but now he couldn't seem to garner any interest in Quentin Pierce and his band of miscreants. Today he'd actually been happy to get a call from Booker Rose about his hemorrhoids, and how whacked was that?

Annie kept the pink velvet sofa and the beds, but shipped off most of the rest of the furniture, including the mermaid chair. She wrapped old blankets around the larger paintings and packed up smaller items in boxes she brought down from Harp House. Judy Kester's son Kurt had to make two trips in his truck to get it all to the wharf. She paid him with the taupe armchair he wanted to give his pregnant wife for her birthday.

Since the new locks had been installed a little over a week ago, there'd been no more incidents at the cottage, although she couldn't be certain whether the locks were responsible or the sign she'd hung. Once Theo was satisfied she could handle a gun, he'd made certain everyone in town knew she was armed, and she'd begun to feel safe again.

Theo wasn't happy about the missing furniture. "I need a place to write," he complained as he surveyed the nearly bare living room.

"You can go back to the turret. I'll be fine here now."

"I'm not going anywhere until we figure out who's been behind this. It's amazing what people tell me when I'm bandaging them up. I keep hoping if I ask the right questions, I'll learn something."

She was touched by his attempts to help her. At the same time, she didn't want him to think she was leaning on him—expecting him to play the hero to her hapless heroine. "You've had enough of needy women," she said. "You're not responsible for me."

He acted as if he didn't hear her. "I'll bring some furniture down from Harp House. There's a bunch of stuff in the attic that nobody's using."

"But do I really need a mummified corpse?"

"It'll make a great coffee table."

He was more than true to his word. She expected him to show up with a desk and maybe an easy chair, but he also brought the round, drop leaf table that now sat in the front window along with four spindle-backed chairs. A small, three-drawer painted chest rested between two overstuffed easy chairs slip-covered in faded navy and white checks. He'd even brought a dented brass lamp shaped like a huntsman's horn.

Mariah would have hated it all—especially the huntsman's lamp. Nothing was modern, or even coordinated, but the place finally felt like what it was—a humble Maine cottage instead of an artsy Manhattan living room.

"I borrowed Jim Garcia's truck in exchange for my medical services," Theo told her. "He had a small accident with his power saw. These lobstermen are so damn stubborn. They'd rather risk gangrene than make a trip to the mainland to see a doctor."

"Lisa was up at the house again," Annie told him. "She's still mad at you for not taking the jelly bean out of Alyssa's nose. I did a Web search and showed her what could have happened if you'd tried to handle it yourself."

"Three other people are pissed at me, but I'm already doing more than I'm qualified for, and they can just deal with it."

Whether he wanted to admit it or not, he was becoming increasingly absorbed in island life. It must be good for him because he seemed to laugh more, and he no longer looked quite as tense. "You haven't killed anybody yet," she said. "That's good news."

"Only because I have a couple of doctor buddies helping me over the phone."

She was so used to thinking of Theo as a loner that she found it hard to imagine him having friends.

AFTER ANOTHER LUSCIOUS BOUT OF sexual depravity, they fell asleep in their separate beds, something that seemed to annoy

Theo more each night. A pounding on the door jerked Annie upright in bed. Shoving her hair from her face, she untangled her legs from the blankets.

"Don't shoot!" an unfamiliar voice called out. She was glad someone was taking her sign seriously, but she still reached in her bedside table for the pistol.

Theo was already at the front door when she got to the living room. The early March winds had picked up and snow tapped against the front window. She kept the pistol at her side as he turned the knob. Judy Kester's son Kurt, the one who'd helped her move the furniture, stood on the other side. "It's Kim," he said frantically. "She's gone into labor early, and the medevac helicopter's grounded. We need you."

"Shit." Not the most professional response, but Annie didn't blame Theo. He gestured Kurt inside. "Wait here." He passed Annie on his way to grab some clothes. "Get dressed. You're going with me."

Chapter Eighteen

Theo clutched his phone to his ear with one hand, the steering wheel with the other. "I know the weather's bad. Do you think I can't see? But we need a helicopter out here, and we need it *now*!"

The wind buffeted the Range Rover, and the taillights of Kurt's truck gleamed like demonic eyes on the road in front of them as they followed him into town. Kurt said the baby wasn't due for another two weeks and that he and his wife had planned to head to the mainland on Friday. "We were going to leave the kids with my mom and stay with Kim's cousin near the hospital," he'd said. "It wasn't supposed to be like this."

Theo seemed to recognize that he was being unreasonable with the person on the other end of the phone because he calmed down. "Yeah, I understand . . . Yes, I know . . . All right."

As he tossed his cell aside, Annie regarded him sympathetically. "Am I tagging along because you don't want me to be alone in the cottage or because you need moral support?"

"Both." His knuckles tightened on the steering wheel.

"Excellent. I was afraid you were bringing me along for my midwifery skills. Of which I have none."

He grunted.

"All I know about childbirth is what I've seen on TV," she said. "And that it's supposed to hurt a lot."

He didn't respond.

"Do *you* know anything about childbirth?" she asked.

"Hell, no."

"But . . ."

"I've had training, if that's what you mean. But you might say I'm missing any real-life experience."

"You'll do great."

"You don't know that. This baby is two weeks early."

Something Annie had already noted, but she attempted reassurance. "This is Kim's third child. She'll know what she's doing by now. And Kurt's mother will be able to help." Judy Kester, with her ready laugh and positive attitude, would be the perfect person to have around in a crisis.

But Judy wasn't at the house. No sooner had they taken off their coats than Kurt told them Judy was visiting her sister on the mainland. "And why should I have expected anything else?" Theo muttered.

They followed Kurt through a comfortably untidy living room strewn with kids' detritus. "Ever since the school burned down, Kim's been talking to me about moving off the island," he said, shoving aside a pair of Transformer figures with his foot. "This sure isn't going to make her change her mind."

Theo stopped in the kitchen to scrub his hands and arms. When he gestured for Annie to do the same, she gave him an *Are you crazy?* look intended to remind him she was only there for moral support. He narrowed his eyes at her, his expression so ferocious she did as he asked, although not without protest. "Shouldn't I stay here to boil water or something?"

"For what?"

"I have no idea."

"You," he said, "are coming with me."

Kurt peeled off to check on his kids. Since they seemed to be sleeping through the whole ordeal, Annie suspected he was doing whatever he could to avoid his wife.

She followed Theo into the bedroom. Kim lay in a tangle of orange and yellow floral sheets. She wore a threadbare pale blue summer nightgown. Her skin was blotchy, her frizzy auburn hair snarled. Everything about her was round and plump: her face, her breasts, and most of all, her abdomen. Theo set down his red canvas EMT kit. "Kim, it's Theo Harp. And this is Annie Hewitt. How are you doing?"

She bared her teeth through a contraction. "How does it look like I'm doing?"

"It looks like you're doing fine," he said, as if he were the most experienced obstetrician in the country. He began unpacking his EMT kit. "How far apart are the contractions?"

The pain eased and she sagged into the pillows. "About four minutes."

He pulled out a package of latex gloves and a blue bed pad. "Tell me the next time you're having one, and we'll see how long it lasts."

His calm seemed to rub off on her, and she nodded.

A couple of celebrity magazines, some children's books, and various tubes of lotion cluttered the glass-topped bedside table closest to her. The other held a digital alarm clock, a pocketknife, and a small plastic food storage container half-filled with pennies. Theo unwrapped the bed pad. "Let's get you more comfortable."

His voice was soothing, but the look he shot Annie told her if she even thought about moving from the room a terrible fate would befall her followed by an even worse fate, followed by total annihilation. Annie reluctantly went to the head of the bed, even less anxious to see what was going on than she suspected Theo was.

Kim was beyond modesty, and Annie doubted that she even noticed how carefully he slipped the bed pad under her hips and arranged the sheet across her knees. She moaned as an especially hard contraction claimed her. As Theo timed it, he gave Annie a series of softly spoken instructions detailing what he expected would happen and what he wanted her to do.

"Fecal matter?" she whispered as he finished.

"It happens," he said. "And it's natural. Be ready with a clean pad."

"And a barf bag," she muttered. "For me."

Theo smiled and returned his attention to his watch. While Kim labored, Annie stayed by the head of the bed, gently stroking her hair and whispering encouragement. Between contractions, Kim apologized for bringing Theo out in the middle of the night, but she didn't once question his obstetrical skills.

After about an hour, things got serious. "I have to push," she cried, kicking the privacy sheet away and letting Annie see more than she wanted.

Theo had already slipped on the latex gloves. "Let's take a look."

Kim moaned as he examined her. "Don't push yet," he said. "Hold on."

"Fuck you!" Kim screamed.

Annie patted her arm. "Attagirl. You're doing great." She hoped that was true.

Theo concentrated on whatever it was he was doing. With the next contraction, he encouraged her to push. "You're crowning," he announced, as calmly as if he were reporting on the weather. At the same time, Annie saw the beads of perspiration on his forehead. She hadn't imagined anything could make Theo Harp sweat, but this was doing it.

The contraction eased, but not for long. Kim gasped.

"I can see the baby's head," Theo said.

A growl caught in Kim's throat. He patted her knee and encouraged her. "Push . . . That's great. You're doing great."

Annie's reluctance to see the birth was gone. After two more strong contractions and with more of Theo's encouragement, the baby's head appeared. Theo cradled it in his hand. "Let's get the cord out of the way," he said softly, slipping his opposite finger inside and sliding it around the baby's neck. "Annie, have a blanket ready. Okay, little one . . . Let me see that shoulder . . . Turn. That's the way. There you go."

The baby slid into his strong, competent palms.

"We've got a boy here," he announced. He tilted the tiny, messy newborn to clear his airway. "Let's give you an eight, little guy."

It took her a moment to remember what he'd said about calculating the baby's Apgar score in the first minute after birth and then again at the five-minute mark to assess the infant's condition. The baby began to cry, a soft little mewing. Theo placed him on Kim's abdomen, took the towel from Annie, and gently rubbed.

Kurt finally came into the room. He went to his wife, and they started to cry together as they took in the sight of their newborn son. Annie would have smacked Kurt in the head for not being there through the ordeal, but Kim was more forgiving. As she gathered the newborn to her, Theo massaged her abdomen. It wasn't long before she had another contraction, and the globby mass of the placenta slipped out.

Annie tried not to look as she handed over the red disposal bag from Theo's kit. He clamped off the umbilical cord and exchanged the soiled pad for a clean one. For a guy with a big trust fund and a lucrative book contract, he didn't mind getting down and dirty.

The baby was a little small, but as a third-time mother, Kim handled him with confidence and soon had him nursing. Theo spent the rest of the night in an easy chair while Annie slept fitfully on the couch. She heard him get up several times, and once when she opened her eyes, the baby was asleep in his arms.

His eyes were closed, and the newborn curled protectively to his chest. She remembered the gentle way he'd dealt with Kim, saw his tenderness with the baby. Theo had been thrust into a daunting situation and handled it like a champion. Fortunately, there hadn't been any complications, but if there had been, he would have kept a cool head and done what he needed to. He'd been a hero, and heroes were her weakness . . . Except this particular hero had once nearly killed her.

IN THE MORNING, KIM AND Kurt thanked Theo effusively as their older children—after Annie had fed them breakfast—climbed on the bed to check out their new brother. With the baby safely delivered and Kim doing well, there was no longer a need for helicopter evacuation, but Theo wanted Kurt to take his wife and the newborn to the mainland that morning to get checked out. Kim flatly refused. "You did as good a job as any doctor, and we're not going anywhere."

No matter how Theo pressed, Kim wouldn't change her mind. "I know my body, and I know babies. We're fine. And Judy's already on her way back to help out."

"Do you see what I have to deal with?" Theo said as they drove back to the cottage, his face creased with fatigue. "They have way too much trust in me."

"Act less competent," Annie suggested, instead of telling him he might be the most trustworthy man she'd ever known. Or maybe not. She'd never been more confused.

She was still thinking about him the next day as she climbed the steps to the Harp House attic. He'd told her to take whatever she wanted for the cottage, and she wondered if any of the seascapes she remembered remained up there. The hinges on the attic door moaned as she opened it. The place was right out of a horror movie. An eerie dressmaker's dummy stood sentry over broken furniture, dusty cardboard boxes, and a pile of faded life preservers. The only light came from a grimy oriel window shrouded in tattered gray cobwebs and two bare bulbs hanging from the ceiling beams.

You don't really expect me to come in here, do you? Crumpet squeaked.

Unfortunately, I can't stay, Peter said.

Leo sneered. *It's a good thing somebody here has a backbone.*

Your backbone is my arm, Annie reminded him, diverting her attention from a creepy plastic-shrouded doll collection that had once been Regan's.

Exactly, Leo resneered. *And here you are.*

The attic held piles of old newspapers, magazines, and books no one would ever read. She stepped around a mildewed canvas sail bag, a broken patio umbrella, and a dusty Jansport backpack to get to some picture frames leaning against the wall. Cardboard boxes peppered with dead bugs blocked the paintings. As she began to move them aside, she spotted a shoe box labeled PRIVATE PROPERTY OF REGAN HARP. Curious, she looked inside.

The box was filled with photos of Theo and Regan as children. Annie unfolded an old beach towel and sat on the floor to look at them. Judging by the crooked composition, they'd taken many of them themselves. They were dressed in superhero costumes, playing in the snow, making faces at the camera. The images were so endearing that a lump grew in her throat.

She opened the clasp on a manila envelope and found it stuffed with more photos. The first was of Theo and Regan together. She recognized Regan's NO FEAR T-shirt from the summer they'd all been together and vaguely remembered having taken the photo herself. As she gazed at Regan's sweet smile, the way she leaned against her brother, she was once again struck by the tragedy of her loss. The tragedy of all the losses Theo had endured, beginning with his mother's abandonment and ending with the death of a wife he must have once loved.

She took in the tousled hair falling over his forehead and the arm carelessly draped around his sister's shoulders. *Regan, I wish you were here to explain your brother to me.*

All the photos in the envelope seemed to have come from that summer. There were pictures of Theo and Regan in the pool, on the front porch, and aboard their boat——the same boat Regan had taken out the day she'd drowned. Annie was overcome with both nostalgia and pain.

And then . . . bewilderment.

She shuffled through the photos more quickly. Her pulse began to hammer. One by one, the photos drifted from her lap and scattered at her feet like dying leaves. She buried her face in her hands.

I'm sorry, Leo whispered. *I didn't know how to tell you.*

AN HOUR LATER, ANNIE STOOD in the bitter wind next to the empty swimming pool. Long cracks fissured the concrete pool walls, and filthy piles of snow and muck littered the bottom.

According to Lisa, Cynthia was planning to fill in the pool. Annie imagined her replacing it with the fake ruins of an English folly.

Theo didn't see her as he emerged from the stable where he'd been grooming Dancer. He was her lover, this wildly seductive man she knew so well yet didn't know at all. Gray snowflakes swirled like ashes in the gloomy air. A sensible book heroine wouldn't have confronted him until she'd gathered her thoughts. But Annie wasn't sensible. She was a mess. "Theo . . ."

He stopped walking and turned to find her. "What are you doing out here?" He didn't wait for an answer but came toward her with that long-legged gait that had become so familiar. "Let's call it a day and go down to the cottage together." The smoky cast in his eyes told her what he had in mind for the two of them to do when they got there.

She huddled into her shoulders. "I've been in the attic."

"Find what you needed?"

"Yes. Yes, I did." She reached in her coat pocket. Her hand trembled slightly as she pulled out the photographs. Five of them, although she could have brought a dozen more.

He stepped up on the cracked pool deck to see what she held. And when he did . . . Pain contorted his face. He turned on his heel, abandoning her.

"Don't you *dare* walk away from me," she cried as he stalked across the yard. "Don't you *dare*!"

He slowed, but didn't stop. "Leave it alone, Annie."

"Do not walk away." She spat out each word. Not moving a step. Staying right where she was.

He finally turned to face her, his words as flat as hers had been vehement. "It was a long time ago. I'm asking you to leave it alone."

His expression was stony, foreboding, but she had to know the truth. "It wasn't you. It was never you."

He clenched his hands into fists at his sides. "I don't know what you're talking about."

"You're a liar," she retorted, not with anger, but as a statement. "That summer. All this time I thought it was you. But it wasn't."

He launched himself toward her, using attack as his defense. "You don't know anything. That day you got dive-bombed by the birds . . . I was the one who sent you to that wreck." He was on the pool deck, looming over her. "I put the dead fish in your bed. I insulted you, bullied you, excluded you. And I did it all on purpose."

She nodded slowly. "I'm starting to understand why. But you're not the one who shoved me into the dumbwaiter or pushed me into the marsh. You didn't take those pups down to the cave or write the note that sent me to the beach." She ran her thumb over the photos she held. "And you weren't the one who wanted me to drown."

"You're wrong." He met her eyes dead-on. "I told you. I had no conscience."

"That isn't true. You had too much." Her throat tightened, making it hard to speak. "It was Regan all along. And you're still trying to protect her."

The proof lay in the photos she held. In each one, Annie had been cut out. Her face, her body—every jagged slash of the scissors a little murder.

Theo didn't move—he stood as straight as ever—but even so, he seemed to fold in on himself, withdrawing to that place where no one could reach him. She expected him to walk away again, was astonished that he didn't. She clung to that. "Jaycie's in some of the photos," she said. "All of her."

She waited for him to stalk away, to explain, and when he did neither, she offered her own conclusion, the one he couldn't seem to utter himself. "Because Jaycie wasn't a threat to Regan. Jaycie didn't try to steal your attention the way I did. You never singled her out."

She could feel him waging an internal war. His twin had died more than a decade earlier, yet he still wanted to protect her from the evidence of the photos. But Annie wouldn't let him. "Tell me."

"You don't want to hear this," he said.

She gave a mirthless laugh. "Oh, but I do. You did those things to me to keep me safe from her."

"You were an innocent party."

She thought of the punishments he'd taken for his sister. "So were you."

"I'm going inside," he said flatly. He was shutting her out, sealing himself up as usual.

"Stay right here. I became a big part of this story, and I deserve to know all of it right now."

"It's an ugly story."

"You think I don't already understand that?"

He separated himself from her, walking to the end of the deck where the old diving board had once been mounted. "Our mother left us when we were five—you know that. Dad escaped by working, so it was Regan and me against the world." Every word he uttered seemed to cause him pain. "All we had was each other. I loved her, and she would have done anything for me."

Annie didn't move. Theo nudged a rusted metal bolt with the toe of his riding boot. She didn't think he'd say more, but he went on, his voice barely audible. "She'd always been possessive, but then so was I, and it wasn't a problem until we were around fourteen, and I started paying attention to girls. She hated that. She'd horn in on my phone calls, tell me lies about any girl I showed an interest in. I thought she was just being a pest. And then things got more serious." He crouched down on his heels to check out the mess at the bottom of the pool, but Annie doubted he was seeing anything except the past. He went on—coldly, without emotion. "She began starting rumors. She made an anonymous call to the parents of one girl telling them their daughter was on drugs. Another girl ended up with a broken shoulder after Regan tripped her at school. Everybody believed it was an accident because they all loved Regan."

"You didn't believe it was accidental."

"I wanted to. But there were more incidents. A girl I'd only talked to a few times was on her bike when she had a rock thrown at her. She fell and was hit by a car. Fortunately she wasn't badly hurt, but she could have been, and I confronted Regan. She admitted she'd done it, then cried and promised nothing like that would ever happen again. I wanted to believe her, but she couldn't seem to help herself." He stood back up. "I felt trapped."

"So you gave up girls."

He finally looked at her. "Not right away. I tried to keep Regan in the dark, but she always found out. Not long after she got her driver's license, she tried to run down one of her best friends. After that happened, I couldn't take any more chances."

"You should have told your father."

"I was afraid to. I'd spent hours in the library reading about mental illness, and I knew something was drastically wrong with her. I even came up with a diagnosis—relationship-based obsessive-compulsive disorder. I wasn't that far from the mark. He'd have had her institutionalized."

"And you couldn't let that happen."

"It would have been the best thing for her, but I was a kid, and I didn't see it that way."

"Because it was the two of you against the world."

He didn't acknowledge what she'd said, but she knew it was true. Saw the helpless boy he'd once been.

"I thought if I made sure she never felt as if anyone was coming between us, she'd be fine," he said. "And I was right, up to a point. As long as she didn't feel threatened, she behaved normally. But the most innocent remark could set her off. I kept hoping she'd get a boyfriend, and then it would stop. They all wanted to go out with her, but she had no interest in anyone except me."

"Didn't you start to hate her?"

"Our bond was too strong. You spent a summer with her. You know how sweet she could be. That sweetness was genuine. Right up to the moment the darkness took over."

Annie pushed the photos into her coat pocket. "You burned her poetry notebook. You had to have hated her to do that."

His mouth twisted. "There was no poetry in that notebook. It held all her most obsessive delusions, along with some venom-filled pages directed at you. I was afraid someone would look in it."

"But what about her oboe? She loved it, and you destroyed it."

His eyes held a weary sadness. "She burned it herself when

I threatened to tell Dad what she'd been doing to you. She saw it as a kind of sacrifice to appease me."

Of everything he'd told her, this seemed the saddest—that Regan's twisted love had compelled her to destroy what had brought her so much pleasure.

"You wanted to protect her that summer," she said, "but you also wanted to keep her from hurting me. You were in an impossible position."

"I thought I had it under control. I'd turned myself into a regular teenage monk—not talking to girls, barely looking at them for fear of what Regan would do. And then there you were, living in the same house. I'd see you running around in your red shorts, hear your chatter, watch the way you played with your hair when you were reading a book. I couldn't avoid you."

"Jaycie was a lot prettier than me. Why not her?"

"She didn't read the same books, didn't listen to the music I liked. I couldn't get comfortable with her. Not that I would have let myself. I trashed her to Regan. I tried that with you, too, but Regan could read my mind."

"It was all about availability, wasn't it? That's what's so ironic. If you'd met me in the city, you'd never have looked at me twice." Theo belonged with beautiful women. He and she were lovers only because of proximity. She tucked her cold hands inside the front of her coat. "After everything you went through with your sister, how could you have fallen in love with Kenley?"

"She radiated independence and self-confidence." He made a mockery of his own words. "Everything I was looking for in a woman. Everything Regan lacked. We hadn't been together for six months when she pressed me to get married. I was crazy about her, so I ignored some misgivings and went along with it."

"Which put you in virtually the same predicament you'd been in with Regan."

"Except Kenley didn't try to kill anyone but herself."

"As a way of punishing you."

He hunched his shoulders. "I'm getting cold. I'm going inside."

The man who'd once stripped off his sweater and stood bare-chested in the snow was suddenly cold? "Not yet. Finish the story."

"I already have." He strode away from her and into the turret.

She pulled the photographs from her pocket. They burned her cold fingers. She gazed at them through the gray swirl of snow, then opened her hands. A gust of wind plucked at her palms and carried them away. One by one, they drifted into the muck at the bottom of the swimming pool.

As soon as Annie went inside, Livia demanded her attention. Annie drew cartoons for her while her mind reeled from what she'd learned and brooded over what she still didn't know. Predictably, Theo had only gone so far with his story. She'd have to pry the rest out of him. Maybe telling it would chip away at the icy wall he lived behind.

She planted a kiss on Livia's head. "Why don't you go do a puppet show for your stuffed animals?" She pretended not to notice Livia's frown as she got up from the table.

Even before she entered the turret, she could hear rock music. She let herself into the living room. The music was coming from Theo's office. She climbed the steps to the third floor and knocked but got no response.

The music was loud, but not so loud he couldn't hear. She knocked again, and when he still didn't respond, she tried the knob. She wasn't surprised to find it locked. The message was clear. Theo had finished talking for the day.

She thought it over. The music switched from Arcade Fire to The White Stripes. Out of nowhere, the screech of a terrified cat ripped through the air, quickly followed by the kind of agonizing sound only an animal in the worst kind of peril could make.

The door flew open. Theo dashed out onto the landing looking for his cat. She slipped inside as he raced down the steps.

He had tossed his coat over the black leather ottoman that sat in front of his writing chair. His desk was neater than the last time she'd been here, but then he'd been doing most of his writing at the cottage. A few CD cases lay on the floor by the easy chair. The telescope stood in the window overlooking the cottage, but now she found the sight reassuring instead of menacing. Theo the protector. Trying to shield his mentally ill sister, rescue his crazy wife from herself, and keep Annie safe.

She heard his footsteps coming back up the stairs, moving with a slower, more purposeful tread. He appeared in the doorway. Stopped there. Gazed across the room at her. "You didn't . . ."

She wrinkled her nose, going for cute. "I can't help it. I have crazy-mad skills."

His eyebrows slammed together. He advanced ominously into the room. "I swear . . . If you pull that on me one more time . . ."

"I won't. At least I don't think I will. Probably not." *Unless I have to,* she thought.

"Just to ease my mind . . ." he said, through gritted teeth. "Where is my cat?"

"I'm not completely sure. Probably asleep under the studio bed. You know how he likes it there."

Theo seemed to realize that—as much as he might want to do her just a little bodily harm, it wasn't in his nature. "What the hell am I going to do with you?"

She went on the attack. "I'll tell you what you're not going to do. You're not going to knock yourself out trying to take care of me. I appreciate the thought, but I'm able-bodied, relatively sane—at least in comparison—and I take care of myself. The way I'm doing it might not be pretty, but I'm doing it, and I'm going to keep on doing it. No heroics are necessary on your part."

"I have no idea what you're talking about."

And maybe he didn't. He seemed to view himself as the villain instead of the protector, but if she pointed that out to him, he'd likely dismiss it.

She plopped down into his writing chair. "I'm hungry. Let's get this over with."

Chapter Nineteen

GET THIS OVER WITH?" ONCE again his eyebrows went on a collision course. "You want to know if I killed Regan."

The only way she could get Theo to tell her the rest was to goad it out of him. "Don't play games with me. You didn't kill her."

"How do you know that?"

"Because I know you, O master builder of fairy houses." And she did. In so many ways she hadn't until now.

He blinked. She cut him off before he could deny what he'd done for Livia. "You put your horror on the page. Now stop trying to distract me with all your phony menace, and tell me what happened."

"Maybe I've told you as much as I want to."

He sneered just like Leo, but she wasn't put off. "You and Regan had both just graduated from college," she said. "And not the same college. How did you manage to pull that off?"

"I threatened to ditch college altogether if she didn't agree that we'd split up. I said I'd backpack around the world without telling anyone where I was going."

She loved that he'd been able to do that much to protect himself. "So you went to different schools . . ." It didn't take a crystal ball to figure out what happened next. "And you met a girl."

"More than one. Don't you have something better to do?"

"Not a thing. Keep going."

He grabbed his coat from the ottoman and tossed it on a hook by the door, tidying up—not because he was a neat freak, but because he didn't want to look at her. "I was like a starving man in a supermarket, but even though our campuses were a hundred miles apart, I was still secretive. Right up until senior year when I fell hard for a girl in one of my classes . . ."

Annie leaned back in the chair, trying to appear relaxed so he wouldn't clam up. "Let me guess. She was beautiful, smart, and crazy."

He managed a vapor of a smile. "Two out of three. She's now the CFO of a Denver tech firm. Married with three kids. Definitely not crazy."

"But you had a big problem . . ."

He shifted a yellow pad on his desk a few inches to the left. "I'd been visiting Regan on her campus as often as I could, and she seemed okay. Normal. By her senior year, she'd even started to date. I thought she'd outgrown her problems." He moved away from the desk. "The family was getting together on the island for the Fourth of July. Deborah couldn't make it, but she wanted to see Peregrine, so I brought her over the week before everyone else was scheduled to arrive." He wandered toward a back window, one that looked out onto the water. "I planned to tell Regan about her the next weekend, but Regan showed up early."

Annie tightened her fingers over the chair arms, not wanting to hear what came next, but knowing she had to.

"Deborah and I were walking on the beach. Regan saw us from the top of the cliff. We were holding hands. That's all." He splayed his hands on either side of the window frame, staring out. "It had rained earlier, and the rocks were slippery, so I still don't know how she made it down the steps so fast. I didn't even see her coming, but the next thing I knew, she'd thrown herself at Deborah. I grabbed her and pulled her off. Deborah ran up to the house to get away."

He turned away from the window but still didn't look at her. "I was furious. I told Regan I needed to live my own life, and she needed to see a shrink. It got vicious." He pointed to the scar by his eyebrow. "Regan's the one who gave me this, not you." He indicated just below the scar a much smaller mark that Annie had barely noticed. "This is yours."

She had felt so good about giving him a scar. Now the sight of it made her sick.

"Regan went wild," he continued. "She threatened me, threatened Deborah. I exploded. Told her I hated her. She looked me straight in the eye and said she was going to kill herself." A muscle twitched in his jaw. "I was so angry that I told her I didn't care."

Pity overwhelmed her.

He wandered toward the window with the telescope, not looking at her, not seeing anything. "A storm was coming in. By the time I got to the house, I'd calmed down enough to know I had to go back and tell her I didn't mean it, even though part of me did. But it was too late. She'd already run down the beach to our dock, and she was climbing into the sailboat. I yelled at her from the steps to come back. I'm not sure she heard. Before I could get to her, she had the sails up."

Annie could see it as if she'd been there, and she wanted to wipe away the image.

"The powerboat was out of the water for repairs," he said, "so I jumped in the water, somehow thinking I could catch her. The surf was strong. She saw me and yelled at me to go back. I kept swimming. The waves were breaking over me, but I could still catch glimpses of her face. She looked so sorry, so apologetic. So fricking apologetic. Then she trimmed the sails and raced out into the storm." He unclenched his fist. "That was the last time I saw her alive."

Annie clenched her fists. It was wrong to hate someone with a mental illness, but Regan had not only destroyed herself and nearly killed Annie; she'd done her best to destroy Theo, too. "Regan got you good, didn't she? The perfect revenge."

"You don't understand," he said with a bitter laugh. "Regan didn't kill herself to punish me. She did it to set me free."

Annie came out of her chair. "You don't know that!"

"Yeah, I do." He finally looked at her. "Sometimes we could read each other's minds, and that moment was one of them."

She remembered Regan's tears over a gull with a broken wing. In her sane moments, she must have hated this part of herself.

Annie knew not to let any of the pity she felt show in her face, but what he'd done to himself was wrong. "Regan's plan didn't work. You still think you're responsible for her death."

He dismissed her sympathy with a harsh slash of his hand. "Regan. Kenley. Look for the common element, and you'll find me."

"What you'll find are two mentally ill women and a man with an overdeveloped sense of responsibility. You couldn't have saved Regan. Sooner or later, she would have destroyed herself. The more troublesome question is Kenley. You say you were attracted to her because she was the opposite of Regan, but is that true?"

"You don't understand. She was brilliant. She seemed so independent."

"I get that, but you must have sensed her neediness underneath all that."

"I didn't."

Now he was angry, but Annie plowed on. "Is it possible you saw your relationship with her as a way to make up for what had happened to Regan? You hadn't been able to save your sister, but maybe you could save Kenley?"

His lip curled. "That psych degree you got off the Internet sure does come in handy."

She'd gotten her insights into human psychology in acting workshops dedicated to understanding a character's deepest motivations. "You're a natural caretaker, Theo. Have you ever thought that writing might be your rebellion against whatever it is inside you that makes you feel responsible for other people?"

"You're digging way too deep," he said harshly.

"Just think about it, okay? If you're right about Regan, imagine how much she'd hate the way you keep punishing yourself."

His barely concealed hostility told her she couldn't push him any further. She'd planted the seeds. Now she had to step back and see if any of them would grow. She walked toward the door. "In case you start to wonder . . . You're a great guy and a halfway decent lover, but no way would I ever kill myself over you."

"Comforting."

"Or lose even a minute's sleep."

"Vaguely insulting, but . . . thanks for the clarity."

"This is the way sane women behave. Tuck that away for future reference."

"I'll be sure to do that."

The sudden constriction in her chest contradicted her glibness. Her heart ached for him. He hadn't come to the island to write. He'd come here to do penance for two deaths he believed were his responsibility. Harp House wasn't his refuge. It was his punishment.

THE NEXT MORNING AS SHE pulled a cereal box from the cupboard, she glanced at the calendar she'd hung on the wall. Thirty-four days down, twenty-six to go. Theo came into the kitchen and told her he had to go to the mainland. "My publisher is driving up from Portland. I'm going to meet with her in Camden and take care of some business. Ed Compton is bringing me back on his boat tomorrow evening."

She grabbed a bowl. "Lucky you. Streetlights, paved roads, Starbucks—not that I could actually afford Starbucks."

"I'll go there for you." He held up one hand as if he knew she'd object to whatever he was about to say. "I know you're armed and dangerous, but I'm asking you to stay at Harp House while I'm gone. This is a polite request, not an order."

He'd tried to take care of Regan and of Kenley, and now he was trying to take care of her. "You're such a girl," she said.

He answered that by leaning back on his heels and glaring at her, every inch of him the embodiment of pissed-off masculinity.

"That was a compliment," she said. "Sort of. The whole nurturing thing you have going . . . ? As much as I appreciate your watchdog attitude, I'm not one of those needy females you tend to collect."

He gave her his baddest badass sneer. "That whip idea you had . . . I'm liking it more and more."

She wanted to rip off his clothes and devour him right there. Instead, she sniffed, "I'll stay at Harp House, girlfriend, just to keep you from worrying."

Her taunt had its desired effect. He took her right there on the kitchen floor. And it was exhilarating.

As much as Annie didn't like the idea of sleeping at Harp House, she agreed to appease him. On her way, she stopped to inspect the fairy house. Using sticks, Theo had built a cantilevered balcony over the doorway. He'd also turned a few clamshells on their sides and scattered some of the paving stones, evidence of a late-night fairy frolic. She turned to face the sun. After enduring so much cold weather, she'd never again take a bright winter day for granted.

The fragrance of freshly baked banana bread met her as she stepped into the kitchen. Jaycie was a better baker than cook, and she'd been making these small treats ever since Annie had confronted her about her husband's death. It was her way of making amends for not confiding her past.

Remnants of construction paper from one of Livia's art projects lay on the table next to the bread. Annie had spent hours on the Internet delving into articles about deep childhood trauma. When she'd come across information about puppet therapy, she'd been especially intrigued. But it was a specialized field with trained therapists, and the articles had made her even more aware of how much she didn't know.

Jaycie came into the kitchen. She'd been on crutches for weeks, but she still moved as awkwardly as ever. "I got a text from Theo," she said. "He's on his way to the mainland." Her voice developed an uncharacteristic edge. "I bet you're going to miss him."

Annie had criticized Jaycie for not being forthcoming, yet

Annie was being equally withholding. But she couldn't imagine announcing they were lovers. Nothing had changed the fact that she owed Jaycie her life. She thought about the day Regan had pushed her into the marsh. Jaycie had been there, but she'd lagged far enough behind that she must not have seen the actual push.

As the afternoon wore on, Annie's mood dipped. She'd grown to look forward to being with Theo at the end of the day. And not just for the incredible sex. She simply liked being with him.

Get used to it, Dilly said, in her normal straightforward manner. *Your ill-advised love affair is going to be over soon.*

Sex *affair,* Annie corrected her. *And do you think I don't understand that?*

You tell me, Dilly said.

Whether Annie liked it or not, this ache she felt at his absence was a wake-up call. She made herself focus on the evening ahead, one she was determined to enjoy. The articles on puppet therapy had been fascinating. She did some more research, then settled down with the ancient gothic paperback she'd brought with her. What better place to read one of her spooky old favorites than at Harp House?

By midnight, however, the story of the cynical duke and virginal lady's companion hadn't worked its magic, and she still couldn't fall asleep. Dinner had been sparse, and there was banana bread in the kitchen. She slipped out of bed and stuffed her feet in her sneakers.

The lamp in the upstairs hallway cast a long yellow shadow up the wall, and the stairs creaked as she made her way into the foyer. A full moon threw blades of silver light through the panes of glass above the front door—not enough to illuminate the area, only enough to emphasize its gloom. The house had never felt more forbidding. She rounded the corner into the back hallway . . . And froze.

Jaycie was making her way toward her apartment, and her crutches were nowhere in sight.

An icy panic paralyzed Annie. Jaycie walked with perfectly erect posture. There was nothing wrong with her foot. Nothing at all.

Annie's ears rang from the memory of the bullet whizzing past her head. She saw Crumpet hanging from the ceiling, the bloodred warning painted on the wall. Jaycie had a motive for wanting her gone. Had Annie overlooked the obvious? Was Jaycie the one who'd vandalized the cottage? Had she fired that bullet?

Jaycie had nearly reached the door of her apartment when she stopped. She looked up, tilting her head ever so slightly, almost as if she were listening for any movement above her. And since Annie was the only person upstairs . . .

Jaycie began to move, not into her apartment but back the way she'd come. Annie cut into the dark kitchen and flattened her spine to the wall just inside the doorway. Her paralysis lost its grip. She wanted to grab Jaycie and shake the truth out of her.

Jaycie passed by the kitchen.

Annie eased out into the hallway in time to see her turn toward the front foyer. Staying well back, Annie followed her, barely avoiding one of Livia's My Little Pony figures abandoned on the floor. She peered around the corner. Jaycie had stopped at the bottom of the staircase. As Annie watched, she slowly began mounting the steps.

Anger and betrayal burned inside her. She pressed the back of her head against the wall. She didn't want to believe it. Didn't want to confront the truth that was staring her in the face. It had been Jaycie all along. Her anger burned hotter. She wasn't letting her get away with this.

She began to pull away from the wall, only to hear Scamp's scoffing voice. *You're going after her now? Just like the most dimwitted heroine. It's the dead of night. There's an arsenal in this house, and for all you know, Jaycie has a gun. She's already murdered her husband. Have you learned nothing from your novels?*

Annie gritted her teeth. No matter how much she hated it, this confrontation had to wait for daylight when she had a cooler head. And a gun of her own. She forced herself back into the kitchen, snatched her coat from the hook, and escaped from the house.

A soft whinny came from inside the stable. The spruces creaked, and a night creature scuttled through the brush. Despite the bright moonlight, the descent was treacherous. She slipped on loose rock. An owl hooted a warning. All this time she'd thought someone was after the legacy, but that hadn't been it at all. Jaycie wanted to drive Annie away so she could have Theo to herself. It was as if Regan's darkness had found a home inside Jaycie.

By the time Annie reached the marsh, her teeth were chattering. She looked back at the house. A light burned from a window in the turret. She shivered, imagining Jaycie staring down at her, then remembered she'd left the light on herself when she'd gone up there earlier.

As she gazed at the massive shadow of Harp House and the glowing turret window, she experienced a moment of the blackest humor. This was just like the cover of one of her old gothic paperbacks. But instead of fleeing the haunted mansion in the dark of night wearing a billowing gossamer gown, Annie was fleeing in a pair of flannel Santa pajamas.

Gooseflesh crept up her spine as she approached the dark cottage. Had Jaycie already discovered Annie had fled? Her anger resurfaced. She'd deal with her tomorrow before Theo could get back and try to take over. This was her fight alone.

Except it wasn't. She thought of Livia. What would happen to her?

The nausea she'd been fighting ever since she'd seen Jaycie walk struck. She fumbled in her pocket for the door key and fit it into the latch. The door gave an ominous squeak. As she let herself inside, she reached for the light switch.

Nothing happened.

Booker had told her how to start the generator, but she hadn't imagined doing it in the dark. She grabbed the flashlight she kept by the door and turned to go back outside when a soft, almost imperceptible sound stopped her cold.

Something had moved on the other side of the room.

Her toes curled in her sneakers. She stopped breathing. The pistol was in her bedroom. All she had was the flashlight. She raised her arm and shot the beam across the room.

Hannibal's yellow eyes gazed back at her, his stuffed-mouse toy clutched between his paws.

"You stupid cat! You scared me to death!"

Hannibal stuck his nose in the air and batted the mouse across the floor.

She glowered at him as she waited for her heartbeat to return to normal. When she was reasonably certain she'd recovered enough to move, she stomped back out into the night. She was not born to be an islander.

You're doing a pretty good job of it, Leo said.

Your cheerleader routine is creeping me out, she told him.

You're reprimanding a puppet, Dilly reminded her.

A puppet who had stopped acting like himself.

She made it to the generator and tried to remember what Booker had told her. As she began to go through the steps, she heard the faintest sound of an engine approaching from the main road. Who would be coming out here now? It might be someone with a medical emergency looking for Theo, except everyone would know by now that he'd left the island. And that Annie was here alone . . .

She abandoned the generator and raced inside to get the pistol from her nightstand. She wasn't absolutely sure she could shoot anyone, but she wasn't sure she couldn't either.

When she returned to the darkened living room, she had the gun in hand. She stood off to the side of the front window and listened to pings of loose gravel. Headlights swept across the marsh. Whoever was driving didn't seem to be making any effort to approach quietly. Maybe Theo had somehow managed to catch a middle-of-the-night ride from the mainland.

Keeping a firm grip on the pistol, she peered around the edge of the window and saw a pickup pull in front of the cottage and stop. A truck she recognized.

By the time she'd opened the front door, Barbara Rose was getting out, leaving the engine running. In the glow coming from the open driver's door, Annie saw the hem of her pink pastel nightgown hanging from under her coat.

Barbara rushed toward her. Annie couldn't see her expression, but she sensed her urgency. "What's wrong?"

"Oh, Annie . . ." Barbara pressed her hand to her mouth. "It's Theo . . ."

A spigot seemed to open in the front of Annie's chest, draining her body of blood.

Barbara clutched Annie's arm. "He was in an accident."

Her grasp was the only thing holding Annie up.

"He's in surgery," Barbara said.

Not dead. Still alive.

"How—how do you know?"

"Someone from the hospital called. The reception was terrible. I don't know if they tried to reach you first. I understood only half the message." Barbara was as breathless as if she'd just run a long distance.

"But . . . He's alive?"

"Yes. I got that much. But it's serious."

"Oh, God . . ." The words came from high in her throat. A prayer.

"I phoned Naomi." Barbara was fighting tears. "She'll take you over on the *Ladyslipper.*"

Barbara didn't ask if Annie wanted to go to him, and Annie didn't hesitate. There was no decision to make. She grabbed the first clothes she could find, and within minutes, they were barreling into town. Annie could live without the cottage, but the thought of the world without Theo was unbearable. He was everything a man should be. He had a brilliant mind and a sterling character. He was a man of conscience: trustworthy, intelligent, and caring. So caring he took on the demons of others as his own.

And she loved him for it.

She loved him. There it was. The thing she'd vowed would never happen. She loved Theo Harp. Not just his body or his face. Not just for sex or companionship. Definitely not for his money. She loved him for who he was. For his beautiful, tortured, kind soul. If he lived, she would stand by him. It made no difference if he were scarred, paralyzed, or brain damaged. She would be there for him.

Just let him live. Please, God, let him live.

The wharf lights were on when they reached the dock. Annie rushed toward Naomi, who was waiting next to the skiff that would take them out to the *Ladyslipper.* She was as grim-faced as Barbara. Wild, awful thoughts swirled through Annie's head. They knew Theo was dying, and neither of them wanted to tell her.

Annie jumped in the skiff. Soon they were racing out of the harbor. Annie turned her back to the retreating shoreline.

Chapter Twenty

M Y HUSBAND IS IN SURGERY." The word tasted all wrong on Annie's lips, but if she didn't identify herself as family, the doctors wouldn't talk to her. "Theo Harp."

The woman behind the desk turned her attention to her computer. Annie squeezed the keys to the Honda Civic Naomi kept on the mainland, a much better car than the clunker she drove on the island. The woman looked up from her computer. "How do you spell the last name?"

"*H-A-R-P*. Like the instrument."

"We don't have anyone here by that name."

"You do!" Annie cried. "He was in a serious accident. The hospital called. He's in surgery."

"Let me double-check." The woman picked up her phone and turned her chair away.

Annie waited, her sense of dread growing by the second. Maybe he wasn't in the computer records because he was already—

The woman set down the phone. "We have no record of him, ma'am. He's not here."

Annie wanted to yell at her, tell her that she should learn how to read. Instead she fumbled for her phone. "I'm calling the police."

"That's a good idea," the woman said kindly.

But neither the local nor state police had any record of an accident involving Theo. The intensity of her relief brought her to tears. Only slowly did that relief give way to comprehension.

There had been no accident. He wasn't hurt. Wasn't dying. He was asleep in a hotel room somewhere.

She called his cell, but it went to voice mail. Because Theo had a habit of turning off his phone at night, even at the cottage, where there was no reception. Whoever had contacted Barbara had done it with the clear intention of getting Annie off the island.

Jaycie.

Barbara had said the call had been hard to understand. Of course it had. But not because of bad reception. Because Jaycie had made sure Barbara couldn't identify her voice. Because Jaycie wanted to get Annie off the island before the end of March so Theo would be hers alone.

The sky had begun to lighten as Annie drove back to the dock where Naomi waited. The streets were empty, stores closed, traffic lights flashing yellow. She could fight—plead extenuating circumstances—but Cynthia wanted the cottage, Elliott was a hardheaded businessman, and the agreement was ironclad. No do-overs. The cottage would return to the Harp family, and whatever his stepmother wanted to do with it would become Theo's problem. Annie's problem would be getting back to the city and finding a place to live. Theo, rescuer of needy women, would likely offer her a room at Harp House, which she'd refuse. No matter how difficult her circumstances, she wouldn't let him see her as another woman in need of rescue.

If only she'd called the hospital herself, but in her panic, that hadn't occurred to her. All she wanted to do now was punish Jaycie for the harm she'd done.

Naomi was sitting in the stern of the *Ladyslipper,* drinking a mug of coffee, when Annie returned to the dock. Naomi's short hair stuck up on one side, and she looked as weary as Annie felt. Annie gave her an abbreviated account of what had happened. Until now, she hadn't spoken to any of the women—not even Barbara—about the conditions surrounding her ownership of the cottage, but it would soon become common knowledge, and there was no longer any need for secrecy. What Annie didn't tell Naomi was that Jaycie had made the phone call. Before she shared that piece of information, she intended to deal with Jaycie herself.

THE *LADYSLIPPER* APPROACHED THE HARBOR at dawn as the fishing boats chugged out to sea to begin their day's work. Barbara and her pickup waited for Annie at the dock, parked not far from Theo's Range Rover. Naomi had called Barbara from her boat, and as Barbara approached Annie, guilt oozed from every pore of her matronly body. "Annie, I'm sorry. I should have asked more questions."

"It's not your fault," Annie said wearily. "I should have been suspicious."

Barbara's repeated apologies on the drive back to the cottage only made Annie feel worse, and she was glad when the ride ended. Even though she'd barely slept, she knew she couldn't rest until she'd confronted Jaycie. Vandalism, attempted murder, and now this. Any hesitation Annie might have felt about involving the police had vanished. She wanted to look Jaycie right in the eye when she told her she knew what she'd done.

She made herself drink a cup of coffee and eat a few bites of toast. Her gun was where she'd left it last night. She couldn't imagine using it, but she also wasn't going to be stupid, not after she'd seen Jaycie climb the stairs toward Annie's room last night. Tucking it in her coat pocket, she left the cottage.

Not even a hint of spring rode on the wind. As she made her way across the marsh, she pictured Theo's farm at the other end of the island. The lush stretch of sheltered meadow. The distant view of the sea. The all-embracing peace of it.

The kitchen was empty. Keeping her coat on, she made her way to the housekeeper's apartment. All this time she'd been trying to repay the debt she owed Jaycie not knowing the debt had been paid in full the first time Jaycie had broken into the cottage.

The door to the housekeeper's apartment was closed. Annie shoved it open without knocking. Jaycie sat by the window in the old rocker, Livia in her lap curled against her mother's breast. Jaycie's cheek rested on her daughter's head, and she didn't seem indignant about Annie barging in. "Livia hurt her thumb in the door," she told Annie. "We're having a little cuddle. Is it better now, muffin?"

Annie's stomach twisted. Regardless of what Jaycie had done, she loved her daughter, and Livia loved her mother. If she turned Jaycie over to the police . . .

Livia forgot about her hurt thumb and lifted her head to see if Scamp was hidden behind Annie's back. Jaycie fingered a lock of Livia's hair. "I hate it when she gets hurt."

With Livia in the room, the heavy weight of the gun in Annie's coat pocket felt more obscene than prudent. "Livia," Annie said, "Mommy and I need to talk about some grown-up things. Will you draw a picture for me? Maybe a picture of the beach?"

Livia nodded, slid off Jaycie's lap, and headed for the small table where she kept her crayons. Jaycie's forehead knit with concern. "Is anything wrong?"

"We'll talk in the kitchen." Annie had to turn away as Jaycie reached for her crutches.

The uneven thump of Jaycie's gait followed Annie down the hall. She thought about how men historically settled their scores in public arenas: the dueling field, the boxing ring, and the battleground. But women's disputes tended to be played out in domestic arenas, like this kitchen.

She waited until Jaycie had come in behind her before she turned to confront her. "I'll take those." She pulled the crutches away so abruptly Jaycie would have fallen if she didn't have two good feet to hold herself up.

Jaycie gave a hiss of alarm. "What are you doing?" Too

many seconds passed before she remembered to balance her weight against the wall. "I need those."

"You didn't need them last night," Annie said flatly.

Jaycie looked shocked. Good. Annie wanted her unbalanced. She dropped the crutches to the floor and pushed them away with her foot. "You lied to me."

Jaycie's face went pale. Annie finally felt as if she were seeing through the invisible veil she lived behind. "I—I didn't want you to find out," Jaycie said.

"Obviously."

Jaycie moved away from the wall, walking with a limp so slight that Annie doubted she would have noticed it if she hadn't been looking for it. Jaycie curled her fingers around the back of the chair at the end of the table, her knuckles white. "That's why you left the house last night," she said.

"I saw you going upstairs. What were you planning to do?"

Jaycie gripped the chair back tighter, as if she still needed support. "I was— I don't want to tell you."

Annie's hurt erupted. "You deceived me. And you did it in the worst possible way."

Misery clouded Jaycie's features. She sank into the chair. "I—I was desperate. That's not an excuse. I know it's not. And I kept meaning to tell you my foot was better. But— Try to understand. I was so lonely."

The residual rawness of being afraid Theo was dead had hardened something inside Annie. "It's too bad Theo didn't make himself available to keep you company."

Instead of hostility, Jaycie displayed only a resigned acceptance. "That was never going to happen. I'm prettier than you, and for a while, I let myself believe that might be enough." Jaycie's words weren't boastful, just a statement of fact. "But I'm not interesting the way you are. I'm not well educated. You always know what to say to him, and I never do. You stand up to him, and I can't. I know all that."

Annie hadn't expected so much frankness, but it did nothing to lessen her sense of betrayal. "Why were you going up to my room last night?"

Jaycie dipped her head. "I don't want to look any more spineless than I already am."

"Not exactly the word I'd use."

Jaycie gazed down at her hands. "I hate being alone in this house at night. It wasn't so bad when I knew Theo was in the turret, but now . . . I can't go to sleep until I've walked through all the rooms, and even then, I have to lock the door on my apartment. I'm sorry I lied to you, but if I'd told you the truth— If I'd told you my foot was healing and I could walk without crutches, that I didn't need your help, you wouldn't have kept coming up here. You're used to your city girlfriends who know about books and theater. I'm just an island girl."

Now Annie was the one feeling unbalanced. Everything Jaycie said had the ring of truth. But what about everything she wasn't saying? Annie crossed her arms. "I left the island last night. But I'm sure you already know that."

"Left the island?" She pretended to be alarmed, as though this was new information. "But you can't do that? Did anybody see you? Why would you leave the island?"

A thread of doubt was beginning to weave its way through Annie's anger. But then she'd always been gullible around accomplished liars. "Your phone call worked."

"What phone call? Annie, what are you talking about?"

Annie held tight to her determination. "The phone call Barbara got saying Theo was in the hospital. That phone call."

She jumped from the chair. "Hospital? Is he all right? What happened?"

Don't let her suck you in, Dilly admonished. *Don't be naive.*

But . . . Scamp interceded. *I think she's telling the truth.*

Jaycie had to be the person behind these attacks. She'd lied, she had motive, and she was aware of all of Annie's comings and goings.

"Annie, tell me!" Jaycie insisted.

She was so adamant, so uncharacteristically demanding that Annie felt even more unbalanced. She bought time for herself. "Barbara Rose got a phone call, supposedly from the hospital . . ." Annie told Jaycie about her trip to the mainland, about what she had—hadn't—found. She spelled out the details coldly and factually as she watched carefully for Jaycie's every reaction.

By the time she finished, Jaycie's eyes were full of tears. "You think I was behind that call? You think, after everything you've done for me, I'd do this to you?"

Annie steeled herself. "You're in love with Theo."

"Theo is a fantasy! Daydreaming about him kept me from reliving everything I went through with Ned. It wasn't real." Tears rolled down her cheeks. "I'm not blind. Do you think I don't know you're lovers? Does it hurt? Yes. Are there times I envy you? Too many. You're so good at everything. So competent. But you're not good at this. You're not good at judging people." Jaycie turned her back on Annie and stalked from the kitchen.

Annie collapsed in a chair, sick to her stomach. How had this gone so wrong? Or maybe it hadn't. Even now, Jaycie could be lying to her.

But she wasn't. Annie knew that.

Annie couldn't stay at Harp House, and she walked back to the cottage. Hannibal greeted her at the door and followed her into her bedroom, where she got rid of the gun. She picked him up and carried him to the couch. "I'm going to miss you, fella."

Her eyes were scratchy from lack of sleep, and her stomach churned. As she stroked the cat for comfort, she gazed around her. Almost nothing was left for her to take when she left the island. The furniture was Theo's, and without a kitchen of her own, she had no need for the cottage's pots and pans. She wanted some of her mother's scarves and the red cloak, but she'd leave the rest of Mariah's clothes on the island. As for her memories of Theo . . . Somehow she'd have to figure out a way to leave them behind, too.

She blinked her eyes against the pain. Giving Hannibal one more scratch under his chin, she set the cat down and went over to the bookshelves, bare except for some tattered paperbacks and her old Dreambook. She felt defeated. Empty. As she picked up the scrapbook, one of the *Playbill*s she'd saved fell out, along with some magazine photos of models wearing sleek hairstyles that, in a fit of teenage delusion, she'd thought she could achieve.

The cat wrapped himself around her ankles. She flipped through the pages and found a review she'd written herself of a play in which she'd been the imaginary star. All that youthful optimism.

She crouched down to retrieve the rest of the things that had fallen out, including two manila envelopes where she'd kept various certificates she'd earned. She looked inside one and saw a heavy piece of drawing paper. She pulled it out and gazed at a pen-and-ink sketch she couldn't remember ever having seen. She opened the second envelope and found a matching drawing. She carried them toward the front window. Each had a signature in the bottom right corner. She blinked. N. Garr.

Her heart skipped a beat. She studied the signatures more closely, took in the sketches, looked at the signatures again. There was no mistake. These sketches had been signed by Niven Garr.

She began frantically searching her memory for what she knew about him. He'd made his mark as a postmodern painter, then ventured into photorealism a few years before his death. Mariah had always been critical of his work, which was odd considering that Annie had found three books with photographs of his paintings right here at the cottage.

She laid the sketches on the table where the light was the brightest. These drawings had to be the legacy Mariah had told her about. And what a legacy!

She sank into one of the spindle-backed chairs. How had Mariah gotten these, and why all the mystery? Her mother had never mentioned knowing him, and he certainly hadn't been part of Mariah's social circle in the days when she'd still had one. Annie examined the details. The drawings were dated two days apart. Both sketches were realistic renderings of a nude female, but despite the boldness of the ink lines and the precision of the shading, the depth of tenderness in the woman's expression as she gazed at the artist gave the drawings a dreamy quality. She was offering him everything.

Annie understood this woman's emotions as if they were her own. She knew exactly what that kind of love felt like. The model was long limbed—handsome, but not beautiful—with

a strong-boned face and a mane of straight hair. She reminded
Annie of old photographs she'd seen of Mariah. They had the
same—

Annie's hand flew to her mouth. This was Mariah. Why
hadn't she recognized her right away?

Because Annie had never seen her mother like this—soft,
young, and vulnerable, her hard edges gone.

Hannibal jumped into Annie's lap. Annie sat quietly, tears
springing to her eyes. If only she could have known her mother
back then. If only . . . Once again, she took in the date of the
sketches—the year, the month. She calculated.

These were done seven months before she was born.

*"Your father was a married man. It was a fling. Nothing
more. I didn't care for him at all."*

A lie. These were the drawings of a woman deeply in love
with the man capturing her image. A man who, according to
the dates, must have been Annie's father.

Niven Garr.

Annie sank her fingers into Hannibal's fur. She remembered photos she'd seen of Garr. His wildly curly hair had
been his trademark—hair so unlike Mariah's, so like Annie's
own. Annie's conception hadn't been the result of a fling, as
her mother had said, and Niven Garr hadn't been married at
the time. His only marriage had come many years later, to his
longtime male partner.

It all became clear. Mariah had loved Niven Garr. The tenderness evident in his depiction of her suggested he'd felt the
same. But not enough. Ultimately he'd had to make peace with
his true nature and leave Mariah behind.

Annie wondered if he knew he had a daughter. Had Mariah's pride—or maybe her bitterness—caused her to conceal
the truth from him? Mariah had been so dismissive of Annie's childhood drawings, so disparaging of Annie's curls and
her childhood shyness. They'd been painful reminders of him.
Mariah's acrimony toward Garr's paintings had nothing to do
with his work and everything to do with the fact that she'd
loved him more than he'd been able to love her.

Hannibal wiggled from Annie's grip. These beautiful

drawings of a woman in love would solve all her problems. They'd bring Annie more than enough money to pay off her debts several times over. She'd have the time and money to prepare for the next part of her life. The drawings would fix everything.

Except that she could never part with them.

The love radiating from Mariah's face, her hand curled protectively across her belly, all of it so tender. These sketches were Annie's true legacy. They were concrete evidence that Annie had been created in love. Maybe that's what her mother had wanted her to see.

IN THE LAST TWENTY-FOUR HOURS, Annie had lost so much, but she'd also found her heritage. The cottage was no longer hers, her financial situation was as dire as ever, and she needed to find a place to live, but she had discovered the missing part of herself. She'd also betrayed a friend. The memory of Jaycie's stricken expression wouldn't go away. She had to go back and apologize.

Don't be a sap, Peter said. *You're such a chump.*

She tuned him out, and even though her body craved sleep, she made her second trek of the day to the top of the cliff. As she climbed she thought about what it meant to be both Mariah and Niven Garr's daughter. But ultimately, the only person she knew how to be was herself.

Jaycie was in her apartment, sitting by the window, staring out into the side yard. The door was open, but Annie knocked on the frame. "Can I come in?"

Jaycie shrugged. Annie took that as permission. She shoved her hands in her coat pockets. "Jayc, I'm sorry. I truly am. There's not anything I can do to take back what I said, but I'm asking you to forgive me. I don't know who's behind what's been happening to me, but——"

"I thought we were friends!" Jaycie said, her hurt raw.

"We are."

Jaycie pushed herself up from the chair and swept past Annie. "I have to check on Livia."

Annie didn't try to stop her. The damage she'd done to

their relationship ran too deep for an easy repair. She returned to the kitchen, intending to stay there until Jaycie was ready to talk. Jaycie appeared almost immediately but brushed past her. Without even a glance in Annie's direction, she opened the back door. "Livia! Livia, where are you?"

Annie was so accustomed to going after Livia herself that she made her way toward the door, but Jaycie had already stepped outside. "Livia Christine! Come back here right now!"

Annie followed Jaycie. "I'll go around the front."

"Don't bother," Jaycie snapped. "I'll do it myself."

Annie ignored her and checked the front porch. Livia wasn't there. She went back to Jaycie. "Are you sure she's not inside. She could be hiding anywhere in the house."

Jaycie's concern for her daughter temporarily eclipsed her anger at Annie. "I'll go look."

The stable door was securely locked. Annie didn't find her in the woods behind the gazebo, and she circled to the front of the house again. The porch was still empty, but as she looked down at the beach, she spotted a splash of pink against the rocks. She rushed toward the steps. Even though Livia stood well back from the water's edge, she shouldn't be down there alone. "Livia!"

Livia looked up. Her pink jacket was unzipped, her hair falling straight around her face.

"Stay right where you are," Annie ordered her as she neared the bottom. "I found her!" she yelled, not certain if Jaycie could hear.

Livia wore her mulish look. She held what appeared to be a piece of drawing paper in one hand and a teepee of crayons in the other. Earlier, Annie had asked her to draw a picture of the beach. Apparently the four-year-old had decided to do it on location. "Oh, Liv . . . You aren't allowed to come down here alone." She recalled the stories she'd heard about rogue waves sweeping grown men into the sea. "Let's go find Mommy. She's not going to be happy with you."

As she reached for Livia's hand, she saw a figure striding down the beach from the cottage. Tall, lean, and broad shouldered, wind rippling his dark hair. Her heart tripped all over itself with the love she felt for him, along with a fierce determination not to let her feelings show. She knew he cared for her, just as she knew he didn't love her. But she loved him enough to make certain her feelings for him didn't become one more guilty burden. For once in Theo Harp's life, a woman was going to look out for his well-being instead of the other way around.

"Hey, Boo," she said as he stopped next to her.

His eyebrow shot up in a dagger of annoyance. "Don't even think of trying to play cute with me. I heard what happened. Are you crazy? What possessed you to take off like that?"

Love possessed me. She forced her rigid jaw muscles to relax. "It was the middle of the night, and I was barely awake. I thought you were hurt. Pardon me for being concerned."

He ignored the barb. "Even if I'd been dying, the last thing you should have done is leave the island."

"We're friends, you ass. Are you telling me that, if you thought I'd been in a terrible accident, you wouldn't have done the same thing?"

"Not if it meant losing the only place I had to live!"

So untrue. He would have done exactly the same thing for any of his friends. That was how he was made. "Go away," she said. "I don't want to talk to you." *I want to kiss you. Smack you. Make love with you.* But more than that, she wanted to save him from his own nature.

He threw up his hands. "All you had to do this winter was one simple thing. *Stay in place.* But could you do that? No."

"Stop yelling at me."

He wasn't yelling, as he immediately pointed out. "I'm not yelling."

But he had raised his voice, so she raised hers. "I don't care about the cottage," she lied. "The best day of my life is going to be the day I leave this place."

"And exactly where do you plan to go?"

"Back to the city, where I belong!"

"Doing what?"

"Doing what I do!"

They kept on like that for a few minutes, their voices getting louder by the second until they both ran out of steam. "Damn it, Annie. I worry about you."

He'd finally calmed down, and she couldn't resist touching him. Her palm to his chest, feeling his heart beat. "It's your nature. Now stop it."

He looped his arm around her shoulders, and they turned toward the steps. "I have something——"

Annie spotted a sheet of white construction paper fluttering across the rocks. Livia was gone.

"Liv!"

There was no response.

"Livia!" She instinctively turned toward the sea, but she'd been standing at enough of an angle that surely she would have seen her if she'd gotten close to the water.

"Did you find her?" Jaycie appeared at the top of the cliff. She was coatless, her voice reedy with near hysteria. "She's not in the house. I've looked everywhere."

Theo had started to move toward the rockslide that blocked the cave, but it took a moment for Annie to see what he had seen, a torn piece of pink fabric lying in a fissure between the boulders. Annie rushed to his side. The cave entrance had been blocked up years ago, but there was an opening in the rocks, an angular space wide enough for a child to get inside. And four crayons lay nearby.

"Get a flashlight!" Theo yelled up to Jaycie. "I think she's gone in the cave."

High tide was a few hours away, but who knew how deep the water already was inside? Annie crouched in front of Theo and leaned into the crevice. "Livia, are you in there?"

She heard the echo of her own voice, the slap of water against the cave walls, but nothing else. "Livia! Honey, you have to answer me so I know you're all right." Did she really think she could demand that a mute child talk?

Theo pushed her aside. "Liv, it's Theo. I found some great shells for the house, but I'm going to need help building the furniture. Can you come out and help me?"

Theo locked eyes with Annie as they waited. They heard nothing.

Annie tried again. "If you're in there, can you make a little sound for us? Or throw a rock so we can hear? Just so we know you're there."

They strained to listen. A few seconds later, they heard it. The soft plop of a stone hitting the water.

Theo began frantically shoving at the boulders, undeterred by the fact that even the smaller ones were too big for one man to move. Jaycie was racing down the steps, flashlight in hand, still coatless. Theo momentarily stopped what he was doing to stare at her as she scrambled toward them over the boulders without her crutches. It wasn't Annie's job to explain, and he went back to work.

"She's in there." Annie moved out of the way so Jaycie could kneel in front of the crevice.

"Livia, it's Mommy!" Jaycie shone the flashlight inside. "Can you see the light?"

Only the waves answered.

"Livia, you have to come out. Right now! I won't be mad. I promise." She spun toward Annie. "She could drown in there."

Theo grabbed a heavy slab of driftwood. He shoved it under the top boulder to make a makeshift lever, then hesitated. "I can't take the chance. If I do shift the boulders, there's no guarantee they won't seal up the entrance even tighter."

Jaycie's cheeks were ashen. She clutched the torn pink fabric from her daughter's coat. "Why did she go in there?"

"I don't know," Annie said. "She likes to explore. Maybe—"

"She's afraid of the dark! Why would she do this?"

Annie had no answer.

"Livia!" Jaycie cried. "You have to come out now!"

Theo had begun digging at the hard sand at the bottom of the crevice. "I'll go in after her, but we have to widen the opening."

"You're too big," Jaycie said. "It'll take too long."

The tip of a wave crested over the rocks and splashed their feet, returning some of the sand that Theo had moved. Jaycie tried to push him aside. "I'm going in."

Theo stopped her. "You won't fit. We need to shift more sand."

He was right. Even though he'd deepened the opening, the seawater kept trying to move the sand back, and Jaycie's hips were too wide. "I have to," she protested. "Right now, she could be . . ."

"I'll do it," Annie said. "Get out of my way."

Even as she pushed Jaycie aside, she wasn't sure whether she would fit, but she stood a better chance than either of them. Theo's eyes met her own. "It's too dangerous."

Instead of arguing, she gave him her cockiest smile. "Out of my way, dude. I'll be fine."

He knew as well as she did that she was the only one of them who had a chance of doing this, but that didn't ease the struggle that played out in his eyes. "You be careful, do you hear me?" he said fiercely. "Don't you dare do anything crazy!"

"Not planning to." She took off her coat and passed it to Jaycie. "Put this on."

She surveyed the tight opening, then pulled her sweatshirt over her head and tossed it aside, leaving herself in only jeans and a bright orange camisole. The cold raised goose bumps on her skin.

Theo dug furiously at the sand, trying to give her more room. She crouched down, wincing as an icy blast of spray struck her. "Liv, it's Annie. I'm coming in with you." She gasped as she lay down in the cold sand. As she pushed her feet inside, she imagined getting stuck in the cave entrance like Pooh in the honey jar.

"Easy now." Theo's voice was unnaturally tight. "Go easy." He did his best to help her maneuver, but at the same time, she detected an almost undetectable resistance, as if he didn't want to let her go. "Careful. Just be careful."

It was a word he repeated half a dozen more times as she threaded her legs through the crevice, then turned her body so that her hips were roughly parallel with the opening. Another wave sprayed her. Theo shifted his position, trying to shield her.

Her sneakers were underwater inside the cave, renewing her fears about the water's depth. Her hips wedged between the rocks. "You're not going to make it," he said. "Come back out. I'll dig deeper."

She ignored him and sucked in her stomach. With the upper half of her body still outside, she pushed as hard as she could.

"Annie, stop!"

She didn't. She bit her lip against the sharp edges of rock and dug her feet into the sand. With a final twist of her shoulders, she was inside.

As Annie disappeared into the cave, Theo felt as though he, too, had been sucked in with her. He passed the flashlight to her through the crevice. He should be the one in there. He was a stronger swimmer, although God knew, he hoped the water inside wasn't deep enough to make that a factor.

Jaycie stood behind him making helpless sounds. He kept digging at the sand. He should be the rescuer, not Annie. He tried not to think about how this scene would play out if he'd been writing it, but the ugly scenario unwound in his head like a filmstrip. If this were a scene in one of his books, Quentin Pierce would be inside that cave waiting for an unsuspecting Annie to become the victim of his next sadistic butchering. Theo never wrote detailed descriptions of the brutal deaths of his female characters, but he planted enough clues so the readers could fill in the cruel particulars for themselves. And now he was doing that in his head with Annie.

The very reason he'd been drawn to writing horror novels mocked him. By creating his gruesome tales of twisted minds, he'd achieved a sense of control. In his books, he had the power to punish evil and make certain justice was served. In fiction, at least, he could impose order on a dangerous, chaotic world.

He mentally sent in Diggity Swift to help her. Diggity, who was small enough to slip through the crevice and resourceful enough to keep Annie safe. Diggity, the character he'd killed off two weeks ago.

He dug faster and deeper, ignoring the bleeding cuts in his hands, calling to her, "For God's sake, be careful."

Inside the cave, Annie heard Theo's words, but she'd been plunged back into her old nightmare. She turned on the flashlight. Erosion had left the water level at the front of the cave deeper than it used to be, already at her calves. Her throat clogged with fear. "Liv?"

She swept the beam around the cave walls, then forced herself to shine it on the water. No torn pink jacket bobbed on the surface. No little girl with straight brown hair lay face-down. But that didn't necessarily mean she wasn't there . . . She choked out the words, "Livie, make a noise, sweetheart, so I know where you are."

Only the lap of water echoed against the granite walls. She moved deeper into the cave, creating a mental image of Livia crouched out of sight in one of the nooks. "Livia, please . . . Make a sound for me. Any kind of sound."

The continuing silence pounded in her ears. "Mommy's right outside the cave waiting for you." Her flashlight caught the ledge at the back that she remembered so well. She half expected to see a sodden cardboard box. The water splashed the top of her knees. Why wouldn't Livia answer her? She wanted to scream with frustration.

And then a voice whispered, *Let me.*

She flicked off the flashlight.

"Turn it back on!" Scamp exclaimed in a shaky voice. "If you do not turn it back on immediately, I shall shriek, and that will be unpleasant for everyone. Let me demonstrate . . ."

"Don't demonstrate, Scamp!" Annie fought the possibility that she was playing out a puppet show for a child who might already have drowned. "I turned it off to save the batteries."

"Save something else," Scamp declared. "Like Pop-Tarts boxes or red crayons. Liv and I want the flashlight on, don't we, Liv?"

A small, choked sob drifted over the water.

Annie's relief was so intense that she could barely manage Scamp's voice. "You see. Livia agrees! Pay no attention to Annie, Livia. She's in one of her moods. Now please turn the light back on."

Annie switched on the light and waded deeper into the cave, her eyes desperately searching for any movement. "I'm not in a mood, Scamp," she said in her own voice. "And if the battery runs down, don't blame me."

"Liv and I plan to be out of here long before your stupid battery runs down," Scamp retorted.

"You're not allowed to say 'stupid,'" Annie proclaimed, her voice still shaky. "It's rude, isn't it, Livia?"

No answer.

"I apologize," Scamp said. "I'm only being rude because I'm scared. You understand, don't you, Livia?"

Another muffled sniffle came from the back of the cave. Annie swung the flashlight beam to the right and traced a narrow shelf that hung just above the waterline and curved around a jutting piece of rock. Could Livia have crawled along that ledge?

"It's very dark in here," the puppet complained. "And that means I'm very scared, so I shall sing a song to make myself feel better. I shall call it the 'Sitting in a Dark Cave' song. Written by me, Scamp."

Annie waded through the thigh-high water as Scamp began to sing.

> "I was sitting in a dark cave
> High on a ledge.
> Hiding away
> Not wanting to stay—ay—ay."

She was so cold, she was losing feeling in her legs.

> "When along came a nice spider
> And sat down beside her
> And said . . .
> Holy cow! What's a nice spider like me
>   doing in a dark cave like this?"

She rounded the edge of a protruding rock and glimpsed a blessed blur of pink huddled on the ledge. She wanted to charge forward and grab her. Instead she ducked back out of sight and aimed the flashlight down into the dark water.

"Annie," Scamp said, "I'm still scared. I need to see Livia right now. Livia will make me feel better."

"I understand, Scamp," Annie said, "but . . . I can't find her anywhere."

"You have to! I need to talk to a kid, not a grown-up! I need Livia!" Scamp grew increasingly upset. "She's my friend, and friends help each other when they're scared." Scamp started to cry in pathetic little sniffles. "Why won't she tell me where she is?"

A wave hit Annie's thighs, and the cave ceiling dripped icy fingers down her spine.

Scamp began crying harder, her sniffles growing more pronounced. Until three soft, sweet words drifted over the water . . .

"I'm right here."

Chapter Twenty-one

ANNIE HAD NEVER HEARD ANYTHING as beautiful as those faint, hesitant words. *I'm right here.* She couldn't spoil this . . .

"Livia," Scamp whispered. "Is that really you?"

"Uh-huh."

"I thought I was alone, with only Annie."

"I'm here, too." Livia's newfound voice had a rusty little rasp from lack of use.

"That makes me feel better." Scamp sniffed. "Are you scared?"

"Uh-huh."

"Me, too. I'm glad I'm not the only one."

"You're not." She couldn't fully form her *r* sounds, and they came out more as *w*'s, the sound substitution so sweet it constricted Annie's heart.

"Do you want to stay here longer, or are you ready to leave?" Scamp asked.

A long pause. "I don't know."

Annie reined in her apprehension and made herself wait. Long seconds ticked by.

"Scamp?" Livia finally said. "Are you still there?"

"I'm thinking," Scamp said. "And I think you need to talk this over with a grown-up. Is it okay if I send Annie to find you?"

Annie waited, afraid she'd pushed too far. But Livia responded with a quiet "Okay."

"Annie!" Scamp called out. "Come over here, please. Livia needs to talk to you. Livia, I'm very cold, and I'm going to get some hot chocolate. And a dill pickle. I'll meet you later."

Annie waded around the rock, praying that her appearance wouldn't make Livia mute again. Livia still had her knees pulled to her chest. Her head was down, her hair hiding her face.

Annie wasn't sure if Jaycie could hear that Livia was safe, but she was afraid to call out for fear of sending Livia spiraling backward. "Hey, goofball," she said.

Livia finally lifted her head.

What had driven a child who was afraid of the dark to come in here? Only something deeply traumatic. Yet when Annie had found her on the beach, Livia had been more petulant than traumatized. Something had to have happened after that, but other than Theo appearing—

Right then Annie understood.

Even though her teeth were chattering, and the ledge was too shallow for any kind of comfort, she hoisted herself up. Wedging in as best she could, she wrapped her arm around the child. Livia smelled of musty ocean, little girl sweat, and shampoo. "Did you know that Scamp is mad at me?" Annie asked.

Livia shook her head.

Annie waited, ignoring the blade of rock digging into her shoulder, holding Livia close, but not explaining.

Finally, Livia's jaw moved against Annie's arm. "What'd you do?"

That voice! That dear little voice. "Scamp said you came in here because you heard Theo and me arguing. That's why she's mad at me. Because we argued in front of you, and arguments between grown-ups scare you."

A barely imperceptible nod against her shoulder.

"It's because of the bad way your dad used to hurt your mommy and because of how your dad died." Annie made the pronouncement as matter-of-factly as she could.

"It scared me." A heartbreaking sniffle.

"Sure it did. It would have scared me, too. Scamp told me I should have explained to you that just because grown-ups argue doesn't always mean something bad will happen. Like when Theo and I argue. We like to argue. But we'd never hurt each other."

Livia cocked her head at Annie, taking that in.

Annie could have lifted her down and waded out with her, but she hesitated. What else could she say to undo the damage? She traced her thumb along Livia's cheek. "Sometimes people argue. Kids and grown-ups. For instance, your mommy and I had an argument today. It was my fault, and I'm going to tell her I'm sorry."

"You and Mommy?" Livia said.

"I was confused about something. But here's the thing, Livia. If you get scared every time you hear somebody argue, you'll be scared a lot, and none of us want you to feel like that."

"But Theo's voice was really loud."

"Mine, too. I was very mad at him."

"You could shoot him with a gun," Livia said, trying to sort out a situation that was too complicated for her.

"Oh, no, I would never do that." Annie tried to find another way. Hesitated. "Can I have a free secret?"

"Uh-huh."

Annie rested her cheek against the top of Livia's head. "I love Theo," she whispered. "And I could never love anybody who tried to hurt me. But that doesn't mean I can't get mad at him."

"You love Theo?"

"It's my free secret, remember?"

"I remember." The sweet sound of her breathing hummed in Annie's ears. She wiggled. "Can I have a free secret?"

"Sure." Annie braced herself, afraid of what was coming next.

Livia turned her head to gaze up at Annie. "I didn't like Scamp's song."

Annie laughed and kissed her forehead. "We won't tell her."

THE JOYOUS REUNION BETWEEN MOTHER and child would have brought Annie to tears if she hadn't been so cold. Theo drew her into a weak patch of sunlight and examined her wounds. She stood before him dressed only in her orange camisole and white panties, her wet wool socks collapsed in origami folds around her ankles. After she'd pushed Livia through the crevice into Theo's arms, she'd discovered that her sodden jeans had picked up just enough extra bulk to keep her from squeezing through, and she'd had to take them off.

Theo checked the long scratch running down her abdomen, joining her other cuts and bruises. His right hand curved around her buttocks to keep her from pulling away, not that she wanted to. "You're all cut up." He pulled off his parka and wrapped her in it. "I swear to God I'm ten years older than I was when you went in there." He pulled her against his chest, a place Annie was more than happy to rest.

Jaycie's gratitude had made her forget her anger at Annie, and she finally wrenched her gaze away from Livia long enough to say, "I can never thank you enough."

Annie tried unsuccessfully to stop her teeth from chattering. "You may not want to . . . after you hear why Livia . . . went in the cave." She reluctantly drew away from the comfort of Theo's chest and moved a few steps closer to Jaycie and Livia, but he came up behind her.

"You can talk to Jaycie later," he said. "Right now, you need to get warmed up."

"I will in a minute." Jaycie was sitting in the shelter of a boulder with Livia curled in her lap, Annie's coat draping them both. Annie looked at Livia. "Liv, I'm afraid I'll say it wrong, so you'd better explain to your mom."

Jaycie hadn't overheard her daughter speak, and she was visibly confused. Livia turned her face into her mother's chest.

"It's okay," Annie said. "You can tell her." But would she? Now that they'd left the cave behind, had Livia lost her need to speak? Annie drew the parka tighter around her and waited, hoped, prayed . . .

The words that finally emerged were muffled, spoken against her mother's breast. "I was scared."

Jaycie gasped. Cupping her daughter's cheeks, she turned her small face up and gazed into her eyes with wonder. "Liv . . ."

"'Cause Annie and Theo was fighting," Livia said. "It made me scared."

Theo's curse was no less heartfelt for being whispered.

"Oh, my God . . ." Jaycie pulled Livia to her again in a fierce embrace.

The tears of joy that filled Jaycie's eyes made Annie suspect she hadn't taken in the content of Livia's words, only the miracle of her daughter's voice. Now, while emotions were high, was the time to rip off the bandage of secrecy that Jaycie had plastered over the past and open the scab that had grown there.

Annie drew courage from the way Theo's body settled protectively against her spine. "You might not know this, Jaycie, but hearing grown-ups argue reminds Livia of what happened with you and her father."

Jaycie's joy dissolved. Her mouth twisted in pain, but Annie pressed on. "When she heard Theo and me arguing, she was afraid I might try to shoot him, so she went in the cave to hide."

Theo spoke vehemently. "Livia, Annie would never do that."

Jaycie slipped one hand over her daughter's ear, symbolically sealing it off. The tightness around her mouth testified that the gratitude she'd been feeling toward Annie was fading. "We don't have to talk about that."

"Livia needs to talk," Annie stated gently.

"Listen to Annie," Theo said, in a remarkable leap of faith. "She understands things."

Livia shook her head, the gesture automatic. Theo squeezed Annie's shoulders from behind. His encouragement meant everything. "Livia and Scamp and I have been talking about how her father scared her," Annie said, "and how you shot him, even though you didn't mean to." The cold had numbed her brain to caution. "Livia might even be a little glad you shot her father—I know Scamp is glad—and Livia needs to talk to you about that, too."

"Scamp?" Jaycie said.

"Scamp is a kid, too," Annie said, "so she understands things about Livia that grown-ups sometimes miss."

Jaycie was now more bewildered than angry. She searched her daughter's face, trying to understand, not able to. Her helplessness reminded Annie that Jaycie was as deeply wounded as Livia.

With no psychotherapist handy, a failed character actress trained in her theater workshops to understand human behavior would have to do. Annie let her spine rest ever so slightly against Theo's chest, not using him as a crutch, merely as comfort. "Scamp would like to understand some things, too," she said. "Maybe she could sit down with both of you tomorrow, and we could all talk about what happened." Annie remembered that her "tomorrows" on Peregrine Island were numbered.

"Yes, I wanna see Scamp!" Livia displayed all the enthusiasm her mother lacked.

"A great idea," Theo said. "Now I think it's time for everybody to get warmed up."

Livia had recovered more rapidly than the adults, and she climbed off her mother's lap. "Will you show me the shells you got for my fairy house?" she asked Theo.

"Yep. But I have to take care of Annie first." He tilted his head toward the top of the cliff. "Want a ride?"

Livia ended up on his shoulders as they climbed the cliff steps to the top.

ONCE ANNIE AND THEO WERE back at the cottage, he filled the tub that was no longer hers and left her alone. She had cuts everywhere, and she winced as she settled into the water, but by the time she got out and slipped into her robe, she was warm. Theo had changed into dry clothes himself—a pair of jeans with a rip across one knee and a long-sleeved black T-shirt he'd stopped wearing because Jaycie had shrunk it in the wash so it outlined every muscle in his chest in a way he didn't like, but that Annie very much appreciated. He patched up her cuts, everything about his touch impersonal. In the space of a day, so much had changed. She'd lost the cottage, accused an innocent woman of trying to harm her, discovered her roots, and helped rescue a little girl. Overriding it all, she'd recognized how much she loved this man she couldn't have.

He made grilled cheese sandwiches for them. As he dropped a big pat of butter into the hot skillet, a clock pendulum ticked away in her head marking the time she had left to be with him. "I called Elliott," he said. "As soon as I heard that you'd been conned into leaving the island."

She tugged the sash of her bathrobe tighter. "Let me guess. Cynthia already knew—thanks to Lisa McKinley—and they were having cocktails to celebrate."

"Right on one count. Wrong on the other. Lisa had called, but there was no celebration."

"Really? I'm surprised Cynthia wasn't already drawing up plans to turn the cottage into a replica of Stonehenge."

"I intended to make him change his mind. Threaten him. Do whatever I could to make sure you kept the cottage for as long as you wanted. But as it turned out, Elliott had made a modification none of us knew about."

"What kind of modification?"

"The cottage doesn't revert back to the family." He abandoned the sandwiches to look at her. "It goes to the Peregrine Island trust."

She stared at him stupidly. "I don't understand."

He turned back and flipped the sandwiches into the sizzling butter with unnecessary force. "The bottom line is, you've lost the cottage, and I'm sorrier about that than you can imagine."

"But why did he change it?"

"I didn't get the details—Cynthia was in the room—but he wasn't exactly happy with what she did to Harp House. My guess is that he wanted to make sure the cottage stayed as it was, so rather than stand up to her, he went to his lawyer behind her back and made the change."

Her head spun. "Mariah never mentioned this."

"She didn't know. Apparently no one knew except the island trustees."

The sound of a vehicle approaching interrupted them. He handed her the spatula. "Keep an eye on these."

As he made his way to the front door, she tried to piece

it all together, but her thoughts were interrupted by a strange male voice at the front door. Moments later, Theo stuck his head back in the kitchen. "I have to go. Another emergency. You shouldn't have to worry about intruders now, but keep the doors locked anyway."

After he left, she sat at the table with one of the sandwiches. He'd used good cheddar with a touch of her favorite coarse brown mustard, but she was too tired to eat or to think. She needed sleep.

The next morning found her as clearheaded as she'd ever been. She had Jaycie's Suburban and drove into town. The collection of dirty pickup trucks in front of Barbara Rose's house indicated that the Monday-morning knitting group was in session. Before Annie had been able to fall asleep last night, she'd had plenty of time to think, and she let herself in without ringing the bell.

Upholstered furniture and knickknacks stuffed the living room. Amateur oil paintings of boats and buoys hung on the walls, along with half a dozen floral china plates. Every tabletop held family photos: Lisa blowing out birthday candles, Lisa and her brother opening Christmas presents. Even more photos showed off the Rose grandchildren.

Barbara commanded the room from a brown and gold platform rocker. Judy and Louise Nelson sat on the couch. Naomi, who should have been on the water by now, had the love seat to herself. Marie, looking as sour as ever, occupied an easy chair across from Tildy, who'd exchanged her fashionable wardrobe for shapeless sweat pants. None of them were knitting.

Barbara jumped up so quickly that the platform rocker bumped against the wall, rattling a china plate featuring a pair of golden retriever puppies. "Annie! This is a surprise. I suppose you heard about Phyllis Bakely."

"No, I haven't heard anything."

"She had a stroke last night," Tildy said. "Her husband, Ben, took her to the mainland, and Theo went with them."

That explained why Theo hadn't returned to the cottage. But Annie hadn't driven into town to find him. She stared at the women, taking her time, and finally posing the question she'd come here to ask. "Which one of you tried to shoot me?"

Chapter Twenty-two

A COLLECTIVE GASP TRAVELED AROUND THE knitting circle. Louise leaned forward, as if her elderly ears had missed something. Judy gave a moan of distress, Barbara went rigid, Naomi set her jaw, and Tildy twisted her hands in her lap. Marie recovered the quickest. Her lips pursed and her small eyes narrowed. "We have no idea what you're talking about."

"Really?" Annie advanced into the room, not caring about tracking the carpet. "Why don't I believe that?"

Barbara reached for the knitting bag by her chair and sat back down. "I think you'd better go. You're obviously upset by everything that's happened, but that's no reason—"

Annie cut her off. "Upset doesn't begin to describe it."

"Really, Annie." Tildy puffed up with indignation.

Annie spun toward Barbara, who'd begun rifling through her knitting bag. "You're an island trustee. But there are six others. Do they know what you've done?"

"We haven't done anything," Naomi said in her sea captain's voice.

Marie grabbed her own knitting bag. "You have no business barging in here and making these kinds of accusations. You need to leave."

"That's exactly what you've wanted from the beginning," Annie said. "To make me leave. And you, Barbara. Pretending to befriend me when all you wanted was to get rid of me."

Barbara's needles moved faster. "I didn't pretend anything. I like you very much."

"Sure you do." Annie stepped farther into the room, making sure they understood that she wasn't leaving. She cast her eyes around the group, searching for the weak link and finding it. "What about your grandkids, Judy? Knowing what you've done, how will you ever look in the face of that little boy Theo delivered without remembering this?"

"Judy, don't pay attention to her." Tildy's order held a tinge of desperation.

Annie focused on Judy Kester with her bright red hair, sunny disposition, and generous spirit. "What about your other grandkids? Do you really think they'll never find out about this? You've set the example. They're going to learn from you that it's okay to do whatever it takes to get what you want, no matter whom you hurt on the way."

Judy was designed for laughter, not confrontation. She dropped her face into her hands and began to cry, the silver crosses at her earlobes dropping against her cheek.

Annie was dimly aware of the front door opening, but she didn't stop. "You're a religious woman, Judy. How do you reconcile your faith with what you've done to me?" She took in the whole group. "How do any of you?"

Tildy twisted her wedding ring. "I don't know what you think we've done . . ." Her voice faltered. "But . . . you're wrong."

"We all know I'm not." Annie felt Theo behind her. She couldn't see him, but she knew he was the one who'd come in.

"You can't prove anything." Marie's defiance didn't ring true.

"Shut up, Marie," Judy said with uncharacteristic vehemence. "This has gone on long enough. Too long."

"Judy . . ." Naomi's voice sounded a warning note. At the same time, she gripped her elbows across her chest, as if she were in pain.

Louise spoke for the first time. At eighty-three, her spine was bowed from osteoporosis, but she held her head high. "It was my idea. All mine. I did everything. They're trying to protect me."

"So noble," Annie drawled.

Theo came to Annie's side. He was scruffy and unshaven, but he carried himself with a tough kind of elegance that commanded everyone's attention. "You didn't trash the cottage by yourself, Mrs. Nelson," he said. "And, forgive me, but you couldn't hit the broadside of a barn."

"We didn't break anything," Judy cried. "We were very careful."

"Judy!"

"Well, we didn't!" Judy said defensively.

They were defeated, and they knew it. Annie could see it in their expressions. They'd been done in by Judy's conscience, and maybe their own. Naomi dropped her head, Barbara dropped her knitting, Louise sagged back into the couch, and Tildy pressed her palm to her lips. Only Marie looked defiant, for all the good it would do her.

"And the truth comes out," Annie said. "Whose idea was it to put my puppet in a noose?" The image of Crumpet hanging from the ceiling still haunted her. Puppet or not, Crumpet was part of her.

Judy looked at Tildy, who rubbed her cheek. "I saw it in a movie," Tildy said weakly. "Your puppet didn't come to any harm."

The side of Theo's arm was solid against her own. "A more important question . . . Which one of you shot at me?"

When no one answered, Theo turned cold eyes toward the woman in the platform rocker. "Barbara, why don't you answer that question?"

Barbara gripped the chair arms. "Of course it was me. Do you think I'd let anybody else take that chance?" She gazed at Annie, her expression pleading. "You were never in any danger. I'm one of the best marksmen in the Northeast. I've won medals."

Theo's response was scathing. "Too bad Annie didn't have the comfort of knowing that."

Judy fumbled in her pocket for a tissue. "We knew what we were doing wasn't right. We knew that from the beginning."

Marie sniffed, as if she didn't think what they'd done was all that bad, but Tildy had come to the edge of her chair. "We can't keep losing our families. Our children and grandchildren."

"I can't lose my son." Louise's gnarled hands gripped her cane. "He's all I have left, and if Galeann makes him leave . . ."

"I know you can't understand," Naomi said, "but this is about more than our families. It's about the future of Peregrine Island and whether we can keep surviving."

Theo was unimpressed. "Spell it out for us. Explain exactly why stealing Annie's cottage was important enough to turn decent women into criminals."

"Because they need a new school," Annie said.

Theo cursed softly under his breath.

Judy sobbed into a crumpled tissue, and Barbara looked away. The boat captain took over. "We don't have the money to build a school from scratch. But without it, we're going to lose the rest of our young families. We can't let that happen."

Barbara struggled to pull herself together. "The younger women weren't so restless until the school burned down. That trailer is awful. All Lisa talks about is leaving."

"And taking your grandchildren with her," Annie said.

Marie's bluster faded. "Someday you'll know what that feels like."

Barbara's eyes begged for understanding. "We need the cottage. There's no place else like it."

"This wasn't impulsive." Tildy spoke with a desperate kind of enthusiasm she seemed to want Annie to share. "The cottage is special because of its view. And every summer, we can easily convert it back into a residential property."

"There aren't enough decent summer rentals to keep up with the demand," Naomi said. "The rental money will give us income we've never had to support the school during the year."

Louise nodded. "And keep up with the road repairs so it's not so hard to get out there."

Rental money was income Annie could never have had because the agreement Mariah had signed had forbidden it. No surprise that Elliott had been more lenient with the islanders than with her mother.

A note of pleading had replaced Naomi's air of command. "We had to do it. It was for the greater good."

"It sure as hell wasn't for Annie's good," Theo said. Pushing his jacket back, he rested his hand on his hip. "You know she's going to the police with this."

Judy blew her nose. "I told you this would happen. All along I said we'd end up in jail."

"We'll deny it," Marie declared. "There's no proof."

"Don't turn us in, Annie," Tildy begged. "It'll ruin us. I could lose my shop."

"You should have thought about that a long time ago," Theo said.

"If this gets out . . ." Louise said.

"*When* this gets out," Theo retorted. "You're trapped. You all understand that, right?"

Marie sat as straight as ever, but tears leaked over her bottom lids. They sagged back into their chairs, reached for one another's hands, pressed their faces into tissues. They knew they were defeated.

Barbara was aging right in front of her. "We'll make it right. Please, Annie. Don't tell anybody. We'll fix it. We'll fix everything so you keep the cottage. Promise us you won't say anything."

"She's not promising anything," Theo said.

The door burst open, and two red-haired little girls raced in. Dashing across the room, they hurled themselves into their grandmother's arms. "Grammie, Mr. Miller got sick, and he barfed. It was so gross!"

"He couldn't get a substitute teacher!" the younger chimed in. "So we all got to go home, but Mom went to see Jaycie, so we came here."

As Barbara gathered the girls in her arms, Annie saw the

tears running down her powdery cheeks. Theo noticed, too. He shot Annie a frown and closed his hand around her arm. "Let's get out of here."

THEO'S CAR BLOCKED THE SUBURBAN in the driveway. "How did you figure it out?" he said as they came down the front steps.

"A woman's perspective. Once you told me about the lease, I knew it could only be them."

"You understand that you have them over a barrel, right? You're going to get the cottage back."

She sighed. "Looks that way."

He heard her lack of enthusiasm. "Annie, don't do this."

"Do what?"

"What you're thinking about."

"How do you know what I'm thinking about?"

"I know you. You're thinking about giving up."

"Not giving up exactly." She zipped her coat. "More like moving on. The island . . . It isn't good for me." *You aren't good for me. I want it all—everything you're not prepared to give.*

"The island is great for you," he said. "You haven't just survived this winter. You've thrived here."

In a way, that was true. She thought about her Dreambook and how, when she'd arrived here, so sick and broken, she'd seen it as a symbol of failure—a tangible reminder of everything she hadn't accomplished. But her perspective had been shifting without her recognizing it. Maybe the theatrical career she'd imagined had never materialized, but because of her, a mute little girl had found her voice, and that was something.

"Drive out to the farm with me," he said, "I want to check on the new roof."

She remembered what had happened the last time they'd visited his farm, and it wasn't the puppets she heard in her head, but her own survival instinct. "The sun's out," she said. "Let's take a walk instead."

He didn't protest. They descended the rutted drive to the road. The boats in the harbor had been out at sea since dawn, and the empty buoys bobbed in the harbor like bath toys. She stalled for time. "How is the woman you helped?"

"We got her to the mainland in time. She has some rehab ahead, but she should recover." The gravel crunched beneath their feet as he steered her across the road by her elbow. "Before I leave, I'm going to make sure some of the islanders start getting their EMT certification. It's dangerous not having medical help here."

"They should already have done it."

"Nobody wanted the responsibility, but with a group of them training together, they'll have each other's backs." He took her hand to guide her around a pothole. She drew away as soon as they reached the other side. As she pretended to fix her glove, he stopped walking and gazed down at her, his expression troubled. "I don't get it. I can't believe you're thinking about giving up the cottage and leaving."

How could he understand her so well? No one else ever had. She would start up her dog-walking business again; work at Coffee, Coffee; and book more puppet shows. The thing she wouldn't do was go on any more auditions. Thanks to Livia, she had a new direction, one that had been taking shape inside her so gradually that she'd barely known it was happening. "There's no reason for me to stay," she said.

An SUV with a missing door and bad muffler roared past. "Sure there is," he said. "The cottage is yours. Right now those women are falling all over themselves trying to figure out how to give it back to you in exchange for your silence. Nothing's changed."

Everything had changed. She was in love with this man, and she couldn't keep staying at the cottage where she'd see him every day, make love with him every night. She needed to rip off the bandage. And go where? She was healthy now, strong enough to figure something out.

They began walking toward the wharf. Ahead of her, the American flag flying from the pole between the boathouses caught the morning breeze. She stepped around a pile of lobster traps and climbed the ramp. "I have to stop postponing the inevitable. From the beginning, the cottage was only a stopgap. It's time for me to get back to my real life in Manhattan."

"You're still broke," he said. "Where are you going to live?"

The easiest way for her to raise rent money quickly was to sell one of the Garr drawings, but she wouldn't do that. Instead she'd call her former dog-walking clients. They were always traveling. She'd done house-sitting before. If she was lucky, one of them might need someone to stay with their animals while they were gone. If that didn't work, her former boss at Coffee, Coffee would probably let her crash on the futon in the storage room. She was physically and emotionally stronger now than she'd been five weeks ago, and she'd figure it out.

"I already have money coming in from the resale shop," she told him, "so I'm not completely penniless. And now that I'm healthy again, I can get back to work."

They bypassed a length of chain attached to one of the granite mooring posts. He leaned down to pick up a loose stone. "I don't want you to leave."

"Don't you?" She said it easily, as if he'd revealed nothing of any importance, but her muscles tensed, waiting for what would come next.

He hurled the stone into the water. "If you have to move out of the cottage while the island mafia fixes their mess, you can stay at the house. Take over as much of it as you want. Elliott and Cynthia aren't arriving until August, and by then, you'll be back where you belong."

This was Theo the caretaker speaking, nothing more, and where she belonged was back in the city reclaiming her life. The boathouse flag snapped in the breeze. She squinted her eyes against the sun glinting off the water. Her stay on the island this winter had been a time to regenerate. Now she saw herself with clearer eyes, saw where she'd been and where she wanted to go.

"Everything is too uncertain for you in the city," he said. "You need to stay here."

"Where you can watch out for me? I don't think so."

He shoved his hands into the pockets of his parka. "You make it sound so terrible. We're friends. You might be the best friend I've ever had."

She nearly winced, but she couldn't be angry with him for not loving her. It wasn't in the cards. If Theo ever did manage to fall in love again, it wouldn't be with her. It wouldn't be with anyone so closely attached to his past.

She had to put an end to this right now, and her voice was as steady as could be. "We're lovers," she said. "And that's a lot more complicated than friendship."

He pitched another stone in the water. "It doesn't have to be."

"Our relationship has always had an expiration date, and I think we've reached it."

He looked more peeved than heartbroken. "You make us sound like spoiled milk."

She needed to do this right. She needed to free herself, but also avoid stirring up his all-too-ready feelings of guilt and responsibility. "Hardly spoiled," she said. "You're gorgeous. You're rich and smart. And sexy. Did I mention you're rich?"

He didn't crack a smile.

"You know me, Theo. I'm a romantic. If I hang around any longer, I might fall in love with you." She managed a shudder. "Think how ugly that would be."

"You won't," he said with deadly sincerity. "You know me too well."

As if what he'd revealed to her about himself had made him unlovable.

She curled her fingers into fists inside her coat pockets. When this was over, she'd feel like shattering into a million pieces, but not yet. She could do this. She had to. "Let me give it to you straight. I want a family. That means as long as I stay on the island when I don't have to, as long as I keep entertaining myself with you, I'm basically wasting time. I need more discipline."

"You haven't said anything about this to me." He seemed annoyed, maybe hurt, but definitely not inconsolable.

She pretended to be confused. "Why would I?"

"Because we tell each other things."

"That's what I'm doing. Telling you. And it's not at all complicated."

He shrugged. "I guess."

The constriction around her heart tightened. He hunched his shoulders against the wind. "I suppose I'm being selfish wanting you to stay."

She'd had enough misery for one day. "I'm getting cold. And you've been up all night. You need some sleep."

He looked down at the wharf, then up at her. "I appreciate what you've done for me this winter."

His gratitude was one more gash to her heart. She turned into the wind so he wouldn't hear the tremor in her voice. "Right back atcha, pal." She straightened her shoulders. "I have to pee. See you later."

As she left him standing on the wharf, she blinked her eyes against the tears she couldn't let herself shed. He'd given up on her so easily. Not really surprising. Duplicity wasn't in his nature. He was a hero, and true heroes didn't pretend to offer what they weren't prepared to give.

She crossed the road to her car. She had to leave the island now. Today. This very minute. But she couldn't. She needed her Kia, and the big car ferry wasn't due for eight more days. Eight days, during which Theo could show up at the cottage anytime he wanted. Unbearable. She had to fix that.

As she drove back to the cottage, she told herself her heart would keep beating, whether she wanted it to or not. Time healed—everyone knew that—and eventually, time would heal her. She'd keep herself focused on the future and take comfort from knowing she'd done the right thing.

But for now, comfort was nowhere to be found.

Chapter Twenty-three

To Annie's relief, Livia hadn't fallen back into muteness, and she happily showed Annie a turtle she'd made from Play-Doh. "I don't know what to say to her," Jaycie whispered while Livia was occupied. "I'm her mother, but I don't know how to talk to her."

"I'll get Scamp," Annie said.

Annie fetched the puppet, grateful for the distraction from her own painful thoughts and fervently hoping Scamp could guide the conversation Jaycie needed to have. She propped the puppet on the kitchen table across from the two of them and turned her attention to Jaycie. "You are Livia's beautiful mother. I don't believe we've formally met. I am Scamp, otherwise known as Genevieve Adelaide Josephine Brown."

"Uh . . . Hello," Jaycie said with only minimal self-consciousness.

"I will now tell you about myself." Scamp proceeded to

lay out her accomplishments, calling herself a talented singer, dancer, actress, housepainter, and race car driver. "I can also catch lightning bugs and open my mouth really wide."

Livia giggled as Scamp demonstrated, and Jaycie began to relax. Scamp continued chattering before finally tossing her yarn curls and saying, "I, Scamp, love free secrets because they help me talk about bad things. Like the bad things that happened to you, Livia, and to your mommy. But . . . Your mommy doesn't know about free secret."

As Annie had hoped, Livia butted in to explain. "Free secret is when you can tell somebody something, and they aren't allowed to get mad at you."

Scamp leaned toward Jaycie and said, in a stage whisper, "Livia and I would very much like you to tell us a free secret. We want to hear about that awful, terrible, horrible night you shot Livia's father and he died dead. And since it's a free secret, nobody can get mad."

Jaycie turned away.

"It's okay, Mommy." Livia spoke as if she were the adult. "Free secrets are very safe."

Jaycie hugged her daughter, tears filling her eyes. "Oh, Liv . . ." She pulled herself together. At first hesitantly, then gradually gaining strength, she talked about Ned Grayson's alcoholism. Using language a four-year-old could understand, she explained how it made him violent.

Livia listened raptly. Jaycie, fearing the effect her words were having, kept stopping to ask if Livia understood, but Livia seemed more curious than traumatized. By the time they were done, she was on her mother's lap getting kissed and demanding lunch.

"First, you must promise to keep talking to each other about this whenever you need to," Scamp said. "Do you promise?"

"We promise," Livia said solemnly.

Scamp stuck her head in Jaycie's face. Jaycie laughed. "I promise."

"Excellent!" Scamp exclaimed. "My work here is done."

After lunch, when Livia wanted to ride her scooter on the front porch, Annie went out with Jaycie and settled on the top step next to her. "I should have talked to her from the beginning," Jaycie said as the scooter bumped over the floorboards with Livia struggling to keep her balance. "But she was so young. I kept hoping she'd forget. Stupid of me. You knew right away what she needed."

"Not right away. I've been doing a lot of research. And it's easier to be objective as an outsider."

"Not a good excuse, but thanks."

"I'm the one who's thankful," Annie said. "Thanks to Livia, I know what I want to do with my life." Jaycie cocked her head, and Annie told her what she hadn't yet confided to anyone. "I'm going to start training to be a play therapist—using puppets to help traumatized children."

"Annie, that's wonderful! It's perfect for you."

"Do you think so? I've talked to some play therapists over the phone, and it feels right." This career fit her better than acting ever could. She would have to go back to school, something she wouldn't be able to afford for a while, but she had a good academic record, and her experience working with kids might help her get scholarship money. If it didn't, she'd apply for a loan. One way or another, she intended to make this work.

"I admire you so much." Jaycie got a faraway look in her eyes. "I've been locked up as tight as Livia—feeling sorry for myself, fantasizing about Theo instead of getting on with my life."

Annie knew all about that.

"If you hadn't come here . . ." Jaycie shook her head, as if she were getting rid of cobwebs. "I'm not just thinking about Livia but about the way you've taken control of your life. I want a fresh start, and I'm finally going to do something about it."

Annie knew all about that, too.

"What are you going to do about the cottage?" Jaycie said.

Annie didn't want to tell her what the grandmothers had done or admit that she'd fallen in love with Theo. "I'm moving out right away and leaving the island on the car ferry next week." She hesitated. "Things with Theo have gotten . . . too complicated. I've had to end it."

"Oh, Annie, I'm sorry." Jaycie displayed no schadenfreude, only genuine concern. She'd meant what she'd said about Theo being a fantasy and not her reality. "I was hoping you wouldn't leave so soon. You know how much I'm going to miss you."

Annie gave her an impulsive hug. "Me, too."

Jaycie was stoic when Annie told her she needed to find someplace to stay until the car ferry arrived. "I can't keep running into Theo at the cottage. I . . . need some private space."

She intended to talk to Barbara about finding someplace temporary. Annie could ask for a golden unicorn, and the grandmothers would come up with a way to find it for her. Anything to buy her silence.

But as it turned out, Annie didn't need Barbara. With a single phone call, Jaycie found Annie a home.

LES CHILDERS'S LOBSTER BOAT, THE *Lucky Charm,* was temporarily moored at the fish house dock while its owner waited for a crucial engine part to arrive on the same ferry that would take Annie back to the mainland next week. Les took good care of the *Lucky Charm,* but it still smelled of bait, rope, and diesel fuel. Annie didn't care. The boat had a small galley with a microwave and even a tiny shower. The cabin was dry, a heater provided a little warmth, and, most important, she wouldn't have to see Theo. In case she hadn't been clear enough yesterday, she'd left a note for him at the cottage.

> *Dear Theo,*
> *I've moved into town for a few days to, among other things, adjust to the depressing (boo hoo) prospect of no longer having mind-blowing sex with you. I'm sure you can find me if you try hard enough, but I have stuff to do, and I'm asking you to leave me the hell alone. Be a pal, okay? I'll handle the Witches of Peregrine Island, so stay away from them.*
>
> *A.*

The note struck exactly the breezy tone she wanted. There was nothing maudlin in it, nothing to make him suspect how long it had taken her to compose, and absolutely nothing to signal how deeply she'd fallen in love with him. She would e-mail him her final kiss-off from the city. *You're not going to believe this, but I've met the most amazing man.* Blah . . . Blah . . . Blah . . . Curtain down. No encore.

Between her emotional turmoil, the noisy squeak of ropes against the moorings, and the unfamiliar rocking of the lobster boat, she had trouble falling asleep. She wished she'd brought her puppets with her instead of leaving them with Jaycie at Harp House for safekeeping. Knowing they were nearby would have been comforting.

Her blankets slipped off during the night, and she awakened at dawn shivering. She rolled out of the berth and pushed her feet into her sneakers. After she'd wrapped Mariah's red wool cloak around her, she climbed up to the pilothouse and walked out onto the deck.

Peach and lavender ribbons streamed in the sky above a pearl gray sea. Waves slapped the boat's hull, and wind caught her cloak, trying to turn it into wings. She spotted something in the stern that hadn't been there the night before. A yellow plastic picnic basket. Holding her hair away from her face, she went to investigate.

The basket held a jug of orange juice, two hard-boiled eggs, a slab of still-warm cinnamon coffee cake, and an old-fashioned red thermos. She knew a bribe when she saw one. The grandmothers were trying to buy her silence with food.

She unscrewed the thermos, releasing a cloud of steam. The freshly brewed coffee was strong and delicious. Sipping it made her miss Hannibal. She'd gotten used to the cat cozying up to her as she drank her morning coffee. Gotten used to Theo—

Stop it!

She stayed in the stern, watching the fishermen in their orange and yellow gear set out on their day's run. The seaweed that grew from the dock's pylons floated in the water like a mermaid's hair. A pair of eider ducks swam toward the wharf. The sky grew lighter, a brilliant crystal blue, and the island she'd resented so much became beautiful.

THE *LUCKY CHARM* WAS MOORED at the fish house dock, but Theo spotted Annie standing at the very end of the ferry wharf dressed in her red cloak and gazing out at the open water like a sea captain's widow waiting for her dead husband to return. He'd left her alone all day yesterday, and that was long enough.

She could have stayed at Harp House. Or at the cottage, for that matter—the island witches hadn't been within a mile of it. But, no. Beneath all of Annie's goodness lay an evil streak. She could couch it any way she wanted, but she'd moved onto Les Childers's lobster boat to get away from *him*!

He stalked down the wharf. A crazy part of him enjoyed his anger. For the first time in his life, he could be totally pissed off at a woman and know she wouldn't collapse into a sniveling heap. Sure, he'd been relieved that things weren't going to get complicated between them, but that had been an instinctive reaction, not reality. Their relationship hadn't expired, as she'd put it. That kind of closeness didn't simply go away. She'd made it clear this wasn't some deep love affair, so what was the big deal? He got the fact that she wanted a family—more power to her—but what did that have to do with them? Sooner or later they'd have to keep their clothes on, but since she wasn't going to find the father of her kids here on this island, she had no reason to end it now, not when it meant so much to both of them.

Or maybe it was just him. He'd always been guarded, but that had gone away with Annie. He never knew what the hell she was going to say or do, only that she was tough instead of fragile—that he didn't have to watch what he said or pretend to be someone he wasn't. When he was with her, he felt as if . . . he'd found himself.

She wasn't wearing a hat, and her curls ran amok as usual. He went badass. "Enjoying your new house?"

She hadn't heard him approach, and she jumped. Good. Then she frowned, not happy to see him, and that hurt in a way that made him want to hurt her back. "How's life on a lobster boat," he said with something he hoped looked like a sneer. "Cozy as hell, I'll bet."

"The views are good."

He wouldn't let her flip him off like that. "Everybody on the island knows that you're living on Les's boat. It's like you're handing the cottage over to those women free and clear. I'll bet they're getting bruises from giving each other high fives."

Her small nose shot up in the air. "If you came here to yell at me, go away. As a matter of fact, even if you didn't come here to yell at me, go away. I told you I had things to do, and I'm not going to be distracted by your"—she flicked her hand at him in a dismissive gesture—"ridiculous gorgeousness. Do you ever look as though you haven't just stepped off the cover of a paperback novel?"

He had no idea what she was talking about, only that it sounded like an insult. He fought the urge to tunnel his hands into her tangle of hair. "How's the search for the love of your life going?" He gave her more of his makeshift sneer.

"I don't know what you mean."

He wanted to pick her up and carry her back to the cottage where she belonged. Where they both belonged. "The reason you dumped me, remember? So you'd be free to find somebody to marry. Les Childers is single. So what if he's seventy? His boat's paid for. Why don't you call him up?"

She sighed, as if he were nothing more than an irritant. "Oh, Theo . . . Stop being a jerk."

He was being a jerk, but he couldn't make himself back off. "I guess my definition of friendship is different from yours. In my life, friends don't just pick up one day and call it quits."

She buried her hands inside the cloak. "Friends who make the mistake of sleeping together do."

It hadn't been a mistake. Not for him, anyway. He stuck a thumb in the pocket of his jeans. "You're making it too complicated."

She glanced out at the sea and then back at him. "I've been trying to do this nicely . . ."

"Then stop!" he exclaimed. "Make me understand why, with no warning, you decided to take off. I want to hear this. Go ahead. Do it ugly."

And she did. In a way he should have expected. By telling the truth.

"Theo, I wish you the best, but— I need to fall in love . . . and I can't do that with you."

Why the hell not? For one horrified moment, he thought he'd spoken the words aloud.

Her gaze was steady. Strong. She touched his arm and said with a kindness that made him want to grind his teeth, "You have too much baggage."

He shouldn't have made her say it. He should have known—did know. He managed a brusque nod. "Got it."

That was all he needed to hear. The truth.

He left her on the wharf. When he got back to the house, he saddled Dancer and pushed him hard. Afterward he spent a long time in the stable rubbing him down, grooming him, concentrating on brushing out briars and picking hooves. For so long, he'd felt as if he'd been frozen inside, but Annie had changed that. She'd been his lover, his cheerleader, and his shrink. She'd forced him to look at his inability to make Kenley happy in a new way—at Regan who'd killed herself to set him free. Somehow, Annie had managed to breach the borders of his darkness.

His hands stilled on Dancer's withers. He stood there thinking, replaying the last six weeks. His reverie was broken by the sound of Livia's voice.

"Theo!"

He came out of the stable. Livia broke away from her mother and ran to him. As she slammed into his legs, he experienced an overwhelming urge to pick her up and hug her. So he did.

She wasn't having it. Planting both her hands against his chest, she pushed back and glared up at him. "The fairy house didn't change!"

Finally, a mistake he could fix. "Because I have a treasure to show you first."

"Treasure?"

He'd spoken without thinking, but he knew right away what it had to be. "Beach jewels."

"Jewels?" Livia breathed wonder into the word.

"Stay right here." He headed upstairs to his old bedroom.

The oversize jar that held Regan's collection of beach glass was stored at the back of his closet, shoved there years ago because, like so much else in the house, it triggered bad memories. But as he pulled it out and carried it downstairs, the edges of his dark mood lifted for the first time all day. The sweet, generous side of Regan's nature would have loved passing on her precious beach stones to Livia, one little girl to another.

As he descended the stairs that his sister had raced up and down a dozen times a day, something brushed past him. Something warm. Invisible. He stopped where he was and shut his eyes, the glass jar cool in his hands, his sister's face vivid in his mind.

Regan smiling at him. A smile that said *Be happy.*

Jaycie left Livia with Theo, and as the two of them added the beach glass to the fairy house, they talked, although it was mainly Livia who did the talking. All the words she'd been storing up in her head seemed to need to come out at once. He was amazed at how observant she was and how much she understood.

"I told you my free secret." She pressed the final piece of glass into the house's new mossy roof. "Now it's your turn to tell me."

By nightfall, he was back in his turret, a lonely prince waiting for a princess to climb the tower and free him. *"You have too much baggage."*

He tried to write but found himself staring across the room and thinking about Annie instead. He didn't want to enter the twisted pathways of Quentin Pierce's mind, and he couldn't deny the truth any longer. Whatever nomadic ghouls fueled his imagination had fled, taking his career with them.

He closed the computer file and leaned back in his desk chair. His gaze fell on the drawing he'd swiped from her. The studious kid with ragged hair and a freckled nose.

Theo's hands moved to the keyboard. Opened a new file. For a moment, he simply sat there, and then he began typing, the words flowing from him, words that had been trapped inside him for too long.

*Diggity Swift lived in a big apartment that looked
down over Central Park. Diggity had allergies, so
if too much pollen was in the air and he forgot his
inhaler, he started to wheeze and then Fran, who
took care of him while his parents worked, made him
leave the park. He already felt like a freak. He was
the smallest kid in seventh grade. Why did he have to
have allergies, too?*

*Fran said it was better to be smart than strong,
but Diggity didn't believe that was true. He thought
it was a lot better being strong.*

*One day after Fran made him come back home
from the park, a strange thing happened. He went to
his room to play his favorite video game, but as he
touched the controller, an electric shock traveled up
his arm and down through his chest into his legs, and
the next thing he knew, everything went dark . . .*

Theo wrote on into the night.

EACH MORNING WHEN ANNIE AWAKENED, she found another burnt offering on the aft deck of the *Lucky Charm*. The
muffins, egg casserole, and homemade granola weren't really
charred, but they were burnt offerings nonetheless—rooted in
guilt, petitioning for her silence, and—in the case of freshly
squeezed orange juice—signaling sacrifice.

Not everything was edible. A bottle of scented hand lotion appeared, then a zippered Peregrine Island sweatshirt with the price tag
from Tildy's gift store still attached. Occasionally, she caught a glimpse
of the giver—Naomi delivering a bowl of chowder, Mrs. Nelson leaving the scented lotion. Even Marie left a pan of lemon bars.

With a decent phone signal available, Annie had begun
contacting her former dog-walking clients. She talked to her
old boss at Coffee, Coffee about getting her job back and about
crashing on the couch in the back room until her first house-
sitting job started. But she still had too many hours to fill, and
the aching sadness wouldn't ease.

Theo was furious with her, and he hadn't come back. The pain of losing him was a circling vulture that refused to fly away. Pain, she reminded herself, that only she was feeling.

She thought a lot about Niven Garr, but she could only handle so much rejection at a time. She wanted to locate his family, but she'd wait until she was off the island and the worst of her misery over Theo had eased.

A couple of the younger women stopped by the boat, curious about why she'd left the cottage, so Annie knew the news about the transfer of ownership hadn't leaked. She muttered something about needing to be close to town, and they seemed satisfied.

Annie's fourth morning on the boat, Lisa hopped on board and grabbed her in a hug. Since she'd always been cool, Annie couldn't imagine where this sudden enthusiasm had come from until Lisa finally let her go. "I can't believe you've made Livia talk. I saw her today. It's like a miracle."

"It was a group effort," Annie said, only to have Lisa hug her again and tell her she'd changed Jaycie's life.

Lisa wasn't her only visitor. Annie was in the cabin washing some underwear when she heard footsteps on the deck. "Annie?"

It was Barbara. Annie draped her wet bra over the fire extinguisher to dry, picked up her coat, and went on deck.

Barbara stood in the pilothouse, holding a loaf of home-made sweet bread in plastic wrap. Her big blond bouffant hairdo had collapsed, and all that remained of her customary heavy makeup was a bloodred slash of lipstick that had bled into the lines around her mouth. She set the bread next to the sonar equipment. "It's been six days. You haven't called the police. Not you or Theo. You haven't told anyone."

"Not *yet*," Annie said.

"We're trying to fix what we did. I want you to know that." It was more a plea than a statement.

"Bully for you."

Barbara tugged at a toggle button on her coat. "Naomi and I went to the mainland on Thursday to talk to a lawyer. He's drawing up the paperwork to make the cottage yours forever."

She looked past Annie toward the fish house, no longer able to maintain eye contact. "All we ask is for you not to tell anyone."

Annie ordered herself to dig in. "You don't have the right to ask for anything."

"I know, but . . ." Her eyes were bloodshot. "Most of us were born here. We've had our disagreements over the years, and not everybody likes every one of us, but . . . People respect us. That's a precious thing."

"Not so precious that you weren't willing to throw it away. And now you want Theo and me to stay quiet so I can get *my* cottage back."

The smeared red lipstick made her complexion ashen. "No. We'll make sure you get it back, regardless. We're just asking you to . . ."

"To behave better than you did."

Barbara's shoulders sagged. "That's right. Better than all of us did."

Annie could only be a hard-ass for so long. She'd made her decision the moment Lisa's two little red-haired girls had raced into their grandmother's living room and flung themselves at her. "Call off your lawyer," she said. "The cottage is yours."

Barbara gaped at her. "You don't mean that."

"I mean it." She couldn't come back here. If she held on to the cottage, it would only be for spite. "The cottage belongs to the island. I don't. It's yours. Free and clear. Do what you want with it."

"But . . ."

Annie didn't wait to hear any more. She wrapped her coat tighter around her and jumped to the dock.

A man was scraping a boat hull. The fishermen floated their boats onto Christmas Beach at high tide, did their repairs, then pushed them back in the water when the tide ebbed. Island life was stripped down like that—dependent on tides and weather, on fish and the whims of nature. She wandered through town, feeling as empty and disconnected as the solitary lobster trap leaning against Tildy's shuttered gift shop.

Her cell rang in her pocket. It was the dealer at the resale shop. She leaned against a weathered sign that advertised chowder and lobster rolls and listened, but what he told her was so incomprehensible, she had to make him repeat it twice.

"It's true," he said. "The money is outrageous, but the buyer is some kind of collector, and the mermaid chair is one of a kind."

"For good reason!" she exclaimed. "It's ugly."

"Fortunately, beauty is in the eye of the beholder."

Just like that, she had the money to wipe out most of her debt. With one phone call, she'd been given a fresh start.

THE CAR FERRY WAS DUE the next afternoon—Annie's forty-fourth day on the island. She had to dash out to Harp House in the morning and pick up the things she'd left with Jaycie—her puppets, the rest of her clothes, Mariah's scarves. After seven nights sleeping on the lobster boat, she was more than ready to live on dry land. She wished that dry land weren't a couch in the back of Coffee, Coffee, but it wouldn't be for long. One of her dog-walking clients wanted her to house-sit while he was in Europe.

A notice on the community bulletin board announced a town meeting that night. Since the issue of the cottage was bound to come up, she wanted to attend, but she needed to make sure Theo wouldn't be there, so she waited until the meeting had started before she went inside.

Lisa caught sight of her and gestured toward the empty chair at her side. The seven island trustees sat at a long folding table at the end of the room. Barbara looked no better than she had the last time they'd been together: her blond hairdo still deflated, her makeup nonexistent. The other grandmothers were scattered around the room, some sitting together, others with their husbands. Not a single one made eye contact with Annie.

The business of the meeting unfolded: the budget, wharf repairs, how to get rid of the island's growing supply of dead trucks. There was speculation about the day's unusually warm weather and the storm that was supposed to accompany it. Nothing about the cottage.

The meeting was beginning to wind down when Barbara stood. "Before we end, I have some news."

She looked smaller without her thick mascara and rouged cheeks. She leaned against the folding table, as if she needed the support. "I know all of you are going to be happy to learn that—" She cleared her throat. "Annie Hewitt has given Moonraker Cottage to the island."

The room buzzed. Chairs squeaked as everyone turned to look at her. "Annie, did you really?" Lisa asked.

"You never mentioned anything about this," Barbara's husband said to her from the first row.

A trustee at the opposite end of the table spoke up. "We just learned about it ourselves, Booker."

Barbara waited for the commotion to settle down before she went on. "Thanks to Annie's generosity, we'll be able to turn the cottage into our new school."

The buzz started again, along with some applause and a whistle. A man Annie didn't know reached around to clap her on the shoulder.

"During the summer, we can rent it out and add the income to the school budget," Barbara said.

Lisa grabbed Annie's hand. "Oh, Annie . . . That's going to make such a difference to the kids."

Instead of becoming steadier, Barbara appeared to be wilting. "We want our younger residents to know how much we care about them." She gazed toward Lisa. "And how much we're willing to do to keep them on the island." She looked down at the table, and Annie had the unsettling feeling she was about to cry, but when Barbara lifted her head, her eyes were dry. She nodded to someone in the room. Nodded again. One by one, the grandmothers she'd conspired with rose to their feet and joined her.

Annie shifted uneasily in her chair. Barbara's lips quivered. "We have something we need to tell all of you."

Chapter Twenty-four

Aｎｎｉｅ'ｓ ｕｎｅａｓｉｎｅｓｓ ｅｓｃａｌａｔｅｄ. Bａｒｂａｒａ ｇｌａｎｃｅｄ helplessly at the others. Naomi ran one hand through her cropped hair, leaving a rooster tail behind. She took a step away from the rest. "Annie didn't give up the cottage voluntarily," she said. "We forced her out."

A confused muttering rippled through the audience. Annie shot to her feet. "Nobody forced me to do anything. I wanted to give you the cottage. Now am I wrong, or do I smell coffee? I move to adjourn the meeting."

She wasn't a property owner, and she couldn't move to adjourn anything, but her need for revenge was gone. The women had done something wrong, and they were suffering from it. But they weren't bad women. They were mothers and grandmothers who'd wanted so much to keep their families together that they'd lost sight of right and wrong. For all their flaws, Annie cared about them, and she knew better than anyone how easily love could make people lose their way.

"Annie . . ." Barbara's natural authority began to reassert itself. "This is something we've all agreed we need to do."

"No, you don't," Annie said. And then more pointedly, "You really don't."

"Annie, please sit down." Barbara was back in charge.

Annie slumped into her seat.

Barbara briefly explained the legal agreement between Elliott Harp and Mariah. Tildy gripped the edges of her scarlet bomber jacket and said, "We're decent women. I hope all of you know that. We thought if we had a new school our kids would stop leaving."

"Makin' our kids go to school in a trailer's a disgrace," a female voice in the back called out.

"We convinced ourselves the end justified the means," Naomi said.

"I'm the one who started the whole thing." Louise Nelson leaned heavily on her cane and looked toward her daughter-in-law in the front row. "Galeann, you didn't mind living here so much until the schoolhouse burned down. I couldn't stand the idea of you and Johnny leaving. I've lived here all my life, but I'm smart enough to know I can't stay without family nearby." Age had weakened her voice and the room fell silent. "If you leave, I'll have to go to the mainland, and I want to die here. That made me start thinking about other possibilities."

Naomi shoved her hand through her hair again, pushing up a second rooster tail. "We're all getting ahead of ourselves." She took over, laying out what they'd done step-by-step, sparing none of them. She described sabotaging Annie's grocery delivery, vandalizing the house. All of it.

Annie sank lower into her seat. They were making her look like both a heroine and a victim, neither of which she wanted to be.

"We made sure we didn't break anything," Judy interrupted, dry-eyed but clutching a tissue.

Naomi detailed hanging the puppet from a noose, painting the warning message on the wall, and finally, firing the bullet at Annie.

Barbara dropped her gaze. "I did that. That was the worst, and I was responsible."

Lisa gasped. "Mom!"

Marie's lips pursed into a buttonhole. "I was the one who came up with the idea of telling Annie that Theo Harp had been hurt in an accident so she'd leave the island with Naomi. I'm a decent woman, and I've never been more ashamed of myself. I hope God forgives me because I can't."

Annie had to hand it to her. Marie might be a sourpuss, but she was a sourpuss with a conscience.

"Annie figured out what we'd done and confronted us," Barbara said. "We begged her to keep quiet so none of you would find out, but she wouldn't promise anything." Barbara held her head higher. "Sunday I went to see her to beg her again to keep our secret. Right then, she could have told me to go to Hades, but she didn't. Instead she said the cottage was ours, free and clear. That it belonged to the island, not to her."

Annie squirmed in her seat as more people turned to look at her.

"At first, all we felt was relief," Tildy said, "but the more we talked, the harder it got to look each other in the eye, and the more ashamed we were."

Judy blew her nose. "How were we going to face all of you day after day, face our kids, knowing in our hearts what we did?"

Barbara straightened her shoulders. "We knew this would eat at us for the rest of our lives if we didn't come clean."

"Confession is good for the soul," Marie said sanctimoniously. "And that's what we decided we had to do."

"We can't change what we did," Naomi said. "All we can do is be honest about it. You can judge us. You can hate us if you have to."

Annie couldn't take any more, and she sprang up again. "The only person who has a right to hate you is me, and I don't, so the rest of you shouldn't either. Now I move to end this meeting right now."

"Second," Booker Rose called out, overlooking Annie's nonresidency issue.

The meeting was adjourned.

Afterward all Annie wanted to do was get away, but she was surrounded by people who wanted to talk to her, thank her, and apologize to her. The islanders ignored the grand-mothers, but Annie didn't doubt that the worst was over for them. It would take the Mainers a while to sort things out in their own minds, but they were a tough lot who admired re-sourcefulness, even if it was ill-advised. The women wouldn't be ostracized for long.

THE SEAS HAD GROWN ROUGHER by the time she returned to the boat, and a bolt of lightning sliced the horizon. It was going to be a wild night, a perfect bookend to the wildness of the night when she'd arrived. By this time tomorrow, she'd be gone. She prayed Theo wouldn't show up to say good-bye. That would be too much.

A wave washed over the stern, but she didn't want to seal herself in the cabin yet. She wanted to watch the storm roll in, soak up its ferocity. She located the boat's foul weather gear. The oversize jacket smelled of bait, but it kept her dry to midthigh. She stood in the stern and watched the violence of the light show. The city isolated her from nature's shifting rhythms in a way the island couldn't. Only as the lightning came closer did she go below.

The cabin lit up, then darkened, then lit again as the storm attacked the island. By the time she'd finished brushing her teeth, she was queasy from the boat's rocking. She sprawled on the bunk without getting undressed, the legs of her jeans still wet. She tolerated the roll as long as she could, but the queasi-ness grew worse, and she knew she'd throw up if she stayed down there any longer.

She grabbed the wet orange jacket and staggered back up to the deck. The rain blasted her through the open end of the pi-lothouse, but that was a price she was willing to pay for clean air.

The boat continued to pitch, but her stomach settled. Gradually, the storm began to move off and the rain eased. A shutter banged against the side of a house. She couldn't get any wetter, so she climbed up on the dock to see if there'd been any damage. Branches were down, and a distant flash of light-ning revealed dark patches on the town hall roof where a few shingles had blown off. Electricity was expensive, and no one kept their porch lights on, but several were burning now, so she knew she wasn't the only one awake.

As she surveyed the scene, she noticed a strange light in the sky. It seemed to be coming from the northeast, near the area around the cottage. The light began flickering like a campfire. But this was no campfire. It was a real fire.

The first thing she thought of was the cottage. After everything they'd gone through, it had been hit by lightning. There'd be no new school. No summer rental money. It had all been for nothing.

She scrambled back on the boat to get her keys. Moments later, she was running down the dock toward the fish house where she'd parked her car. The rain would have turned the road into a quagmire, and she didn't know how far she could get in her Kia, only that she had to try.

Lights had come on in more houses. She spotted the Rose pickup truck backing away from the house, Barbara in the passenger seat. Booker must be driving. The truck wouldn't have any trouble navigating the road, and she ran toward it.

She slapped the side panel before they could get away, and the truck stopped. Barbara spotted her through the window, opened the door, and moved over so Annie could get in. She didn't ask for an explanation, so Annie knew they'd seen the fire, too. Rain rolled off Annie's jacket. "It's the cottage," she said. "I know it."

"It can't be," Barbara said. "Not after everything. It just can't be."

"Calm down, both of you," Booker ordered, turning out onto the road. "There's a lot of woods over there, and the cottage sits low. More likely some of the trees were hit."

Annie prayed he was right, but in her heart, she didn't believe it.

The truck had lost its shocks long ago and wires gaped from a hole in the dashboard, but it navigated the mud better than Annie's car ever could. The farther they traveled, the brighter the orange glow grew in the sky. The town had only one fire truck, an old pumper truck that Barbara told her wasn't running. Booker swung into the lane that led to the cottage. The landscape opened up, and they could see that it wasn't the cottage on fire. It was Harp House.

Annie's first thought was of Theo, then of Jaycie and Livia. *Dear God, let them be safe.*

Barbara grabbed the dashboard. A shower of sparks exploded into the sky. They jolted up the drive. Booker parked the truck well back from the fire. Annie threw herself out and began to run.

The fire was ravenous, devouring the wooden shingles in snarling gulps, its hot claws greedy for more. The piles of newspapers and magazines stored in the attic had been the perfect tinder, and the roof was nearly gone, the skeleton of a chimney already visible. Annie saw Jaycie huddled near the top of the drive, Livia at her side. She raced toward them.

"It happened so fast," Jaycie exclaimed. "It was like an explosion hit the house. I couldn't open the door. Something fell and blocked it."

"Where's Theo?" Annie cried.

"He broke a window to get us out."

"Where is he now?"

"He—he ran back into the house. I yelled. Told him not to go."

Annie's stomach pitched. There was nothing inside important enough for him to risk his life. Unless Hannibal was there. Theo would never abandon anything that was in his care, not even a cat.

Annie started toward the house, but Jaycie grabbed the sleeve of her foul weather jacket and held on tight. "You're not going in there!"

Jaycie was right. The house was too big, and she had no idea where he'd gone. She had to wait. Pray.

Jaycie picked up Livia. Annie was dimly aware of more trucks arriving, and of Booker telling someone there was no saving the house.

"I want Theo," Livia wailed.

Annie heard the shrill whinny of a terrified horse. She'd forgotten about Dancer. But as she turned toward the stable, she saw Booker and Darren McKinley already going inside.

"They'll get him," Barbara said, rushing up next to her.

"Theo's in the house," Jaycie told her.

Barbara curled her hand over her mouth.

The air was hot and full of smoke. Another beam fell, sending up a meteor of sparks. Annie watched numbly from the drive, her fear growing by the second, a filmstrip playing in her head of Thornfield Hall burning. Of Jane Eyre coming back to find a blind Edward Rochester.

Blind would be good. Annie could deal with blind. But not dead. Never dead.

Something brushed against her ankles. She looked down and saw Hannibal. She snatched up the cat, her fear escalating. Even now, Theo could be dodging the flames searching for him, not knowing the cat was already safe.

Booker and Darren struggled to get Dancer out of the stable. They'd wrapped something around his head to mask his eyes, but the panicked horse smelled the smoke and fought them.

Another piece of roof caved in. Any moment now, the house could collapse. Annie waited. Prayed. Held the cat so tight it howled in protest and wiggled out of her arms. She should have told Theo she loved him. Told him and damned the consequences. Life was too precious. Love was too precious. Now he would never know how well he'd been loved—not with smothering demands or insane threats, but enough to be set free.

A figure emerged from the house. Hunched. Amorphous. She raced forward. It was Theo carrying something in each hand and gasping for air. A window exploded behind him. She reached his side, tried to support him. Whatever he was carrying struck her in the legs. She tried to take it away from him, but he wouldn't let go.

The men came to his side, pushing her out of the way and dragging him to clean air. Only then could she see what he'd brought from the burning house. What he'd gone back inside to rescue. Not the cat at all. Two red suitcases. He'd gone back to retrieve her puppets.

Annie could barely absorb it. Theo had gone back into

that inferno to rescue her silly, beloved puppets. She wanted to scream at him, kiss him until neither of them could breathe, make him promise never to do anything so foolish again. But he'd broken away from the men to get to his horse.

"My fairy house!" Livia screamed. "I want to see my fairy house."

Jaycie tried to quiet her, but it had all been too much for the four-year-old, and she was past reasoning. Annie couldn't do anything for Theo right now, but maybe she could help with this. "Did you forget?" She touched Livia's flushed cheek and drew her face close. "It's nighttime, and the fairies might be there. You know they don't want people to see them."

Livia's small chest shook as she sobbed. "I want to see them."

So many things we want that we can't have. The fire hadn't gotten as far as the fairy house, but the area had been badly trampled. "I know, sweetheart, but they don't want to see you."

"Can you—" She hiccuped. "Can you bring me in the morning?" Annie hesitated too long, and Livia started to cry. "I want to see the fairy house!"

Annie glanced at Jaycie, who looked as exhausted as her daughter. "If the fire is out and it's safe," Annie said, "I'll bring you in the morning."

That satisfied her until her mother started making plans to spend the night in town. The wailing began again. "Annie said she'd take me to see the fairy house in the morning! I want to stay here!"

A hoarse male voice spoke from behind them. "Why don't the three of you spend the night in the cottage?"

Annie swung around. Theo looked as though he'd emerged from hell, blue eyes blazing from a soot-blackened face, cat cradled in his hands. He held Hannibal out to her. "Take him with you, will you?"

Before she could say anything, he was gone again.

BARBARA DROVE ANNIE, JAYCIE, AND LIVIA to the cottage. Annie deposited Hannibal inside, then went to retrieve the two red suitcases from the truck bed. Everything else that she'd stored at the house was gone: her clothes, Mariah's scarves, and her Dreambook. But she had her puppets. And, pressed between heavy cardboard in the bottom of each of her suitcases, she had the Niven Garr drawings. Far more important, Theo was alive and safe.

An explosion of sparks lit up the night like the devil's sideshow.

Harp House had fallen.

ANNIE GAVE UP HER BED at the cottage to Jaycie and Livia and slept on the couch herself, leaving the studio for Theo, but by early morning, he hadn't returned. She went to the front window. Where Harp House had once lorded it over all of them, only plumes of smoke rose from the ruins.

Livia appeared in the pajamas she'd had on the night before and rubbed her eyes. "Let's go see the fairy house."

Annie had hoped the four-year-old would sleep in after last night, but the only person still in bed was Jaycie. She'd also hoped Livia would forget about the fairy house. She should have known better.

She gently explained that someone might have accidentally stepped on the house during the fire, but Livia wasn't having it. "The fairies wouldn't let that happen. Can we go see it now, Annie? Please!"

"Livia, I'm afraid you're going to be disappointed."

Livia screwed up her face. "I want to see!"

By evening, Annie would be back on the mainland, and instead of leaving behind a child with happy memories of her, she'd be leaving behind a disappointed one. "All right," she said reluctantly. "Get your coat."

Annie had already dressed in a pair of Mariah's too short pipe-stem trousers and a black pullover. She added the foul weather jacket that smelled of smoke and scribbled a note to Jaycie. As she herded Livia outside in her coat and pajamas, she remembered she hadn't given her breakfast—not that much was left in the kitchen. But when she suggested they eat first, Livia refused, and Annie didn't have the heart to argue.

Someone had parked Jaycie's Suburban by the cottage.

Annie fastened Livia in her car seat and drove off. Theo's car was parked near the top of the cliff where it had been last night. She parked behind it and helped Livia out. Keeping a tight grip on the four-year-old's hand, she walked with her the rest of the way to the top.

The gargoyles and the stone turret had survived, along with the stables and garage. But nothing was left of the house except four brick chimneys and a section of staircase. Beyond the ruins, she could see the ocean. The house no longer blocked the view.

It was ironic that Livia spotted Theo first, since Annie hadn't been able to think of anyone else. Livia broke away and ran to him, the cuffs of her pajamas dragging. "Theo!"

He was filthy. Unshaven. He wore a too-small navy jacket one of the men must have lent him, and his jeans were ripped at the calf. Annie's heart constricted. After all he'd been through—all he had to do—there he was, crouched in the mud, rebuilding Livia's fairy house.

He gave the little girl a smile so weary it drooped. "The fire made the fairies mad. Look what they did."

"Oh, no." Livia planted her hands on her hips like a miniature adult. "They were very, very bad."

Theo gazed at Annie. Dirt had settled into the creases around his eyes, and one of his ears was completely black. He'd risked his life to save her puppets. So like him. "You've been here all night," she said softly. "Bearing witness to the fall of the House of Harp?"

"And trying to keep the sparks from the stable."

Now that he was safe, her compulsion to reveal her feelings for him gave way to reality. Nothing had changed. She wouldn't sacrifice his well-being simply to unburden herself. "Is Dancer all right?" she asked.

He nodded. "He's back in his stall. How's our cat?"

Her throat caught. "Our cat is just fine. Better than you."

Livia studied what he'd done. "You're making a path. The fairies are gonna like that."

He'd made the new house lower and wider, and instead of the stone pathway, he'd been pressing pieces of the smoothed beach glass in a half-moon around the entrance. He handed some of the glass to Livia. "See what you can do while I talk to Annie."

Livia hunkered down. Annie had to clench her hands to keep from brushing them over Theo's face. "You're an idiot," she said with a tenderness she couldn't hide. "Puppets are replaceable. You're not."

"I know what they mean to you," he said.

"Not as much as you do."

His head cocked.

"I'll watch Livia," she said quickly. "Go to the cottage and get some sleep."

"I'll sleep later." He gazed at the ruins of the house and then back at her. "You're really leaving today?"

She nodded.

"Now who's the idiot?" he said.

"There's a difference between running into a burning house and leaving for the mainland," she pointed out.

"Both have a big downside."

"I don't think leaving has a downside for me."

"Maybe not for you. But it sure has one for me."

He was exhausted. Of course he cared about her leaving. But caring wasn't the same as loving, and she wouldn't mistake his fatigue for a sudden unlocking of his heart. "Unless you start hooking up with more crazy women, you'll be fine," she said.

His smile, weary but genuine, took her aback. "It should bother me hearing you talk about them that way."

"But it doesn't?"

"Truth is truth. Time for me to man up."

"It has nothing to do with manning up," she said. "It has to do with accepting the fact that you can't save everybody you care about."

"Fortunately for me, you don't need saving."

"Darned right I don't."

He rubbed the back of his hand over his jaw. "I have a job for you. A paying job."

She didn't like where this was headed, so she tried to deflect him. "I knew I was good in bed, but I didn't know I was that good."

He sighed. "Have some compassion, Antoinette. I'm too tired to keep up with you right now."

She managed to roll her eyes. "Like you ever could."

"This is work you can do from the city."

He was going to offer her a pity job, and she couldn't bear it. "I've heard about Skype sex, but it doesn't appeal to me."

"I want you to illustrate a book I'm working on."

"Sorry. Even if I were an illustrator, which I'm not, I don't have any practice drawing disemboweled humans." Oh, she was on a roll, all right. Rolling right over her heart.

He sighed. "I've barely slept in a week, and I can't remember the last time I ate. My chest hurts. My eyes feel like sandpaper. I have a blistered hand. And all you want to do is make jokes."

"Your hand? Let me see it." She reached for it only to have him slip it behind his back.

"I'll take care of my hand, but first, I want you to listen to me."

He wasn't going to let it go. "No need. I already have more work than I can take on."

"Annie, just once could you not give me a hard time?"

"Maybe someday, but not today."

"Annie, you're making Theo sad." Neither of them realized Livia had been paying attention to them. She peered around Theo's legs. "I think you should tell him your free secret."

"I don't!" She gave Livia a death glare. "And you'd better not, either."

Livia peered up at Theo. "Then you better tell her *your* free secret."

He stiffened. "Annie doesn't want to hear my free secret."

"You have a free secret?" Annie asked.

"Yes, he does." Livia puffed up with four-year-old self-importance. "And I know it."

Now Theo was the one giving Livia the death glare. "Find some pinecones. A lot of them." He jabbed his hand toward the trees behind the gazebo. "Over there."

Annie could only stand so much. "Later," she said. "We need to get back to the cottage and see if your mom's awake."

Livia's face turned into a thundercloud. "I don't want to go!"

"Don't give Annie a hard time," he said. "I'll finish the fairy house. You can see it later."

The fire had disrupted Livia's world. She hadn't had enough sleep, and she was as cranky as only an overstimulated four-year-old can be. "I'm not going!" she cried. "And if you don't let me stay, I'll tell your free secrets!"

Annie grabbed her arm. "You can't tell a free secret!"

"You absolutely can't!" Theo exclaimed.

"I can!" Livia retorted. "If they're both the same!"

Chapter Twenty-five

T HEO COULDN'T GET HIS BRAIN to work. He stood there like one of the Harp House gargoyles, his feet frozen to the ground, as Annie somehow managed to get the recalcitrant four-year-old to the car. He watched dumbly as she drove away.

"I can! If they're both the same!"

Annie had been crystal clear when she'd said he had too much baggage. But he didn't feel that way now. The smoldering ruins of the house represented everything he was leaving behind. Everything that kept him from seeing into his own heart and being the man he wanted to be. He loved Annie Hewitt from the depths of his soul.

Annie had told Livia she loved him? What exactly had she said? Because he had a sinking feeling she didn't mean the same thing he meant.

Reality had slapped him in the face the same day he'd found Regan's beach glass. When Livia had demanded he tell her what she called a "free secret," the words had slipped out of him as freely as his breath. He felt as if he'd loved Annie since he was sixteen—and maybe he had.

"You have too much baggage."

Annie's words had turned him into a coward. He had a dismal track record with women, and for all her cracks about his money, she didn't want any of it. If she ever found out he was the one who'd bought that damned mermaid chair, she'd never forgive him. All he could give her was his heart—something she'd made clear she didn't want.

But he wasn't such a coward that he wouldn't put up a fight. He'd planned to give her until the last day to cool off from their argument at the wharf. He'd intended to make the best breakfast of his life and take it to her on the *Lucky Charm* this morning. Somehow, he'd figured out he could convince her his baggage was a thing of the past—that he was free to love her, whether or not she could love him in return. But the fire had screwed everything up.

He needed a clear brain. A few hours' sleep. Definitely a shower. But he didn't have time for any of that. Annie had to feel his urgency as powerfully as he did. It was the only way he could convince her not to give up on him.

Good luck with that. You've already blown it.

His lack of sleep had gotten the best of him. Now he was hearing her puppet Scamp. He turned his back on the ruins of Harp House, headed for his car, and raced down to the cottage.

She was already gone. She'd handed Livia over and sped toward town as if her life depended on getting away from him. Anxiety gnawed at the pit of his stomach as he took off after her.

The Suburban was no match for his Range Rover, and he caught up with her quickly. He honked, but she didn't stop. He kept honking. She had to hear, but—not only didn't she stop—she sped up.

I told you, the damned puppet said. *You're too late.*

Like hell I am! They were on an island, and she'd reach town soon. All he had to do was be patient and follow her. But he didn't want to be patient. He wanted her now, and if she couldn't understand how serious he was, he'd show her.

He bumped the rear end of the Suburban. Not hard enough to make her swerve. Just enough so she knew he meant business. Apparently so did she because she kept driving. The Suburban was a piece of crap with so many dents another couple wouldn't matter, but the same couldn't be said for his Range Rover. He didn't care. He bumped her again. And again. Finally, the Suburban's only surviving brake light flared on.

The car lurched to a stop, the door flew open, and she threw herself out. He jumped out, too, only to hear her scream, *"I don't want to talk about it!"*

"Fine!" he shouted back. "I'll do the talking. I love you, and by damn I'm not ashamed of it, and you may not have as much baggage as I do, but don't pretend you don't have some with all those losers you attached yourself to."

"Only two!"

"And only two for me, so we're even!"

"Not even close!" They were fifteen feet apart and she was still screaming. "My two were self-centered assholes! Yours were homicidal nutcases!"

"Kenley wasn't homicidal!"

"Close enough. And all I did after my breakups was watch *Big Bang* reruns and gain five pounds! That's not the same as doing penance for the *rest of your life*."

"Not anymore!" He was shouting as loud as she, and he hadn't moved, either. His brain was jumbled. His throat raw. Every part of his body ached. She, on the other hand—with her electrified hair and blazing eyes—looked like a vengeful goddess at the height of her powers.

He stalked toward her. "I want a life with you, Annie. I want to make love with you until you can't walk. And have kids with you. I'm sorry it took me so long to figure out, but I'm not exactly used to having love feel good." He poked his finger in the rough direction of her face. "You talked about being a romantic. Romance is nothing! It's a tiny word that doesn't come close to what I feel for you. And I know sooner or later you're going to find out about that damned chair, but that's the way I do things! And from now on—"

"Chair?"

Shit. Now he was looking into both flaring nostrils and flaming hazel demon eyes.

"*You're* the one who bought the chair!" she exclaimed.

He couldn't show any weakness. "Who the hell else loves you enough to buy that ugly piece of crap?"

Her mouth was open again, and he was so wrung out that even his hair hurt, but he kept at her. "The job offer I have for you is *real.* I started a new book—one you'll actually like—but I don't want to talk about that now. I want to talk about us making a life together, and my getting a chance to show you that what I feel is bright and strong without any shadows hanging around. That's what I want to show you."

He yearned to tell her about Diggity. And tell her again that he wanted kids with her, in case she'd missed it the first time. He wanted to kiss her until she was dizzy. Make love with her until she couldn't think straight. He would have done all that by now except she sat down. Right in the middle of the muddy road. As if her legs were useless. That put an end to his tirade as nothing else could have.

He went to her. Knelt next to her. A watery beam of sunlight found its way through the trees and played hide-and-seek with her cheekbones. The honey brown snarl of curls he loved so much had launched a full-out skirmish around her face—the most beautiful face he'd ever seen, brimming with life, animated with all the emotions that made up who she was.

"You okay?" he asked.

She didn't respond, and Annie without words scared him, so he plunged back in. "I want a life with you. I can't imagine a life with anyone else. Will you at least think about it?"

She nodded, but it was a wobbly nod, and she didn't look certain about it. If he backed off, he might lose her forever, so he told her about Diggity and how he wanted her to illustrate the book he was writing for kids instead of adults, and how much his new readers would love her quirky sketches. He sat with her in the middle of the muddy road and told her love had always meant catastrophe to him and that was why it had taken him so long to label what he felt for her—the ease, the connection, the tenderness. He'd almost choked on that last word, not because he didn't mean every syllable, but because—even for a writer—saying a word like *tenderness* out loud made him feel like he should turn in his man card. But she had her eyes glued to his face, so he said it again and then followed up by telling her how beautiful she looked when he was inside her.

That definitely got her attention, so he introduced a little smut. Lowered his voice. Whispered in her ear. Told her what he wanted to do to her. What he wanted her to do to him. Her curls tickled his lips, her skin flushed, and his jeans got way too tight, but he felt like a guy again, a guy hopelessly at the mercy of this woman who played with puppets and helped mute little girls talk again and rescued him from his own hopelessness. This quirky, sexy, utterly sane woman.

He touched her face. "I think I've loved you since I was sixteen."

She cocked her head, as if she were waiting for something.

"I'm sure of it," he said more firmly, even though he wasn't sure at all. Who could look back on their teenage years and be clear about anything? But she wanted something more from him, and he had to give it to her, even if he had no idea what it was.

Out of nowhere, he heard a puppet's voice. *Kiss her, you dumbass.*

There was nothing he yearned to do more, but he reeked of smoke, his face was coated with oily soot, and his hands were filthy.

Just do it.

And so he did. He tunneled his dirty hands through her hair and kissed her breathless. Her neck, her eyes, the corners of her mouth. He kissed her lips as if his life depended on it. Kissed their future into her. All they could have and all they could be. The soft sounds they made together became a poem to his ears.

Her hands clasped his shoulders, not pushing him away, drawing him closer. He lost himself in her. Found himself.

When their kiss finally ended, he kept his grubby hands cupped around her now equally grubby cheeks. Soot smudged the tip of her nose. Her lips were swollen from their kiss. Her eyes shimmered.

"Free secret," she whispered.

His stomach twisted into its tightest knot. Slowly he released his breath. "Make it good."

She pressed her lips to his ears and whispered her secret.

It was good. Really good. In fact, it couldn't have been better.

Epilogue

T HE SUMMER SUN SKIPPED OVER the crests of the waves and bounced off the masts of a pair of sailboats tacking into the wind. Cobalt blue Adirondack chairs sat on the garden patio, which had been positioned well in front of the old farmhouse to afford the best view of the distant ocean. Roses, delphinium, sweet peas, and nasturtium bloomed in the garden nearby, and a curving path led from the stone patio back across the meadow to the farmhouse, which was twice as big as it had once been. A grove of trees sheltered a small guesthouse off to the left where an ugly mermaid chair rested on the postage stamp porch.

On the garden patio, a market umbrella, folded against the early-afternoon breeze, rose from the center of a long wooden table large enough to accommodate a big family. An old stone gargoyle with a Knicks cap perched crookedly on its head had once guarded a house at the other end of the island. Now it crouched protectively near a clay pot overflowing with geraniums. The detritus of a Maine summer lay all around: a soccer ball, a pink riding toy, abandoned swim goggles, bubble wands, and waterlogged sidewalk chalk.

A boy with straight dark hair and a scowl sat cross-legged between two of the Adirondack chairs talking to Scamp, who was peering at him over the arm of one chair. "And . . ." the boy said, ". . . that's why I stomped my feet. Because he made me very, *very* mad."

The puppet shook her yarn curls. "Horrors! Tell me exactly what he did again."

The boy—whose name was Charlie Harp—impatiently shoved his dark hair off his forehead and puffed up his cheeks in outrage. "He won't let me drive the truck!"

Scamp pressed her cloth hand to her forehead. "That *blackguard*!"

A long-suffering sigh came from the next chair. Scamp and Charlie ignored it.

"Then . . ." Charlie added. "He got mad at me just because I took my turbo car away from my sister. It was *mine*."

"In*sane*!" Scamp made a dismissive gesture toward the curly-haired toddler napping on an old quilt in the grass. "Just because you haven't played with that car for years is absolutely no reason for her to have it. Your sister is nothing but a bother. She doesn't even like you."

"Well . . ." Charlie frowned. "She kind of likes me."

"Does not."

"She does! She laughs when I make funny faces and when I play with her and make noises, she goes crazy."

"*Très intéressant,*" said Scamp, who still had a thing for languages.

"Sometimes she throws her food on the floor, and that's pretty funny."

"Hmmm . . . Perhaps . . ." Scamp tapped her cheek. "No, forget I said anything."

"Tell me."

"Well . . ." The puppet tapped her other cheek. "I, Scamp, am thinking that your turbo car is really a baby toy, and if anybody saw you playing with it, they might think you yourself are a——"

"They won't think nothing because I'm giving that baby toy to her!"

Scamp regarded him with openmouthed astonishment. "I should have thought of that. Now, I believe I shall compose a song to—"

"No song!"

"Very well." Scamp sniffed, deeply offended. "If you're going to be like *that* I'm going to tell you what Dilly said. She said you can't be a real superhero until you learn how to be nice to little kids. *That* is what she said."

Charlie didn't have a good counterargument, so he picked at the bandage on his big toe and returned to his prime grievance. "I'm an island kid."

"Tragically, only in the summer," Scamp said. "The rest of the time you're a New York City kid."

"Summer counts! It still makes me an island kid, and island kids get to drive."

"When they're *ten*." This voice, deep and assertive, came from Leo, who was Charlie's second favorite of the puppets—a lot more interesting than boring old Peter; or stupid, silly Crumpet; or Dilly—who was always reminding him to brush his teeth and stuff.

Leo peered at Charlie over the arm of the next chair. "Island kids have to be at least ten to drive. You, *compadre,* are six."

"I'll be ten soon."

"Not that soon, thank G—goodness."

Charlie glared at the puppet. "I'm really mad."

"Sure you are. Super mad." Leo circled his head one way and then the other. "I've got an idea."

"What?"

"Tell him how mad you are. Then look really pitiful and ask him to take you Boogie-boarding. If you look pitiful enough, I bet he'll feel so bad that he'll take you."

Charlie wasn't born yesterday. He looked past Leo to the man holding him. "Really! Can we go right now?"

His father set Leo aside and shrugged. "The waves look good. Why not? Get your stuff."

Charlie jumped up, and raced toward the house, his legs

pumping. But just as he got to the front step, he stopped and whipped around. "I get to drive!"

"No you don't!" his mother countered, slipping Scamp from her arm.

Charlie stomped inside, and his father laughed. "I love that kid."

"Now, there's a surprise." Charlie's mother gazed at the sleeping baby. The toddler's wild honey-blond curls couldn't be more different from her brother's stick-straight dark hair, but the children shared their father's blue eyes. They also had their mother's irreverent personality.

Annie leaned back in the chaise. Theo never got tired of looking at his wife's quirky face. He reached over and took her hand, running his fingers over the diamond-encrusted wedding band she'd declared too lavish but loved all the same. "What time do we get rid of them?"

"We're dropping them off at Barbara's at four. She's giving them dinner."

"Leaving us the whole evening for drunken debauchery."

"I don't know about the drunken part, but there will definitely be debauchery."

"There'd better be. I love those little demons with all my heart, but they sure do play havoc with our sex life."

Annie curled her fingers around his thigh. "Not tonight, they won't."

He groaned. "You're killing me."

"I haven't even started."

He reached out for her.

As Annie felt his hand in her hair, she wondered if it was wrong of her to love playing the femme fatale so much. To love the power she had over him—a power she used only to keep the shadows away. He was a different man from the one she'd seen seven years ago standing on the staircase holding a dueling pistol. They were both different. This island she'd once hated had become her favorite spot on earth, a refuge from the busyness of her normal life.

In addition to working privately with troubled children, she conducted puppet-training seminars for doctors, nurses, teachers, and social workers. She'd never imagined loving her work so much. Her main challenge was balancing it all with the family that meant everything to her and the friends she cherished. Here on the island, she had time to do the things that sometimes slipped past her the rest of the year, like the tenth birthday party she'd thrown for Livia last week when Jaycie and her new family had visited from the mainland.

She turned her face into the sunlight. "It's so nice just sitting here."

"You work too hard," he said, not for the first time.

"I'm not the only one." It wasn't entirely surprising that the Diggity Swift books had become so successful. Diggity's adventures took his young teen readers to the edge of horror without pushing them into the pit. Annie loved that her goofy drawings inspired her husband and pleased his readers.

Charlie came barreling out of the house. Theo rose reluctantly, kissed Annie, grabbed one of the cranberry nut cookies from the container he'd found on the farmhouse doorstep that morning, gazed down at his sleeping daughter, then headed for the beach with his son. Annie drew her heels up onto the chair seat and hugged her knees.

In her old gothic paperbacks, the reader never got to see what happened to the hero and heroine when real life set in and they had to deal with all its messiness: household chores, children squabbling, head colds, and the challenges of dealing with extended family—his, not hers. Elliott had mellowed with age, but Cynthia was as pretentious as ever, and she drove Theo crazy. Annie was more tolerant because Cynthia was an astonishingly good grandmother—much better with children than with adults—and the kids loved her.

As for Annie's family . . . Niven Garr's widowed sister Sylvia, along with Niven's longtime partner Benedict—or Grampa Bendy—as Charlie called him, would be arriving soon for their annual summer visit. At first, Sylvia and Benedict had been suspicious of Annie, but after a DNA test and some awkward early visits, they had become as close as if they'd always been part of each other's lives.

Tonight, though, it would just be Theo and herself. Tomorrow they'd pack up the kids and drive to the other end of the island. She imagined them waving at the family from Providence who'd rented the schoolhouse cottage for the season, then heading up the badly rutted drive to the top of the cliff and the island's best view.

The outbuildings of Harp House had been demolished long ago, the swimming pool filled in for safety. Only the vine-covered turret remained of what once had been. She and Theo would lie on a blanket sampling a good bottle of wine while Charlie ran free as only an island kid could. Eventually Theo would pick up their daughter, kiss the top of her head, and carry her to an old spruce stump. He'd crouch down, gather up the beach glass that was still scattered there, and whisper in her ear.

"Let's build a fairy house."

Fall in love with *New York Times* bestselling author

SUSAN ELIZABETH PHILLIPS

THE CHICAGO STARS/BONNER BROTHERS BOOKS

IT HAD TO BE YOU
978-0-380-77683-2

When she inherits the Chicago Stars football team, Phoebe Somerville knocks heads with handsome Coach Dan Calebow.

HEAVEN, TEXAS
978-0-380-77683-4

Gracie Snow is determined to drag the legendary ex-jock Bobby Tom Denton back home to Heaven, Texas, to begin shooting his first motion picture.

NOBODY'S BABY BUT MINE
978-0-380-78234-5

Dr. Jane Darlington's super-intelligence made her feel like a freak growing up and she's determined to spare her baby that kind of suffering. Which means she must find someone very special to father her child. Someone very . . . well . . . . *stupid*.

DREAM A LITTLE DREAM
978-0-380-79447-8

Rachel Stone is a determined young widow with a scandalous past who has come to a town that hates her to raise her child.

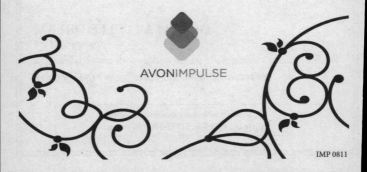